good Graces

A novel by

KI STEPHENS

Cover Design: Books and Moods

Editing: Sandra Dee at One Love Editing

This book is intended for an 18+ audience. For a complete list of content warnings, please visit my website www.kistephens.com

For the ones who left the water—
and came back for something braver.

Playlist

THE NIGHT WE MET | LORD HURON	♥	3:28
ALL I WANT | KODALINE	♥	5:06
MR. FORGETTABLE | DAVID KUSHNER	♥	3:07
PRAY | LAUREN SPENCER SMITH	♥	2:58
WHERE'S MY LOVE | SYML	♥	3:22
HARD SOMETIMES | RUEL	♥	4:29
ALL I EVER ASKED | RACHEL CHINOURIRI, SOMBR	♥	3:38
DO I WANNA KNOW? | ARCTIC MONKEYS	♥	4:32
COULDN'T MAKE IT ANY HARDER | SABRINA CARPENTER	♥	3:00
LOVE ME NOT | RAVYN LENAE	♥	3:33
SWEET HEAT LIGHTNING | GREGORY ALAN ISAKOV	♥	4:46
SPRING INTO SUMMER | LIZZY MCALPINE	♥	4:23
BEST | GRACIE ABRAMS	♥	3:53
KISS ME | DERMOT KENNEDY	♥	3:49
WE HUG NOW | SYDNEY ROSE	♥	4:09
SOMETHING, SOMEHOW, SOMEDAY | ROLE MODEL	♥	3:36
STRANGERS | MT. JOY	♥	3:13
THINKING 'BOUT LOVE | WILD RIVERS	♥	3:19
YOU WERE GOOD TO ME | JEREMY ZUCKER, CHELSEA CUTLER	♥	3:39
UR SO PRETTY | WASIA PROJECT	♥	2:12

Chapter One
WARREN

The kitchen is suspiciously quiet.

Which, on a Saturday morning, can only mean one thing. Something's wrong.

Usually, this place is brimming with energy. Namely, Liam Donovan stomping around like a golden retriever in human form, laughter echoing down the hall, dramatic gasps, lips smacking against other lips. The kind of noise that makes a single man seriously consider eating breakfast in his car.

But right now? There's nothing but the low hum of the fridge and the sound of my spoon scraping the bottom of my cereal bowl. *Weird.* Maybe his girlfriend didn't spend the night for once. Or maybe they ascended to some higher plane of coupledom where they no longer need oxygen. Or noise.

I barely have time to enjoy the peace before he's strolling in, shirtless, blond hair a mess, grinning like he spent the night dreaming of himself. And he probably did.

My cousin is the effortless, easygoing type. He's also shamelessly, ridiculously obsessed with his girlfriend, Birdie Collins. Practically worships the ground she walks on, which—whatever. Not my business. But if he ever starts calling her his "baby bird" unironically, I'll have to stage an intervention.

Liam stretches, groaning like his body physically hurts from all the affection, then beelines for the fridge. "What's up, big guy?"

"Nothing," I mutter around my spoon.

I like Liam. He's a good guy. Annoying, too chatty, constantly in my space—but decent. I didn't think we'd ever end up as roommates, but last semester, my old apartment had a mold problem, and I needed out. My landlord was a jackass, my upstairs neighbor's shower leaked into my bedroom, and I got sick of breathing in possible spores every night.

I suppose I could've moved home, but that was never a real option in my mind. Not because it wasn't available to me—it was. A big, pristine house with polished floors and curated furniture. But I could never really call it mine.

Liam is only my cousin by marriage. Three and a half years ago, my mom married his uncle, Daniel Donovan. She moved us into his fancy house with the kind of furniture you aren't actually supposed to sit on and a fridge stocked with wine you're not meant to drink.

I only lasted a single summer there before getting my own place near Dayton's campus.

And God, that summer was a strange sort of hell. Living in a stranger's home, walking on eggshells, trying—no, *needing*—to be liked by this new man in my mother's life. Not because I gave a shit about him but because I knew it would be easier for her if I didn't make things worse.

Daniel's a fine man. A nice man. But I knew from day one we'd never have any sort of meaningful relationship. *What grown man is gonna want to bond with some other guy's adult kid?* I wasn't some impressionable preteen desperate for a father figure—I was eighteen. A pseudo-adult. Too old to be folded into a new family like a lost sock.

So, I left as soon as I could. And I don't think either of us was particularly upset about that. Maybe my mom was. But she has enough bridges to mend without worrying about the ones I burned.

Still, it makes Liam part of my family, in a way. Not in the way that matters but in the way that's written into marriage certificates and tax filings. The two of us are very different people. He grew up with wealth. He benefits from it, even if he rejects it. And that's the thing about privilege—you don't have to like it for it to still work in your favor.

Liam's dad, David, belongs to the art world. My stepdad? Finance. The kind of money that makes more money while you sleep. And yet, for all the ways Liam and I differ, living with him is easy. Easier than I expected, anyway.

"Where you off to this early?" Liam asks, finally looking at me. His brows pinch together, taking in the club polo I'm wearing. It's stiff, boxy—regulation navy blue with a stitched logo over the chest. A layer I'll strip off as soon as I'm safely situated on the pool deck.

I sigh. "The club."

Liam stares, blank as an empty canvas.

"The country club," I say, slower this time. "The one I've been working at all summer."

He blinks. "Doesn't ring a bell."

I pinch the bridge of my nose. *How is he like this?* "The Sycamore Club."

"Oh." He leans against the counter, eyes flicking up in recognition. "Right. My parents are members there."

"No shit," I say flatly. "So are mine."

He snaps his fingers, pointing at me like that actually just clicked for him. "Right, right. That tracks."

I shake my head, rinsing my bowl in the sink. "You've never been, have you?"

Liam scoffs. "Me? At a country club? What the hell would I even do there?"

There's golfing, swimming, tennis, brunches. All sorts of ways for a rich, legacy kid to occupy his time. But Liam's more interested in soccer and Birdie than schmoozing over overpriced mimosas. I like that about him.

But it still makes him oblivious to half the shit he was born into.

Like how places like Sycamore weren't built for guys like me to work at—they were built for guys like him to belong to.

I don't dignify his willful ignorance with an answer, just scrub my bowl, set it on the drying rack, and grab my keys. I still hear him rambling behind me as I push out the door and head to work.

I pull out of the driveway and onto the main road, the engine of my dark blue 2008 Toyota 4Runner rumbling under my hands. It's old, a little banged up, but reliable. The kind of car I don't have to think about.

I bought it when I was sixteen and haven't had a reason to trade up. That's the way I prefer things. Trustworthy and reliable. Not prone to sell you out or steal from you at the first opportunity.

The Sycamore Club is only about thirty minutes from campus, tucked into a stretch of rolling green that smells like fresh-cut grass and money. I've made this drive hundreds of times, though not in the last two years.

I worked there the first summer my mom and I lived with Daniel. He got me the job. Said it would be "good experience," a way to earn my own money instead of "sitting around the house." Not that I had any intention of doing that. I was already itching to get out of there, to stop feeling like a guest in what was meant to be my own home.

So, I took it. Lifeguarding is easy enough. Made sense, given I'd been swimming my whole life.

I don't come from the same world as most of the club's members, but I can hold my own in the water. My old coach used to joke that I was born with gills, the way I moved through a pool. But the truth is, swimming is one of those things that quiets my brain. The rhythm of it, the repetition. The way you can push yourself to exhaustion without saying a single word.

The Sycamore pool isn't like the ones I train in during the school year. Those are cold, cracked, built for grind. The club's lap lanes are practically spa-like. They're heated and clean, surrounded by umbrella-shaded loungers and expensive sunglasses. Everything here is meant to look effortless.

I didn't work at the club the last two summers, though. I needed space. Last year, I stayed in Dayton to train and knock out a few summer courses, and the year before that, I did construction with my uncle—long hours, shit pay, but honest work that kept me away from here.

But I came back this year because I needed the money. One last stretch before senior year starts. Four more weeks of shifts before I head back to school.

The drive is smooth, the kind where you don't have to think much. It's early enough that the sun is still working its way up the sky, but the heat is already pressing down—thick, humid, the kind of North Carolina stickiness that turns asphalt into lava and melts a popsicle in under ten seconds.

I don't mind it.

Some of the staff complain, but I'd rather bake under the sun than be stuck inside. Sitting there with my sunglasses on, silently scanning. It's meditative, in a way. Letting the world move around me, being still, being watchful.

When I pull into the club's parking lot, it's already filling with luxury cars—Range Rovers, Mercedes, the occasional Tesla. I park in the staff lot, away from the pristine lineup of the members' "weekend toys."

The walk from the lot to the staff entrance is lined with white rosebushes and perfectly manicured hedges. I push through the side gate and into the employee check-in area, where a handful of other lifeguards are already gathered, some sipping coffee, some staring dead-eyed at the time clock like they're willing it to fast-forward.

I swipe my ID, clock in for my shift, and then head toward the pool deck.

There's an Olympic-sized lap pool on one side and a more

casual family pool on the other, complete with a waterslide, a shaded splash pad, and a shallow end where toddlers scream like they're being actively murdered.

I grab my rescue tube from the equipment shed and make my way to the lifeguard stand. The seat is high, perched over the pool like a watchtower. I climb up, settle in, push my sunglasses down over my eyes.

From up here, everything looks smaller. The members, the kids, the perfectly laid-out lounge chairs, the expensive umbrellas shielding people from a sun they paid good money to vacation under.

It's still early, so the crowd is light. A couple of kids paddle around in the shallow end. A woman in a wide-brimmed hat is reading a paperback by the cabanas, her toes perfectly pointed like she practiced the pose before sitting down.

At the far end of the lap pool, a guy in his forties is doing a slow, methodical freestyle. Probably someone who used to be an athlete and refuses to let it go. I can see it in the way he moves. He's determined and stubborn, unwilling to surrender the rhythm.

I could see myself like that someday. Still swimming laps at eighty, chasing the calm of the water even when everything else starts to fall apart.

I watch his form out of habit, noticing the inefficiencies, the drag, the way his elbows are just a little too low on his stroke. He'd get smoked in a real race, but there's something admirable about the effort.

A few other guards are stationed around the deck, chatting in between scanning the water. The job is equal parts boredom and hyperawareness. You spend ninety percent of it waiting for nothing to happen and ten percent responding the second something does.

Most of the time, it's nothing serious. A scraped knee, a kid who forgot they don't actually know how to swim. But the second you let yourself get too comfortable, you miss something.

So, I keep scanning from one side to the other. The heat wraps around me, but I don't move. My resting asshole face in full effect. Some might call it brooding; I call it waiting.

A kid in floaties clings to the edge of the shallow end, his dad scrolling his phone instead of watching him. A group of teenagers splashes each other, pretending to flirt while pretending not to flirt. A woman in a high-cut one-piece and a floppy hat orders a frozen cocktail from the poolside bar, tilting her sunglasses down to scan the deck.

I keep scanning. Keep watching. Keep not thinking.

And then I double take. My brain glitches for half a second, the sun pressing down a little heavier. Something in me short-circuits.

Standing near the entrance to the pool deck is Quinn Rose.

Long dark hair spills over poised shoulders, skin sun-kissed, glowing like she's absorbed every second of the summer. But it's the uniform that gets me most. The navy polo, the khaki shorts, the visor hooked to her bag. The same caddy uniform she wore that first summer we met.

She's got a towel slung over her shoulder, a water bottle in one hand, her bag in the other, and a permanent scowl on her face. A bit of a warning wrapped in a hell of a first impression.

Quinn has always been the most magnetizing force in any room. The kind of person you feel before you see. Even now, people glance at her as they walk past, like they can't help it, like something about her demands it.

She's a force. A storm. A reckoning.

It's been over two years since I've seen her, nine-hundred-something days since I told her I never wanted to again.

Chapter Two

QUINN

WHAT IN THE absolute fuck is Warren doing here?

No one had the good sense to tell me he'd be back at Sycamore this summer. No one thought they needed to. They either assumed I could handle it or wanted to play a cruel joke on me. I was a last-minute addition to the staff. Someone must've figured the overlap was unlikely or just didn't care enough to check.

I spent the first half of the summer traveling around South America. Bouncing between hostels, chasing sunsets like they were answers, pretending I had life figured out. It was meant to be my last hurrah before senior year. But those plans disintegrated halfway through, along with my savings and any sense of direction I thought I had.

So, I came home. And when you're home, you need a reason to stay.

Four weeks. That's all I needed. Not just to keep busy but to stay afloat. The job at Sycamore had never been some throwaway gig. It was money for groceries when the meal plan didn't stretch far enough. For tampons, for hair products, for textbooks I couldn't ask my parents to cover. For everything small that adds up until you're drowning in it.

I told myself I'd work hard, keep my head down, save what I could before term started again. And of all the things I prepared myself to deal with this summer—low tips, drunk customers, the occasional grabby hand—my terminally grumpy ex-boyfriend wasn't one of them.

I keep walking, my pace even, my posture poised, like I don't have a storm brewing under my ribs. Like my pulse didn't just trip over itself. Like the sight of him doesn't rip open old wounds I never bothered stitching up.

I'm only on the pool deck because I need the starter kit from the storage closet. A pack of new scorecards, fresh tees, the clipboard they keep locked up because some asshole keeps stealing pens. Normally, I'd cut across the side lot to the caddy shack instead, but I was already passing through. It made sense to grab everything now. It was an efficient and practical thing to do.

Unavoidable, really.

I feel Warren's gaze before I even look at him. It's a slow, heavy drag across my skin, like a hand pressing against the center of my back.

I stare right back at him. Not a glance or a flicker, either. I give him a full-bodied, unflinching stare as I walk, daring him not to look away first.

Warren sits on his guard stand, elbows on his knees, sunglasses covering those sharp, cutting eyes. But the moment he lifts them, pushing the frames up onto his head, the breath leaves my lungs.

He's cold and emotionless. Shuttered the way I expected him to be. It's as if every piece of warmth he used to offer me—every smirk, every breathless whisper in the dark—has been scrubbed clean.

But my body? My traitorous, foolish, still-remembering body? It reacts anyway. To him. To all of it. There's a flash of heat, then something far more dangerous.

The rough slide of his hands gripping my hips. The low, filthy words whispered against my ear as he pounded into me. The heat of him, the weight of him, the way we used to fit together like it was inevitable.

Nights spent tangled up in each other's bodies, our minds just as wrecked and ruined.

He watches me. I *feel* him watching me.

But then, just as easily as he lifted them, he lowers his sunglasses back into place, settles back into his chair and looks away from me. If I didn't know better, I'd say he didn't feel anything at all.

Something inside me goes rigid, and I keep walking. Straighten my spine, tighten my grip on my bag. I trudge forward like it doesn't matter, ignoring the sharp, slicing sense of disappointment.

By the time I reach the storage closet, my chest is a mess of tangled wires. Frustration, embarrassment, something else I refuse to name. Something hot and bitter, lodged deep inside my chest.

One of the new guys is already there, sorting through sunscreen bins like he's afraid to mess anything up. So, I do what I do best. I bury and freeze it. Cover it up with something easier to swallow.

I flash a slow, lazy smirk at the new guy. He's cute in a forgettable kind of way. Dark hair, lean build, eager smile that says he'd absolutely let me ruin his day if I wanted to.

"You gonna get that for me?" I ask, nodding toward the closet door.

He straightens instantly, fumbling for the key and rushing to unlock it.

Too damn easy.

I pluck the supplies off the shelf, tossing a breezy "Thanks, sweetheart" over my shoulder before strutting back across the deck.

I keep my head held high, my shoulders back, not looking at Warren or allowing myself think about the way he looked right through me.

I walk across the club grounds, cutting a direct path toward the caddy shack with my supplies in hand. My fingers tighten around the clipboard, my nails pressing against the smooth plastic. I won't let this shake me.

It's only four weeks. I've worked here every other summer since I was sixteen. I know this place. The shortcuts, the schedules, the way the smell of freshly mowed grass mixes with sunscreen and overpriced cologne.

I used to like it here, on occasion.

The caddy shack is the same as always. It's dim, slightly musty, the faint scent of sweat and sunscreen clinging to the walls. The long wooden bench against the back wall is already half-occupied, a few guys lounging around, checking the tee sheet and waiting for assignments.

I step inside, drop my bag in the corner, and take a slow breath.

"Rose."

I glance up. Mikey, one of the older caddies, is leaning against the lockers with his arms crossed. He's been here longer than I have. He's in his late twenties, permanently tanned, smirks like he knows more than he lets on.

"You're back," he says, giving me a slow once-over.

I grab a fresh pencil from the supply bin, arching a brow. "Observant as ever."

He grins, unbothered. "Didn't think you'd be working this summer."

I shrug. Neither did I.

One of the newer guys—skinny, nervous energy, fresh out of high school—glances between us. "You guys know each other?"

Mikey snorts. "Kid, everyone here knows Quinn."

I roll my eyes, grab my name tag from the cubby, and clip it onto my polo. "Tee sheet updated yet?"

Mikey nods toward the whiteboard. "You're with some of the regulars. Davis, Mancini, and Beckett."

I barely suppress a groan. Businessmen in their forties who like to talk more than they play. The type who tip well enough but spend half the round trying to flirt.

I take my caddy bib from the wall hook, slide it over my head, and check the time. It's barely past eight, which means I've got a long shift ahead. Four hours in the sun with a trio of windbags and no real escape. Perfect.

The sun is brutal by midmorning, bearing down in thick, unrelenting waves as I trail behind my assigned golfers. The course is sprawling, impossibly green, stretching out under the kind of summer heat that makes the air feel sticky.

"Damn," Beckett mutters as we approach the next hole, swiping his sleeve across his forehead. "Hot as hell out here today."

It's been hot every day. But sure.

I pull a bottle of water from my bag, take a sip, and keep walking.

Davis lines up his shot, adjusting his stance, shifting his weight. He takes too long and swings too hard, sending the ball slicing off into the rough.

Mancini claps him on the back. "Tough break, man."

Davis exhales sharply. "Quinn, be honest with me. That was a shit swing, right?"

I fight the urge to sigh. "My job isn't to comment on your form."

Beckett chuckles. "That's a yes."

Davis shakes his head, laughing to himself. "You're too sharp for this job, Rose."

Yeah, well. Sharp doesn't pay my bills.

We move on, the game stretching out in long, slow intervals. Their conversation shifts from business deals to vacation homes, to their stock portfolios, to a poker game one of them lost big in last week.

I tune most of it out. I've spent years perfecting the art of appearing engaged while caring about absolutely nothing. That is, until Davis turns his attention back to me.

"So, just summers here?" he asks, casually adjusting his glove. "Why don't you work during the school year, too?"

"Busy saving the world up at Dayton," I say lightly.

Mancini nods. "Smart girl. Focus on your studies. What's your major again?"

"Business," I lie.

Beckett whistles. "Damn. You're gonna have half the country club hiring you once you graduate."

"Sure," I say, forcing a polite smile. "If they pay well."

They laugh, and Davis shakes his head. "You know, I like you, Rose. You remind me of my daughter—sharp as a whip, doesn't take shit from anyone."

"Must run in the family," I deadpan.

He grins.

We keep moving. I check the time. Only two more hours until my shift is over.

I keep my steps measured, my grip firm on the handle of the golf bag slung over my shoulder. The heat presses down thickly. It's the kind that settles deep in your bones and makes the air itself feel too heavy to breathe.

I fight the urge to shake my hands out, to press a palm against my chest to make sure my lungs haven't shrunk in the past five minutes. *Not now. Not here.*

I give a slow exhale through my nose.

I'm tight and buzzed with strain, but this isn't anything new.

Davis swings again. This time, the ball arcs clean, landing just shy of the green. He grins, pleased with himself, and they all start moving again, talking about some real estate deal or stock dip or whatever the hell else rich men like to complain about.

I don't listen. I keep my head down, count the holes left in my shift, roll my shoulders like that'll loosen the slow, breathless pressure that's begun creeping in.

The fairway curves around the edge of the pool deck, and I catch a glimpse of white chairs, striped umbrellas, the glint of water sparkling under the midafternoon sun. And there's Warren again. Still on his lifeguard stand, still watching the water like it's the only thing in the world worth looking at.

The moment my gaze snags on him, his head tilts, just slightly.

I snap my attention forward, jaw clenching.

No. No way in hell am I going to let him think he still has that kind of pull over me. The kind that sees through every defense, every carefully constructed wall. The kind that never really left, no matter how much I told myself it did.

Sure, I'm the one who fucked up. Who made the wrong choice. Who ruined everything. And I spent so many nights wishing I could just apologize, explain it all away and fix it. That I could go back and undo what I did.

But it doesn't work like that. For Warren, grudges root deep and make a home in his bones. It would have been foolish to think he'd ever want to hear me out.

So, if he wants to pretend I don't exist, then by all means, let him.

I adjust my grip on the golf bag and keep walking forward.

By the time the round ends and I finally make it back to the clubhouse, my muscles are aching, my shirt sticking to the small of my back. My patience is wearing thinner by the second. Somehow, I managed to keep my chest from tightening past the point of no return, so I'd consider that a win.

The blast of cold air-conditioning hits like a shock, and I shudder, sweat cooling against my skin too fast. I roll my shoulders, trying to shake the sensation as I make my way toward the staff area.

The break room is mostly empty, just a couple of other workers scrolling their phones or gulping down bottles of water. I head straight for the counter, grab a plastic cup, and fill it to the brim with ice water.

The first sip burns in the best way. I brace my hands against the counter, exhaling slowly.

Then something shifts behind me. A presence I'd know anywhere.

Warren doesn't say anything right away. He moves to the sink, fills a cup of his own, and then takes a slow drink like we're not standing three feet apart for the first time in two and a half years.

I stare ahead, eyes fixed on the ice melting in my glass, counting each drop like it might keep me steady. My jaw tightens, my shoulders stay stiff.

The silence stretches too long, and eventually, his voice cuts through it. "Didn't think you'd be here this summer."

I don't turn my head to face him. I can't. "Didn't think you cared."

A beat of silence, then, "I don't."

Without another word, he turns and walks away. I get it, he wants me to think I mean nothing to him. Maybe that I never did.

I stand there, jaw clenched, gripping my cup so hard it crinkles in my hand. A sharp pulse of anger, regret, and something dangerously close to heartbreak lodges itself in my throat. It's all I can do to swallow it down, bury it deep and keep on moving.

But I know better. I know *him*. If Warren really didn't care, he wouldn't have said anything at all.

Chapter Three
WARREN

The water in the training pool is cold and perfect.

I push through my stroke, arms cutting through the lane, each kick driving me forward. I'm fast and efficient. My breath is steady, my muscles tight but strong, each motion a carefully measured calculation of power and endurance.

I crave this. I savor it. The drag of water against my skin, the rhythmic churn of my body gliding forward, the momentary burn of oxygen deprivation before I roll for another breath.

It's 5:04 a.m., and I'm already ten laps in.

I didn't set an alarm this morning because I didn't need to. My body always knows. Years of training have made this muscle memory and instinct. I could do it in my sleep, could time my strokes without thinking, could pull myself through lap after lap while my brain stays blissfully blank.

No distractions or unwanted thoughts slipping through the cracks.

Fifty meters. Flip turn. Fifty meters back.

The water dulls everything. It mutes the world and quiets my mind, which forces me to focus on the mechanics. The rotation of my shoulders, the angle of my entry, the precision of my kick.

This is what I know, what I trust. The one thing in my life that's never let me down, never betrayed me or left me standing in the wreckage of something I couldn't put back together.

Five strokes, breathe. Five strokes, breathe.

I kick harder, propelling forward, lungs burning but steady, muscles tight but capable. I go until the strain in my limbs is the only thing I can feel, until my heartbeat drowns out the whisper of anything else trying to break through.

Because as long as I'm swimming, I'm not thinking.

I don't stop until my arms are screaming and my pulse hammers in my throat. My body demands air in a way that makes it impossible to ignore. I grip the wall, fingers digging into the slick tile, drag in a lungful of breath. Only then, does the tension in my chest finally ease.

And just like that, Quinn's there.

Not physically or in any real, tangible way. But in my fucking head, where I don't want her, where I refuse to let her take up space.

It's a quick flash of something unwelcome and unrelenting. Soft fingers pressing against my chest, dragging down the center of my sternum. The heat of her, flush against me, breath warm as she whispered my name like it was something to be savored.

"Warren, please, baby . . ."

I slam it down. Shut it off.

I pull myself up out of the water, bare feet slapping against the tile, water streaming off my body as I grab the towel from the bench and whip it over my shoulders. The thick cotton sticks to my skin, absorbing the heat from my workout, but it doesn't do anything to wipe her from my head.

Fucking Quinn.

I don't let myself linger on it for too long.

I rake a hand through my wet hair, grab my gear, and make my way to the showers, flipping the nozzle straight to cold, letting the icy water crash over me in sharp, punishing relief. It works for about five seconds before she's back again.

She's intrusive like that, always has been, slipping through the cracks.

I don't think about her. I mean, I haven't for years. Okay, *fuck*, I've done my best not to think about her. And I never would have taken the job at Sycamore if I had known she'd eventually show face.

I would have picked something else, taken an internship I didn't want, hell, even gone back to construction work if it meant not having to see her again. I don't like dealing with the reminder of something I've spent nearly three years trying to erase.

I scrub a hand over my jaw, let out a sharp breath, and flip the water off. I don't bother reaching for the cheap bodywash in my bag. I just stand there, dripping, watching the rivulets of water spiral down the drain like they might take the last twenty-four hours with them.

But they don't. They never do.

Someone should have told me, shouldn't they? I've always had a good, if not at least amicable, relationship with the Sycamore manager, Robbie.

When I reached out about coming back for the summer, I asked him point-blank.

"Quinn still working there?"

"Nah," he said. "She's not coming back this summer."

And that was the only reason I agreed.

But what he failed to mention—what he either forgot or chose not to tell me—was that she must have changed her mind. That somewhere along the way, her plans fell through, and they offered her a spot to finish out the last month of the season.

Now she's back there, and I'm rattled.

Because if I'd known Quinn Rose was going to be walking around the same damn club, wearing the same uniform, working the same job, throwing the same smug little smirks at guys who don't know any better—

I would have stayed far, far away.

I get dressed, shove my damp towel into my bag, and head for the exit. Outside the locker room, I breathe slowly, the way I was trained to do in the water. The way I always do when something creeps up on me that I don't want to deal with.

A swimming staple, a therapy trick.

I brace a hand against the doorframe, roll my shoulders, and shake it off. This person is not my problem. Not anymore.

When I make it to my car, I let muscle memory guide me to the last place I should be going right now. Oakview Assisted Living Facility.

It's a straight shot from campus, one I used to make more often, back when the guilt got to be too much. Now, I come here about once a month.

Not often, but enough to remind myself he's still kicking. No matter what's happened between us, the man inside is still my father. My blood.

But that doesn't mean I forget. And visiting him doesn't mean I forgive him, either or that I let go of all the shit he's put me through.

The missed pickups. The stolen money. The excuses that ran out long before I stopped answering his calls. The way I used to wait—*always fucking wait*—for him to change, to be better, to give a shit about anything other than his next fix.

But addiction doesn't work like that. It chews people up and spits them out hollow, takes the good and replaces it with hunger. And even now, sitting in a place like Oakview, surrounded by four walls that are meant to keep him safe, I wonder if there's still some part of him that's looking for an escape.

I pull into the lot, cut the engine, and sit there for a second, fingers tight around the wheel. My shoulders stiff, tension coiled up between them.

I could leave. I could put the car in reverse, drive straight home, and pretend I didn't feel the familiar pull of obligation. It's some sick, twisted sense of loyalty that never quite goes away.

But I wanted a distraction, and maybe this counts. Hell, maybe it's the only thing that ever does.

So, I grab my bag, lock the door behind me, and head inside.

The place smells like sanitized air and stale coffee. It's quiet, save for the low hum of a daytime talk show playing from the common room. The receptionist recognizes me, offers a small nod, but doesn't stop me as I pass.

She knows why I'm here.

I make my way down the hall, shoes scuffing against linoleum, and push open the door to Room 114.

My dad is sitting in his recliner, half-asleep, the TV blaring some old western at a volume far too loud. His hair is thinner than I remember, the deep-set lines in his face more pronounced.

For a second, he doesn't notice me.

Then his head turns, bleary gray eyes locking on mine. The same gray eyes I used to see every day when I was a kid. The same ones I looked up to before I realized they were always looking past me, searching for something else. A fix or a way out. Another goddamn excuse.

"Well, look who decided to show," he mutters, rubbing a hand over his jaw, eyes dropping to the cheap plastic watch on his wrist. "What's it been this time? Three weeks?"

Four, actually. But I don't say that. I drop my bag by the door, cross my arms over my chest, and say, "You need anything?"

It's the same question I always ask. The safest one. The one that keeps us both from saying anything we don't want to.

He shrugs, scratching at his wrist. "More smokes."

I exhale sharply. "You know you can't have those in here."

"Doesn't mean I don't want 'em."

I don't respond to that. Instead, I reach into my bag, pull out a pack of electrolyte drinks, a few high-protein snacks, the small things I know he'll take, even if he pretends not to care. I set them on the table beside him.

He spares them a glance, then looks back at me. "Still swimming?"

"Yeah."

He nods. "You gonna make Nationals this year?"

I roll my shoulders. "Yeah, maybe."

I'm a good swimmer. A great one, even. But I peaked early—back when I was fifteen, winning Junior Nationals and collecting medals like candy. Now? I'd be lucky to hit an A-cut during the regular season.

The Olympics were never in the cards for me, not really. Those dreams belonged to a younger version of me who didn't know better yet.

"That's good, kid."

The words land awkwardly, like he's not sure if he should be saying them at all. I think he's still trying to figure out what being a father is supposed to mean when you haven't really been one in years.

His road here was a slow descent. It started with drinking—heavy, often, and always justified. Then came the pills. And when those weren't strong enough, he found something stronger. Meth, eventually. That's the kind of drug that can rewire your entire life.

He had a few strokes not long after that. Drug-induced, the doctors said. One of them left him with hemiplegia. Partial paralysis on his left side.

After enough ER visits and too many botched attempts at rehab, Oakview became the only option he had left. A long-term care facility where they could monitor him full-time. Where he could be watched and where he'll probably spend the rest of his miserable life.

"You leading the Sunday service today?" I ask dryly, nodding toward the Bible sitting untouched on his bedside table.

He lets out a raspy chuckle. "Wouldn't that be a sight."

I smirk. "I'd pay money to see it."

His mouth twitches. "That the only way I'm getting you to church?"

"Maybe."

He huffs a laugh, shaking his head. "Still a heathen."

"Still your kid."

A beat of silence. Something uneasy and unspoken settles between us, like it always does. The kind of silence that says everything we're not ready to. Without offering more, without trying to fill it, I check my watch, pick up my bag, and step back toward the door.

"I'll see you soon, Dad."

"I'll believe it when I see it."

I lift a hand in a half-hearted wave and step out into the hallway.

This is the way it always goes. We have the same conversation with the same unspoken bullshit hanging in the air. For me, it's a cycle of resentment, obligation, and something close to pity. It's a shame we're both too proud to call it what it is.

By the time I pull into the driveway back home, the sun has climbed higher, burning off the last traces of morning cool.

I step into the house, kick my shoes off by the entryway, drop my bag at the base of the stairs, and head straight to my room. It's only 10:47 a.m., but I'm already exhausted. Emotionally, mentally, all of it.

I have the rest of the day ahead of me, but no real plan for how to spend it. I could go back to the pool, but I already put in my meters this morning—no point in overtraining. Could lift, but my muscles are still worn from the week. Pushing too hard now means paying for it later.

What I should do is catch up on the grad school applications

I've been putting off, but the thought of staring at another blank essay prompt makes my head ache. And not in the productive, push-through-it kind of way. More like shut-my-laptop-before-I-toss-it-out-the-window kind of way.

I need to figure out my next step. Need to lock in a plan and actually commit to something.

I've spent four years studying kinesiology, training like hell, working my ass off to keep my grades solid and my body stronger. I've done everything right—on paper.

But now that graduation's creeping closer, I still don't know if I want to go straight into grad school or take a shot at something else. Not the Olympics. I'm not that guy. But maybe something short-term.

A club circuit, maybe. Training part-time while I coach. It would be a way to stay in the water a little longer, just until I'm sure I'm ready to let it go.

I should sit down today and at least start an application. Pick a program, write the damn essay, and get it over with.

Instead, I stretch out on my bed, muscles finally starting to loosen, and let my eyes close for a second. But then—soft footsteps, a thud against the wall, the quiet creak of Liam's mattress. A low, familiar laugh.

My jaw tightens as I roll onto my side and yank my pillow over my head.

Birdie's with him. I can hear it—the rustle of sheets, the way she murmurs something under her breath, his answering chuckle, the muffled press of lips meeting skin.

I sigh, dig the heel of my hand into my eye, and force myself to shut it all out.

Fuck.

There goes Quinn again. The sound of her laugh muffled against my neck, the scrape of her teeth as she smiled into a kiss, the heat of her bare legs tangled with mine under my sheets.

Between us, it wasn't just sex. It was her. All of her. The best and worst of us, colliding.

I turn over again, restless. My ceiling fan spins in slow, useless circles.

There are a thousand things I should be worrying. Instead, I'm focused on the feeling that creeps in when everything else goes quiet. The gnawing sense of hunger, the echo in an empty room.

God, I am so fucking lonely, aren't I?

Chapter Four

QUINN

I DON'T APPRECIATE SHARED living or bonding with roommates.

I have them, technically. Two of them—Alyssa and Jordan. They were looking for a third during their sophomore year, and after a few polite interviews and one awkward group dinner, we decided to stick it out for the rest of college.

It's a mutual arrangement. One that works because I keep my space, and they keep theirs.

They're nice enough. Alyssa's pre-law, Jordan's on the club volleyball team. They study together at the kitchen table, swap mascara before going out, huddle up on the couch with their matching fuzzy blankets to binge-watch reality TV.

I exist adjacent to all of that.

I don't borrow clothes or sit in on study sessions. I don't braid anyone's hair while dissecting the finer points of the latest love triangle on *The Bachelor*. But when they need me—really need me—I show up.

Last fall, when Jordan's long-distance boyfriend dumped her over FaceTime? I handed her my best bottle of whiskey, let her sob into my sweatshirt, and helped her torch the hoodie he'd left at our place.

When Alyssa bombed her mock trial and spent three days convinced she'd never get into law school? I left a bottle of wine and a brutally annotated copy of her argument on her desk with one note: *This sucked. Try again.*

I'm not warm or cuddly. But I'm loyal. And I suppose that counts for something.

"Where the hell have you been? Back from traveling for three days and already off the grid?"

Alyssa's sprawled on the couch when I walk in, laptop open, case notes scattered across the coffee table. She peers over her screen, arching a brow.

"Just been at work," I say, kicking off my shoes.

"At Sycamore?" Jordan chimes in, stepping out of the kitchen with a protein shake. "Thought you weren't going back this summer."

Yeah, well. Plans change.

"Figured I might as well squeeze tips out of men who either think I'm their daughter reincarnated or want to fuck me. And sometimes, in a really gross way, *both*."

Jordan nearly chokes. "Ew. Though, at least the icky rich old men will tip you just for breathing. That's the dream."

Breathing? More like constant pandering coupled with the opportunity to leer at my tits. And while I do have a great set of them, it'd be nice if a man could make eye contact before pretending to care about my thoughts on market trends.

Besides, the tips are rarely generous unless I flirt like I mean it. And even then, they still hand me fives like they're doing me a favor.

Alyssa grins, stretching her arms over her head. "Please tell me you're still stringing them along with the business major thing."

"Obviously."

She laughs and shakes her head. "I swear, one day, some guy is gonna ask about your portfolio, and you're gonna have to admit you don't actually know what a mutual fund is."

"Oh, please," I say, grabbing a water bottle from the fridge. "The day a man at Sycamore asks me a serious question about business is the day I retire."

They laugh because they know I'm right. The guys who come to the club aren't interested in actual conversations. They want someone who nods at the right moments, laughs at their bad jokes, and lets them think they're more important than they are.

It's easier this way. People love what they can recognize.

A girl studying business? She's smart. Savvy. Marketable. Sexier because she's ambitious.

A girl studying English literature? She's useless in their minds.

So, I let them think I'm one thing when I'm another. It's a harmless lie but it's also a method of survival.

Alyssa shakes her head, amused, and turns back to her laptop. Jordan plops onto the couch beside her, flipping through a magazine.

I take my water to my room and quietly kick the door shut behind me. The solitude is familiar, and it's easy because I like being alone. I always have. It's sort of peaceful in a hollow, echoing sort of way.

I drop onto my bed and let my head tip back against the wall, the quiet settling over me like a second skin. My desk is a mess. Books are stacked in uneven piles, loose papers with half-written annotations, my laptop open to a creative writing project I abandoned three days ago.

It's hard for me to focus lately, but I still love stories. I always have. I love the way they work, the way people reveal themselves in fiction without realizing it. The way words can be used as both a weapon and a shield.

But I don't talk about it. Not because I'm embarrassed but because it doesn't fit the version of myself I like to give people.

When I was younger and my parents' attention narrowed in on my little brother—when their concern, their energy, their love seemed to orbit only him—I had stories. I had magical worlds and classic poetry. I had historical romance and gothic heartbreak. I had characters who felt like they existed solely for me. They listened when no one else did.

I stretch and grab my notebook, flipping to the dog-eared page where I left off. This is how I drown out the world. By getting lost in someone else's.

Four weeks. That's all I need. Four weeks of working, reading, and keeping my head down. Then the summer will be over, and my ex-boyfriend will be nothing more than a memory again.

Monday morning comes too soon, too hot, too much like déjà vu.

The air is already stifling by 9:00 a.m., the kind of heat that clings to your skin and makes your clothes feel like a punishment. Somewhere in the distance, a golf cart whirs to life, tires crackling over gravel. A slow reminder that summer doesn't care how tired you are.

Everything moves in a haze. Lazy swings. Half-hearted conversations. The lull of another long, sun-bleached morning at the Sycamore Country Club.

I avoided the pool deck today. I skipped the break room and didn't even glance at the storage closet. But that avoidance has an expiration date, and I know it. Eventually, Warren will be somewhere I can't sidestep. Eventually turns out to be now.

I'm halfway through my first shift when Warren walks past the gate.

He's dressed in uniform, near-black hair still damp from an early swim. He has the same broad, carved-out back as he moves past the cabanas with a towel slung over one shoulder, muscles shifting and rippling.

Of course, I notice. Of course, I look. And it makes my pulse stutter in that way I hate. My grip tightens on the scorecard in my hand.

I'm mad that he's here and that I still react to him this way. I'm mad that it still gets under my skin, no matter how many times I've told myself it won't.

I drag my eyes away and force a breath out, trying to shake it.

He's just a guy. A coworker. Interchangeable and forgettable the way most guys are.

But that's a lie, and I know it.

Warren Mercer isn't just a guy. He's the boy who once knew every corner of me, the only one who ever really understood how I worked. He was the sharpest mirror I ever stood in front of—and now, all he sees when he looks at me is the girl who broke his trust.

And maybe that's all I deserve.

I refocus my attention, shift my bag higher on my shoulder, and tune in to the conversation happening between my golfers.

". . . if you're not playing to win, you're just donating money," Beckett is saying, adjusting his grip on his club. "Last time I played with Mark, he lost six grand on a bet because he thought he could outdrive me."

"Some of us play for the sport, not the wallet," Graham replies, lining up his shot.

Beckett snorts. "You say that now, but the second you lose a couple grand to me, you'll be rethinking your stance."

I barely suppress an eye roll. Different day, same conversation.

I shift my weight, already overheated, my water bottle half-drained, my chest tight in the way that means I need to slow down, regulate my breathing, and take a damn break. But I don't have time for that.

I force another sip of water, nod when one of the guys makes some offhanded comment in my direction, and keep moving. My pulse quickens, and I go light-headed.

By the time we reach the turn, the heat is oppressive, a thick, smothering weight pressing against my ribs. My fingers tingle. My chest feels like it's full of cotton.

Shit. I need my inhaler.

I tell my group I'll meet them at the next tee, then duck off the path, cutting through the maintenance lot toward the club's storage shed. It's shaded here, away from the worst of the heat, the air marginally cooler beneath the awning.

I sit up on the wooden storage table, bracing myself as I dig through my bag with shaky fingers. When I find my inhaler, I hold it to my lips.

One puff. Hold. Two. Deep breath in. Hold. Exhale.

The relief comes slowly, the tightness in my chest loosening with every controlled inhale. My vision sharpens. My pulse evens out. I close my eyes for a second, focusing on my breath, grounding myself in the quiet hum of cicadas, the muffled sounds of golfers in the distance, the low, familiar rasp of—

"You good?"

My eyes snap open.

Zane—one of the younger pool attendants, all easy charm and too much curiosity—is standing a few feet away, arms crossed, head tilted.

I straighten quickly, clearing my throat. "Yeah. I'm fine."

His gaze flicks to the inhaler. "Didn't know you had asthma."

"I don't exactly advertise it," I mutter, shoving it back into my bag.

He studies me for a second, then takes a step closer and props one hand against the table beside me. He's tall—not Warren tall, but close enough to feel a little too confident about it.

"You should pace yourself," he says, teasing. "Can't have you dropping on the back nine. One of the regulars might think it's their heart giving out."

I roll my eyes. "I'm fine."

He grins and reaches out, fingertips brushing lightly against my elbow, like he's about to nudge me or say something else—

"Zane. Shift change."

My stomach knots instantly.

We both glance toward the door, where Warren stands, arms crossed, his posture relaxed but his eyes sharp. He's watching us, but he's also measuring the shape and the distance between Zane's hand and my body.

My face burns.

Warren's gaze moves slowly between us, assessing the scene.

Zane, ever oblivious, just smirks. "Hey, Mercer. I'll be right there in less than a minute—just finishing up."

Warren doesn't look at him. Doesn't even blink. He tips his head slightly, eyes fixed on me now. "If thirty seconds is all you need, by all means. Finish."

His tone is smooth, but there's something razor-edged beneath it.

I straighten, bracing myself. "Don't be such a dick."

He lifts a brow and finally flicks his gaze toward Zane. "I'm not the one getting handsy in the equipment shed."

"We weren't doing anything," I snap.

Zane laughs. "Guess I'll see you around, Quinn."

I keep my eyes locked on Warren until Zane disappears.

Warren steps forward, close enough that I have to tilt my chin up to meet his eyes. The space between us shrinks into a narrow, focused point.

"You're real quick to defend yourself." His gaze drops to my mouth, then back to my eyes. "Why's that?"

I huff. "For someone so committed to avoiding me, you sure love to stick around."

Warren gives a knowing smirk.

The kind that says he sees right through me. That he knows exactly how much this is driving me up the wall. That no matter how hard I try to act unaffected, he can still spot the truth in my eyes.

Then, just like that, he steps back. He's calm and in control, like he didn't just invade every inch of my personal space and leave me reeling.

He shakes his head once and walks off without another word. Somehow, that pisses me off more than anything else.

By the time I make it back to my group, the tightness in my chest has eased, but the frustration lingers, buzzing under my skin like static. Thankfully, the rest of the round passes by without incident.

I move on autopilot—haul the clubs, smile when expected, nod at conversations I'm not really listening to. But my thoughts won't relent.

They circle, restless, dragging me right back to the look in Warren's eyes. The tension in his voice. The edge in the way he said my name.

He says he doesn't care, says I don't matter, but something slipped through the cracks just there—a flicker or a fracture of feeling.

And for a girl who's spent the last two years trying not to feel anything at all, that's dangerous.

Chapter Five

WARREN

THE CLUB IS ALREADY FILLING up when I step into the dining room. White tablecloths, polished silverware, servers moving smoothly between tables with trays of mimosas and fruit plates.

It's still early, but that doesn't mean much here. Sycamore mornings start with espresso, neatly pressed linens, and weekend warriors talking too loudly about their golf handicaps. It's a performance—one they've all rehearsed a hundred times.

I catch sight of my mom first, seated near the window, her hands wrapped around a steaming cup of coffee, a plate of untouched croissants between her and my stepdad. She looks relaxed, content in a way I don't remember from when I was younger.

Her hair is pulled into a neat twist, her nails freshly done. Those are small details, but they say everything. She's not struggling anymore. She's not scrubbing coffee stains out of her uniform or counting tips in the back of a diner.

She's taken care of now, which is why I don't totally begrudge Daniel.

He's sitting next to her, reading something on his phone, a perfectly ironed golf polo stretched across broad shoulders. The picture of a man who's got it all under control. He's never been unkind to me, never once treated me like a burden, and he's certainly never tried to act like my dad.

He looks up first, nodding when he sees me. "Look who's on time."

Mom turns and smiles. "Warren, sweetheart."

I slip into the chair across from them, letting the club's signature too-expensive, too-stiff cushions swallow me. A server appears almost instantly, dropping a menu in front of me.

"Your usual, Mr. Mercer?"

I almost sigh. The fact that I even have a usual here is embarrassing. I've worked at Sycamore on and off for years, but I've never belonged here. Still, I nod.

"Yeah, thanks."

Mom tilts her head. "How's the summer job treating you?"

I fight the urge to scrub my temples. "It's fine."

Daniel snorts. "That's convincing."

I shoot him a look. "What do you want me to say? The pool's wet. The members are rich. The lifeguard chair is still uncomfortable as hell. Nothing's changed."

Mom hums, her knowing gaze flicking between me and my stepdad. She sees everything, always has. But she also has the good sense not to press me on it. Instead, she stirs a bit of sugar into her coffee. "And swimming? Training?"

I nod, absently drumming my fingers against the table. "It's been good. I've been hitting all my splits, times are solid. If I keep it up, I've got a shot at Nationals. Probably a B-cut, but it's doable."

I've been there once before—sophomore year. Barely made the cut, swam the 200 free like my life depended on it, and placed somewhere in the middle of the pack. Solid, not spectacular.

It wasn't like Junior Nationals, where I used to win heats and hit the podium. Back then, people thought I had a real shot at going pro. Now? I'm consistent and strong. My coach still calls me one of our best. But sometimes I wonder if that's just experience talking—or if I really did peak five years ago.

Daniel sets his phone down, finally giving me his full attention. "That's big."

I shrug. "Would be."

He considers me for a second, the way he always does when he's about to say something that he thinks I won't like. "And after that?"

I grab my water, taking a slow sip, buying time. "What do you mean?"

He leans forward, resting his forearms on the table. "After the season. After graduation. You've been putting off your grad school applications, haven't you?"

Mom presses her lips together like she wants to intervene but doesn't.

I set my water down, shifting my weight. "I've still got time."

Daniel doesn't call me out on the lie, but he doesn't let it slide, either. "Warren, we've talked about this."

Yeah, we have. Countless times. He thinks he's helping, but if I'm not self-motivated, then a pep talk from my stepdad isn't going to flip a switch in me overnight.

I glance out the window, watching a pair of golfers lazily tee off, trying not to feel cornered. Daniel and I don't fight. We don't argue. But I know this is his way of pushing me—nudging me toward a decision, a plan, a path forward.

I know he's right. I should've sent in my applications already. I should be lining up my future instead of waffling between the safe option—grad school—and the unknown of a swimming future.

I exhale through my nose, keeping my expression blank. "I'll figure it out in time."

Daniel holds my gaze, then dismisses it. "Alright."

That's another thing I like about him: he knows when to let things drop.

The server returns, setting my plate in front of me. I ordered eggs, toast, turkey sausage. Load up on protein, they say. It makes for a better season. I stab my fork into the yolk, watching it bleed across the plate.

Mom switches gears. "I ran into your manager, Robbie, last week. He had very good things to say."

I snort. "Yeah, I haven't disappointed anyone yet. Or pissed them off, I guess."

Daniel chuckles. "Sounds about right."

I glance at him, then back down at my plate. He's joking, but it still stings. Maybe because once upon a time, he had a real reason not to trust me. A reason I gave him.

I push my food around, keeping my voice casual. "Yeah, well, not much trouble to get into as a lifeguard."

Mom doesn't react, but I can feel the shift in the air. The weight of what we're not saying. Because three summers ago, I wasn't just the kid whose new stepdad pulled some strings to get him a cushy job at the club. I was the kid who got caught stealing from him afterward.

Daniel clears his throat. "I'm glad it's working out."

Mom smiles, reaching across the table to squeeze my wrist. "I'm proud of you, sweetheart."

Daniel nods, lifting his mug. "Same."

And I believe them. I do. Even if they've got a million things to worry about—bigger things, heavier things—it still feels good to be seen. To be told I'm doing okay, even if I'm not sure I believe it myself most days.

We finish eating, conversations shifting to lighter things. Gossip about the club members, some story about a guy who got caught cheating at poker last week, Mom reminiscing about a trip she wants to take after I graduate.

And for a moment, everything feels easy and normal. For once, there isn't this quiet pressure building beneath the surface. But then I check the time, and I realize I only have fifteen minutes left until my shift.

The second I stand up, stretching, adjusting my uniform, I know what's coming. Like fucking clockwork, that low-grade sense of dread creeps up again. The kind that tightens in my chest and coils low in my gut.

I exhale sharply, shake it off. It doesn't matter. *She* doesn't matter.

I drop a few bills on the table. It's enough to cover my meal, even though I know Daniel would pay for me without a thought. He'd put it on his Sycamore tab and call it a day. But it's the principle. I always earn my keep.

Mom stands, pressing a kiss to my cheek. "Don't work too hard."

"Try not to let anyone drown," Daniel adds.

Outside, the heat slams into me like it's got something to prove. Another scorcher. Another long shift ahead. I roll my shoulders, try to center myself, then round the corner toward the pool deck.

And there's Quinn again.

She's wearing that same knowing smirk, shoulders braced.

Whatever semblance of patience I walked out with? It vanishes, just like that.

I'm right back to square one.

The rest of my shift passes in a flurry of chlorine, sunscreen, and mindless routine.

Hours spent perched on the guard stand, sunglasses shielding my eyes, watching over a pool full of kids cannonballing off the diving board, retirees wading through the shallows, and club members who don't understand that no running rule applies to them, too.

It's fine, easy work. If I don't think too hard, it's almost peaceful. Almost.

Because every once in a while, my gaze catches on the course beyond the gates. The flash of a navy polo, the swing of a golf bag over a shoulder, the sharp sound of a club cracking clean against a ball.

I go through the motions—rotating shifts, hydrating, tossing a couple of swim rings back to kids who keep floating too far out. I nod along as one of the younger lifeguards rambles about his plans to try out for his college swim team. I wipe sweat from my brow and keep my focus locked straight ahead.

I make it through unscathed.

Or, at the very least, without snapping.

By the time I clock out, the sun is sinking low, bleeding orange and pink across the sky. My shoulders ache with the weight of the day, but there's a strange relief in it. Another shift finished means another paycheck earned. I'm one day closer to the end of summer and to getting back to school, where things make more sense.

I head toward the parking lot, keys in hand, already running through tomorrow's shift in my head.

Oh, fucking hell.

Quinn's sitting on the hood of my car, arms braced behind her, ankles crossed, gaze turned toward the sky. She's completely at ease. If she hadn't spent the day haunting the edges of my focus, I'd almost think she arrived here by apparition.

Her long, dark hair is pulled into a loose braid over one shoulder, strands escaping and curling against her sun-kissed skin. High cheekbones, full lips, those deep, cutting brown eyes that have always seen too much. Always too sharp, too knowing.

And still—God help me—the most devastatingly beautiful woman I've ever laid eyes on.

I grit my teeth. "You're gonna dent it."

Quinn tilts her head slightly, as if considering the thought for the first time. "What? This mint-condition, top-of-the-line, 2008 Toyota 4Runner?"

My patience snaps. "Get off my damn car, Quinn."

She huffs a little, unimpressed, but she does it. She slides off with an exaggerated stretch.

"We should talk," she says, brushing imaginary lint off her shorts.

I move closer and yank open the driver's side door. "We shouldn't."

She steps into my space, close enough that I can smell her sunscreen and whatever shampoo she uses. Okay, it's fucking cherry almond. I'm not gonna pretend I don't know that. I remember exactly what it smells like on her skin, in my sheets, on my hoodie that she used to steal.

"I'm so tired of this, and it's only been three shifts."

I don't answer as I move around her, hand braced on the door handle, ready to get in and drive away. But then she moves, too, cuts me off and plants herself firmly in front of me.

"I'm serious, Mercer," she says, crossing her arms. "This has got to stop. I get that you can't stand me. I get that you'd rather I disappear into the ether forever, that you're unbelievably mad at me. But can you just put on an act for the next few weeks to make this experience tolerable for the both of us?"

Something inside me—something I thought I buried a long time ago—finally pushes to the surface. "You think I'm *mad*?"

Quinn blinks, bracing herself.

I shake my head, a hollow laugh slipping past my lips. "I stopped being mad a long time ago." Then I look her straight in the eye and say the biggest lie I've ever told. "Now I just really don't fucking care about you."

The words leave my mouth with a grand sense of finality. And I wish—God, I wish—they were true. But the second they land, the second I see something fractured flicker across her face, I know I fucked up.

She tilts her head, arms still crossed. "Did you forget that I know exactly what it looks like when you don't care?" she murmurs. "This? This is not that."

"We hooked up for a while, and then . . . whatever." I shrug, work my way through a heavy swallow. "It was three years ago. What else do you want me to say?"

"Hooked up?" Her voice is sharp, low. Not loud, but enough to make my chest tighten. "You loved me, Warren. I know you did."

"And you fucked me over," I snap. "So, what's that say about *you*?"

She doesn't back down. She never does. She stands in front of me, too close, the sunset throwing golden halos across her sharp cheekbones, the familiar glint of pride in her eyes. She's holding herself steady and unflinching.

She's daring me to shrink first.

But I won't. Not with her looking at me like that. She pretends like she still knows me. Still knows exactly how to wreck me. And maybe—for some inane, self-destructive reason—I still want her to.

But I know exactly how it ends because I've already lived through the wreckage once before. It doesn't burn out clean. It lingers. It rots through everything you try to build after.

That's why I can't let myself go back to her. Because deep down, I know I wouldn't survive her twice.

Chapter Six

THAT FIRST SUMMER

WARREN

This job was handed to me. Arranged as a favor from my new stepdad to help me get on my feet, to keep me occupied before starting college. He called it a good opportunity. A way to earn my own money and to get used to responsibility.

As if I haven't been responsible for as long as I can remember. For my deadbeat dad and his endless money-spending habits, for my mom when she finally fell apart, for myself when it became obvious no one else was going to be.

I've been managing shit on my own for years.

But I took it because there wasn't a good reason not to. Lifeguarding at a country club? Easy hours, decent pay. Beats hauling bricks or sweating through a landscaping job in the middle of July.

It's only my second week, and I'm still figuring things out. Who's in charge, who slacks off, which members to avoid, which coworkers to actually acknowledge. I don't care much either way. I want to keep my head down, do the job, and then go home.

That is, until a furious voice slices through the heat.

"Are you fucking kidding me?"

I turn my head toward the sound. There's a girl about my age standing by the cart path. She's tall and athletic. A long dark braid swings over one shoulder. Her skin is sun-warmed, her frame all lean lines and sharp edges. She's really fucking gorgeous.

She doesn't notice me as she storms off. Her steps are clipped, shoulders tight like she's ready to shatter something. Or *someone*.

She stops at the staff shed, yanks a clipboard off the hook, and stares it down.

I should keep moving. Whatever she's pissed about isn't my problem and it's definitely not my business. But for some reason, I don't. I stand there like a dipshit, watching her flip through the pages, muttering curses under her breath.

She's mad, and it's not the kind of anger that fades quickly, either. It's rooted, wound tight and deep. I can't see what's on the clipboard and I don't know what she's looking for, but she clearly hasn't found it there.

I'm not the type to start small talk, especially not with someone mid-rage spiral. But for some reason, my mouth moves before my brain catches up.

"Rough day?" I ask.

She snaps her head up, eyes already narrowing. "Who the hell are you?"

I raise a brow. "New guy. Lifeguard."

Her eyes drag over me like she's trying to decide if I'm worth acknowledging. Then she exhales sharply, shaking her head. "Right, the Donovan kid?"

I wince. "Mercer. Daniel's my stepdad."

"Great. A *step*-nepo baby. Just what we need here."

"Nice to meet you, too," I mutter.

She doesn't laugh or even look at me again as she flips through the clipboard, fingers drumming impatiently against the edge.

I could leave. I could keep walk out of here like a normal person. But something about her keeps me rooted in place. I want to understand her, want to know what's gotten under her skin.

"Something wrong?"

She lets out a humorless laugh. "You mean besides the fact that this job is an endless exercise in suffering?" She flicks the clipboard toward me. "Someone switched my assignments. I was supposed to be with the high rollers this week—good tippers, good money. Now

I'm stuck caddying for a bunch of washed-up guys who call me sweetheart and think it's a compliment."

I frown. "That sucks."

"No shit," she mutters.

She's still fuming. I can see it in the way her jaw clenches, the way her fingers twitch like she's two seconds from chucking the clipboard into the nearest hedge. It's kind of impressive, honestly.

I lean against the shed, watching her. "You look like you're about to kill someone."

She tilts her head, eyes flashing. "Yes, and I still might."

For some reason, I grin. I like that about her, like that she doesn't fake it.

She catches it, frowns harder. "What?"

"Nothing." I shake my head. "You're just—"

Bitter. Rude. Furious at the world.

And I want you anyway. Badly, in fact. Desperately, if the way my pulse spikes just from standing this close is any indication.

"You're kind of terrifying. It's weirdly appealing."

She scoffs and steps past me. "Not worth the effort."

And then she's gone. But I already know, down to my bones, I'm completely fucked.

Chapter Seven

QUINN

I PUSH through the apartment door, kick it shut behind me, and drop my bag onto the floor with a little too much force. My shoulders are tight, my pulse still uneven. My skin is damp with sweat, and I know it's because I overdid it out there.

I yank the elastic from my hair, shaking loose the long braid that's been pressing against the back of my neck all day. It sticks slightly to my skin, heavy and damp. The heat of the day hasn't quite let go of me yet.

Alyssa and Jordan are sprawled across the couch, picking at takeout cartons, half watching some trashy reality show. It's one of those fake dating competitions where everyone has the same haircut and too-white teeth, where the women act like falling in love on a sponsored yacht is the pinnacle of human experience.

Jordan barely glances up, arching a brow. "That bad, huh?"

I grab a water bottle from the fridge, crack it open, and take a long sip. Shrug. "People are annoying."

Alyssa stretches, her tank top riding up slightly as she lifts her arms over her head. Soft brown skin peeks above her waistband, glinting faintly with leftover body shimmer. "Must be really annoying if it got to *you*."

I wrinkle my nose. "What's that mean?"

Jordan snickers, digging through the takeout box with her chopsticks. "It's just that you usually don't give a shit about anyone."

I force a smirk, tilting the bottle back again. "Still don't."

It's not a lie. It's just not the whole truth.

I cross the kitchen, letting the cold water press against the heat of my palm. It's grounding, a small relief. But my thoughts still buzz, Warren's voice still sitting there at the base of my skull, looping through every last word.

I stopped being mad a long time ago. Now I just really don't fucking care about you.

He said is so flatly. A lie that somehow still managed to land like a fist between my ribs.

I exhale through my nose. Slam the water bottle down on the counter. My chest feels tight again, like I've been holding something in for too long, and now there's no room left to breathe.

Alyssa doesn't look away from the screen, but she catches it anyway. "You good?"

"Fine."

She hums, unconvinced, but doesn't push.

Jordan tosses her chopsticks into the takeout box, leaning back against the couch cushions. "You know what you need?"

I don't look at her. "A million dollars and a secluded island?"

She snorts. "Close. You need to hit something."

I blink, turning toward her. "What?"

Alyssa perks up. "Oh, you could try that old boxing gym down the street. Emberline, I think it's called."

Jordan nods. "Yeah, I pass right by it on my way to work. It's a little old and dingy, but it's legit. You should check it out."

I scoff. "Right. Because what I really need is a mouthguard and a reason to sweat more."

Alyssa grins. "No, but you *do* seem like you'd enjoy punching things."

I shake my head, but something about the suggestion sticks. Not because it's a good idea. Not because I actually want to go. But because I *do* want to hit something.

The thought lingers as I start absentmindedly cleaning the kitchen, picking up discarded napkins and stacking takeout cartons that aren't mine. I don't really care about the mess, but it gives me something to do. Something to control.

Alyssa watches me from the couch, expression vaguely amused. "Quinn, you know we have a dishwasher, right?"

I rinse out a coffee mug that isn't mine, shake the water off my fingers. "You guys are animals."

Jordan rolls her eyes, flipping to another channel. "Oh, the horror. God forbid a crumb touches your sacred countertop."

I don't respond, just wipe down the counter and keep moving.

I like Alyssa and Jordan. They're good people. They're fun and easy to live with. But they haven't gotten to know me well, just like I haven't bothered getting to know them. Not on a deeper level, anyway.

They know I work at Sycamore every summer. That I'm an English lit major. That I can drink tequila without flinching. They think I'm tough and unbothered, the kind of person who doesn't dwell.

And I let them think that. Because people don't ask questions when they think they already have the answers. The moment you hand someone the real parts of yourself—the messy parts—they get to decide what to do with them.

Keep them. Twist them. Discard them when you become inconvenient.

So, I keep my cards close. I offer up just enough to be understood, never enough to be truly known. That way, the inevitable rection doesn't sting so much.

The apartment is quiet by the time I make it to my room. My roommates have gone to bed, leaving behind silence and the occasional creak of the walls settling. It's dark but humming with the kind of tension that doesn't let you rest.

I should sleep, or try to, at least. But it's useless. So, I lie there, staring at the ceiling, hands fisted in the sheets, chest tight with the weight of everything unsaid. Warren's words are still there, pressing in on me.

I stopped being mad a long time ago.

I scoff into the silence. He's such a lousy little liar. I squeeze my eyes shut, turn onto my side, and try to will myself to sleep until something else creeps in.

It's a flash of a memory. A gut punch.

Warren and I are tucked away under the shadow of the Sycamore's clubhouse awning, hidden from view but not enough to be entirely safe. Rain drenches us both, dripping from his hair, his breath warm against my lips.

His hands grip my waist, voice rough.

"Christ, Quinn. You're trying to kill me."

I sit up so fast it makes me light-headed. Cursing under my breath, I throw off the blankets, shove my feet into my sneakers, grab my bag. This restless, spiraling bullshit is eating me alive.

I need to do something. Need to *hit* something, actually.

I think of Emberline. And then, not even five minutes later, I'm slipping out the front door, careful not to let it slam behind me.

Outside, streetlights flicker—some buzzing faintly, others already dead—leaving patches of darkness along the cracked sidewalk. Somewhere in the distance, a siren wails, stretching long and low before fading into the night.

I check the time. 10:42 p.m.

I pray that the gym is still open at this hour. Because if I don't do something—move, run, fight—I'm going to lose my mind.

I take the stairs down, two at a time, and step out onto the street, the heat still clinging to the pavement. The city is different at night. It's a little sharper and dangerous. Still, I'm not afraid to be out here alone.

I've spent the last three years wandering around at night by myself.

I keep my pace even and steady, my breath measured as I jog down the street.

I stopped being mad a long time ago.

I push harder, pick up speed, let my muscles strain with the effort.

Now I just really don't fucking care about you.

I suck in a sharp breath, ignoring the way my chest tightens, the slow burn climbing up my ribs. I'm fine. It's fine. I just need to move enough to quiet the noise in my head.

The gym appears at the end of the block. A squat, nondescript building with a faded sign that reads: EMBERLINE BOXING CO. It's the kind of place that doesn't care about aesthetics. Old-school. No frills.

I slow my stride, jogging to a stop in front of the door. My hands brace on my knees as I catch my breath, lungs dragging air. I've been walking miles all summer, but this kind of movement hits different.

I'm in decent shape, just not the kind that holds up under a sprint.

I dig into my bag and pull out my inhaler, take a quick puff, wait for the tightness in my chest to ease. The lights inside are still on, but I hesitate, shifting my weight, my pulse still uneven.

What the hell am I doing here?

I should turn around, go home, and sleep it off. But something about the thought makes my skin itch, makes the anger coil a little tighter in my chest. So, before I can overthink it, I pull the door open.

There's a worn-out ring in the center of the floor, ropes sagging slightly at the corners. A few beat-up dummies stand in a crooked line near the wall, arms stiff at their sides. Speed bags hang in a lopsided row by the back wall.

In the far corner, a heavy bag swings gently, still moving from the last person who took something out on it. Every few seconds, a low grunt echoes from somewhere behind a partition, followed by the sharp thud of glove on leather.

I take a hesitant step inside, feeling instantly out of place. It's not polished or welcoming. And I don't like feeling unsure of myself.

"You lost, kid?" The voice is rough, sandpapered with age as it cuts through the quiet.

I glance over. The man is probably in his sixties—wiry but solid. He's nursing what's left of a cup of coffee, scowl etched deep into his face like it's been there for years. His T-shirt, once black, is now faded to a dull gray, the Emberline logo barely legible beneath the wear.

His unimpressed eyes sweep over me from head to toe. If I had to guess, I'd say he's seen a hundred girls like me walk through that door and bolt just as fast. He already knows I don't belong here.

I lift my chin. "I was just—"

"Leaving?" he cuts in, one brow raised, daring me to confirm it. "Yeah, figured."

Something about his tone pisses me off. My chin tilts, shoulders going stiff.

"I was actually gonna say I'm just checking the place out."

His mouth twitches in amusement. He huffs a short laugh, then tosses me a pair of old, beat-up gloves from behind the counter.

"First day's free," he says gruffly. "You look like you need to get a hit in."

The gloves are heavy, the leather worn. They smell like old sweat and chalk, and I'm not sure if that's comforting or deeply disgusting. I blink down at them, then back at him.

"Er, I don't exactly know what I'm doing."

He shrugs. "Good. That means you won't think too hard."

I chew on the inside of my cheek. I could still leave. I should leave, actually. I should definitely, absolutely not stay. But I'm too proud to back down now.

I exhale slowly. "Okay."

He nods toward the far wall. "Locker room's through there. Wraps are in the bin. Tape up first."

I nod back, forcing my steps forward before I can change my mind.

The locker room is dimly lit, the overhead bulb flickering like it's on its last leg. I step inside and scan the space. There are dented metal lockers, an industrial fan humming lazily in the corner, and a plastic bin filled with rolls of hand wraps. Nothing that tells me what the hell I'm doing.

I crouch down, pull a roll free, and hesitate. I've seen this before—on TV, in documentaries, the occasional YouTube rabbit hole—but watching and doing aren't the same thing.

I fumble with the material, trying to figure out where to start, how tight to pull, how to keep it from bunching awkwardly around my wrist.

The first attempt is too loose. The second cuts off my circulation. The third . . . better. Not perfect, but good enough.

I glance up, catching my reflection in the mirror above the sink. My hair's a mess, my tank top clinging to the damp skin at the small of my back. There's something unfamiliar in my own expression. Tension, maybe, or anticipation.

I'm not sure if I'm waiting for this to explode in my face or if I'm excited about the prospect of letting something out for once. Of hitting back.

I pull on the gloves he gave me, flexing my fingers against the padding. They're still heavy, still smell like someone else's fight.

But when I curl my hands into fists, something about it feels . . . right.

I need this, I think. Need to do something for myself.

Fifteen minutes later, I'm standing in front of a heavy bag. My muscles are loose, but my mind is coiled tight, waiting for the inevitable second where the doubt will creep back in.

"Hit it," the old man calls from his perch behind the counter.

I turn, blinking at him. "What?"

He gestures lazily with one hand. "You're standin' there like it's gonna hit you first. Get on with it."

I glance back at the bag and shift my stance. My fingers twitch inside the gloves.

Of course, it lands wrong. An awkward thud, my wrist bending too much on impact. A dull shock shoots up my arm, and I fight the urge to shrivel up and retreat, to shake it off and pretend I wasn't just embarrassingly bad at something so basic.

"You ever thrown a punch before?" The man—he still hasn't told me his name—steps closer, arms crossed, weight shifted slightly to one side.

"Not really."

He grunts. "Again."

I adjust my stance, shake out my hand, then try again. This time, it feels better. Still not good, but better.

"Not bad. Keep your wrist straight. Don't let your shoulders get sloppy."

I reset and punch again. Harder. Then again. Faster.

Without overthinking, I just hit. Over and over, breath coming in sharp bursts, fists slamming into the bag with more force, more certainty. I don't stop until my lungs are burning, my arms aching, my heartbeat thudding in my ears.

The tension in my chest finally starts to uncoil.

I step back, hands braced on my knees, sweat dripping from my temple, muscles trembling from the effort. I fumble for my inhaler without thinking, take a quick puff, and press the back of my hand to my forehead.

The old man doesn't say anything about it, and I don't care if he does.

The release is sudden and startling. I expected to feel ridiculous, self-conscious. Instead, I feel a hell of a lot lighter.

"You've got something to work with."

I tense at the pseudo-compliment. "Yeah? And how would you know?"

"I own this place. Been doing this shit longer than you've been alive. Seen enough to know when someone's got too much fight bottled up for their own good."

I wipe my forehead, still catching my breath. "Yeah, well, I don't really have time for this. I'd rather get more sleep."

"Oh? You just spent an hour proving otherwise."

I glance at the heavy bag. At my shaking hands and the space I carved out for myself here. That hour of chaotic training was real and raw and mine. It was something I wanted to do.

But it's not something I *need* to do. I'm busy, tired, and spread much too thin already. I have other things to do—bills to cover and plans to salvage. Priorities that should always come first.

I shouldn't come back here again, should I?

Fuck. I already know I will.

Chapter Eight

WARREN

THE WATER SHOCKS my system the second I dive in. It's sharp and bracing, trying to scrape clean everything I've been carrying with me. Regret, frustration, the weight of my conversation with Quinn. It all dulls under the surface.

By the second lap, the noise in my head finally quiets. The ache in my chest doesn't disappear, but it fades enough to breathe around it. The pull of the water gives me something else to focus on. A clarity I can't find anywhere else.

Each stroke cuts a little deeper through the static. The push off the wall, the stretching and the breathing. Nothing matters except the next turn ahead. I'm not thinking about what I should've said. I'm not thinking about the way Quinn looked at me or how fast I caved when she got close again.

It's just me and the lane now. Ten 200-meter repeats. Descending intervals. The kind of set that leaves no room for doubt, no space for anything except the burn in my shoulders and the tight coil in my core. Staying ahead of the fatigue as the steady tick of the pace clock pushes me forward.

I've been swimming since I was eight years old. My mom signed me up for summer league after I nearly broke my arm falling out of a tree in the backyard. She said I needed something to burn off energy and to keep me out of trouble. I rolled my eyes at the time, but the second I hit the water, something in me clicked.

The world disappeared around me. Everything slowed down to just my body, my breath, my control—it all suddenly made sense. And by the time I was ten, I wasn't just good at swimming. I was winning.

By high school, the sport was everything to me. I had morning practices before the sun was up, afternoon doubles, weight training, and dryland workouts. I qualified for Junior Nationals at sixteen, state champion in the 200 and 400 free by seventeen.

Scouts started watching. Schools started calling.

Dayton University gave me the best offer by far. The best training and a real chance to push myself further.

Now, I'm a senior. It's my final year and my last shot.

I'm no longer the prodigy or the one to watch.

I'm still good—damn good—but not NCAA champion or Olympic circuit material. I'm not the kind of swimmer who racks up NIL deals or has SportsCenter knocking. And that's okay. I've made my peace with it.

I still chase the time clock like it owes me something. I still crave the quiet clarity that comes with pushing my body to its edge. I don't need medals to prove I'm getting better, either. I just need the water and the semblance of peace it gives me.

I finish my last rep and grip the pool's edge, dragging in lungfuls of air. My arms shake, my pulse pounds, my whole body hums with exertion.

That was good, but not good enough.

I duck under, run a hand over my face, and let the water mute everything for a few seconds longer. When I finally pull myself out, I check the time again. Another tenth of a second shaved off.

Faster, but not fast enough.

The thought sticks as I grab my towel, rake it over my head, and make my way to the locker room. I used to swim like I was chasing something. Now it feels more like I'm trying to outrun it.

My body's wrung out, but my mind is already on to the next thing. Because if I qualify for Nationals again this year, then what?

And if I don't?

I shake it off, exhaling hard. No point chasing questions I can't answer yet. Turning over possibilities doesn't make them any more certain. It's just mental noise. And that won't make me faster. It certainly won't make the decision any easier when the time comes.

I'd be better off putting my energy where it actually matters—training.

By the time I get back to the house, I only have about thirty minutes left before I need to head to the club. The door's unlocked. Of course it is. Liam and his girlfriend are already up.

"Don't stress, baby, we've got plenty of time."

"Yeah, uh-huh, you said that twenty minutes ago."

I step into the kitchen to find Birdie pacing near the fridge, tucking her short bob into place while Liam leans against the counter, watching her with obvious amusement.

She huffs, adjusting the strap of her tote bag. "I told you I wanted to be there *early*."

"And we will be." He reaches out, easily tugging her toward him by the belt loop of her jeans, pressing a quick kiss to her temple. "Promise."

Birdie exhales, tension visibly unwinding under his touch. "I know. I just hate feeling rushed."

"I know you do." He kisses her temple again, easy and familiar. He's done it a thousand times before. "But you're gonna kill it today. And I'll be right there after practice to pick you up, yeah?"

Her expression eases into something small and warm. "Yeah."

I shake my head. "How much PDA can two people possibly squeeze into a morning?"

Liam tilts his head. "We're inside our own home. How is that PDA?"

I gesture vaguely between them, rubbing my temple. "I wasn't meaning it in the literal sense."

Liam's green eyes glint. "Right. So, you're just jealous, then?"

"No," I say flatly, popping the cap on my drink. "Merely trying not to choke on the sheer amount of heart eyes happening in this room."

Liam smirks and tosses an arm over his girlfriend's shoulder. "Can't help it. I'm very in love."

Birdie laughs. "It's true. Have you seen his Birdie shrine?"

Liam's brows skyrocket. "I actually don't have one of those, but you've just given me a brilliant idea. Can I have a lock of your hair?"

I roll my eyes. "Jesus Christ."

Birdie snickers but doesn't move away, her attention flicking back to her bag.

Liam watches her, still smiling, before glancing over at me. "Good practice?"

"Decent." I down half a bottle of water and bite into an apple. "Times are still improving."

"Times. Right. Like, five meters per second or whatever."

I snort. "Yeah, I'm twice as fast as the world record holder."

Birdie shakes her head. "You two are both major dorks."

"Dorks with elite athletic ability," Liam corrects, then checks his phone. "Shit, okay, we really *do* need to go."

Birdie sighs. "That's what I *said*."

I raise a brow. "You're training him, slowly but surely."

She smirks. "Someone has to do it."

Liam dramatically winks at me as Birdie drags him toward the door, still muttering about punctuality. "Later, Flipper," he calls.

"Try not to get fired today," Birdie adds.

"Try not to let him make a public spectacle of his devotion to you," I shoot back.

She grins over her shoulder. "Too late."

They leave, Birdie talking about her internship, Liam listening with the kind of attention that would make any other guy seem whipped but just makes him look steady. He's never once questioned where he stands with her.

It must be nice, I think, to love someone like that without hesitation. To be loved right back and not wonder what's coming next.

A few minutes after they're gone, the house settles into silence. The good kind, the kind that usually helps me focus. But today, it just sits there, loud in all the wrong ways.

I toss my empty bottle into the sink and rake a hand through my damp hair.

Fifteen minutes until I have to be at Sycamore. Fifteen minutes until I'm back in the same orbit as the girl I can't stop thinking about and can't seem to forget.

I grab my keys, square my shoulders, and try to remember how to act like she doesn't matter.

On the pool deck, the heat clings, but it's different today. There's no blazing sun or sharp glare bouncing off the water. The sky is overcast, clouds stretched dense and unmoving across the horizon. It's still hot and humid, but with that deceptive edge that makes it easy to forget the burn creeping up on bare skin until it's too late.

Sweat beads at the back of my neck, slick under the collar of my uniform. My sunglasses slide slightly down the bridge of my nose, and I push them back up, shifting in my chair to find some position that doesn't make my lower back hate me.

The afternoon crowd is already restless. Not just the kids but the adults, too. Tensions fraying under the weight of too much sun, too many overpriced drinks, too many egos clashing over whose poolside lounge chair was technically reserved first.

From my perch, I clock it all.

The way the lifeguard stationed at the shallow end is already starting to look drained. The way a group of bored teenagers near the diving board are eyeing each other, hyping up whatever foolish idea they're about to attempt next. The way a dad with an expensive-looking watch is gesturing a little too aggressively at one of the servers, probably pissed that his drink wasn't cold enough.

It's the kind of day where patience wears thin, where someone's bound to snap over something ridiculous. The kind of day I hate the most.

I scrub my temples, resisting the urge to check the clock again. It doesn't matter. The shift will drag at the same pace it always does. Slow and uneventful.

A flicker of motion catches my eye in the deep end. A kid, maybe eight, is pushing off from the wall. I sit up straighter. He's moving with a distinct lack of confidence. It's not the kind of control you want to see in the deep section.

I don't need to see his face to recognize the signs—arms slowing, body tipping slightly off balance, the effort suddenly outweighing the ability. Then, just as I shift forward, ready to blow my whistle, a bigger kid rockets past him.

The wake slams into the smaller one, water splashing straight over his head.

One second. That's all it takes.

The younger kid gasps, eyes wide, panic blooming across his face as he flails for the surface. Then he goes under.

My body reacts before my brain fully registers it. I'm out of my chair, whistle piercing through the air. I hit the water hard, cool blue closing in around me as I cut through the lane with sharp, efficient strokes. It's instinct and training that gets me there.

I reach him fast, my rescue tube already against my chest. I slip it between us, guiding his arms over the top so he can float while I keep hold. His breathing is ragged, mouth open as he gasps and coughs, but he's conscious and responsive, at least.

I angle us toward the shallow end, kicking steadily as I tow him back.

"You're okay," I tell him. "I've got you."

A couple of other patrons are already moving. Someone's getting the parents. I hoist the kid onto the deck, kneeling beside him as he coughs up water, his eyes wide and wet and panicked.

"You good?" I ask, giving him a second to breathe. "Can you tell me your name?"

He nods shakily. "Owen Satterly."

"Alright, Owen." I shift back, letting him sit up. "You're safe now. But no more deep end unless you're with an adult, yeah?"

Another nod, this one more embarrassed than scared. I sit with him for another minute until his breathing evens out, until his parents arrive, fussing and thanking me a hundred times before leading him off with a towel wrapped tight around his shoulders.

The second they're gone, I exhale, rolling my shoulders.

It wasn't that bad. A routine save, nothing I haven't handled before. But I suppose you never get used to the fear of the *what-ifs*.

We've had worse here. A kid slipped past the ropes last summer, went under so fast no one saw until it was almost too late. Took three of us and an ambulance before he came back up breathing.

That must be why it's enough for management to call it for the day. The pool's too crowded, too chaotic, and Robbie—our manager—doesn't like taking unnecessary risks. He blows the final whistle and calls for maintenance to shock the water, using it as a tidy excuse to shut everything down until morning.

By the time I'm drying off and heading to the staff room, Zane's just showing up for his shift. He takes one look at my damp hair and smirks.

"You finally fall in, Mercer?"

"Kid needed a pull," I mutter, shaking water from my ears. "Pool's shut down. Did no one tell you?"

Zane groans. "I hauled my ass here for what? To stand around and look pretty?"

I snort, but my attention flicks to the schedule taped up on the wall. I already know what it says. I checked it this morning. And yesterday. And possibly the day before that, too.

Quinn was supposed to be caddying for the Mancini group, but I haven't seen a glimpse of her all day. In fact, the Mancinis are with Mikey—I saw them together when I came in this morning.

I shouldn't notice and I certainly shouldn't care. But the empty space where she's supposed to be? I feel it anyway.

"Where's Quinn?" I ask, voice even. "She's on the schedule."

Robbie glances up from the paperwork he's stacking. "Called out."

I nod, but something tightens in my chest.

Robbie studies me, a slow smirk tugging at the corner of his mouth. "You gonna act like you haven't been tracking her whereabouts like it's your second job?"

I let out a dry, humorless laugh. "I'm not tracking anything. She was just supposed to be here."

He chews on the inside of his cheek and sighs. "Look, I probably should've told you she was coming back. Thought about giving you a heads-up. But I didn't want to lose you."

I keep my posture relaxed, my tone flat. "You probably would have."

Robbie's lips twitch.

I grab my bag and head for the door.

Then he adds, "It was a family thing."

I pause. Turn back. "What?"

"That's why Quinn called out. Said it had something to do with her little brother. Some kind of emergency."

I know her brother, Wesley. He must be a junior in high school by now.

He's sharp like she is, but he was born early. He spent months in the NICU, small and fragile in ways Quinn never was. Even after he got stronger, there were always complications. Seizures and a heart condition meant his body never let him feel completely safe in it.

I remember the hospital visits. The middle-of-the-night phone calls. The way Quinn used to balance everything—school, work, life—like she was always bracing for something to go wrong.

She never talked about it much. Not in full detail, anyway. But I didn't need the details to know she needed support.

I saw it in the way her hands clenched when her phone rang late at night, how her shoulders locked tight with tension before she even looked at the screen. In the way exhaustion sat heavy beneath her eyes some mornings, the dark circles she never quite managed to cover up. In the way she never let herself rest, like the moment she did, the world would pull the rug out from under her.

I saw it in the way she loved her brother. Fiercely, protectively, like it was stitched into her bones. And now, something's gone wrong.

I swallow hard. "What kind of emergency?"

Robbie shrugs. "Don't know. She just called out last minute, said she couldn't come in."

I nod slowly, distracted, forcing my fingers to loosen around the strap of my bag. "Alright. Thanks. I'll see you tomorrow."

It's not my business anymore. I know that. But it doesn't stop my stomach from knotting or my mind from racing through worst-case scenarios. It doesn't stop the part of me that still cares. Still worries.

Outside, the heat presses close, heavy and unmoving. I step into it and pause.

This was supposed to be a simple summer job. A paycheck and

nothing more. Even when Quinn showed up here gain, I told myself I could manage it. Keep her on the periphery and let her blur into the background.

But Quinn's never been background noise.

And no matter how much I want to be indifferent, I'm not. I could never be.

Chapter Nine

QUINN

Hospitals have a way of pressing into my skin, of making the hairs at the nape of my neck stand on end. The cold sterility of the air. The low, mechanical hum of machines. The scent—sharp, antiseptic, too clean.

I hate it all.

I've spent enough time in places like this to know that the worst moments of my life don't come with dramatic soundtracks or flashing warning signs. They happen quietly. In waiting rooms, in hallways, in cramped hospital chairs.

In the lull between doctors' visits, where I sit there, staring at the speckled tile, waiting for someone to tell me something definitive. It rarely comes.

Wesley stirs beside me, shifting against the thin hospital sheets. He's been out for the last hour, breathing slow, his dark curls a mess against the pillow. The IV line taped to his arm looks out of place on him. I hate that, too.

I glance at the monitor above his bed, tracking the soft beeps of his heart rate. Normal.

He's fine, Quinn. It was only a seizure.

It wasn't even the worst one he's had, but it was bad enough. He collapsed in the middle of the kitchen, his head smacking against the tile. By the time Mom got to him, he was already coming out of it, confused. Dad carried him to the car while she called ahead to the hospital.

They kept him overnight for observation, running the usual tests. Checking his heart and watching for anything they might've missed.

He'll go home today, they told us. And that's what I keep reminding myself, that at least he's stable for the time being.

But I know how this works. Stability doesn't mean safety, and fine doesn't mean forever.

The bed creaks as Wesley shifts again, his eyelids fluttering. He groans.

"You're still here?"

"Nah," I murmur with a tiny half-assed smirk. "You're hallucinating."

"Damn. Kinda hoped I was."

I flick the side of his arm, careful of the IV. "Asshole."

Wes huffs a laugh, but it turns into a wince as he moves too fast.

"Slow down," I warn, my smirk fading. "You good?"

He presses his fingers to his temple. "Yeah. Just . . . headache."

I nod, leaning back in the chair I've spent too many hours in. It's uncomfortable as hell, but I'm used to it by now. I've spent too many nights in chairs like this, memorizing the shape of worry and what it feels like to wait.

Mom and Dad stepped out to get coffee, promising to be back in ten minutes. They left together, which means they'll be gone for at least thirty. Mom will linger by the counter, asking about caffeine levels in the decaf, Dad will get caught up reading the news on his phone.

For now, it's just me and Wesley.

He squints at the window, where weak morning light is starting to filter through the half-drawn blinds. "What time is it?"

"Almost eight."

His brows furrow. "You stayed all night?"

I roll my shoulders, trying to stretch out the stiffness. "So did Mom and Dad."

"Yeah, but they're—" He cuts himself off, biting his lip.

They're *them.* The ones who have always been by his side, through every appointment, every hospital stay, every emergency. The ones who dropped everything, rearranged their entire lives around making sure he was okay.

Me? I was just the extra set of hands. The built-in backup.

I watch as he shifts again, slowly adjusting to sit up.

"I'm fine, you know," he says softly. "You don't have to babysit me, too."

"Right. Because the whole *collapsing in the kitchen* thing was just for fun."

He rolls his eyes. "It wasn't that bad."

"Tell that to Mom. Pretty sure she aged another ten years."

He sighs, rubbing at his temple. "I just hate this shit."

Yeah. Me too, kid. I don't say it out loud as I press my lips together, leaning forward to prop my elbows on my knees.

"You scared them."

He glances away. "I know."

I run a shaky hand through my hair. "You scared me, too."

He blinks, caught off guard for half a second before covering it up with a smirk. "Didn't think anything scared you."

"Yeah, well." I exhale through my nose, looking back at the monitor again. Still normal. Still fine.

A beat of silence stretches between us before his smirk fades. He picks at the edge of the hospital blanket, looking a whole lot younger than seventeen. In fact, he looks like the kid I used to read stories to in the back seat of Mom's car, not the teenager who just got his learner's permit and now has to wait at least three months to drive again.

"I really am okay," he says, quieter now.

"I know."

Another beat. Then, "But you look like shit."

I snort. "Wow. Thanks, Wes."

"Just saying. You could've at least changed your clothes. The Sycamore polo has seen better days."

"I didn't exactly plan for an overnight stay."

He gives a crooked smile, but there's something softer beneath it. Something grateful.

The door creaks open then. Mom and Dad step inside, two coffee cups in hand. Mom looks exhausted, her bun a little looser than it was last night, worry still etched between her brows. But she smiles when she sees Wesley awake.

Dad steps in behind her, his expression harder to read, but I know that look. The quiet concern, the wheels turning in his head, already planning the next appointment, the next precaution.

"Morning," Mom says, setting one of the coffee cups on the bedside table. "How are you feeling, sweetheart?"

Wes shrugs. "Fine."

Mom presses her lips together, clearly debating whether or not to argue. She doesn't. Just reaches for his hand, rubbing gentle circles over his knuckles.

Dad's eyes flick to me. "You should go home, Quinn. Get some rest."

I stretch my arms above my head, feigning indifference. "I'm fine."

Mom frowns. "Honey, you were here all night."

"So were you."

She sighs, looking between me and my brother. I don't know why they've suddenly decided that my presence is optional, like it hasn't always been expected. I've built a second skin out of showing up.

Dad shifts, rubbing a hand over his jaw. "We appreciate you staying," he says carefully. "But you don't have to carry this, Quinn."

A familiar weight settles in my chest. I know they mean well. I know they're saying it because they care. But that's the thing—I've always carried this. It's part of who I am. It's not going to end just because I'm graduating college soon and suddenly they've decided I've done enough.

They can pretend the balance was ever even, pretend I didn't spend years trying to prove I mattered too. But that doesn't erase the past.

I push to my feet and grab my bag. "I'll head out. Just let me know when he gets discharged."

"Text us when you get home," Mom says.

I sling my bag over my shoulder. "Will do."

Wes watches as I step toward the door, something flickering in his expression. It's hesitation, maybe. A kind of guilt that doesn't belong to him but is there anyway. I don't wait for him to say anything. If he opens his mouth, it'll just make it harder to walk out.

So, I push through the door and let it swing shut behind me.

The hallway is bright and clean, stretching out in a sterile blur of white tile and muted colors. Soft greens. Powder blues. The kind of palette meant to calm kids down but just makes everything feel like a waiting room inside a cartoon.

The walls are lined with painted murals: smiling animals, rainbow kites, a sun with wide cartoon eyes. It's all a little too cheerful, a little too forced. This place is trying too hard, I think, to make you forget where you are.

It's the Hawthorne Children's Hospital, which is why the murals make sense. Doesn't make them any less weird. Or babyish. Or kind of haunting when you've grown up walking these halls.

I've been here more times than I can count. First as a wide-eyed kid trailing after my parents, later as a teenager keeping Wes entertained between appointments. The faces change—new nurses, new doctors, new scared parents—but the feeling doesn't.

I pass a small girl clutching a stuffed elephant, her IV pole rattling quietly beside her. Her mom murmurs something soft as they head toward the playroom. Another kid, maybe six or seven, sits in a wheelchair, staring blankly at an iPad. His arms are thin, covered in faded hospital bracelets.

Wesley was once just like them, all wiry limbs and quiet bravery. He grew, got stronger, and outlived the worst predictions. Now he's taller and more sarcastic than ever. Sprawled across that hospital bed like he owns it, tossing out jokes to make me roll my eyes.

He *seems* older.

But seventeen isn't grown. It's barely anything at all.

And if seventeen still counts as a kid, then what does that make me?

I'm twenty-one. Technically an adult. Old enough to be on my own and to make decisions that matter. Old enough to be working, studying, building something for myself. But most days, I still feel like I'm waiting for someone to hand me the blueprint.

I don't stop at the waiting area or glance at the receptionist. I don't acknowledge the low murmur of nurses at the desk as I walk out, straight through the automatic doors and into the thick summer air.

Outside, I blink against the sudden light. The heat hits instantly, clinging to my skin after too many hours breathing stale, filtered oxygen. I move on autopilot—cross the lot, unlock the door, slide in behind the wheel.

The drive home blurs past. Stoplights, street signs, late-morning traffic. I couldn't recount the route if I tried. My brain stays back at the hospital, stuck somewhere between the beep of a heart monitor and the feel of Wesley's too-cold fingers brushing mine.

I pull into the lot outside my apartment complex, cut the engine, and sit there with my fingers curled tight around the wheel.

The AC hums, blowing lukewarm air that barely touches the sticky weight pressing down on me.

I should go inside. Take a shower and sleep. Pretend I didn't just spend the last twenty-four hours in a hospital room pretending to be fine.

But the thought of walking through that door, of stepping into a quiet apartment where everything is normal—where my roommates are probably stretched across the couch watching trashy TV and complaining about who forgot to buy oat milk—feels impossible.

I can't bring myself to do it.

Instead of heading in, I climb out of the car.

It's just a quick walk down the street. Five minutes, tops. By the time I reach the gym, my pulse is already thrumming, but not from the pace. It's something else. Something wired and restless buzzing under my skin.

Inside Emberline, it's louder than before, the whole place crowded with movement and noise. Bodies cut between stations, gloves crack against the pads, and effort hangs in the air like heat.

The energy feels different from the last time I was here. It's not only the older regulars, the worn-down men who've been showing up for years out of habit or stubbornness. There are younger fighters now too, sharp-eyed and restless, carrying themselves like they've still got something to earn.

It makes me pause. That awkward, out-of-place feeling creeps in again. But then I remind myself—everyone starts as an outsider. You fake it until you don't have to, right?

And more than anything, I want that feeling back. The one I had after that first night. After I spent an hour taking it all out on the bag, after the adrenaline left my system and my body finally went quiet. I've been chasing that silence ever since.

I need it now more than ever.

The owner's behind the counter again, arms crossed. He

doesn't greet me or ask why I'm here. He tips his chin toward the lockers, and I take that as a sign that I'm allowed.

I make my way over, drop my bag onto the bench, pull my hair into a knot, and start taping up. When I finally step onto the mats, he's already waiting.

"Good," he says. "You came back."

I roll my shoulders. "Yeah. Found a gap in my schedule."

His expression stays dry. "Sure. That's why."

I don't bother replying. My eyes drift past him to the ring where a pair of guys are sparring. They move like their bodies already know exactly what to do. It's fast and controlled.

I want that. I want to be good enough to let it out without overthinking every move. I want to stop holding it all in.

I want to hit something and finally feel free.

Without me asking for it, the owner steps in and taps the inside of my elbow.

"Last time, I let you go at it. Wanted you to feel it, to let it out. But if you keep throwing wild-ass punches like that, you're gonna blow out your shoulder before you even figure out what you're doing."

I press my lips together. I don't like being called out, but he's not wrong. My body still aches in places I didn't know existed.

He gestures toward the bag. "Hands up."

I square my stance, lifting my fists, and he steps in again to adjust my elbow.

"Keep them tighter. You're leaving yourself wide open."

He moves behind me and presses two fingers to my spine.

"Straighten up. Engage your core. You're not throwing from your arms. You're throwing from here."

I exhale and shift my weight. He steps back, letting me find it on my own. When I punch this time, it feels much more intentional.

He gives a short grunt of approval. "Better. Again."

I throw punch after punch until my arms feel like lead, until my legs tremble with exhaustion, until the sharp edge of everything dulls just enough.

By the time I peel my gloves off, the owner has drifted back to his desk. My body hums with the same tired relief as last time. There's a steady burn in my muscles, a dull ache in my knuckles.

It feels good.

For a minute, I lean against the wall, dragging my hands down my face.

"Hey," I say quietly.

He glances up, eyes narrowed like he's expecting me to complain or quit.

"Thanks," I mutter. "For . . . you know." I gesture vaguely, unsure how to explain that I needed this. That I was unraveling when I walked in, and now, somehow, I feel like I've been stitched back together. "For today."

His expression softens. "Right. I'll see you again in a couple days, then."

I should say no, should remind him I don't have time for this. I can't afford to spend my nights in a dingy gym throwing punches at a bag. I need to sleep more and focus more on my priorities.

"Yeah," I say instead. "See you soon."

I step outside into the cool night air, still feeling the sting in my palms. It's sharp, but the tension I've been dragging around all day feels quieter now. Someone's finally turned the volume down.

I fish around in my pocket for my phone, half expecting it to be dead. I haven't checked it since yesterday morning—since the second I got the call about Wesley. I texted Robbie, my manager, a quick "Family emergency. Can't come in." Then I shoved my phone away and forgot about it.

Now, as the screen lights up, I blink at the notifications. I have ten missed texts. A few are from my roommates. Some from my mom. One from Robbie, checking in. But none of them matter quite as much as the one at the bottom.

WARREN

heard about Wesley. hope he's okay.

I stare at it, unblinking, my heartbeat thrumming somewhere in my throat. Warren fucking Mercer texted me. For the first time in two and a half years, he reached out to say something that wasn't sharp or loaded or angry.

He reached out to *check on me.*

I swallow hard, my fingers hovering over the screen. I shouldn't care. It's a simple message—nothing heavy, nothing that should make my chest feel like it's folding in on itself. But it does. And when I scroll up, just to see it, I find the last thing he ever sent me.

WARREN

Quinny, please.

I remember exactly where I was when I first read it. I was sitting on the steps outside my dorm, my heart lodged somewhere between my ribs, my mind a hurricane of what-ifs and too-late regrets.

I ignored it. Not because I wanted to and not because I didn't have anything to say. But because, by then, it didn't really matter. Warren had already made up his mind about who I was and what I was worth.

Maybe he was the one to say the final words, but I was the one who really ended it. I was a girl with too many secrets and a habit of breaking things that mattered.

That's why I let the message sit there, unanswered. A final period on something that had once been everything. I spent a long time wishing I hadn't. Wishing I'd fought harder or that he would have listened.

But now he's the one reaching out to *me*.

I have no fucking clue what to do with this. The way I still feel him everywhere. The way his voice sneaks into my head when I'm alone, low and certain, like he's standing right behind me. I still ache for something I told myself I didn't need.

And I hate that a single text is enough to make me feel like I'm standing on those steps all over again, drowning in the same regrets.

Chapter Ten

WARREN

QUINN DIDN'T ANSWER my text. I don't know why I expected her to or why I even bothered to send it at all.

What did I think was gonna happen? That she'd suddenly decide to open up, to let me in again? That she'd text back and say, *Thank you for checking in, Warren,* like we were civil, like we were people who actually knew how to be gentle with each other?

Ridiculous. Foolish. My own fucking fault.

But maybe it's worse than I think. Maybe she hasn't even looked at her phone because she's spent the last few days in the hospital waiting on news that didn't come.

My stomach twists, and I force myself to give her the benefit of the doubt. There's no point spiraling yet. If she misses another shift today, I'll find some other way to reach her.

Only she doesn't.

She's already there by the time I walk in, smiling at the Davises like nothing happened. Joking with one of the servers. Laughing, even, like the silence between us is nothing more than a thing I imagined.

When I step inside, she doesn't so much as glance in my direction. And that pisses me off to no end.

God, what the fuck is wrong with that woman?

I should let it go. I know I should. But every time I see her, it's like a live wire sparking beneath my skin, my whole body tensing on instinct. She flips some old switch I forgot I still had, and worse, I think she delights in it.

She knows exactly how to dig her nails into my brain and squeeze until I'm thinking sideways.

I shake it off, shove my sunglasses higher on the bridge of my nose, and step onto the pool deck. It's early still, and the place is calm. A few retirees drifting through their laps, toddlers squealing in the shallow end while their moms half watch, half scroll.

It's quiet enough that I start to think today might not be a complete disaster.

At ten, Robbie flags me down, and my stomach dips. I know, the second I see that apologetic grimace on his face, that I'm about to get screwed.

"We're consolidating coverage," he says, nodding toward the pool. "Barely anyone swimming, so we've got Kayla running both stations."

I glance toward the shallow end. Kayla, the youngest lifeguard on staff, is already perched on the stand.

"And?" I ask, dread curling in my gut.

Robbie claps a hand on my shoulder. "That means you're on drinks duty."

I blink. "No."

"Yes."

I exhale hard. "I hate serving drinks."

"I know." Robbie's already walking off, grinning. "Think of it as character-building, Mercer."

I grumble a curse under my breath but don't argue. What's the point? I'd rather not miss out on a full shift again. Yesterday, when they shut the pool down early, I lost three hours of pay. Not exactly devastating, but still annoying as hell.

I'm here to make money. So, if I have to play waiter for entitled assholes, then fine—I'll do it. Although most of them can't even be bothered to say please when they order their overpriced cocktails.

Management does this sometimes. Reallocates lifeguards to other "hospitality duties" when it's slow. It's the club's way of making sure no one's just sitting around.

And I hate it.

Hate being in the middle of people and making small talk, pretending to care about drink orders and whether someone's cocktail has exactly the right ratio of ice to liquor. I'd rather be up in the chair, baking in the sun, watching the water, not talking to anyone.

Now, I'm stuck slinging drinks for a bunch of trust fund kids and country club moms who think boundaries are optional.

I step behind the outdoor bar, already irritated, already counting down the minutes until I can go back to not doing this.

To my great surprise, the first half hour goes fine. I'm serving mostly iced teas and lemonades, a single mimosa, and a vodka tonic. It's quiet, manageable, almost enough to trick me into relaxing.

Then, right on cue, the poolside moms show up. Two of them, already tipsy despite the fact that it's barely noon. They have designer sunglasses perched on their noses, sheer cover-ups barely concealing expensive bikinis, and flashy rings that sparkle in the sun.

"Oh," one of them purrs, sliding up to the bar. "Where have *you* been hiding?"

Her friend tilts her head, appraising. "You're new."

"I'm not," I say flatly, already reaching for the vodka.

She smirks, leaning her elbows on the bar. "Must've been before my time, then."

I grab two glasses, fill them with ice, and pour.

Her friend hums. "You play sports? You look like you could pick me up and not break a sweat."

I keep my expression blank. "I swim."

The first one drags her nails over the rim of her glass. "Mmm. Swimmers' bodies are the best."

Her friend giggles. "Toned, lean, so much *stamina*."

Jesus Christ. I slide their drinks across the bar, resisting the urge to rub my temples.

"Anything else?"

The first one grins, tipping her sunglasses down to peer at me. "What's your name, sweetheart?"

I level her with a look. "It's on my name tag."

She laughs, eyes flicking to my chest, to the small WARREN stitched onto my polo.

"Oh, I like that," she muses. "Strong name."

The friend nudges her. "You're terrible."

I exhale through my nose. "Right. Enjoy your drinks."

The first one lingers, taking a slow sip of her cocktail before leaning in again, voice all sugar and amusement. "You ever give private lessons, Warren?"

I stare at her as her friend dissolves into laughter. "Oh my God, Victoria, stop."

I turn, grab the bar rag, and start wiping down the counter. Because apparently, pretending I didn't hear her is the only way this conversation ends.

Victoria pouts. "Aw. Don't be like that. I bet you could teach me a lot."

That's it, I'm done. I don't even bother hiding my disinterest as I flash the most bland, dead-eyed look I can muster and say, "Have a great day."

I turn my back and start taking inventory, hoping they'll take the hint.

Eventually, they saunter off, giggling, and I let out a slow exhale.

The damp cloth smears condensation from abandoned glasses, the scent of citrus clinging to my fingers. I scrub harder than necessary, trying to burn off the irritation, the embarrassment, the faint flush that crept up my neck the second she leaned too close.

I'm used to people looking at me. I'm not used to feeling cornered by it.

Only four more hours left.

I roll my shoulders, refocus, and grab a clean glass.

I should be on the stand, perched above the pool with nothing but my own thoughts and the occasional whistle to keep kids in check, not pouring vodka sodas for sunburned moms who flirt out of boredom.

As I reach for a bottle of Tito's, a flash of movement catches my eye. Dark hair and a frantic stride.

Undeniably, impossibly, that's Quinn.

She's moving fast, slipping through the door to the break room and disappearing behind it. Is she upset? Hiding? Avoiding me again? She obviously doesn't want to be seen, but the second I realize it's her, I'm paying attention anyway.

I press my palm against the counter, grip the edge. I've already done enough. I sent the text and checked in with her. She didn't respond to me. That should be enough.

She's not your business anymore.

I exhale sharply as I drop the rag. And then, like the goddamned fool I am, I chase after her.

The break room is dim, a little hideaway from the glare of the afternoon sunshine. The overhead fan hums, stirring the thick air, but it does nothing for the warmth curling in my gut.

Quinn's got her back to me, arms braced against the sink, shoulders drawn tight. She's breathing fast and shallow, like she's trying to get enough air but can't quite manage it.

My chest tightens. It must be her asthma.

She's always been reckless with it—pushing herself too hard, pretending she doesn't need help. Like using her inhaler in public is some kind of weakness she can't afford.

I step forward, already on edge. "Jesus, Quinn, do you even have your inhaler?"

She startles, whipping around like she didn't realize I was there. Her eyes are red, face pale beneath her tan. "I—yeah. It's fine."

"Fine?" I scoff. "You're wheezing. Just take the damn thing."

She bristles. "I said I'm fine."

I cross my arms. "Right. Because hiding out alone in a break room gasping for air is totally fine. If you'd just tell Robbie you need more breaks or—"

"No," she snaps, turning back to the sink. Her fingers curl around the edge, white-knuckled. Like if she holds on hard enough, she won't fall apart.

A single tear slips down her cheek. She wipes it away in half a second, fast and fierce, but I still see it.

Something coils low in my gut.

I step closer, my voice low. "It's not asthma, is it?"

She squeezes her eyes shut. Takes a slow breath in, then slower out. She's trying to bury something deep before it breaks the surface.

"Quinn," I try again.

"It was just one of the regulars. He, uh . . . he got a little handsy with me earlier. That's all."

Every part of me locks up. I don't speak or move or breathe. I can't.

"It wasn't— I mean, it was just—" She lets out a hollow little laugh, sharp and small. "You know how it is here."

Rage spikes so fast it makes me dizzy. I step in, close enough to see the dampness still clinging to her lashes, the way her hands tremble and her breath snags in her throat.

"Who?"

She exhales sharply. "Warren—"

"Who the fuck was it?"

Her gaze flickers, wary. "It's not a big deal."

Not a big deal. Not a big fucking deal.

My fingers curl into fists. "Don't do that," I say gruffly. "Don't brush it off."

She huffs, wiping at her cheek again. "And what do you want me to do? File a formal complaint? Go to Robbie?" She lets out a humorless laugh, shaking her head. "He's middle management, Mercer. He has no real clout here. You and I both know that."

I clench my jaw, grinding my teeth. "That's bullshit."

She looks at me then, something exhausted settling into her expression. "The members are king."

Yeah, I already know that. I know how this place works. How the money, the power, the connections all run one way. How guys like Robbie, guys like *me*, are disposable in the grand scheme of things.

And it makes me fucking sick.

My pulse hammers in my skull, breath sharp as I try to bite back the fury crawling under my skin. Because this—this is exactly why I shouldn't have chased after her.

Quinn Rose has always had the ability to wrap herself around my ribs, squeeze tight, and make me forget how to breathe. No matter how much time has passed between us, no matter how far I've tried to push her out, she's still under my fucking skin.

I don't know how to get her out.

"Give me a name here, Quinny. Something to work with."

She lets out a short breath. "You can't do anything. You'll get fired."

I grit my teeth because I know she's right. The members here can do whatever the fuck they want without consequence, and people like us are expected to just take it.

Smile. Nod. Keep our heads down.

And yet, I want to go apeshit.

I want to grab the guy by the collar, shove him up against the cabana, and make sure he never so much as looks at Quinn again. But that's not what she needs right now.

So, I do the only thing I can. I move closer, reach for her face, and wipe away the damp track of a tear before she can do it herself.

I tilt her chin up. "No one touches you without your permission and gets away with it. I don't give a fuck what their last name is."

Her mouth parts slightly, her breath catching. I can feel it—the way she's wavering, the way she almost lets herself lean in. And for half a second, it's like nothing has changed between us at all.

It's like we're eighteen again and she's sneaking into my bed after a long shift, curling into me like I'm the only safe place she's ever known. If only I still got to have that piece of her. If only she'd still let me.

Then she blinks, and it's gone. Whatever was there—whatever crack had finally started to let the light in—she slams it shut.

She swallows. "I'm fine."

She's made up her mind but she's still reeling, I can see it. Pushing now would just make things worse.

I exhale hard, running a hand through my hair. "You gonna be okay?"

"Yeah. All good."

"If that changes, you come find me."

She stares ahead, cheeks flushed. "It was Beckett, by the way."

Preston fucking Beckett.

He's the kind of guy that makes this whole place pretend not to notice. He's had everything handed to him since birth and walks around like he owns the air the rest of us breathe. I'm sure he's never faced a single consequence in his entire fucking life.

A slow, deliberate breath pushes past my lips. My fingers flex at my sides. And then, with Quinn's voice still echoing in my head, I make a choice I already know is a bad one.

"Warren, wait—"

I don't stop, don't even look back, as I march straight to the overflow lot behind the maintenance building.

Beckett usually parks there, even though it's not technically for members. The man thinks he's too important to circle the front lot like everyone else. Too important to follow the rules. I know for a fact the cameras don't reach the back corner near the fence, and that's exactly where I'm headed.

It doesn't take me long to find his car. A silver Maserati Ghibli —sleek, smug-looking—parked crooked, eating up two spaces.

I crouch low, grab the small blade off my key chain, and jam it straight into the sidewall of his tire. It's not enough to fully slash it but enough to ensure that the second he pulls out of here, it blows.

Then I toss the blade back into my pocket and head right back to the bar. I've got a few more drinks to sling before I can go home.

Chapter Eleven

QUINN

WARREN'S TEXT is still there, unanswered, sitting on my screen, glowing in the dark like it's waiting for me to do something about it.

WARREN

heard about Wesley. hope he's okay.

It's ridiculous how much I want to respond to him.

Because twice now—twice in two days—he's made it feel like no time has passed between us. Could it be possible that we could find our way back to something that didn't hurt this much? Could I crack myself open and let him bleed back into my life, filling all the spaces he used to belong.

Because I want that. I want it so fucking bad.

But maybe I'm letting myself get hopeful when two inconsequential instances don't mean anything. That in the grand scheme of the last two and a half years, a couple of soft moments can't outweigh everything else. Because that's what it's been—two and a half years of silence.

We've crossed paths a time or two at Dayton, though neither of us ever stopped long enough to acknowledge it. The university is big, but not *that* big. We walk the same quad, share the same sidewalks. It's easy to blend into the crowd, easier still to keep our heads down.

The first time I saw Warren after the breakup, he was sitting alone on a bench in Navy Square, staring out over the fountain, shoulders hunched like the weight of something invisible was pressing down on him.

I thought about approaching. Sitting beside him, saying something, *anything*.

But then I thought about the way his jaw would tighten, the way his eyes would shutter. I thought about how fast he'd leave. So, I ran first.

I saw him again last year, passing by the intramural training building. He was walking out, hair damp, a Dayton swim duffel slung over his shoulder.

My heart stuttered. I had the first syllable of his name on my tongue, my lips parting, ready to call out. But then I froze, and the moment slipped through my fingers like it never belonged to me in the first place.

I turned before he could see me. Before I could see the way he'd look right through me, the way he'd remind me of what I already knew. That whatever we were—real and raw and *everything*—I destroyed it.

And yet, I wonder if he ever saw me, too. If he ever spotted me in the nooks and crannies of his day. If his gaze ever snagged on me, even just for a second, before slipping away. Is it possible for him to be oblivious to my presence when I've never been able to ignore his?

Maybe it's easier for him. Cleaner, too. Because he can put it all in a box labeled "mistake" and never look at it again. Because he can't forgive me. *He won't.* And no matter how good things were between us before, that hasn't changed.

I know that. So why does it still ache?

I flip onto my side, then onto my back again, my sheets twisted around my legs, restless energy burning through my skin. My ribs feel too tight, my chest too full.

I should be thinking about Preston Beckett. About the way his hand landed on my waist earlier today, the too-firm squeeze that dropped down to my ass, the way his mouth pressed into my ear when he leaned in to whisper about how he liked having me back at Sycamore.

I should be pissed off about it. I am pissed off about it. Grossed out, disturbed, violated.

But the worst part? The part I can't stop circling back to?

The way Warren's hand felt on my face afterward. Soothing, reassuring. His thumb sweeping over my cheek, wiping away a tear I hadn't even realized had fallen. The way he looked at me—not like I was something to be handled or dismissed, but like he really saw me.

For a moment, I was still the girl he met and chose. I was still *his*.

I press the heel of my palm against my sternum, forcing the thought out of my head. It doesn't mean anything. It can't. Proximity forced us into that moment. It wasn't fate, it wasn't some buried longing on his part, and it sure as hell wasn't because he still cares.

I flip my phone over, screen down, and roll onto my stomach. As I press my forehead into the pillow, it takes everything in me not to cry.

Loving Warren Mercer had come so easily to me back then. Instinctively, like second nature, like gravity itself. Like stepping into warm water and letting myself sink.

But losing him? That had been the hardest fucking thing I've ever done.

Even now, there's a part of me that still waits for him. Still looks for him in crowds and aches in the quiet spaces where he used to be.

I scrub my fingers over my jaw. Before I can talk myself into doing something reckless—something like texting him back—I shove the phone under my pillow and push the covers off.

I can't just lie here. I need to move.

I climb out of bed and make my way into the dark apartment, bare feet soft against the floor. My whole body still feels overstimulated, skin prickling like I'm holding myself together a second too late.

There was a time when Warren was the steadiest thing in my life. The person I reached for without thinking. The one place I could land, every single time. Now he's the exact thing I can't let myself want, which would almost be funny if it didn't hurt so much.

I stand in the kitchen for a second, swallowing around the knot in my throat before I flick on the kettle. Maybe that's all I need. Something ordinary. Something with steps I don't have to think about. If I keep my hands busy, maybe my mind will stop circling him long enough for me to breathe.

So, I pull down a mug. Drop in a tea bag. Pour the water and watch steam rise in slow, wavering ribbons toward the cabinets. I've done this enough times that the ritual lives in my body now. It doesn't fix anything, but it gives me something to follow.

Because there's too much I can't control. Warren. Preston Beckett. The past. All that guilt I've carried around for years, heavy and familiar as a stone tucked behind my ribs.

But this I can manage. The kettle clicking off. The mug warming my palms. The sharp, herbal smell rising with the heat. One careful sip, then another. It is not peace, exactly, but it's close enough to pass for comfort in a night like this.

Behind me, there's a shift in the room. A soft rustle of fabric, the quiet creak of the couch. I turn my head enough to see Jordan curled up on the cushions, phone in hand, her attention half-absorbed in whatever she's watching.

I hadn't even noticed her there.

"Can't sleep?" she asks.

I shake off my shock, shifting against the counter. "Oh. Nope."

She stretches before setting her phone down on the arm of the couch. "Tea?"

I nod toward the kettle. "Yeah, want some?"

There are approximately three things I know about Jordan: she plays volleyball, she loves reality TV, and Chinese takeout is her comfort food. But we haven't had a lengthy conversation, a real heart-to-heart, since that weird night last year after her boyfriend unceremoniously dumped her.

I grab another mug from the cabinet, dunk a tea bag inside, pour the steaming water in. By the time I bring it over, she's moved slightly, making space next to her on the couch.

I hesitate, just for a second. It feels strange to sit here beside her in the middle of the night. But Jordan doesn't say anything as she accepts the mug with a quiet thanks, so I lower myself onto the other side of the couch and leave a foot of space between us.

Even so, I still feel the warmth of her, the slight shift of the cushion beneath us.

It doesn't come easily, but I force myself to settle. To not think about the last time I sat with someone like this in the middle of the night. Two and a half years ago.

Warren's hand used to rest on my knee, his shoulder pressing into mine as he leaned back, so close I could feel the rise and fall of his breath.

Jordan doesn't press for conversation, which I appreciate. She blows on her tea, taps through something on her phone, and lets the quiet stretch between us, soft and unobtrusive. It's a kindness I didn't realize I needed.

I sip my tea, let the warmth curl in my chest. It's strange how rare this feels. How much of my time is spent alone, wrapped up in my own mind, refusing to let anyone too close.

After a minute, Jordan finally asks, "How's your brother? You just spent the night in Hawthorne, right?"

My whole chest clenches like she's pried it open.

I stare down into my tea. "Yeah, he had a seizure. Hit his head."

Jordan finally looks up, her brows pulling together. "Shit. Is he okay?"

I nod, forcing my voice even. "Yeah. Home now."

"That must've been scary."

It was. Even though I'm used to it, even though it's happened countless times before. I still spent the whole night bracing for bad news. Sitting in that hospital room, staring at his IV, waiting for the other shoe to drop. Wondering if this would be the time things didn't go back to normal.

Jordan doesn't say anything else. She's giving me space to fill the silence if I want to.

I don't. Because the longer I sit here, the itchier I feel. My skin doesn't fit quite right on my body. I'm not used to opening up to people, and I don't think now's the right time to try.

I clear my throat. "It was fine. Thanks for asking."

"If you ever wanna talk, you know I'm here."

"Yeah, yeah. Feelings. We'll circle back."

She gives a quiet laugh. "You're so annoying."

"I know."

She shakes her head and settles deeper into the couch, her focus shifting back to her phone. It's not her fault I can't open up like a normal girl.

I drain the rest of my tea and push to my feet. "Night."

Jordan lifts a hand in a lazy wave as I disappear down the hall, back to my room and into silence. The phone still sits on my bed, face down, Warren's text unanswered.

School starts in just over two weeks. Maybe I can pull it together and regroup by then. I can try to be productive and convince myself I'm still on track.

I pull my summer reading from the stack and open *Wuthering Heights*, hoping maybe this time I'll be able to force my way into it.

I skim the first few pages, but nothing sticks. My eyes move over the words while my mind slips somewhere else entirely, drifting so far from the story I may as well not be reading at all.

After a minute, I let out a quiet breath and close the book, sliding it back onto the pile.

What I reach for instead is the one I always seem to return to. I love classic literature. I do. But poetry has always felt more like mine. There's nothing wasted in it. It can be intimate without softness, precise without losing feeling, honest in a way prose sometimes dances around.

Emily Dickinson: Collected Poems.

The spine is cracked, the pages worn soft from years of being turned over in my hands. The edges curl where I've dog-eared my favorites. The margins are lined with faint pencil marks, thoughts I never quite committed to ink but needed to leave behind.

I thumb through the pages, my fingers skimming over worn paper.

"I like a look of Agony,
Because I know it's true—"

There are some things you can't fake. Some things you can't lie about.

"Water, is taught by thirst."

My fingers still.

That one. That was always the one.

I read the rest, the words settling into me like an old ache.

"Land—by the Oceans passed.
Transport—by throe—
Peace—by its battles told—

Love, by Memorial Mold—
Birds, by the Snow."

This one has always been my favorite because it makes sense of the hard things. The idea that absence teaches us everything. That knowing comes from missing, from losing, from living without.

And Warren knew that, too.

That first summer we met, he started memorizing the ones I liked best, even though he didn't care about poetry himself. He'd tilt his head at me from across the break room at Sycamore, drop a single mangled line into the conversation just to see me react.

"You make it too easy," he'd said once, grinning at the way my shoulders tensed.

"You butcher poetry for sport," I'd shot back.

And then, later, when we were at the Sycamore pool together, he undid me in a way I didn't know how to come back from. It was after hours during the first weekend of July. He whispered a few words of poetry in my ear, pressed me into the tiles, the water slick between us, the air thick with chlorine and the heat of July.

That was the moment, I think, that I knew I was his.

That no matter how much I pretended otherwise, no matter how many times I told myself otherwise, Warren Mercer had already slipped beneath my chest, made a home inside my hollow heart. He'd settled there.

And I never wanted him to leave.

Chapter Twelve

THAT FIRST SUMMER

QUINN

The pool's been closed for over an hour now. The lounge chairs are stacked and the cabanas long empty. The icy blue water is a still, glassy surface reflecting the glow of the security lights.

Warren and I shouldn't be here.

If anyone catches us, we're both screwed. But Warren had smirked at me after our shift, tossed his towel over his shoulder, and said, "Meet me at the deep end after lockup."

And now, here we are. Breaking rules like it's foreplay.

I perch at the pool's edge, toes dipping into the water. It's warm, even at night, the heat of the day still clinging to my skin. I lean back on my outstretched arms, legs dangling into the deep end, eyes locked on Warren's blue-gray gaze just below.

He's in the pool, arms hooked over the edge, watching me. He's bare-chested, dark hair damp and slicked back, eyes steady on mine.

"You gonna make me wait all night?"

I roll my eyes. "Patience, Mercer."

I slip into the water, the chlorine-slick surface sliding up my skin as I push off the wall. Warren drifts backward, keeping his eyes on me. There's a challenge in them. A dare.

For a moment, we just float there without words. The sounds of the night fill the space—the hum of cicadas, the distant rush of traffic, the occasional lap of water against tile. It's the kind of night that makes recklessness feel inevitable.

I dip my head back, letting myself drift.

"Did you actually have a reason for dragging me out here, or was this just an elaborate plot to get me in a swimsuit?"

He hums, lazily treading water. "Would you believe me if I said both?"

I scoff and flick some water in his direction. He laughs, dodging easily, then kicks off. It only takes him a single powerful stroke to cross the distance between us.

He's close enough that I can see the water beading on his shoulders, the way his collarbones cut sharp against his skin. Close enough to count the flecks of navy blue in his eyes.

I swallow thickly. "You know, if this is the part where you try to drown me, you're gonna have to work harder than that."

He doesn't laugh or smirk as he watches me and says, "*I dwell in Possibility*."

A shiver slides down my spine. It's not just the words; it's the way he says them. They're both a question and an answer—a vow made just for me.

My breath catches. "You got it right this time."

He gives a half smile. "Figured you'd appreciate the effort."

I do. *God, I do.*

Warren Mercer isn't the kind of guy who recites poetry for no reason. And hearing him say the words I love most—softly, intentionally, with his mouth this close to mine—might actually be the sexiest thing I've ever experienced.

I skim my fingers over the surface of the water. "You planning on finishing the poem, or was that all you could memorize?"

His fingers gently brush against the curve of my jaw.

I tilt my head slightly. My pulse beats against my throat, water lapping quietly around us. He's all I see, all I feel. A breath wrapped in skin and want.

His thumb traces the curve of my mouth. A featherlight touch, but it sets my skin on fire.

He moves lower, trailing along my jaw, down the slope of my throat. His fingers graze my collarbone. I feel it everywhere. My breath catches, and I tilt my chin up for him to kiss me.

He watches, mouth curving, eyes flickering with something dark and knowing.

Then, low and hushed, like he's sharing a secret only I get to hear:

"For Occupation—This—
The spreading wide my narrow Hands
To gather Paradise."

The words land like a spark to dry kindling. My stomach twists, thighs pressing together against the ache curling deep inside me. I want him. I *need him.* Biblically, spiritually, in a way that feels carved into my bones.

When he pulls back, I blink, heart dropping.

He pushes away from me and glides backward through the water like none of this just happened. But I know it did. I could never forget it. The way he touched me with hungry hands, looked at me with burning eyes, and spoke to me with the words my soul knows by heart.

I stare at him, breath uneven, a little stunned.

Rivulets of water slide down his chest, carving paths over firm muscle, his broad shoulders cutting through the glow of the security lights. Dark, nearly black hair falls onto his forehead, still dripping, framing his sharp jaw.

He looks like a fucking dream. A cruel one. A merciless one.

God, I'm wrecked. I'm unraveling, and he's going to have me.

He already does.

Whatever game we've been playing, he's won. A thousand times over, he's won.

Chapter Thirteen

WARREN

THE SYCAMORE STAFF are gathered in the employee break room. We're pressed shoulder to shoulder, all thirty-something of us, and I'm about to combust with the effort of keeping my expression neutral.

Robbie stands at the front of the group, arms crossed over his chest, looking uncharacteristically serious. Beside him is one of the upper managers, a guy whose name I never bothered to learn, the kind of middle-aged golf dad who runs this place like a kingdom.

He steps forward, clears his throat, and lets his gaze sweep over all of us.

"We've got a problem," he says, voice clipped. "Yesterday, a guest's car was vandalized in the parking lot. Slashed tire, clean through."

Silence. No one moves. No one even breathes.

I keep my face blank, arms loose at my sides. Lying doesn't come easily to me, but I've learned to act from the best. To steady my breath when the heat crawls up my neck.

"Whoever did it needs to come forward now," the manager continues. "If you do, we'll deal with this internally. But if we have to investigate? If we have to pull security footage and turn this into a police matter?" He lets that sink in. "Then whoever's responsible will not only be fired but also fined and possibly face jail time."

Still, no one speaks. The waitstaff glance at each other. The grounds crew leans back like they're trying to disappear into the wall, waiting for someone to twitch the wrong way, for someone to break.

Zane, standing a few feet away from me, shifts his weight. "How do they know it was an employee?"

The manager's mouth flattens. "The guest parked in the overflow lot behind the staff building. It's not officially restricted, but most members don't even know it exists. Whoever slashed the tire would've had to know where the cameras don't reach. Which means they knew the layout."

"Is it possible it wasn't on purpose?" one of the tennis instructors asks. "Could've been a nail or something."

"No," Robbie says flatly. "It was a singular slash. Deliberate. Like from a knife."

I stare straight ahead while they keep talking. Threats. Promises. A reminder that Sycamore's reputation comes before any of us. Their voices blend into the background, dull and slow, like a radio set to the wrong frequency.

"Y'all are dismissed," the manager says finally. "But let us be clear. If anyone knows anything and doesn't come forward, you'll be implicated, too."

There's a shuffling of bodies as people move toward the exit, murmuring under their breath. I'm the first one out, slipping through the doorway and into the hall like I'm in a hurry to get to my next shift.

Then, slender fingers pinch around my wrist and tug hard.

I glance down to find Quinn beside me. "Follow me," she mutters, already moving.

I don't argue.

She leads me past the staff lockers, around the back of the maintenance shed, a narrow strip of concrete between the building and the wooden fence that blocks the club from the road. It's secluded back here.

She turns on me the second we stop, scanning the area before lowering her voice. "Word on the street is it was Preston Beckett's car."

I tilt my head, feigning interest. "Huh."

Her glare sharpens. "Huh? That's all you have to say?"

I shrug. "Seems like he had it coming."

Her lips press together. "I know it was you."

I raise a brow, amused. "Yeah?"

"It had to be."

I don't confirm it. She knows I did it. I know she won't say a word. But it's better left unsaid. So, I pivot to something else. "You still never answered my text, by the way."

She flinches. "Wesley's okay. Of course he is, or I wouldn't be here."

"So, your phone *does* work, then?"

"Stop deflecting."

I lean against the fence, arms still loose, giving her nothing. "It doesn't matter who did it. It's already been done."

"But Beckett's going to blame me," she says, urgency threading her voice.

She must've done something—reprimanded him in the moment or said something after. I figured she bottled it up and let it all loose in the break room, alone, like she always does. But maybe I was wrong. Maybe she said something he didn't like, and now he's looking for payback.

"Why?"

"Because I snapped at him." She clears her throat. "When he grabbed my ass, I snapped."

A slow, simmering heat rises in my chest. I rein it in. Breathe slow and deep and count to four. I want to tell her that he deserved more than a snapped warning, more than a dirty look and a sharp word.

That I'm proud of her for standing up for herself and that I wish I'd seen it happen so I could've backed her up. But I can't go there or say those sorts of things to her. Not anymore.

"You're always snappy," I say lightly. "Part of your charm."

"Yeah, maybe."

I glance down. Her fingers are still curled around my wrist and haven't moved. I shift and press my thumb lightly against the inside of hers, tracing the warm skin of her pulse point.

Her breath catches, just slightly, and I don't let go.

"I'm glad about Wes," I murmur. I can give her that. It's safe and careful enough. "That he's okay." I hesitate, then add, "I hope you're okay, too."

Her mouth parts, her grip twitching. "Are *you* okay?"

I blink slowly. "Why wouldn't I be?"

She studies me for a beat, then huffs in disappointment. "Right."

I tap my watch. "We should get back. Wouldn't want to give upper management a reason to start snooping around."

Her lips twitch, and something dry slips into her tone. "As you wish, Clyde."

I huff a quiet laugh, shaking my head. "Alright, Bonnie."

I'm the one who steps back first, letting go of her wrist. She follows a beat later, her fingers brushing over the place I held, as if she can still feel me there.

Neither of us says another word. We just head back to work, pretending nothing happened, pretending we didn't come dangerously close to splitting something open and letting the past pour through.

My cell phone won't stop ringing.

It's been buzzing in my pocket since I left Sycamore, but I ignored it on the drive. I also ignored it when I pulled into the lot behind my building, gripping the steering wheel for a full minute before I could get out of the car. I continued to ignore it as I fumbled my way inside the house, still tasting the sourness of rage on the back of my tongue.

But now I've been sitting here for ten minutes, parked in the empty lot behind the training center, watching the screen light up again.

Dad. Dad. Dad.

I already know what this is about. The missed calls stack up—three, four, five. He never leaves a voicemail. He just keeps calling, again and again, like if he persists, then maybe I'll cave the way I used to.

I should let it go to voicemail. I should shove the phone deep into my bag and pretend I didn't see. Instead, I press Accept and bring the phone to my ear.

"Yeah?"

There's a half-second pause before his voice filters through.

"Hey, kid." A breath. "Took you long enough."

I don't respond.

He exhales sharply, like I'm the one being difficult. "What the hell are you so quiet for?"

Silence, again.

"They raised my meal plan rates again," he continues, voice dipping into that same, familiar strain—exasperated, put-upon, like the hardship is something happening *to* him, not because of him. "Damn near seventy extra a month now. Can you believe that? I told them I can't afford that shit, but do they care? No. Place is a damn scam, Warren."

I press my fingers to my temple. "That's what your disability checks are for."

"They barely cover it as is."

"And whose fault is that?"

He scoffs. "Oh, fuck off. You're real quick to judge, huh?"

I grit my teeth because this is the cycle. This is always the cycle.

He calls. He asks. And when I don't immediately cave, he turns it around on me, like I'm an asshole for not handing over whatever scraps he's looking for this time. I'm supposed to feel guilty or something, but I don't.

I exhale slowly, forcing my voice even. "I can't help you, Dad."

"You really gonna do that to me?"

The words hit their mark, like they always do. It's a subtle thread of disbelief, like the very idea that I could say no is absurd. This is my *dad* we're talking about here, not some lowlife addict looking for his next hit.

My fingers tighten around the steering wheel. "Sorry."

"Seventy bucks isn't gonna ruin you, kid."

He's right, it wouldn't. I could send it right now. I could open my banking app, transfer the money, and it wouldn't set me back in any significant way. But that's not the point.

Because it's never just once. It's never just seventy bucks, either. It's the next thing, and the thing after that. It's the calls and the guilt and the way he always, *always* makes it feel like I owe him something, like I should be grateful he even stuck around after my mom divorced him.

A muscle jumps in my jaw. "I can't," I say again. "I won't."

"You never let me starve before."

I close my eyes. There it is. The gut punch. The thing he's been holding in reserve, waiting for the moment he needs to twist the knife a little deeper.

Because even though he hasn't been a real father to me in years, he knows I remember what it was like. Not when we all lived under the same roof, not when Mom was still trying to hold everything together. But after she finally kicked him out.

After the excuses ran thin and the broken promises stopped being something she was willing to piece back together. He ended up living in a run-down trailer out on Ashwood Road, parked on some old friend's property, surviving off whatever odd jobs he could scrape together between drinking himself to sleep.

I remember the first time I saw it. The sagging porch steps and the busted screen door. The way everything smelled like mildew and stale cigarettes. I was sixteen then. Mom told me I didn't have to go. That it wasn't my responsibility. But I went anyway.

Because he was still my dad. The man who raised me and taught me how to throw a spiral and dive off the deep end. And back then, I didn't know how to separate loyalty from love.

I'd show up once a week with groceries—canned soup, sandwich bread, packs of ramen. It was the bare minimum I could. Nothing that would stretch my part-time paycheck too thin.

And every time, he'd laugh, like the whole thing was funny.

"What, you don't think I can feed myself?" he'd ask.

But there'd be nothing in the fridge except a half-empty bottle of whiskey and an expired carton of milk. I wanted to help because I felt obligated to. And I didn't want him to suffer if I could do something about it.

That's what he's counting on, even now. That I'll still be the kid who couldn't walk away.

I exhale hard through my nose. "You're not gonna *starve*."

"Right. I forgot you're all grown up now. You've got it all figured out, don't ya?"

I clench my jaw, gripping the wheel until my knuckles ache.

I should hang up. I shouldn't have bothered answering in the first place.

But then he sighs, voice dipping into something closer to familiar. "Look, I get it. You're busy. Just—" A beat. "Just come by to see me soon, alright? We'll talk then."

I press my lips together. It's unfair because I know—no matter how much I want to be done with this, no matter how many times I say no—there's still a part of me that will always care about him.

And he knows it, too.

I close my eyes, swallow the sharp thing lodged in my throat.

"I'll see you soon," I mutter, then end the call.

The quiet that follows settles hard and fast, pressing in with a finality that feels impossible to argue with. I tip my head back against the seat, jaw tight, breath unsteady. Once, a moment like this would have cracked me open and sent me spiraling for days.

Now there's almost nothing but exhaustion. A dull, hollow numbness spreading through me where the panic used to live.

And somehow, that feels worse.

Chapter Fourteen

QUINN

Two weeks is all we have left before summer ends. Then, I'll finally be able to walk off this godforsaken fairway for the last time and leave it behind me forever.

Unless, of course, I come back here next season.

It'd be pathetic, wouldn't it? To graduate and still be working at this overpriced playground? But a job's a job. And money's money. English lit degrees don't exactly come with a golden ticket to financial security.

I could teach, I suppose. I could write something, query in hopes of securing a literary agent. Or I could spend the next ten years waiting tables while I figure it all out.

I adjust my bag, shifting the weight across my shoulders as I lead Davis and Mancini down the green. It's an overcast morning, heavy with heat, the kind that seeps into your skin.

The sun's tucked behind a thick layer of gray, which should make the air feel cooler, but it doesn't. It just makes everything stickier, thicker. It makes it much harder to breathe.

I press my tongue against the roof of my mouth, checking in with myself. My chest is tight, but not too tight. My breathing is even, but I know better than to trust it. Humidity like this always makes it worse.

I ignore it, adjust my grip on the clubs, and keep moving.

Beckett isn't here today. Thank God.

I noticed the second I checked the schedule this morning, the second I stepped onto the course and saw only the two older regulars waiting for me. It's a small mercy. One I won't spend much time questioning. Maybe he's busy or out of town somewhere. His annual visit to the underworld.

I don't care. So long as it means I don't have to see him, hear him, pretend I don't want to claw his eyes out for touching me. Besides, I'd rather not be questioned about the whole tire debacle and accidentally give away something I shouldn't.

Davis lines up his shot, adjusting his grip. Mancini huffs, watching him struggle.

"Jesus, just hit the damn thing already."

Davis ignores him, takes the swing. The ball soars through the air.

Mancini claps him on the shoulder. "Nice. Should've done that the first time."

Davis flips him off. "Let's see you do better, then."

Mancini grins, stepping up. He likes to act like he's a laid-back guy, like he doesn't take this seriously, but I know better. They all do. This shit is their bread and butter. The only thing they have going for themselves.

They might not play for anything more than bragging rights and a few bucks here and there, but that's enough to make it worthwhile.

I step back, shifting my bag, keeping my breathing measured as they play. I'm hyperaware of the way my lungs pull a little too hard with each inhale, the way my skin feels flushed and heavy, like I'm wearing the humidity as a second skin.

I glance toward the golf cart, where my water bottle is tucked into the side compartment. It's not far. I should grab it and take a second to cool down and reset. Instead, I draw a slower breath, press my tongue to the roof of my mouth again, and keep moving.

No one likes a caddy who slows things down.

The round stretches on, shot after shot, hole after hole. My steps grow more automatic. The air gets thicker. Every blade of grass feels like it's sweating.

When I make a joke about charging hazard pay for a round this slow, something in the air between them shift. The rhythm changes. The banter dies off. A beat of quiet slips in, sharp and purposeful.

Davis adjusts his glove. Mancini takes a little too long lining up his next shot. They exchange a glance. One of those looks. A silent handoff of whatever thought they've both been sitting on.

I feel it before they say anything. That prickle across the back of my neck. The slow, creeping sense that whatever comes next, I'm not going to like it.

Mancini clears his throat, shifts his stance like it'll make this easier. "So, uh . . . we heard about Beckett's car."

My heart skips. I keep my expression blank. "Oh?"

Davis nods, adjusting his glove. "Yeah. Apparently, someone slashed the tire on his Maserati. Real clean cut. Almost surgical."

I grip the strap of my bag tighter. "And?"

Mancini shrugs. "Well, there are a few theories floating around."

I don't respond as I lead them toward their next shot.

Keep your head down. Keep moving.

Davis exhales, feigning casual. "He's saying it was you."

I stop. Slowly, I turn. "Excuse me?"

Davis shrugs. "Yeah. Says you've had it out for him. That maybe you're a little, you know . . . scorned."

It's so absurd I almost laugh. I openly blink at them, gripping my bag so tight my knuckles ache.

Mancini glances at Davis, then back at me. "So, did you two . . .?"

The implication lands like a slap. They're asking if I slept with a man twice my age and then got mad when he wouldn't commit.

It's so ridiculous it could be a stand-up routine if these men were capable of comedy.

I shake my head, disbelief curling in my chest. "Are you seriously asking me that?"

Davis lifts his hands, mock innocence. "Hey, we're just trying to understand the situation."

A flicker of heat rushes to my cheeks. Not from the sun or from exertion. From the sheer, searing humiliation of standing here, on this perfectly trimmed patch of grass, while two grown men casually toss around scathing rumors. It's not harmless, no matter what they think.

I keep my voice even, but it takes everything I have. "There is no situation."

Mancini whistles low under his breath, dragging a hand through his hair. "So, it's not true? You and Beckett?"

I blink, stunned all over again. I thought the implication had been offensive enough. I didn't expect them to double down.

"No," I snap. "God. No."

Davis lets out a low chuckle like I've just confirmed something, and I feel it again—that sharp, crawling sensation under my skin. I'm suddenly too visible, though everything they're seeing is being filtered through someone else's lies.

"Well, he's telling everyone you freaked out," Davis adds. "Started screaming at him on the green last week. Something about boundaries?"

I go still. My breath falters.

So that's it. He twisted it. Warped it into something else. Of course he did. Of course the version he's telling has me emotional, dramatic, irrational. A girl who overreacted to something so benign. A girl who slashed a tire out of spite.

My jaw tightens. "He touched me."

They both blink, the bravado slipping slightly from their faces.

Mancini shifts his stance. Davis actually has the nerve to look uncomfortable.

I should stop. Should let it drop.

"He grabbed me. Without my permission. And when I told him not to, he laughed."

Silence ensues. Thick and heavy.

Davis clears his throat. "Shit. I mean . . . that's not what he said."

"Yeah." I toss my bag to the ground, eyes hard. "No kidding."

Mancini and Davis go still. I feel the full weight of the implication, the thickness of the moment pressing in around us, sticking to my skin like sweat. I shouldn't have said it. I should have kept my mouth shut. Because now, it's real.

It's more than just Warren that I've admitted it to.

Mancini is the first to truly react. His lips press together. He doesn't know what to say, doesn't know how to hold this in his hands. I wouldn't expect him to.

Davis looks away, jaw tight.

And then Mancini clears his throat. "You want us to get someone else to finish the round?"

It throws me off. The way he says it. A painfully neutral offer for me to have a way out.

I bristle. "You'd rather not deal with me now that you know?"

Davis shakes his head. "No. We still want you. You're the best," he says simply. "You've always been the best."

Mancini nods. "And Beckett's a dog."

The comment is so quiet, so certain, I don't know what to do with it. There's a sting behind my eyes—the kind that comes when someone unexpectedly believes you, when you didn't even know you were waiting for it.

I blink it back and swallow it down.

Davis glances at Mancini, then back at me. "We'll handle him. Get him to drop the tire thing."

I study them, waiting for the punchline. Waiting for them to laugh or brush it off. For them to say something that proves this is still just entertainment to them. But, to my great surprise, they don't.

Mancini huffs. "Fucking dipshit's gonna ruin his own life sooner or later."

Davis nods. "Might as well make it sooner."

And just like that, the round continues. I laid something bare, and they let it settle for all of five seconds before moving on.

That's what gets me—not their reaction or their quiet solidarity. But the knowledge that it won't stick. That this won't change anything for any of us.

Because at the end of the day, they're still his friends and I'm still in the peripheral. I'm another story that will flatten into anecdote. Something they'll reference once or twice, then forget.

It won't live in them the way it lives in me.

And I won't ask it to. Because letting them forget is easier being the girl who made it into a bigger thing than it needed to be.

I DON'T KNOW why I said yes to this.

It's been two years, and I can count on one hand the number of times I've spent time with Alyssa and Jordan outside our apartment. Not because I think it would be a bad time—it wouldn't.

We get along well enough and always keep things easy. We make enough small talk to fill the space, never pushing past the edges of something safe.

I prefer it that way. Surface-level and simple. I like the kind of connection that doesn't require work or vulnerability. What I don't like is the weight of being known, and then discarded.

And yet, when they threw out the invite this morning—one of those casual, throwaway things, a flippant *hey, we're doing happy hour later if you wanna come*—I didn't do what I always do. I didn't deflect or give them my usual, *nah, maybe next time* or *I've got work in the morning*.

I just said, *sure*.

The second the word left my mouth, their eyes widened, surprised I'd actually said yes. The invitation, I assume, had been more of a courtesy than something they expected me to accept.

I shrugged it off, pretended it was no big deal. It was completely out of character for me to say yes, but that doesn't mean we need to dwell on the reasons.

Now, hours later, I'm on a bus heading to meet them in the next town over.

They're like that. Economical girls. City girls. The kind who take public transit without thinking, who thrift their entire wardrobe and know which bars have half-off martinis before six. The kind who can throw together an outfit in five minutes and still look effortlessly pretty.

I can be that girl for one night, too.

The ride is short, but I still find myself fidgeting. I adjust my bag, check my phone, even though there's nothing to check. No texts from Wesley, which means he's fine. Nothing from work. Nothing from—

I shove my phone back into my pocket before I let my mind wander too far.

The bar is tucked onto a quiet street, all glass windows and moody lighting, with a name I can't remember. Inside, the air smells like citrus and warm bread, and there's a hum of conversation under the slow, thrumming beat of some indie song I don't recognize.

Alyssa and Jordan are already at a high-top table near the window, a wooden charcuterie board spread out between them, two nearly empty cocktail glasses on either side.

Jordan sees me first. Her eyebrows lift in slight surprise before she schools her face, smiling. "You made it."

Alyssa turns. "Damn, I was about to put money on you bailing."

I smirk as I drop into the empty seat beside them. "I can turn around now if you'd prefer."

Jordan kicks my shin lightly under the table. "Shut up."

I roll my eyes but settle in. The lighting is warm, the scent of toasted rosemary drifting from the board in front of me. There's a tiny jar of fig jam, some briny-looking olives, a neat stack of thin crackers.

Alyssa gestures toward the spread. "We already ordered. But get a drink. We're staying for a couple rounds."

I nod and let them fall back into easy conversation—some guy Jordan met at the gym, the playlist Alyssa's been obsessing over, their half-formed plans for a beach trip that may or may not happen before classes start. It's light, familiar, but it feels like I'm watching from the outside.

I think I missed too much time with them to fully fall back in.

It's not their fault I've kept my distance. And now, I don't know how to close it.

The waiter swings by, and I order something simple—a gin and tonic, easy to sip, easy to keep my hands busy.

Alyssa presses her hands to her cheeks. The slight flush of pink over her freckles tells me she's already a bit tipsy. "So, what's with you actually agreeing to come out with us? Is the world ending? Did you get fired?"

Jordan nudges her. "Don't scare her off."

I shake my head. "Just felt like getting out for a bit."

Alyssa hums, skeptical. "And you chose us?"

"Would you rather I didn't?" I ask.

"Nah, I'll take it," she says with a grin. "And I'm fully prepared for you to ghost us again for another three months."

Jordan snorts. "That's ambitious. Try six."

I roll my eyes and take a slow sip of my drink. They fall into another round of chatter—Jordan ranting about her stats professor, Alyssa reenacting a particularly awful Hinge date—and I offer the occasional hum or half laugh to let them know I'm listening.

It's strange, this whole thing. Sitting here, half-wrapped in the warmth of their voices, their jokes, the clink of glasses and hum of conversation around us. It's simpler than I thought it might be. Undemanding. A version of connection I forgot I might still be capable of.

So, I let myself have it, at least for tonight. I press my fingers to the cool curve of my glass and stay exactly where I am.

Chapter Fifteen

WARREN

The pool's shut down for cleaning, which means the afternoon swim block is cancelled and the staff is on break. The lifeguards, the servers, even a few of the golf course attendants are all crammed into the break room for a fifteen-minute breather.

More importantly, there's cake.

Zane turned twenty-one today, and Robbie brought in some shitty store-bought thing with way too much frosting. No one cares that it's not good. It's free, and it's chocolate.

"Happy legal drinking age to you!" Robbie singsongs. "Hope you're ready for the worst hangover of your life."

Zane just shoves another bite of cake into his mouth. "You know I've been training for this moment."

"I don't doubt it," Robbie says and slaps him on the back. "But you're still on shift for another four hours, so no birthday beers until then."

Zane groans, tossing his head back dramatically. "It's like you *want* me to suffer."

"Anything else would be a lie," Robbie says.

There's some scattered laughter, the kind that comes easy when you're in the second half of your shift, when the worst of the heat has already passed and all you have to do is get through the final few hours.

The room starts to thin out after a few minutes. People trickle back toward their posts, some heading out for smoke breaks, others just trying to squeeze in a few minutes of quiet before the pool reopens.

I hang back because it's a lot cooler in here. The AC cuts through the heat that's been baked into my skin all afternoon.

Quinn hangs back, too. Coincidence, maybe.

She lingers near the table, one hand wrapped around a paper plate, picking at the last bite of cake. She's in no rush to leave, and neither am I.

Zane, still planted in his seat, tips his chair back and grins up at her. "So, Rose. Now that I'm officially legal, how about I take you out for a real drink?"

Quinn arches a brow. "Oh yeah? You think you can keep up with me?"

Zane smirks, tilting his head. "I know I can."

She laughs, humoring him.

My jaw tightens.

He isn't touching her or crowding her space. But he wants to. It's obvious in the way his knee edges closer to hers, the way his voice dips low like he's trying to carve out something private between them.

And she's letting him. Maybe just for fun or because she knows I'm still here, leaning against the wall like I don't care, watching them. Maybe because she wants to piss me off.

If that's the case, she's doing a damn good job of it.

Quinn tilts her head, studying Zane like she's actually considering it. "What's your drink of choice, birthday boy?"

Zane grins. "Rum and Coke."

Quinn wrinkles her nose. "Figures."

"Figures?"

"You seem like the type to order a drink with training wheels."

Zane lifts his hands, flashing a lazy grin. "Hey, I like my alcohol masked by soda. Nothing wrong with that."

"Mmm, sure," Quinn says. "But if we're going out, you're drinking what I drink."

"And what's that?"

She leans back in her chair, all slow, deliberate confidence. "Whiskey, neat."

I watch as Zane swallows, his bravado slipping just slightly. "Damn. Straight to the point, huh?"

Quinn smiles without showing her teeth. The kind of smile that dares you to underestimate her. Her skin glows under the harsh break room lighting, a sheen of sweat catching on her collarbones, on the curve of her neck where a stray curl sticks to her skin.

The ugly Sycamore polo does nothing to hide the slope of her waist, the way her hips rest easy in those cutoff shorts. She looks sun-drenched and unbothered, like heat itself, and I can't stop looking at her.

"Only way worth drinking it," she murmurs.

Zane clears his throat and recovers fast. I don't know how he does it. Maybe he's too stubborn to flinch, or maybe he just hasn't figured out what kind of fire he's playing with.

"Alright, fine. Whiskey neat it is," he says. "But only if you promise to let me drive you home afterward."

My teeth grind.

Of course he said that. Of course he's trying to be charming, responsible, whatever. I know his type—boyish smiles and big talk with nothing solid beneath it.

Quinn's fingers tap against the table, calm and easy. "Oh, you'd drive me home, too? That's cute, Zane. But I don't need anyone taking care of me."

"I don't doubt it," Zane says, still grinning. "But you know. Just in case."

I could leave. I should. This is getting ridiculous, and the heat under my skin is only getting worse.

I stay planted, arms crossed, back against the wall. Watching her watch him. Because sooner or later, she's going to look over here, and I'll feel it like a spark to the spine.

That's how it's always been between Quinn and me. No matter the time, the silence, the distance we try to wedge between us, our eyes always find each other.

It was like that from the first day. Instant and reckless. Magnetic in the worst and best ways. And it hasn't changed. If anything, it's heavier now and more dangerous. Like a rip current under the surface—silent, surging, always threatening to pull us under the second we stop pretending we're swimming away.

She doesn't have to call attention to it or let it linger. But there's a flicker, a glance, a fraction of a second where her eyes meet mine, and everything inside me tightens.

She shifts back to Zane, lifts her drink, hides a smirk behind the rim.

Zane, oblivious as ever, keeps talking. "I'm serious about tonight. One drink. Maybe two. I'll even let you pick the place."

Quinn tilts her head. "Oh, I don't know. You seem a little young for me."

Zane huffs. "Yeah, okay. Like you're so ancient."

"I've been twenty-one for a while, and you just got here. There's a difference."

"You're six months older than me," he grins. "That's nothing."

She taps a finger against her lip, feigning deep thought. "Maybe you're right. Maybe I should lower my standards."

Zane laughs, low and easy, soaking in the attention like sunlight.

I don't realize how tight my fists are until my nails dig into my palms.

It's fine. It's all just harmless flirting. It's Quinn being Quinn. I know that look in her eye. I know the way she plays these games. It's just enough to make someone want more and to keep the ball in her court.

She's doing it for fun. Maybe even for sport. But part of me wonders if she's doing it for me. Just to see if I'll react. She wants to know if I still care.

I shouldn't.

I do.

She used to flirt like that with me, too. Incessantly. Flagrantly. For sport, sure, but also for real. And it was always *real* between us. Hot, heavy, soft, sweet—somehow all of it at once. Everything. Until it wasn't. Until it was nothing. And I'd gotten used to that. I learned to be content with that.

But now, watching her do it with someone else? Even if it's fake, even if it's just for fun?

It makes me want to smash something.

Zane opens his mouth again, but before he can make another move, Robbie leans his head in through the door, one brow raised in exaggerated exasperation. "Evans. You done embarrassing yourself yet?"

Zane startles, twisting toward him. "What? No. Not yet."

Robbie sighs. "Wrap it up and get back to work."

Zane groans but stands, stretching theatrically. "Don't think this over, Quinn," he says with a wink. "I'm not giving up that easy."

She lifts her glass in a mock salute. "I'd expect nothing less."

He disappears through the door, and now it's just us. That's not an accident, either.

I could've left before him and let the moment pass. Let her drift back into the version of my life I've spent two years trying to keep her in—distant, irrelevant, done. But I didn't.

I've been doing this for weeks now. Letting myself fall back into her gravity. Allowing convenience to masquerade as coincidence. Watching her when I think she won't notice. Waiting around like some part of me is hoping for something I'm not allowed to want.

Quinn leans back in her chair, crossing one leg over the other, dragging a fingertip through the condensation on her glass. "Something you want to say to me, Mercer?"

I exhale through my nose, push off the wall. "Not really."

"Good," she says, smirking. "Because if I wanted a lecture, I'd go call my mom."

I arch a brow. "Wasn't planning on giving you one."

She scoffs. "You sure looked like you wanted to."

I fold my arms and tip my chin. "You really gonna go out with him?"

"Maybe."

Bullshit. I shake my head, turn toward the door. "Whatever."

"Aw." Her voice shifts, all honeyed edges and barbed sweetness. "Are you jealous, Warren?"

For a long, stretched-out second, I don't move. I stare straight ahead, pulse pulsing in my throat, jaw tight. I don't have to look to know she's still watching me. Still locked in, unblinking and unwavering.

She doesn't give me a chance to answer.

"I mean, it would be cute if you were."

Now, I look. She's propped on her elbow, chin in her palm, eyes dark and gleaming. Amused, maybe. Satisfied and daring me to retaliate.

If I let her have the last word, then she's got the upper hand. I can't let it go.

I step close enough that she has to tilt her chin up to keep looking at me, and then I let the moment stretch. The tension builds, tight and restless, neither of us willing to give an inch.

"You like getting under my skin, don't you?"

She smiles, slow and smug. "What was it you said to me, once upon a time? You're fun to mess with?"

I shake my head. "Try someone less likely to bite back."

"Oh?" she says, tilting her head. "And you think you can handle teeth?"

I lean in, just enough for my breath to stir against her cheek. "I know Zane Evans can't."

Her lips part slightly. It's enough for me to see the way her breath catches. And then she pulls back a fraction.

"Yeah, well," she murmurs, voice light, almost airy. "Not everyone's got your ego, Mercer."

The moment breaks. The heat, the tension, the way she was watching me like she was waiting for me to do something—it all splinters like a thread pulled too tight.

I should be relieved. Instead, I'm beyond irritated.

"For the record, you don't have to be worried anymore."

I arch a brow.

She shrugs. "Beckett's dropping the whole tire thing."

I tilt my head. "Yeah?"

"Yeah."

I let that settle, watching her for a beat. The tire was never the part that worried me. I knew exactly what I was doing when I took the knife to it. If it had cost me the job, so be it. I'd have done it anyway.

The only part that mattered was her.

Still, there are no cameras in the back lot. No witnesses or real proof other than a clean slash to an expensive tire and a guy with too many enemies to know where to point fingers.

Nothing will come of it. There were never going to be any real consequences—unless Beckett made some ridiculous accusation against Quinn. And even if he did . . . well. I have a feeling the rest of the club would take her side.

Still, I nod. "Good to know."

She exhales, eyes flicking down to her drink, then back up. Her lashes are thick and dark, framing amber eyes. Her pupils are blown just slightly, lips parted, a hint of color high on her cheeks.

She looks flushed and sated. The same way she used to look after hours tangled up in my sheets, breathless and wrecked, her hands in my hair.

I feel it like a muscle twitch. It's instinct that I don't bother fighting anymore. A jolt that forces me to remember something I haven't let myself think about in too long.

Quinn tilts her head, watching me in that way she does when she's trying to stay in control. She's waiting, I think, to see if I'll cave first. Always playing a game I never seem to win.

"You gonna keep standing there," she murmurs, "or are you gonna go be useful somewhere?"

I lean in and knock my knuckles against the table. Slow. Deliberate. Close enough to catch the shift in her breath. Close enough to watch her throat move when she swallows.

"Careful, Rose."

She bats her lashes. Feigns innocence. "Of what?"

I let my gaze drag over her. "You keep looking at me like that, I might start thinking you want something from me."

Quinn scoffs, rolls her eyes, but the flush at her ears is impossible to miss.

I push away from the table and step back, finally walking out of the break room. I don't look back, but I don't need to. I already know she's watching me go.

Chapter Sixteen

QUINN

I'M LYING on the couch, one sock on, one off, staring at the ceiling, contemplating whether or not I have the energy to start a movie, when a knock sounds at the door.

I groan, roll onto my side, and shout, "Did you forget your key?"

Jordan left half an hour ago, something about meeting Alyssa at the farmer's market to "gather seasonal inspiration"—which sounded suspiciously like an excuse to go people-watching and make up stories about strangers.

One last impatient knock and I'm officially annoyed.

I sigh, push myself up, and shuffle to the door. To my complete surprise, it's my brother, Wesley, standing there. He's all bright-eyed and restless, like he's been up for hours just waiting for an excuse to bother me.

I don't get the chance to ask what he wants because right beside him, looking way too pleased with himself, is our dad. "We're stealing you for the day," he says.

I blink. "Are you?"

Wesley shoves past me into the apartment. He surveys the space, frowns. "Yeah. You're coming."

Dad leans against the doorframe, arms crossed. "Mom's at work. Wes and I are bored. You're free. No excuses."

Mom's a nurse at the outpatient facility on Maple Grove. She's been at the same place for nearly two decades, working twelve-hour shifts that stretch into fourteen more often than not. She never complains about it. Not out loud, anyway.

Dad, on the other hand, took a more flexible job a few years back. Remote consulting, mostly, which let him be there for Wes whenever he needed it. All the doctors' visits, the therapies, the unpredictable bad days. And even though Wes is better now, even though he's stronger, healthier, steadier, they still watch him like he could break at any moment.

That's why he's been bored out of his mind all summer. Our parents still don't let him stay out past nine. He has to check in every hour when he's with friends. He handles it well enough, but I can tell it eats at him. The lack of freedom, the invisible line he's not allowed to cross.

I didn't even have a real curfew when I was his age.

I huff out a laugh. "There are a lot of assumptions happening here."

Wes plops onto the couch and makes himself comfortable. "And yet, here we are."

I glance between them, trying to decide how much energy I have to fight this. Because I do want to spend time with them. I was sort of craving a day alone to recharge, to exist in my own space without anyone else's expectations. But I love my family, and I haven't spent much time with Wes lately.

Once school starts, I'll have less time to spare, and chances like this will get harder to come by.

Dad gives me a knowing look. "It's just lunch, Quinn. Get your shoes."

I roll my eyes, but it's half-hearted at best. Because I know myself. I know I'll go, and I know I'll enjoy it. I'm just arguing because it's part of the ritual—part of how I soften the yes.

"Fine," I say, "but I'm picking the place."

A nicer place is out of the question. Not because my dad would say no. He'd try to swing it, act like it's nothing, but I'd see it.

The pause before he reached for the check. The quiet calculation behind his eyes. He'd blink, then bury it.

We've never been particularly flush. Between the medical bills and the job shifts, things have always been tight—held together by resourcefulness and a lot of pretending.

And Wes, sweet as he is, assumes everything's fine. He's still a kid. He doesn't know what it means to stretch a paycheck or what it costs to act like you're not.

That's why I always suggest something casual. Something cheap enough not to leave a mark. I don't want Dad to wince when the bill hits the table, and then do his best to hide it.

Maybe I wouldn't micromanage so much if I didn't feel a little guilty. He's an adult; he knows when and where to spend his money. But the truth is, I know what it feels like to take from him without asking. And I still carry that weight in a place I try not to examine too closely.

For the most part, I was an okay kid. A helpful sister and a dutiful daughter. But we all have our faults—and mine was knowing how easy it was to take what wasn't offered.

Wes snorts. "Yeah, yeah. Let's go, princess."

I grab my bag, lock the door behind me, and follow them down to the car.

We end up at Maggie's, a hole-in-the-wall diner we've been going to for as long as I can remember. The kind of place with laminated menus, a too-loud jukebox in the corner, and a waitress who's probably been here since the dawn of time.

Wes orders pancakes with extra chocolate chips and whipped cream, even though it's the middle of the day. Our dad doesn't stop him.

"You're gonna knock out in the booth," I warn, watching as he drowns them in syrup.

Wes shrugs, unfazed. "At least I'll die happy."

Dad shakes his head, then turns his attention to me. "How's

work?"

It's an easy, neutral question. The kind that fills the space, that keeps the conversation moving without actually meaning much. I mean, what else is he supposed to ask me?

We don't talk much. Not because we're distant or because anything's wrong. Just because, lately, it feels like we don't know what to talk about anymore.

And yeah, asking how work is going is classic father-daughter small talk, but still, it feels a little . . . I don't know. Hollow.

I shrug, picking at the edge of my menu. "Same as always."

Dad waits for me to elaborate. I don't.

"Quinn's a big deal at Sycamore," Wes says around a mouthful of food. "She gets the members' orders right nine times out of ten. Real impressive."

I shoot him a look. "I'm not even a server. Also, I hate you."

"No, you don't." He grins. "You love me."

I don't answer because he's right. The love I have for Wes could probably crack concrete. It's loud, stubborn, impossible to ignore. When we were kids, I used to sit outside the bathroom door while he threw up, just to make sure he wasn't alone.

Even now, I catch myself checking in on him whenever we're together—watching the way he moves, listening for anything in his voice that might mean a bad day is creeping in.

Dad shakes his head. "Are you gonna go back next summer?"

The question is soft, but the weight behind it isn't. Will you still be at that dead-end job after you've graduated? Are you staying where it's safe because it's easy or because you're scared to want more?

"Maybe," I say. "Haven't decided."

Dad nods, but there's something inscrutable in his expression. I get the reaction. He's never said it outright, but I think he wants more for me. Not because Sycamore is a bad job, not because he thinks I'm wasting my time.

He believes I have the potential to do something else. Something bigger. And now that Wes is stable, now that the worst seems behind us, I think he wants me to start moving again. To stop holding my breath.

Wes swipes a finger through the whipped cream on his plate. "You could always come work for me."

I scoff. "Oh yeah? What are you offering?"

"Personal assistant," he says. "Pays in movie nights and unsolicited life advice."

I flick a wadded-up napkin at him. "Sounds like a scam."

Wes gasps, hand to his chest. "How dare you. I am a fantastic boss."

Dad snorts. "Yeah? And what's Quinn's first task as your personal assistant?"

Wes hums, dragging his fork through the syrup on his plate. "Fetch me a new napkin."

I roll my eyes. "Right. Because that's what my resume's missing—experience in napkin retrieval."

Dad chuckles, shaking his head. "Overqualified already."

I huff, picking at the edge of my toast. "Might as well start now, right? Gotta get used to working jobs that don't fulfill me so the disappointment doesn't hit too hard later."

Dad's smile falters. It's subtle, but I catch it. Strange how much he's paying attention today. It's almost as if he's actually listening, not just waiting for his turn to speak.

My parents have never been good at reading between the lines, at catching the cracks in my facade, so why start now? It's not their fault. They believe what I let them see. I've spent years making sure they don't look too closely.

Thankfully, Wes changes the subject for us. He launches into a story about some new game he's obsessed with, a fantasy epic that involves quests and guilds and whatever other nerd shit he's into.

I half listen. I don't care about the mechanics or the lore, but I do like the sound of his voice when he talks about things he loves. It's comforting. Steady. Like background noise I don't have to think about. Something solid in a world that never really stops shifting.

"Sounds fake," I mutter when he tells me his rogue can cast illusions.

"Sounds jealous," Wes tosses back.

Dad smiles, shakes his head. "I don't know how you two make me feel old when I'm not."

I hum. "You *are* old."

Wes grins. "You do make that weird groaning noise when you sit down."

Dad groans dramatically just to prove a point. "Keep talking like that, and I'm leaving you both here."

Wes and I share a look and then immediately fall into exaggerated, innocent smiles—mirror images of faux obedience. I spear the last bite of my eggs, popping it into my mouth while Wes makes a show of licking syrup off his fork. Dad shakes his head, amused, reaching for his coffee.

"Enjoy this while you can, kid. Sugar catches up with you."

Wes smirks. "Yeah, is that why your knees sound like popcorn? From the *sugar*?"

Dad narrows his eyes, about to fire something back, but then his phone buzzes against the table. He glances at the screen and sighs. "Work. Gimme a sec."

He mutters something under his breath before he disappears around the corner, leaving my brother and me alone in the booth.

We don't say much as we sit there, bored, picking at what's left on our plates without really eating. My toast's gone cold. Wes drags the tines of his fork through a smear of syrup, absently tracing lines into it like it's a maze.

"I'm done with this sugar bomb," he says eventually, pushing his plate away. "Want to go outside?"

I nod, and we slide out of the booth, wandering toward the

diner's entrance.

The air is thick with heat, but the clouds keep the worst of it at bay. The smell of asphalt, grease, and faint cigarette smoke lingers in the parking lot. Weirdly enough, I like the smell. It's familiar.

We end up at one of the weathered picnic tables near the lot, kicking at scattered pebbles as we sit. The diner's neon sign hums faintly in the background. Wes leans back on his palms, tilting his face to the sky, soaking in the warmth.

"So," he says, not looking at me. "You okay?"

I should be the one asking him that. I'm older. I'm supposed to be the one checking in, the one steady enough to carry the weight. But maybe he sees the same thing in me that I've always seen in him. A flicker of something frayed at the edges, trying to pass as whole.

"You always ask me that."

"Yeah, and you never answer me for real."

"It's just been a long summer."

"Yeah?" he asks. "Why?"

I pick at a splinter on the edge of the picnic table. "I was traveling."

"I know that." He side-eyes me. "But then you weren't."

My throat tightens. "I ran out of money."

He gives me a long, unimpressed look. "That's really the answer you're going with?"

It's the answer I've given everyone. The one I've repeated so many times that maybe, if I say it enough, it'll turn into something true. But Wesley's never been the type to take things at face value. He likes to press me, to see how much I'm willing to give before I shut down completely.

"Well, for what it's worth," he says, not giving me the chance to lie again, "I like having you home."

Something in my chest twinges. He means it. That even though I don't live there anymore, there's a comfort in me being close. A steadiness that settles him and makes things feel less fragile for all of us.

"Can you come by next weekend?" he asks. "To the house?"

"Next weekend?"

He shrugs. "Yeah. Mom's making that pork thing you like. We could hang out."

Something in me hesitates. Not because I don't want to go but because sometimes being home makes me feel too much like the version of myself I don't know what to do with anymore. The girl who always said yes. The daughter who never spoke up. The sister who held everything in and called it love.

"I'll try," I say.

Wes squints. "That's code for no."

I huff. "It's not. I just—" I exhale, pressing my fingers into the wood. "I have the big end-of-summer banquet at Sycamore. All hands on deck."

He frowns. "Banquet?"

I nod. "Last fancy event before school starts again. Everyone's required to be there."

He tilts his head. "So, like, black tie? Are you going to be wearing a dress?"

I snort. "No. I'll be in a cater waiter uniform, which is exactly as ugly as it sounds."

"So you'll look just as tragically over it as you always do, then?"

I shove his shoulder. "Shut up."

He laughs, but then, a little softer, "You're sure you'll try?"

"Yeah, Wes. I'll try."

Dad steps out of the diner just as a group of kids on bikes loop past the lot, their laughter cutting through the quiet. He's tucking his phone into his pocket, scanning the lot until his eyes land on us at the picnic table.

"All paid up. You kids ready to go?"

Wes stretches his arms over his head, groaning like he's been doing something strenuous instead of sitting here for the past ten minutes. "Yeah, let's hit it."

The drive back is hushed. Dad's got the radio low, some classic rock song humming through the speakers. Wes scrolls on his phone, humming along to the melody, and I lean my head back against the window, letting my eyes drift shut for a moment.

It's nice and simple. One of those drives where you don't have to fill the silence because it's not uncomfortable. Twenty minutes later, Dad's easing the car into a spot near the curb outside my apartment complex.

"You need anything before we go?" Dad asks, glancing at me in the rearview mirror.

I shake my head. "I'm good."

Wes twists around in his seat, watching me like he wants to rib me but thinks better of it. He smirks, tapping the side of his head. "Don't forget about next weekend."

I roll my eyes. "I said I'd try."

"We'll be expecting you."

I unbuckle my seat belt and step out of the car, a strange dip settling low in my stomach, as if the ground's shifted without warning. I wave them off as Dad pulls away, taillights glowing red until they disappear around the corner.

Inside, I pause just past the threshold, keys still clenched in my hand. It was a good afternoon. An easy, familiar outing that used to leave me steady. Instead, there's a restless edge under my skin now, something that lingers as I stand there in the quiet of my apartment, waiting for the other shoe to drop.

Summer's slipping, and with it the rhythm I've been hiding inside. School is coming back into view, along with everything I've managed not to think about. All of it feels close enough to touch.

And then there's the part I've been avoiding.

The distance I built on purpose, something I told myself was safer, has started to feel a lot more like loneliness.

Chapter Seventeen

WARREN

The banquet is exactly what I expected. Loud, overpriced, and crawling with people I have zero interest in talking to. Another Sycamore production dressed up to look impressive.

The ballroom's been transformed for the night. Round tables draped in white linen, candles flickering in low crystal holders, floral arrangements that probably cost more than my monthly rent. It smells like old money in here—expensive perfume and too many glasses of champagne.

Servers in identical black uniforms slip through the crowd like shadows, balancing flutes of sparkling wine while conversations rise and fall in carefully modulated tones. Loud, practiced laughter echoes off the walls.

I adjust my tie for the fifth time, resisting the urge to tear it off completely. The uniform is stiff, the collar too tight, the sleeves cut wrong for my shoulders. If I wasn't required to be here, I'd already be in the parking lot, halfway to home.

I exhale through my nose and scan the room, already counting the minutes until I can disappear out the back.

Daniel and my mom are standing near one of the high-top tables, deep in conversation with some board member I vaguely recognize. My stomach tightens on instinct.

I knew they'd be here. Of course I did. But that doesn't stop the old reflex from kicking in—shoulders tensing, breath hitching.

I'm bracing the same way I did back when I was eighteen,

pressed into a blazer that doesn't quite fit, hoping I could get through their wedding night without embarrassing anyone.

Daniel looks like he belongs. He always does. The man's a natural at this kind of thing—smooth, unshakable, the type of person who always knows what fork to use and which senator's kid goes to which Ivy League school. He's got that polished charm that makes people nod along when he speaks, no matter what nonsense he's spewing.

My mom, though, she's still figuring it out. Still trying to match his poise, his polish, his place in rooms like this. She looks beautiful—always does—but there's a hesitancy in her smile, a split-second lag in her responses. She doesn't laugh too loudly or drink too much so she can avoid drawing attention.

Like me, she's hyperaware of the fact she wasn't born into this. Only she still thinks she can pass if she's careful enough.

I glance away before either of them can spot me. Before I have to pretend I'm comfortable here too. It's been nearly four years, but it still feels strange to watch my mom in spaces like this.

Not because I don't want it for her. I do. She's happy now. She doesn't have to stretch every paycheck or come home from work completely wiped out. She doesn't flinch when the phone rings, doesn't have to count dollars at the grocery store.

But it's hard to forget how things used to be.

She used to come home from work bone-tired, her scrubs wrinkled, her eyes rimmed red from exhaustion. It's hard to reconcile that with the woman standing here now, hair smooth, dress elegant, sipping from a glass of champagne.

It's not a bad thing, I guess. Just a different one.

I take a breath, square my shoulders, and step up beside them.

Her face lights up, the lines around her eyes softening with something gentle. "Warren," she says, touching my arm. "There you are. I was starting to think you were avoiding us."

"Would I do that?" I say flatly.

Daniel lets out a quiet laugh and claps a hand on my shoulder. "Wouldn't be the first time."

"Surprised you came to this one," I say, my eyes flicking to my mom. "Aren't you a little tired of the club?"

She exhales, half-amused. "Daniel said it would be fun."

Daniel grins. "And she's humoring me."

I laugh. "Lucky you."

He gives me a knowing look. "How's work going?"

"Fine as usual," I say, scanning the room. "Just serving drinks, avoiding assholes. Same old, same old."

"Ah," Daniel hums, narrowing his eyes slightly. "I assume by 'assholes,' you mean my peers?"

I flick my gaze toward him. He's perceptive—always has been. I don't know if it's the years of managing people or just something built into him. The way he watches and notices.

"Among others," I mutter.

My mom frowns and smooths a crease in her dress. "I thought you didn't mind working here."

I shrug. "I don't. Doesn't mean I have to like everyone."

Daniel doesn't push the subject. "The girls are here," he says. "You've seen them at holidays, but I don't think you've actually caught up in a while."

He ushers the two teenagers toward us.

Daniel's daughters from his first marriage, Chloe and Claire, are fraternal twins, now fifteen. We all lived in the same house the summer before I started college. They were absolute menaces back then. Always eavesdropping and snooping. Always up to something.

I've seen them since, of course. Thanksgiving, Christmas, the occasional family dinner. But it was never like that summer. That summer, they were eleven, curious about everything, and I was the older almost-brother they didn't know what to do with.

"We see you on TV sometimes," Chloe says. "Well, not TV-

TV, but YouTube clips from your swim meets. Your mom puts them on the big screen."

I raise an eyebrow. "Uh . . . cool?"

The quieter one, Claire, adds. "You should let us come to a meet sometime. We'd make really embarrassing signs."

"Yeah, something like *Go, Warren, Go!* but with, like, really aggressive glitter."

I sigh, scrubbing a hand down my face. *Jesus Christ.*

Daniel smirks, eyes glinting with amusement. "They're a lot."

I chuckle. "Yeah, I can see that."

My mom is smiling, watching the interaction like it's the best thing she's seen all night. She looks genuinely happy. She likes that I'm trying, slotting myself into this version of a family, even if I'm still figuring out where I belong.

"Alright," I mutter. "This has been fun, but I gotta get back to serving."

My mom squeezes my arm. "Don't work too hard, okay?"

I offer a half smile before stepping back and disappearing into the crowd.

The Sycamore banquet is still in full swing. The hum of conversation rides over the clink of glasses and the shuffle of designer shoes across marble floors. I weave through a group of members and make my way toward the bar.

I should be working. Clearing tables, checking trays, pretending I care about making this place run smoothly. Instead, I lean against the polished edge of the bar and contemplate how long I can stand here while doing nothing at all.

Quinn stands to my right, waiting on a drink order, her back to me. The hem of her uniform clings to her hips in a way that makes it impossible not to notice. Her hair is pulled into some kind of loose knot, but a few strands have slipped free, curling down the back of her neck.

I let my gaze linger there, unabashedly watching her.

We're wearing the same stiff black uniform, bland and shapeless, designed to make us blend in. On her, it doesn't. On her, it moves like a second skin. She shifts her weight, balancing a few empty glasses at the edge of the bar.

She's so fluid and practiced. Her body already knows what to do before her mind has to ask. There's something about it that catches me off guard, the ease of it, the precision. She hasn't done this for years, and yet it comes back to her as if it never really left.

Her eyes flick to mine and she tilts her head, assessing. When she smirks, it's a small thing, barely there, but it hits exactly where she means it to. With that single look, she pulls me back in with the same old force. There's no distance left between attraction and memory.

I take a step closer, not even thinking about it. No hesitation or second-guessing. It's instinct that guides me there.

Because it's her.

Because it always is.

By the time we're skin to skin, she's already facing the counter again, fingers tapping a slow rhythm against the tray in front of her.

"Took you long enough," she says, still not looking at me.

I scoff as I lean back. "Didn't realize we were on a schedule."

She tsks. "You're always on my schedule, Mercer."

A breath sticks in my throat. It's a joke. A throwaway line, meant to tease, to poke at the tension strung tight between us. But I don't laugh because she's right.

I've spent the last two years pretending we don't exist on the same timeline. Dodging run-ins, sidestepping conversations, avoiding the inevitability of this—us. And yet, here I am, leaning against the bar, standing too close, watching the way her fingers trace aimless patterns in the condensation on the counter.

She tips her head toward the ballroom. "How's your night going? Enjoying the spectacle?"

I let out a short laugh. "Oh, yeah. This is exactly how I wanted to spend my Friday night. Wearing a crooked tie and making sure some guy named Richard—also known as Dick—doesn't get served the wrong scotch."

She smirks. "Don't forget your mingling duties. I saw you earlier, schmoozing it up with Stepdaddy Dearest."

I exhale, rolling my shoulders. "Yeah, well. Can't avoid family forever."

Something flickers across her expression. I can't miss those tell-tale signs of hers. The slight press of her lips. The way her fingers stall for a beat before moving again. She's never been close with her parents, not in the way people like to pretend they are. But Wesley—he's the exception.

She loves him with a kind of protectiveness that borders on fierce. She'd take on the whole damn world, I think, just to keep it from touching him.

She shifts her tray to her other hand. "You look good in a tie."

I raise an eyebrow. "Yeah?"

"Not as much of a mess as usual."

I huff out a sound caught between a laugh and a scoff. "High praise, Rose."

She waves a hand. "I'm feeling generous tonight."

The bartender finally slides her order across the counter—a fresh tray of whatever overly sweet martinis are trending this week. Quinn grabs it with ease.

"You need a hand with that?"

She scoffs, shifting the tray. "What, you think I can't handle a few drinks?"

"I think you're a little off your game," I say, smirking as I lean in.

Her glare sharpens, jaw tight. "I could carry three of these with one hand while balancing on a barstool."

My voice drops. "You're wobbling, baby."

She exhales sharply through her nose. I can tell I've landed somewhere close to a nerve, and before she can fire something back, I press my thumb to the inside of her wrist.

The touch is light, almost nothing. Her breath hitches anyway, and I feel the thud of her pulse against my skin. Her eyes flick up to mine, and something in them shifts—electric, unguarded. She's on the edge of unraveling, and I'm the one who's done it to her.

I should pull back, step away, pretend none of this has happened. Instead, I let my thumb draw slow, quiet circles against her skin.

She still doesn't pull away.

"You always do this," she whispers. "You get in my head."

I tilt my head, brush the edge of her sleeve with the pad of my thumb. "Do I?"

She swallows thickly. "You make it impossible to think straight."

I let my fingers shift slightly, enough to skim the inside of her palm. She blinks, snapping out of a trance, suddenly realizing how close we are, how much weight is pressed into this tiny, stolen moment.

Her throat bobs, lips parting slightly.

She whimpers, so quiet I barely hear it, and it's like a fuse catching fire.

She's hoping I might kiss her. Remembering what it felt like.

I remember it, too. Kissing her was one of the best things I've ever done. One of the only things I've ever willingly dreamed of.

I lean in, close enough for my breath to ghost over her cheek. "Say the word, Quinn. Say the word and you can have me again."

I press my palm fully over hers, feel the way her breath stutters, the way her pulse hammers against her wrist. One more shared glance, and we'd fall all the way in.

Then she yanks herself free. Both hands return to the tray.

She won't look at me as her chest heaves.

"Quinny?"

Her fingers tighten around the tray, and then—just like that—she's gone, slipping back into the crowd, disappearing into the hum of conversation, into the careful, curated spectacle of the night.

Leaving me standing there, my skin still burning from where it met hers.

Chapter Eighteen

THAT FIRST SUMMER — THE LAST NIGHT

WARREN

It's too late to be out here, and we both know it.

The sky's gone black, the stars burning low and steady above us, flickering in and out of sight behind thin streaks of cloud. The grass is cool beneath the blanket we dragged from my trunk, but the warmth of the day still lingers in the dirt, rising in lazy waves.

There's a pond to the right of us, maybe fifteen yards off. It's a runoff catch that the grounds crew carved out years ago to keep the lower fields from flooding. Now, it's overgrown and murky, full of bullfrogs and dragonflies, with the occasional beer can half-sunk in the reeds.

But tonight, it's kind of pretty. Reflecting pieces of the sky.

Quinn's stretched out beside me, flat on her back, her arm draped loosely over her stomach. Her hair's fanned out over the blanket, dark against the faded plaid, and she smells like sunscreen and mint gum and cherry almond shampoo.

We've been here for hours. Long enough for the bonfire we half built to sputter out, leaving behind nothing but ash and embers.

"You're gonna miss me," she says lightly.

I snort, shifting onto my side to face her. "Yeah?"

She grins, her eyes still on the sky. "So much."

I let my fingers drift across her arm, tracing the ridge of her wrist bone. Her skin is warm, sun-kissed and soft. "You're acting like I'm never gonna see you again. We're going to the same school."

Quinn hums, unconvinced. "It'll be different."

"You mean because I won't get to watch you sass entitled rich guys for tips?"

She turns her head, arching a brow. "Please. That's your favorite show."

"I mean . . ." I shrug. "It's pretty good."

Her grin widens. "Told you. You're gonna miss me *so* much."

I let my fingers wander higher, curling lightly around her elbow, my thumb brushing the inside of her arm. Her pulse flutters beneath my fingertips, unsteady.

"Very true," I say.

This summer has been its own little world. Familiar, self-contained. It's been easy for us to hold on to.

At work, we move like clockwork—circling each other, trading quips, slipping notes into each other's pockets when no one's looking. And outside of work, it's the same. It's steady. Something I can trust to make sense, no matter what else doesn't.

Our time together has been contained. A set number of days stretched across shifts at Sycamore, late-night drives, and mornings spent lying in the grass behind the club, still half-asleep. Even if we didn't want to crawl inside each other's skin, we'd still be practically forced to.

The job keeps us in each other's orbit. But all of that's about to shift.

College is different. It's loud and sprawling, full of people and choices and space. No shifts to anchor us. No break room glances. At Dayton University, there's an open campus and too many directions we could go.

Even now, with her lying next to me, close enough to touch, the thought of losing this—of losing her—wraps tight around my ribs.

"You're gonna miss me, too," I murmur.

Her eyes drop, fingers tracing something invisible against my arm. "Maybe."

I smile, trailing my touch lower, down to her wrist. "Maybe?"

She exhales slowly, buying time. "I'm not good at . . ." Her voice dips. "At keeping people."

I know what she means. She doesn't have to explain.

I've seen it in the way she keeps her distance even when she's standing right next to someone. Her messages often go unanswered, her friendships left half-formed. If she never gets too close, she thinks it won't hurt as much when people leave.

If she doesn't hold on, then she can't be the one dropped.

"You won't lose me," I say.

"You promise?"

"I promise."

She swallows, her gaze rising to meet mine.

I reach up and tuck a piece of hair behind her ear. Her eyes flick to my mouth, but I don't move to kiss her. Not yet. I let my fingers drift down instead, brushing her jaw, skimming the side of her throat, tracing the gentle dip of her collarbone.

Her breath hitches, her body stills, and her amber eyes go soft and dark all at once.

"You always do that," she whispers.

"Do what?"

"Get in my head. Touch me like . . ." She hesitates, like saying it aloud might crack something open. "Like you're memorizing me."

I smile. "Maybe I am."

I've been memorizing her all summer—every freckle scattered across her shoulder, the faint scar on her thumb, the curve of her spine when she leans over the pool rail. The sound she makes when she laughs too hard. The way she looks at me when she's trying not to.

We've spent weeks like this—kissing until we're dizzy, pressing into each other behind storage sheds and late-night corners, her hands in my hair, mine under her shirt. Always skimming the edge but never falling over it.

And God, do I want her. All of her. Her fire, her bite, the mess she tries to hide and the softness she doesn't know how to offer.

But more than anything, I want *this*. This closeness between us.

Before the summer ends, I want to be irreplaceable to her.

My hand drifts lower, tracing the thin strap of her tank top where it curves against her shoulder. She exhales, breath shaky, and her fingers hook into the belt loops of my jeans.

She closes the space between us, her lips brushing mine, soft and warm with the faint taste of Dr Pepper. It's not a desperate kiss.

This one is slow, the kind of kiss that feels like a conversation.

Her fingers slide into my hair, nails grazing my scalp, and I groan low in my throat. My hand slips under the hem of her shirt to find the bare skin of her waist.

She's warm everywhere. In her breath and her skin. But also, in the way she leans into me like she was always meant to fit there. My hand slides higher over her ribs, fingertips brushing the edge of her bra.

Quinn makes a soft, breathy sound against my mouth, something caught between a sigh and a whimper, and it damn near undoes me.

I pull back enough to see her face. My breathing is rough, uneven. "You okay?"

She swallows, blinking like I've knocked something loose in her head. "Yeah."

I smile and run my thumb over her bottom lip. "You sure?"

Her eyes flick to my mouth again. "Yeah, but I might die if you don't kiss me again."

I laugh, low and rough, and put my lips where she needs them

—deeper this time, like I'm trying to pour every unspoken thing straight into her mouth.

She pulls me closer, one thigh sliding between mine. Her nails dig into my shoulders as my hand slips down her side, fingers curling around the back of her thigh. Her breath grows ragged. Her mouth softens, slows.

I'm losing myself in her. In the weight of her body, the heat of her skin, the soft sounds she keeps giving me like secrets. She shifts halfway on top of me, her fingers tangled in my shirt.

It's too much. It's not enough.

I drag my thumb down her side, following the curve of her waist. "Quinn," I murmur.

"Mmm?"

"I—"

The words stall in my throat when her hands slide under my shirt, palms hot against my ribs. My head tips back, and her mouth finds my neck, leaving slow, open-mouthed kisses over my pulse.

Her hand drifts lower, teasing along my stomach before brushing the waistband of my jeans. Then she cups me through the fabric, fingers tracing every inch, every line.

My cock twitches. My whole body tightens.

"Jesus," I groan, fingers digging hard into her hip.

I'm not going to waste this by coming in my pants.

Quinn laughs breathlessly, her mouth still against my throat. Her teeth scrape just enough to make my pulse stutter. "Told you you'd miss me."

"Don't start," I mutter.

Fuck. I didn't know it could feel like this. Not like *this*.

Not easy in the sense of simple because Quinn Rose is anything but. She's sharp where I'm soft, defiant where I hesitate. She pushes, she dares, she burns. She's a storm I never saw coming and never want to outrun.

But this moment—her mouth on mine, her fingers fisting my

shirt, her breath catching in my ear—feels easy. It's something I don't have to explain. It's something that's always been ours, even before it began.

That's what terrifies me most. The hope that it'll still feel like this when summer ends. That whatever this is won't fall apart once we leave this stretch of heat and chlorine and quiet corners behind.

Because I don't know how I'd handle losing her. I don't know how I'd survive going from this to nothing at all. From the heat of her breath to cold silence. From everything she is to the empty space she'd leave behind.

She's everywhere. I wake up thinking about her. When I scan the pool deck, I'm just waiting to spot her ponytail in a crowd. My body fucking shifts when she's close, like it's already tuned itself to her.

And if I lose that—if I lose *her*—I don't know how to stop looking. I don't know if I ever could.

Chapter Nineteen

QUINN

The first day of classes always feels like stepping onto a treadmill already set at full speed. No warning or easing in before hitting an immediate, breathless sprint.

I've done this three times before. Three different Augusts spent walking these same paths, sitting in these same too-warm classrooms, scrawling my name on too-thick syllabi. But this time feels . . . different. Heavier somehow.

I feel I'm holding my breath, waiting for something to knock the air from my lungs.

I spent the weekend convincing myself that walking away from Warren was the right call.

After our almost-moment at the banquet, I spent the rest of the night dodging him—ducking into side halls, slipping behind columns, eyes fixed on my tray like I didn't feel his gaze trailing me.

I left fifteen minutes early, dumped my uniform in the back room, and hurried to my car. I thought I could outrun whatever I'd almost let happen. A kiss from him, maybe. A crack in the armor, definitely.

I doubt I'd survive that same heartbreak twice.

I'd barely survived it the first time. The chest-splitting ache that clung to me for months, like I'd swallowed something sharp and couldn't get it out. It took me too long to rebuild myself after that. Too long to figure out how to stand on my own.

And besides, Warren's . . . different now. He's harder. More closed off, less forgiving.

He was always grumpy—a little rough around the edges, a little too quick to snap—but there was a big part of him that was softer, too. A part of him that let things go, that knew when to cut people slack.

But now that sharp edge has dulled into something else entirely. He's stopped bothering to shake things off. I wonder if he decided it's easier to hold on to the anger than figure out what to do with it.

That's why it's better, I think, if I let him go once and for all.

If anything, staying away is the kindest thing I could do for either of us.

I repeat that to myself all the way to my second class. It's a literature lecture I'm TA-ing this semester with Professor Lang. A small win but one I'm proud of. Her class is competitive and being chosen felt like proof I've done something right.

The room's still half-empty when I get there, students trickling in with coffee cups and notebooks, scrolling their phones or swapping lazy conversation. I tuck myself off to the side, perched in a chair near the whiteboard.

It's part of my job to check the roster, mark off participation points, and keep an eye on the general chaos.

So, I let my gaze drift, scanning familiar faces I half recognize from past semesters. There's the girl who's always overdressed for class, the guy who showed up half-drunk to every final last year and somehow still passed.

And then, second row down, third from the aisle—Warren.

I blink, half-convinced I'm imagining him. But no, he's there, leaning back in his chair, a ballpoint pen spinning idly between his fingers, dark hair still damp like he barely made it out of the shower before bolting across campus.

Why is he here?

In *my* class.

I look away fast, heart stuttering. I press my fingers hard against the notebook in my lap.

It's fine. It's whatever.

Maybe it's a fluke. A scheduling accident or some weird overlap in graduation requirements. A kinesiology major shouldn't need a 200-level literature elective. But now that I think about it . . .

I do remember him complaining about an English class freshman year. Something about hating metaphors, calling symbolism a scam. Maybe this is a retake. Something he put off until the last possible second. Maybe that's all this is. Just bad timing, bad luck.

I'd like to think it's a coincidence. That it doesn't mean anything. But some part of me—the foolish, reckless part—isn't so easily convinced.

Because what if it *isn't* an accident? What if us working together again this summer wasn't random? What if this class, this moment, this entire stretch of tangled timing is the universe's way of nudging us closer again, just to see what we'll do?

There's some invisible hand that keeps reshuffling the deck, determined to place us in each other's path. It's like the universe is hell-bent on giving us one more chance, even if we don't know what to do with it.

Because now that he's walked back into my life, I can't figure out how to unfeel him. Can't unknow what it was like to be his.

There's a Dickinson line from one of her letters that's always stuck with me: "*I am out with lanterns, looking for myself.*"

That's what it feels like sometimes. That there's a version of myself I can't access anymore. One that existed before Warren Mercer touched me, held me, looked at me like I was something precious.

Professor Lang starts reading through the syllabus, snapping me out of it. Warren finally glances up from his notebook. Those blue-gray eyes scan the room lazily.

Then his gaze lands on mine.

God, I can't look away. I'm stuck, caught in the space between his eyes and mine, between the memory of his hand on my wrist and the sound of my nickname on his lips last Friday night. I can still feel the warmth of his fingers, the rough scrape of his voice, and my stomach twists so hard it's all I can do not to flinch.

He doesn't smile at me or smirk. He stares. And then, slowly, like he's giving me a chance to break first, he raises one eyebrow. It's a flick of movement, subtle and knowing.

I force myself to look away, dropping my gaze to my notebook so fast my pen nearly slips from my fingers. My pulse is hammering, my fingers clenched too tight.

It's fine. It's nothing.

I spend the rest of class hyperaware of every shift in his chair, every time his pen scratches against paper, every lazy drag of his fingers over the edge of his notebook. It's as though my brain's decided it's impossible not to track him, impossible not to feel the weight of his presence from across the room.

By the time Lang dismisses class, my nerves are shot. I gather my things with shaking hands and haphazardly stuff my notebook into my bag.

I need to get out of here. Get outside and breathe in fresh air.

If I wasn't so painfully tuned to him, I'd have thought I might have hallucinated. All that *wanting* making a fool of my senses.

I'm already halfway to the door when I hear Warren's voice call my name.

It would be nice, wouldn't it, if I could pretend I didn't hear him? I only spent the last hour agonizing over the way he kept looking up from the back of the room, gaze flicking toward me. He noticed me noticing him. That much is obvious.

I don't think I'm getting out of this unscathed.

I turn, one hand still clutching the strap of my bag.

Warren's standing a few feet away. His backpack's slung over one shoulder, and there's a crease on his cheek from where he must've been sleeping earlier. A ridiculous detail for me to notice.

"What?" I say, and I'm aiming for indifference, but it comes out tight.

He studies me, eyes dragging over my face like he's piecing something together. He must be remembering Friday night, too, remembering how I bolted before I let myself do something drastic.

Either that, or I've got something in my teeth.

"I didn't know you were TA-ing this class," he says finally.

"Yeah, well," I say, shrugging. "Surprise."

His mouth twitches. "Guess I'll have to make sure I don't slack off, then."

"Don't worry, I won't be grading your papers."

"Good," he says. "Wouldn't want you playing favorites."

"Yeah, nepotism is exactly what I'm known for."

He gives a soft, breathy chuckle, the kind that feels like it's meant for just me.

Unbidden, my brain pictures us lying back in that field again on the last day of summer, starlight flickering low over the grass, me tucked against his chest and him tracing slow circles against my naked spine.

I shift my bag higher on my shoulder and say, "Didn't know you were suddenly into literature."

His smile falters. "I needed the credit."

"Right," I say, and I mean to leave it there, I really do. "That the only reason you're here?"

He scratches the back of his neck. "What are you asking me?"

I hate that my pulse jumps. Some soft, silly part of me wants to believe there's more to this.

"I'm not asking anything."

I barely make it three steps toward the door before his hand finds my wrist. I stop like I've hit a wall. Something in me short-circuits at the warmth of his fingers on my skin, and I'm physically incapable of moving forward.

"Quinny," he says softly.

"Don't call me that."

His grip tightens enough to hold me there.

"You don't have to act this way," he says. "Weren't you the one that said *we should talk*?"

I frown. "Weren't you the one that said you *really don't fucking care about me*?"

His gaze dips to my mouth, then back to my eyes. "I lied. You know I did. Look, Friday night, I think we both—"

"I don't have time for this."

I walk forward with his hand still wrapped around my wrist.

He trails after me like a dog with a leash.

I don't stop until we're halfway down the hall, tucked around the corner where no one else can see us. The air smells faintly like chalk dust and stale coffee, and the flickering overhead light is already giving me a headache.

His thumb is still pressed against the inside of my wrist. If he holds on long enough, I wonder if he'll figure out how to sync his heartbeat to mine and make me stay.

"We let our past and the proximity get the best of us these last few weeks," I say, keeping my voice low. "I get that. But it's long over between us."

"You think I don't already know that?"

I sigh. "Then why are you wasting your time trying to hash this out?"

"I'm gonna be in your class all semester long."

"It'll be fine. It'll be normal. I hardly interact with TAs in my regular classes. That's the thing about teachers' assistants and students—they stay in their lanes. But don't—" I shake my head, swallowing hard. "Don't make this into something it isn't."

"So, you can be the bigger person at the club? Sit and wait for me on the hood of my car, tell me to be civil, but I can't request the same from you?"

"This is *school*, Warren."

"What's that got to do with anything?"

"It's different here," I snap. "It's not summer. It's not Sycamore. It's real life."

"Sycamore is real life, too," he says, voice tight now.

"It is—" I start, but words tangle in my throat.

Because it is. It *was*. Sycamore was early mornings and endless shifts and aching feet and sunburns that linger until October. It was frustration and sweat and whispered conversations in dark break rooms. But it was something else, too. Something that feels too big to name.

"You're right," he says before I can answer. "The time to hash things out was winter break freshman year. But you did what you do best. You disappeared."

"You forced me to. You shut me out."

He lets out a quiet, humorless snort. "No one could force you to do anything, Quinn, but sure, let's leave it at that."

"It's better this way. We can be normal in class, obviously, but I think we should just leave this summer behind us."

"And that first summer, too?"

I freeze. My fingers twitch in his hold. "I don't—"

"I thought we could work things out," he says gruffly. "After all this time, I don't know why I let myself think that. Don't know why I let myself hope you'd changed."

"You're the one who changed," I whisper. "It's like I don't even know who you are anymore. You could be a stranger standing in front of me, and I wouldn't know what you wanted."

He stares, vibrating with anger.

Maybe I've said something crueler than I meant to. Maybe I've pushed too hard.

"Right." He lets go of my wrist, his hand falling to his side. "I'll see ya in class, Quinn."

I swallow hard, curling my fingers into a fist to stop them from shaking. "See ya, Warren."

I stand there, alone, watching him walk away. His shoulders are tight, his head low. He's spent every last bit of effort trying to hold this together, and now he's got nothing left to give. I squeezed all the fight right out of him, haven't I?

It's supposed to be better this way—clean and simple. But it doesn't feel better. It feels like something inside me's been scooped out and replaced with static. Sharp and restless and wrong.

"Warren."

He pauses but stays rooted to the spot, hands in his pockets, waiting.

"I didn't really mean that."

He tilts his head. "Which part?"

"The part where I said I didn't know you. I do. I always will."

I want him to understand that even if I fucked up, it had nothing to do with him. That I know we can't be together again, but that it's not his fault. It never was. And if I could be the girl he needed, I would do it in a heartbeat.

There's nowhere he could go, nothing he could change, that would stop me from knowing him—and wanting him exactly as he is.

Chapter Twenty

WARREN

THE POOL DECK smells like chlorine and sweat, the kind that sticks no matter how many showers I take. It clings to my skin, settles in my clothes, lives in my hair. I breathe it in until the smell disappears.

It's the first day of team practice, and the noise already feels like a headache waiting to happen. Half the guys are still dripping from warm-up laps, tracking puddles across the tile. The rest hang around the edge of the pool and talk over each other.

"Alright, you overcooked noodles," Coach Voss calls out. "We're starting with a 400 IM. Let's see who actually remembers how to swim."

There's some groaning before guys start stripping off shirts and sliding into their lanes. I'm adjusting my goggles when I hear the ruckus of my least favorite teammate.

"Hey, Mercer! You taking it easy on us today or what?"

I glance up to find Reed Hawkins grinning over at me. He's a backstroke specialist with a strong underwater phase and a sharper mouth. He likes to rile people up, throw them off their rhythm. It might work on some of the younger guys but it doesn't work on me.

"You want me to slow down?" I ask. "Didn't know you needed a head start."

His grin stretches wider. "Man, I can't tell if you're funny or just a dick."

"Could be both," I mutter, pulling my cap over my head.

Most guys on the team respect me well enough. They know I'm good—maybe not the fastest anymore, but consistent and reliable. I've never been the loud one, never needed to shout or lead the locker room pep talks.

I prefer to fly under the wire.

When Coach offered me the captaincy last season, I turned it down. I didn't want it. Didn't want to be the guy everyone looked to. I'd have to be responsible for team dinners and leading stretches and pretending I cared about anything other than showing up, swimming fast, and then going home.

Those aren't the things I like about swimming, anyway. It's a team sport on paper, but the work is mine. My lane. My time.

Still, I know what they say about me. That I keep to myself. I show up to practice, push harder than anyone else, and leave before anyone can ask if I want to grab lunch after. It's not wrong. I just don't see the point in pretending.

Coach blows his whistle, and I hit the water fast, arms cutting through the surface, body falling into the rhythm I know better than anything else. Kick. Reach. Pull. Breathe.

The tension bleeds out of me as I move. Every doubt and distraction. Every tiny inconsequential thought—gone. It's just me and the lane line now. Nothing else matters.

By the time I finish the set, I'm winded but steady, chest heaving as I haul myself out of the pool. Hawkins is still slogging through his last two laps.

"Taking it easy on me, huh?" I call out, dripping water onto the deck.

He sputters something about his shoulder being sore, but I'm already halfway to my towel.

Maybe I'm not the rising star anymore. The scouts aren't watching me like they used to. But I put in the work this summer. I showed up every morning. I put in extra hours on non-work days.

While half the team was off drinking or sleeping in, I was in the water.

I'm drying off when my buddy Lyle jogs up. He's soaked, breathless, and annoyingly chipper. He slaps my shoulder hard enough to sting.

"Damn, man," he says, grinning. "You gonna make us look bad all season or just the first day?"

I smirk. "Just setting the bar."

Lyle laughs, but it's easy, no edge behind it. He's been my closest thing to a friend on the team since freshman year. I like him because he doesn't push.

"You're in shape," he says. "Even after summer break."

"Didn't take a break," I say, shrugging. "Pool was still there."

Lyle snorts. "You know, some of the guys are pretty unhappy with you. They know you turned down the captaincy last year, and now you're back outpacing everybody."

I snort. "Yeah?"

"They say you're too good to care. That you think you're better than us."

I wipe the water from my face, taking my time before answering. "They can think whatever they want."

I push harder than they do. Train longer and give up more. Gaines and Ruiz could be just as good—maybe better—if they gave half a shit outside of meet days. There are other guys on this team who'll probably make Nationals with an A-cut this year, so no, I don't think I'm better than everyone.

I just know I'm reliable. I'll always show up.

Omar is the only senior who pulls weight in and out of the water. He shows up early, too. Checks on the freshmen. Keeps the energy up when a set drags. That's why he's captain now. That's why he earned it, and why I felt good about turning it down.

Lyle studies me for a beat. "I figured you'd say that."

We're halfway to the locker room when Coach calls, "Mercer, hang back!"

I backtrack, stopping at the edge of the pool deck. "Yeah?"

"Gaines is out for at least a month—shoulder injury," Coach says. "I'm moving you to third leg in the freestyle relay, and you're gonna lead off the medley with backstroke. I want you first in the water, and I'll have Omar anchoring."

I blink. That's . . . unexpected. Backstroke isn't my specialty. I've been anchoring since sophomore year, ever since my split got fast enough to clean up whatever mess the rest of the relay left behind.

When I'm swimming first, there's no one to chase. There's no adrenaline spike from a tight finish or cleanup mission. I'm the one setting the tone, not closing the gap. One bad turn and I screw the rest of the relay before it even starts.

That's part of why I take it so seriously.

And Hawkins is supposed to be the alternate there, so either Voss doesn't trust him, or he's testing me.

"Alright," I say, shrugging my towel higher on my shoulder.

"You sure you're good with that?"

"I said alright."

Coach narrows his eyes like he's waiting for me to crack. But there's no shot I'll tell him what I'm actually thinking. What would be the point? It's not like I can say *Hey, Voss, I don't really trust anyone else to finish the way I would.* Or *Yeah, putting me first is fine, but you better hope the guys behind me don't screw it up.*

He's made his decision, and I'm just here to follow it.

"You know—" Coach says softly. "Being the best doesn't mean much if you're always swimming alone."

When you race solo, there are no missed turns or bad handoffs. No one else dragging your time down. Maybe I'm lonely outside the pool, but at least in the water, I'm in control. That counts for something.

"Just keep your head straight," Coach says, voice quieter. "This is still your season if you want it."

Maybe if things were different, I would allow myself to want it. I know I'm fast enough to win, but I don't want to carry anyone else's weight. I don't want to be responsible for leading if I can't guarantee an outcome.

Being captain would mean more than just showing up and swimming hard. It would mean taking charge. Being visible. Letting people rely on me and risking what happens if I fail them.

I've spent the last three years avoiding everything that comes with being part of a team. The small talk. The bonding. The nights out after practice. The part where trust isn't just implied—it's required.

Maybe that's why the pressure never really lets up. Why it coils tighter after every practice and meet. Our coach looks at me like I'm supposed to lead when I barely know how to follow.

Ten minutes later, I let the shower scorch my back, hoping the heat will unwind something in my chest. It doesn't. The tension sticks, clinging like chlorine—sharp and stubborn—and no amount of heat or steam can burn it off.

I should be thinking about the season and the change in relay. About how Voss is already testing me by switching my spot in the lineup. About how Hawkins and the others have been running their mouths about my attitude, my so-called ego.

But I'm thinking about Quinn again. Her eyes finding mine in that classroom. The way her pulse fluttered beneath my fingers when I grabbed her wrist. The way she's been flashing hot and cold —too sharp one minute, too soft the next—like she doesn't know what to do with me anymore.

I scrub a hand down my face. *Jesus.*

I wasn't meant to see her again once we both finished the season.

When I enrolled in Lang's section last spring, I knew Quinn's major—of course I did—but I wasn't expecting her to be the one standing at the front of the room, watching as I half-heartedly skimmed the syllabi like I couldn't feel her gaze burning into me.

And now I'm stuck with her once again. Twice a week. Two hours of her clipped voice, her presence, her sharp little comments when someone asks a question that's already been answered five minutes earlier. Two hours of pretending I'm not still holding on to some tiny sliver of whatever the hell we once were.

Meanwhile, she's decided to act like I'm nothing more than another student with a notebook and a bad attitude. I could deal with Quinn being angry. With her getting in my face, snapping back like she used to. I know how to fight with her.

Hell, in between all the messy, heated, tangled-up moments, we were always bickering about something—who could carry the most trays through the banquet hall, who could fast-talk their way out of a double shift, who could get the most half-hearted praise from Robbie by cutting corners in the clean-up room.

But this forced, hollow silence she wants to impose? That's usually my wheelhouse. Now that she's the one doing it, I don't know how to handle it.

I can't figure out how to meet her in the middle when she won't give me anything to work with. When less than a month ago, she was the one begging for me to just talk to her.

I know she's not the only one who's been hot and cold. I'm guilty of the same. And I've been doing it often—pushing and pulling, giving just enough to keep her guessing, then retreating before she can get too close.

So, I can't blame her for walking away last Friday night.

Because I almost didn't let her. If she had looked at me a second longer, if she had stayed just a breath closer, I would have found a way to kiss her. I know I would have.

God, I've spent two years convincing myself that's not what I want. But in that moment, I would have given in to her. I would have let myself forget how complicated we are, how badly we ended.

If she had just let me, I would have kissed her like none of it mattered.

I towel off, still fuming, and yank on my clothes. My Wednesday schedule is brutal, starting with early morning practice and running straight into back-to-back classes until two in the afternoon.

Kinesiology keeps me moving—anatomy, biomechanics, sports physiology—the kinds of classes that actually make sense. Everything is mechanical, built to work the way it's supposed to.

But English is another story.

I already withdrew from this class freshman year. It was one of the five credits Dayton lets you drop without it affecting your record. I still don't know what literature has to do with human movement and performance, and honestly, I don't really care.

But since Dayton won't let you graduate without checking off your core requirements, here I am, sitting through lectures about metaphors and themes like any of it matters to me.

Sitting in that room twice a week—pretending Quinn isn't five feet away, pretending I don't still know exactly how her voice sounds when she's teasing or pissed or whispering my name in the dark—is enough to make my brain short-circuit.

Monday, I spent the whole period watching her instead of the slides on the screen. I sat there like some clueless, lovesick fool, tracking every flick of her pen, every time she tucked her hair behind her ear.

Tap, tap, tap—faster when she's nervous, slower when she's calm. That's how I knew she was out of her element last Friday night because her hands were so ungodly still.

I shake the thought off and head to class, cutting across the quad.

The English building is already buzzing by the time I get there, students clustered in doorways, voices rising and falling in a low hum. I head inside and slide into my usual seat, second row from the back. It's far enough to stay out of sight but close enough that I can still see Quinn.

And yeah, I know how that sounds. But this isn't about missing her or wanting access to stare at her during class.

It's not.

Though, if she's going to sit up front where I can see her, I'd be lying if I said I wasn't going to look.

She's already in her seat beside the podium, flipping through her binder, her hair twisted up in a loose knot. She's wearing one of those oversized sweaters she used to steal from my room, soft and slouchy, the sleeves shoved up to her elbows.

It's infuriating.

Because even now—while she's ignoring me, pretending none of the stolen glances or tense conversations or almost-moments from the last few weeks ever happened—I still know her better than anyone. I know the way her fingers twitch when she's second-guessing something. The way her shoulders tense when she's trying too hard to seem unbothered.

I still know every facet of her, intimately.

How could ever forget?

Chapter Twenty

WARREN

THE STACK of papers on my desk is piling up. First-week assignments are short and low-stakes, the kind of thing students rush through in twenty minutes, hoping their half-hearted thoughts will pass as introspection. Most of them will.

Lang's prompt was simple enough:

Choose a passage from this week's reading that resonated with you—a line, a sentence, even a single word—and write 250 words on why it stood out. What did it make you think about? How does it connect to something in your life, past or present?

Most of the responses are predictable: breakups, moving away from home, losing a pet. Some are barely more than a paragraph, like the students thought the word count was just a suggestion. Others overcompensate with flowery language stretched thin across an entire page.

I've been working through them for over an hour now, bouncing between coffee sips and mindless scrolling whenever my focus dips. But I'm down to the last few pages—the last handful of names—and I know what's coming.

I've been telling myself I wouldn't look at the names at all while I'm grading. It's none of my business and I shouldn't care. Still, I haven't been able to keep myself from checking,

No matter. I think I'd know his writing or his words anywhere, anonymous or not.

I couldn't bring myself to confess the conflict of interest to Professor Lang. It would've been unprofessional and awkward. I didn't want to deal with it. Didn't want to make it a thing. So, I left it alone.

Which means I should skip his work, at least for now. I should slide it to the bottom of the stack and forget about it until tomorrow. Instead, I flatten the page against my desk and start to read.

"The line about 'letting go of what's already lost' reminded me of the way summer ends. It's slow at first, then all at once. You blink, and it's over. Like the sun setting without warning, even when you swore you were paying attention. The ache of knowing you had more time than you thought, and still wasting it. Or maybe just not using it right."

My pulse stutters.

There's more. Two hundred words more that tell me about Warren as a wide-eyed kid who looked up to a dad who broke more promises than he kept. Then, later, to a jaded teen who stopped believing in second chances.

Then, eighteen, when he started pretending none of it touched him at all.

Two hundred words that dance around regret without naming it outright. He hints at something unfinished, something cut off too soon.

I read it again, slowly this time. Is he trying to tell me something? Give me some clue, some sign or indication that he's not talking about what I think he's talking about.

If he thought I wouldn't be reading this, then maybe that's the only reason he let himself be honest.

My chest tightens, and suddenly, I'm back at Sycamore. Back

in that last patch of fading summer sunlight. His arm is stretched behind his head, my fingers curling in the grass beside him. His voice dips low when he says *we've still got time.*

You blink, and it's over.

I press my palm hard against my desk.

It's not about me. It's not. It's just a damn paper. A few vague thoughts about a reading assignment. He probably dashed it off ten minutes before class and hasn't thought about it since.

I slip the cursed piece of paper to the bottom of the pile, like if I can just bury it beneath enough pages, I'll forget the way it makes my stomach twist.

I need to get the hell out of here.

I grab my bag from the corner of my room, pull on my sneakers, and step out into the apartment's dimly lit hallway. Jordan and Alyssa are curled beside each other the couch, a blanket tangled around their legs, the TV flickering soft blue light against the walls.

"You heading out?" Jordan sleepily asks.

An empty wineglass balances on the arm of the couch, and Alyssa's half-asleep against her shoulder. They're dressed up, makeup smudged, watching some comfort movie they've seen a dozen times before. They must've gone out earlier.

"Yeah," I say, tightening my ponytail. "I've got . . . stuff."

Jordan cocks a brow. "Emberline again?"

I shrug. "I like it there."

She doesn't press, but I can feel her watching. I know she's noticed the late-night gym runs, tracked the pattern without saying much. I've given her just enough to quiet the questions. I've told her that it clears my head, that it makes me feel strong.

But I haven't told her the whole truth. That I enjoy the stillness of it even more than the strength. There, I'm able to quiet the noise in my head—by moving fast, hitting hard, burning through every thought until there's nothing left but breath and muscle and calm.

Is that the way Warren feels, I wonder, when he's out there in the pool?

"You sure you don't wanna stay?" Jordan asks, gesturing to the screen. "We're watching *The Proposal* again. Come suffer with us."

I smile, but it's tight. "Next time."

They exchange a knowing look as I slip out the door, footsteps quick down the stairs.

The boxing gym is nearly empty when I get there, just a few stragglers lingering by the heavy bags. The place smells like sweat and rubber, the faint tang of disinfectant hanging in the air. It's not quite deserted, but quiet enough that I can breathe.

The guy at the front desk barely looks up as I pass. There's no sign of the owner—Marcus, finally learned his name last week—and without him around, I feel a little less like I need to prove I belong here. Not that I've been trying to impress him exactly, but his presence sharpens something in me. Makes me stand straighter and hit harder.

Warren's words echo again, low and sharp in the back of my mind. *You blink, and it's over.* Five words, stitched into me like thread pulled too tight.

I roll my shoulders back. God, I need this.

At the lockers, I wrap my hands—thumb looped first, snug over the knuckles—and make my way to the bags. The first punch lands sharp enough to jolt my wrist. The second lands harder. The third starts to feel like relief.

For a while, it's just the rhythm. The steady pound of my fists against leather and the dull ache crawling up my arms. I relish the weight of my own body, the crack of my knuckles finding the target.

"For a rookie, you've got a good arm."

I turn, breathing hard.

The unexpected intruder has dark, wavy hair, a few piercings, and fingers wrapped in bandages. He's lean but solid, the kind of build that speaks more to control than brute strength. Definitely a fighter.

"Yeah?" I drag my glove across my face. "Could've fooled me."

"You're pulling back too soon," he says. "That's why you're not landing clean."

I frown. "I'm landing just fine."

The little hoop in his left ear glints. "Yeah, but you could hit harder."

I almost laugh, but something about him stops me. He's probably my age, maybe a year or two older, with faint shadows under his eyes and a cocky sort of confidence that says he's been doing this for a while.

"Show me," I demand, stepping back from the bag.

His eyebrows lift. He unwinds his bandages as he moves, hands bare and calloused when he squares up beside me. "You're cutting yourself short," he says. "Here—step in closer."

I do.

"Now, shift your weight," he says, hand hovering near my shoulder. His fingers ghost along the sleeve of my shirt, and I swear I catch the hint of a smile when I glance at him. "Feel it in your hips, not just your arm. When you pull back, don't rush. Let your knuckles sink in first."

I follow his instructions, shifting forward again. When I throw the next punch, the sound cracks sharper.

"There you go," he says. "Better."

I grin, just a flicker of one, but it surprises me. "Are you a trainer?"

"Nah," he says, shaking his head. "Not yet, but I do work here."

"Dayton student?"

"Used to be."

"Is that right?" I pause, waiting for him to elaborate.

He doesn't. "Keep your shoulders loose," he says instead. "You're too tense. You're thinking too much."

I huff. "Yeah, well. That's kind of my thing."

He snorts a laugh. "Noted. Are you here often?"

"Sometimes," I say. "Late nights."

"Best time to be here. Quiet. No one watching." His gaze flicks to the far wall of mirrors. "No one to impress."

"Exactly," I mutter. "I'm Quinn, by the way."

"Gage," he replies, offering a hand. His palm is rough against mine, fingers worn from years of whatever brought him here. "I don't wanna ruin your flow, so . . . I'll see ya around, yeah?"

"Sure."

He flashes a crooked smile. "Looking forward to it."

I don't get the chance to answer. He's already turning away, slipping through the ropes and stepping into the far ring. I'm not sure if he was taking a break or just saw an opening to step in and help, but either way, he's gone now.

I stay long enough to run a few more rounds at the bag, testing the shift in my form. The way my weight settles, the way each punch sinks deeper and sharper. It feels like something's clicked into place.

By the time I peel off my gloves, I'm drenched and breathless. My arms burn, muscles tight with effort. I stagger to the lockers, unwrap my hands, and rinse off in the grimy sink.

Once I'm done, I shove my damp clothes into my bag and step out into the night.

A light drizzle falls and wets my lashes. It clings to my hair, beads along my skin, washing away the last of the sweat. I walk the few blocks home, the air thick with concrete and rain, the world quiet under the soft patter of water on pavement.

When I reach my apartment, I'm calmer and looser, but still carrying a restlessness I can't shake. The girls' doors are shut, a faint glow slipping out from beneath their frames. The place feels hushed, still holding the warmth of their earlier movie night—popcorn in the air, a half-empty wineglass on the counter.

Eventually, I sit at my desk and open my laptop. It's the middle of the night, but I've been behind on my own assignments while juggling TA work. I open a new Word doc. The blinking cursor stares back at me, taunting.

No time like the present to tackle my first-week assignment in creative writing.

I think I can knock it out in an hour or two. I need to write something simple and reflective, and it helps that I already know what I want to say. Or at least I think I do.

Sadly, while I write, the words keep slipping sideways, never landing quite right. My fingers hover over the keys, then drop away again.

I lean back, dragging both hands through my hair.

Just write something, Rose. Anything.

You blink, and it's over.

Warren's paper is still sitting on my desk, the edges crumpled and curling like a frown beneath the others. I pull it from the pile and smooth it flat against my knee. This time, I don't let it blur past like a blink or a passing thought.

I let it sit and settle in. I let it marinate.

The ache of knowing you had more time than you thought, and still wasting it.

That's the part that gets me. The part that makes my chest go tight because I know what that ache feels like. Acutely, desperately.

We're two sides of the same coin.

The twisting realization hits me again. Warren has always been the one person I never had to pretend with. Even when we were fighting, snapping at each other across the dish pit, stealing glances during breaks, needling each other just to pass the time, it was always real.

With him, I could be sharp and soft in the same breath, restless and steady all at once. Somehow, he always understood. He saw *me.* Not the polished version I showed everyone else but the pieces I could never quite hide.

I've spent two and a half years pretending I don't miss him. These past few weeks pushing him toward me and then pulling away like I can't decide what I want.

And now, with his careful words pressed against my lap, I know what I have to do. My phone rests in one hand, the screen glowing dimly. My thumb hovers over his name in my contacts.

When it comes to Warren, I don't have to wonder what it would be like to be known. To be my whole, unapologetic self. I never did.

So, with his words sitting there like a brand on my heart, I do the only thing I can do. I reach back across the tether.

Chapter Twenty-Two

WARREN

This girl is a fucking menace, I swear to God.

She's texting me at two in the morning on a Friday night. She thinks this is normal and acceptable. Like she didn't shove my own angry words back in my face the other day. Like she didn't draw me in and then bolt like I was something she regretted picking up.

QUINN

didn't know you were such a poet

That's all it says. No context or follow-up to the seven random words that practically roll their eyes at me through the screen.

I stare at my phone like maybe if I look hard enough, I'll find the real message hidden between the letters. But she leaves me nothings else. No breadcrumb trail to follow or tiny hint about what the hell she's thinking.

It would be wise for me to turn my phone face down on the nightstand and forget she ever sent it. But, like the lovesick fool I am, I'm already sitting up, my pillow shoved behind me, fingers ready to reply.

I'd finally managed to fall asleep, too—after an hour of listening to Liam and Birdie going at it from across the hall, their muffled laughter and low voices filtering through the thin walls. I'd shoved a pillow over my head, swore at the ceiling, and eventually drifted off.

And now this.

WARREN

you drunk?

I type it out, but I don't hit Send. Delete it.

you okay?

Delete that, too.

That question isn't the right one. Not for her, not for *us*.

what the hell is that supposed to mean?

I stare at the screen, half expecting her to ignore me. Half hoping she will. But three dots blink back almost immediately.

QUINN

it means you're not as hard to figure out as you think

I huff out a laugh. Humorless. Exhausted.

WARREN

yeah? enlighten me then

QUINN

we've still got time

My stomach twists, sharp and sudden, like someone reached inside and yanked something loose. *We've still got time.*

I know what she's doing now. I know what she's remembering.

It was the last day of our first summer together. I said it to her then because I meant it. Because I believed we'd figure it out, that whatever we were building wouldn't fall apart the second things got hard.

But that's not what happened. We spent six months together,

and then it ended. Her silence. My pride. We didn't run out of time; we wasted it. Let it rot between us while we acted like it didn't matter.

I drag a hand down my face.

She's messing with me. She has to be. This is classic Quinn. She tosses a match, watches it burn, and then pretends it wasn't her that lit it.

WARREN

go to bed, quinn

QUINN

I don't want to. I want to talk about . . . keeping our eyes open

WARREN

stop being cryptic

QUINN

your paper. I read it. It was good, but . . .

My chest pulls tight. A door slams shut behind me. I'm locked in now, I think, no way out except through whatever she says next.

I want to shake the answer out of her, demand she just say what the hell she means instead of making me chase her through half-formed metaphors and memories.

But this is Quinn. It always has been. She doesn't do easy or hand out clean truths. She speaks in fragments and half steps, in loaded silences and unfinished thoughts.

I've always liked that about her.

And she wasn't even supposed to read my paper. Told me herself she wouldn't. Looked me dead in the eye and said it like a promise. But I sort of hoped she would anyway. Hoped she was bluffing. Lying, maybe. The way she always does when she's scared of saying too much.

WARREN

are you going to finish the thought or just circle around it?

Another pause. Longer this time. Long enough that I think maybe I've pushed her too far. Maybe she'll leave it alone now and this whole thing will finally die the death it should've had two years ago.

QUINN

it felt unfinished

I stare at the screen.

Unfinished.

I scrub a hand down my face, heart thudding hard. She's right. It was unfinished. Not because I couldn't figure out how to end it but because I didn't want to end it.

I used the whole damn assignment to talk about her. About me. About us. All the ways we fit and fought and fell apart.

WARREN

maybe it was supposed to be

QUINN

and maybe I still want you

Fuck. *Fucking hell.*

I can't breathe. I can't move. I sit there, staring at my phone like the words might shift and rearrange themselves, like they might turn into something else if I look long enough. But they don't. They stay right there. Blunt and impossible and real.

I still want you.

She must be drunk, or bored, or messing with me. It would be easier to write this off as a mistake, to pretend it's just Quinn playing with matches again. But I know better.

Because this? This isn't Quinn being careless.

This is Quinn being brave.

QUINN

if I promise to just snap myself out of it . . . to stop pretending I don't care and then acting like I do . . . would you meet me somewhere? just to talk, to lay it all out there. say the things we should have said during winter break our freshman year?

I read it again. And again. Until the words blur. Did I conjure this all up by sheer force of will? Because Quinn doesn't ask for things. Not like this. She's too stubborn, too proud. She always leaves first. Always makes sure she's the one walking away.

But here she is, offering me the chance to hurt her first.

I don't know what that means. If this is about closure or second chances or something else entirely. But I do know this: whatever she's offering, I'm not strong enough to turn it down.

WARREN

now?

QUINN

it's 2 o'clock in the morning. what do you think this is, mercer? a booty call?

I snort, dragging a hand down my face. Only Quinn could drop something that heavy and follow it up with a crude joke.

WARREN

then when?

QUINN

tomorrow. our field with the pretty blue flowers. around noon? you know the one x

I know it. A stretch of grass and wildflowers, a small pond tucked past the tree line where the fireflies hovered like embers.

Where we lay on our backs and whispered under the stars and the world goes quiet just for us.

It's where we slept together for the first time.

WARREN

yeah. I'll be there

The phone is ringing when I wake up. Loud, jarring, vibrating against my nightstand like it's got a personal vendetta. I blink at the screen, still half dreaming, half-convinced I've been imagining things since—

Dad. Dad. Dad.

My stomach twists.

I let it ring three times. It's long enough to consider ignoring it, long enough to remember that ignoring him never works. He just keeps calling, keeps wearing me down until I break.

I grope for the phone and hit Accept, voice still rough with sleep. "Yeah?"

"Warren? Jesus Christ, finally."

I sit up straighter, dread settling low in my gut. "What's wrong?"

"I need you to come down here."

"What happened?" I ask, already swinging my legs over the side of the bed, pulling on yesterday's jeans.

"It's—it's the staff, alright? They're trying to screw me over again. Bunch of goddamn crooks, I swear to God. They're threatening to call the cops if I don't calm down, and—hell, I'm calm, Warren. I'm so fucking calm. But they're pushing me. Trying to make me out like I'm the one causing problems when I'm just—damn it. You just need to come down here."

I shove my feet into my sneakers. "What did you do?"

"I didn't do anything!" he snaps, incredulous. "They're just—look, can you just get here?"

"I'm on my way," I mutter, already grabbing my keys.

I'm not the best at de-escalation, but I'm the only one he'll listen to. The only one he still recognizes on his worst days. I have to go. Even knowing what it costs me every time.

The drive to Oakview goes about as well as I'd expect. Unbidden, the old memories to start clawing their way back in.

The yelling. The slammed doors. The nights I sat on the curb outside our house, staring down the street, waiting for my dad to come back. The way he'd stumble in reeking of whiskey, slurring apologies that never meant anything.

I shake it off and grip the wheel tighter.

He's sober now—or close enough. The booze isn't what's messing with him anymore. It's the strokes he brought as a result and the damage they left behind. This half-formed version of him, foggy and fractured, is like a puzzle with the edges blurred.

But that doesn't make him harmless. Not even close.

By the time I pull into the parking lot, my chest is tight, every breath scraping like gravel in my throat. I park, kill the engine, and sit for a second, fingers flexing against the steering wheel.

I should've stayed in bed and let him handle this one thing himself. But I know better. If I don't deal with it now, it'll just spiral. He'll call again and again until I either give in or he does something worse.

The front desk nurse barely glances up when I walk in. The low buzz of daytime TV filters from the common room, mixing with the faint scent of antiseptic and stale coffee.

"He's in the lounge," she says flatly. "Good luck."

I find him in the corner, arms crossed. He looks like a little kid caught misbehaving. It's a ridiculous sight. His face is flushed, jaw clenched. The air around him feels off—charged and brittle. One wrong word could snap it. I know that well enough.

A nurse stands nearby, waiting for backup.

"What happened?" I ask.

"They're trying to take my goddamn watch."

I blink. "Your watch?"

He shoves his wrist toward me, showing off the cheap plastic band I bought him last year. The one he insisted he needed after missing too many appointments.

"They said I can't wear it," he growls. "Said it's against some policy. Bullshit. It's a damn watch, Warren."

I glance at the nurse, who meets my eyes with something like quiet pleading.

"It's the alarm," she says gently. "He keeps setting it during quiet hours. We've asked him to turn it off, but he refuses."

"I need it," my dad cuts in, louder now, pulling attention from across the room. "I need the reminders. My meds, meals—how else am I supposed to keep track?"

His frustration sharpens, turning brittle. I know that tone. It's the one he used to get before a door slammed, before things got broken.

"Dad," I say carefully. "You can't keep waking people up in the middle of the night."

"I didn't mean to!" His voice spikes. "It's not my fault! They're just looking for a reason to ride my ass—"

"That's not true," the nurse says, calm but firm. "We've tried to compromise—"

"You call this a compromise?" He surges halfway out of his chair, palm slamming down on the table. "I can't even—"

"Stop," I snap.

The word cuts the room in half. He freezes, breath ragged. For a second, I think he's going to explode again. But then his face crumples. All the fire in his eyes burns out, and what's left is hollow. Scared. It's like he's already forgotten what he was fighting for.

"I'm trying," he mutters. "I'm trying so goddamn hard."

It's frustrating because I know he thinks that's true. That he's really doing his best, even now, when his hands are shaking and his words keep slipping sideways. Even now, when everything feels like one step forward, two steps back.

"I'll fix it," I say finally, voice flat. "I'll talk to the staff. Just calm down."

I don't wait for him to answer. I turn on my heel and find the nearest nurse.

"I'm sorry," I mutter, voice low, jaw tight. "He's . . . having a rough morning." The words taste hollow in my mouth. Not an excuse—never that—but something to soften the edges, something to make her stop looking at me like I'm the one who's supposed to fix him.

She nods tightly, exhaling. I know this isn't the first time she's had to deal with something like this. "We'll let him keep the watch if he promises to silence the alarm," she says. "But if it goes off again, we'll have to take it."

"Got it." I push a hand through my hair. "I'll make sure he knows."

On the way back to his room, my dad is quiet. He passes me the watch without a word. I hold it in my palm, flick through the settings, and shut the alarm off. Then I hand it back. He straps it on with slow, deliberate fingers, like he knows this small thing is keeping him tethered.

By the time I leave Oakview, my head's pounding. Tension curls sharply between my shoulder blades. The sky has turned a sullen gray, clouds hanging low.

I check the time—11:43.

I'm supposed to be meeting Quinn. Right now, at our field.

I blink hard, forcing her from my thoughts. I don't know if I can handle it. Whatever we're meant to say to each other. Whatever mess we're supposed to untangle out there in the middle of the wildflowers. I need time to breathe and to clear the smoke from my lungs.

I pull out of the lot, knuckles tight on the wheel, and my phone buzzes on the dash.

QUINN

you're still coming, right?

I grip the wheel tighter. My pulse kicks. Part of me wants to ignore her. I could tell her that something came up. Tell her I can't make it, that today isn't the day. But I can't.

Because I know what would happen. The way I know my breath in the water or the burn in my legs when I push past the wall. The way I know exactly how it feels to touch her and mean it.

I'd lose my one opportunity for candor.

And no matter how many times I tell myself it'd be easier to let her go, to erase the field from my memory like it never mattered—I can't and I won't.

Chapter Twenty-Three

QUINN

I SHOULDN'T BE this nervous.

It's ridiculous, really. The way my pulse keeps stuttering, the way my fingers keep tugging at the sleeves of my sweater. It's like I'm eighteen again, back at the club, trying too hard to act like I have everything figured out.

Because that's how it started, didn't it? Me pretending I didn't care. Pretending I was too sharp and sure of myself to bother getting attached to anyone. Especially not some swimmer with a smart mouth and a grin that made my chest go tight.

I exhale hard, shifting my weight from one foot to the other. The field looks different now. More overgrown than I remember, the grass taller, wildflowers blooming in thick clusters where bare patches of earth used to be. The old log we used to sit on is still there, half-hidden beneath tangled vines.

It's a little run-down, a little forgotten, but still beautiful. Still *ours*.

I don't know what I'm doing here really. Last night was impulsive. One painfully honest text sent in a moment of weakness, of hope, of wondering *what if*.

What if we had just talked things out instead of trading jabs and dodging real conversations?

What if I'd let him kiss me after the banquet instead of pulling away?

What if I'd stopped being scared and just tried? Tried to be loved? Tried to be seen, fully and without restraint?

I swallow hard, eyes flicking toward the path that cuts through the trees.

Warren is late.

I don't know what I was expecting. Some grand entrance, maybe. Or for him to already be here when I arrived, leaning against the log and looking at me like he always does—like I *matter* to him.

I pull my phone from my pocket, thumb hovering over his contact. Still no reply to my last desperate text: *you're still coming, right?* Maybe I should try one more time. One last reach across the tethered space between us.

Before I can type anything, his footsteps crunch through the gravel path.

I glance up to find a disheveled, tense version of Warren.

He's wearing a gray T-shirt, damp in spots. He's been sweating, his hair still rumpled from whatever strange morning he's had. There's a tightness in his jaw, a restless coil in his shoulders.

Has he been fighting a storm just to get here?

"You're late," I say, trying to keep it light. "Figured you might've bailed."

"Didn't bail," he mutters, dragging a hand down his face. "Just got held up."

Something's wrong. I can feel it.

I hesitate, swallowing back the question that wants to come out —*What happened? Are you okay?*—because I already know he won't answer it. Not right now with the kind of weight he's carrying in his shoulders.

I stuff my hands deeper into my pockets, rocking back on my heels.

"Well," I say. "I guess I should thank you for showing up."

Warren huffs out a breath, part laugh, part exhale, and shakes his head.

"Yeah," he says dryly. "Would've been easier to just ignore you."

The words are sharp. A little too close to mean.

I flinch before I can stop myself. "Look, if you didn't want to come—"

"That's not—" He cuts himself off with a sharp breath, like he's trying to reel something back in. "I didn't say that."

I frown. "Then what are you saying?"

He stands there, arms stiff at his sides, gaze flicking toward the horizon. If he's searching for a way out, he should take it. Leave me to my misery.

"You text me out of nowhere," he says finally. "Tell me you want to talk. Like this is easy. Like there's still something between us that isn't already shattered."

I blink, caught off guard by the sudden bite in his voice. "I'm trying, Warren."

"Yeah?" His mouth twists. "Feels more like you're playing games again."

"I'm not."

"Sure," he mutters, and the bitterness in that word cuts straight through me.

My stomach turns. This isn't how it was supposed to go. I didn't expect him to be smiling, but I thought maybe we'd find some middle ground. Some thread to pull.

"I just . . ." I shake my head. "I don't know, okay? I don't know what I'm doing here or why I even texted you last night. I just—"

"You just what? Changed your mind? Thought you'd see if I'd still jump when you snapped your fingers?"

I suck in a breath, stepping back like he's shoved me. "That's not fair."

"Yeah? Neither is this."

I gnaw at the inside of my cheek. "If you didn't want to come—"

"I did want to come. Jesus, Quinny. Of course I wanted to come." His voice breaks at the end, the sound cracked and uneven. He's hanging on by a thread, and I'm about to snap it.

I hate that sound.

"I'm sorry," I say finally, softer now. "I didn't mean to—"

"You never mean to," he cuts in. "But you do. Every damn time."

The wind shifts, rustling through the tall grass. The blue wildflowers brush my ankles, soft and fragile, taunting me. I look down at them instead of him.

"This place," I murmur. "I thought maybe . . . I don't know. I thought maybe we could talk here because it's where we had our firsts."

I remember that night the way I remember my own name. The way he kept pausing, breath held like he didn't want to mess anything up. The way his fingers trembled when he reached for me. He was scared I'd laugh or something.

But I didn't. Because I loved him. And I loved that he was nervous. I loved that for all his bravado and easy charm, Warren Mercer had never done this before.

And I never told him it was my first time, either.

He assumed it wasn't. I let him believe that because he seemed so certain. Because I thought it would make things easier and I didn't know how to say it without feeling like I was risking too much.

For the first time since he showed up, I wonder if his hesitation isn't just about me or us. If maybe whatever's been following him since this morning, whatever has wound him up so tight, is something else entirely.

"I'm not playing games," I say softly. "I just . . . I don't know how to do this."

His gaze flickers back to mine. "Me neither," he admits.

We sit there, the air thick between us, words unsaid piling up like stones.

"I'm tired," Warren says eventually. "I really don't know if I can do this today."

"Then don't."

I start to push myself up, thinking maybe this was a mistake. Maybe it was too little, too late. As usual, my indecisiveness has chipped away at whatever chance we had left until there is nothing solid to stand on.

"No, wait, stay," he says. "Just . . . stay a little longer."

I sit, and neither of us speaks. The wind shifts through the grass and there's a faint rustle of leaves overhead. It's peaceful, in a way.

We were good once. Better than good.

When summer ended, we worried it wouldn't last. We were afraid that without the blazing afternoons and stolen hours between shifts, we'd start slipping apart. That things would get harder once school started with classes, schedules, and friends pulling us in opposite directions.

But we didn't slip. We flourished.

We walked to class together, grabbing coffee from that spot near the quad where he always ordered the same thing—black, no sugar. I'd sit on the floor of his dorm room, flipping through his kinesiology notes while he stretched before morning practice.

We spent weekends tangled up in bed, half-dressed and lazy, my fingers tracing the dip of his collarbone, his mouth finding my pulse like he was trying to memorize the beat.

We were happy.

And then over winter break, it all unraveled.

I did something fucked-up, something desperate, and he reacted. Of course he did. But before that, before I ruined it, it was real. It was *everything*.

"We were so good together," I say finally. "Before the split . . . we were good."

"Sure, until we weren't."

"You didn't ask me to stay," I whisper. "Back then, you didn't ask."

"You fucked me over, and then you pushed me away. You told me to leave. You didn't try to fix it after that."

"I knew you wouldn't forgive me. You never even gave me a real chance to explain myself."

"Explain what?" His head snaps toward me, voice sharp. "That you stole from my family and then lied to me about it?"

"I know what I did," I say. "I'm not excusing it."

He exhales hard, dragging a hand down his face. "I texted you. Once. I wanted to know why, Quinn. I needed to know why. And when you didn't answer, I just . . ."

"You just gave up."

His gaze hardens. "I didn't give up. I got the message. You weren't gonna say a damn thing. What was I supposed to do? Chase you down? Beg you to make it make sense?"

"Maybe!" My voice breaks. "Maybe you were supposed to give me more than one text. Maybe you were supposed to try."

"I did try," he snaps. "I spent weeks trying to make sense of it. Trying to believe it wasn't what it looked like. I thought maybe you took it for Wesley—maybe you were desperate, or scared, or something. But no." He lets out a cold laugh. "It wasn't for your brother. It was just you being selfish."

"That's not fair."

"Isn't it?" He stares at me, daring me to argue. "Because I trusted you. I let you in. I let myself believe that you were—" He breaks off, dragging a hand through his hair. "I thought you were different."

"I never meant to hurt you."

"Then why?" His voice cracks, raw and open in a way that makes my chest ache.

I take a breath. It shakes on the way in. "There was this submission fee," I say. "For a writing contest. A big one. The kind that could've actually led to something."

His face goes blank. "A writing contest."

"I know how it sounds," I say quickly. "I know it was silly and selfish and—and ridiculous. But I'd been eyeing it for months. I didn't have the money, and I knew I couldn't ask my parents."

It wasn't some astronomical amount. But I knew that if I asked my parents, they would look at me like I was being impractical. Not because they were cruel but because they wouldn't see it as important. Not compared to Wesley's medical appointments, his therapy, his tutoring.

Dad might've tried to make it work, but they wouldn't have understood. It would have just been another thing for them to worry about, another dollar they didn't have to spare.

And I got that. I really did.

"So, you stole from me."

"From *Daniel*," I correct quietly. "I didn't plan it. It just . . . it just happened. You made some joke—something careless about how he wouldn't even notice the money missing, and I thought—"

"And you thought what?" His voice sharpens, rising with disbelief. "That it wouldn't matter? That when I covered for you like you knew I would, he'd still look at me the same? Because guess what, Quinn—he didn't."

I flinch. "I know."

"No, you don't," he says, and this time, it's a low burn. "You don't know what it took for me to convince my mom I wasn't just like my dad. You don't know what it felt like to have my stepfather look at me like I was some lying, thieving screwup, too."

I stare down at my lap, my fingers knotting in the fabric of my jeans. "I didn't know," I whisper. "I didn't know it would fall on you like that."

"You didn't think," he says flatly. "You didn't think about me at all."

"That's not true. I thought about you constantly. About how you probably hated me. How you'd never want to see me again. How I'd ruined the one good thing I had, and there was no way to fix it."

"You could have tried. You could have explained, or apologized, or—something. But instead, you just disappeared. You didn't even give me the chance to understand."

"I thought you wouldn't forgive me, anyway," I say. "I thought—"

"You thought it'd be easier if I really did hate you."

I press my fingers hard against my temples, trying to push back the burn rising behind my eyes. "I'm sorry," I whisper. "I'm so sorry. I didn't want to lose you. But I didn't know how to keep you, either."

"I needed you to fight for me. I needed you to want to fix it."

"I did," I say, my throat tight. "I still do."

For a second, I think maybe this is it—maybe this is the part where he softens, where we start piecing things back together. All that time apart could have been bridged by one simple truth.

"I can't go back," he says. "I don't know how to trust you again."

I feel it like a slap, sharp and sudden, stealing the breath from my lungs. "You don't have to trust me. Just . . . don't give up on me yet."

He looks at me for a long time, blue-gray eyes steady, jaw tight. "I can't keep chasing something that's already gone. I can't keep wanting this more than you do. It might actually kill me this time."

I swallow hard. "You're wrong about one thing. I never stopped wanting this, never stopped wanting you."

"Yeah? Then prove it."

Chapter Twenty-Four

WINTER BREAK — THE LAST NIGHT

QUINN

I SHOULD TELL HIM.

I should've told him two weeks ago when I did it. When I stood there with three crisp bills in my hand, stomach twisting so hard I thought I might throw up. When I told myself it's not that big of a deal, that Daniel Donovan wouldn't even notice, that Warren wouldn't care—not really.

But I didn't.

And now we're here, back at my parents' house, curled up in my old room, and the words are stuck, lodged somewhere between my ribs.

Warren's lying on my bed, one arm flung behind his head, the other hand scrolling lazily through his phone. He's so relaxed—so calm—that it makes me feel even worse.

I should just tell him. I should say, *Hey, so funny thing* . . . and get it over with. Because it's three hundred bucks. Pocket change to someone like Daniel. Warren's always ragging on guys like him anyway. Rich, spoon-fed club dads with too much money and not enough sense.

He'll understand.

Except . . . I don't know if he will.

Because Warren's not like that. He's got this thing about honesty and integrity. This stubborn, hardwired belief that if you don't have trust, you don't have anything at all. I've heard him say it a dozen times.

And I should have remembered that before I shoved three bills in my purse and told myself it didn't matter. I'd stolen before, not for money but for attention. And this time, it seemed harmless.

My stomach twists again, punishing me. I shift beside him, fingers curling into the fabric of my comforter. My throat's dry. I swallow hard.

"Hey," I say quietly.

Warren hums, still focused on his phone. "Hmm?"

"I need to—"

His phone buzzes three times.

He frowns, muttering something under his breath as he sits up. I catch a glimpse of the screen—Mom. "Shit," he says. "Hang on."

He swipes to answer, and I sit up with him, heart hammering.

"Hello?" A stilted pause, then, "Yeah, I'm fine. Why?"

The voice on the other end rises. It's a little anxious, a little urgent. I can't hear the words, but I can hear the tone.

"What?" Warren asks sharply. "What are you talking about?"

More talking. More pauses. It's starting to unravel, I can feel it, this whole awful thing unspooling right in front of me.

"Missing money? From where?"

My stomach turns to ice. I didn't get the chance to explain, to warn him. It's my fault, my silence. I should have never done it, but after I made my choice, I should have clued Warren in.

"Mom," Warren says, pacing now. His steps are tight, clipped. "What are you even asking me right now?"

I watch him pace, listen to the way his voice strains—low and tight and confused. "No," he says. "No, I didn't take it." He pauses. "Why would I—?" He stops pacing, scrubs a hand down his face. "Yeah. Yeah, okay. We'll figure it out when I get back to your place."

I should say something. I should stop this before it spirals.

I whisper his name, trying to cut in, but he keeps pacing. Keeps talking.

"I don't know," he says, his voice climbing. "I don't know, Mom. I'll talk to Daniel when I get home, okay?"

"Warren," I say again, louder this time.

He finally turns. The confusion in his face guts me.

"I'm sorry," I whisper. "It's my fault. I . . . I took it."

The air stalls, the world's holding its breath. Maybe I can still fix this.

But then his face changes. He goes rigid, his whole body braced.

He mutters something into the phone and then hangs up. His fingers stay clenched.

"You're kidding," he says hoarsely. "Please tell me you're fucking kidding."

"I'm not." My voice is barely audible. "I took it."

He shudders. "Why?"

The truth catches in my throat. "I just—" I break off. "I don't know. I needed it."

"For what?" His voice cracks, sharp and furious. "For what, Quinn?"

I open my mouth, then close it again. The reason feels too small, too selfish to say out loud. It would only make this worse.

He stares at me. "You can't even say it?"

"I can't explain it right now," I murmur. "Just go home. Talk to your mom. Tell them I took it, and then . . ."

"And then what?" His eyes narrow. "You think that fixes this?"

"I don't know," I say, barely holding it together. "I don't know."

"I'm not gonna tell them it was you," he says, voice low and tight. "Just give me the money back. I'll figure something out."

"I can't."

He stares at me. "You *can't*?"

"I spent it. It's gone."

He looks at me like he doesn't recognize me at all. "You spent it," he echoes. "On what?"

"It doesn't matter."

"It matters to me."

I shake my head. "Just go, Warren. Go talk to your mom. Fix it."

His feet stay planted. "I . . . can't believe you did this."

"I know."

I'm not surprised I did it. It's been a few years, but I got used to it—taking small things from my parents when I felt invisible. Not money, not at first. Small things that were enough to make them notice. Enough to feel like I existed for more than being the quiet one, the good one.

So no, I'm not shocked I did it. But I knew Warren would see me differently once he found out.

Maybe that's part of the reason I went through with it. Not just because I needed the money or because I was selfish. But because some twisted part of me wanted to wreck it. To ruin the only good thing I had before it could ruin me.

"I can't believe you—" He cuts himself off, jaw tight. "I just . . . I can't believe *you*."

"I'm sorry," I say, because it's all I have left. "I'm really sorry."

"That's not enough." His voice goes quiet and empty. "I don't know how to reconcile this, Quinn. I don't know how to look at you and see the same person I trusted. The same person I loved."

His words land like a blade to the ribs. "Then don't," I whisper. "If that's what you need—if letting me go makes it easier—then do it."

"Fine, I will." He rakes a hand through his hair, almost trembling with it. "I don't think I can come back from this. I don't want to see you again after today. It's over."

I nod slowly, my throat burning. "I figured."

He grabs his keys from my desk, shoves his phone into his pocket, and walks out without a word.

I don't follow. I don't call after him. I just sit there, staring at the space he left behind, the echo of him still clinging to the air.

This was inevitable, wasn't it? I always wreck things when I get too close.

Warren was never mine to keep, anyway. Good things rarely are.

Chapter Twenty-Five

QUINN

"How CAN I prove it to you?" I tilt my head, breath shaky. "I asked you to meet me here. I told you the truth. What else can I give you?"

"Honesty," Warren says roughly. "All of it."

I swallow hard. "This isn't easy, you know."

He stares at me, waiting silently. It's like he's bracing himself for whatever comes next, and somehow, that's worse than yelling.

"The truth is—" I gulp, low and rough in my throat. "I started stealing back when I was thirteen. When I was just a kid, drowning in the background. Because I didn't know how else to make my parents notice me. Because Wesley was always the one who needed them more. And I get that—God, I get that. He's my brother, and I love him, and I know he's been through hell."

I blink hard, swallowing against the tightness in my throat. "But sometimes . . . sometimes I just wanted to matter, too. I wanted to be the one they worried about, the one they paid attention to." My voice falters. "And the worst part is, it worked. For a minute, anyway. Every time I did it, it was like . . . I don't know, like I'd found this twisted little shortcut to being seen."

Warren exhales through his nose, his eyes flicking away from mine. "You felt invisible."

"Yeah," I whisper. "And it's not an excuse. I know that. I knew it then, too. But when things got hard—when Wesley got sick, or my parents were too busy, or I felt like I was disappearing again . . .

I'd slip back into it. Not because I wanted the money or the stuff but because I wanted the rush. The second they realized something was missing, it was like I existed again. Like I wasn't just the kid who could take care of herself. Like I actually mattered."

I let out a shaky breath. "I stopped, though. For a long time. By the time I met you . . . by the time we started dating, I hadn't done it in a while. I thought I was past it, like it was just some awful phase I'd outgrown.

"But then there was the contest. And I kept telling myself I'd figure it out, that I'd scrape the money together somehow. But the deadline was coming up, and I didn't know what to do."

He grimaces. "And then Daniel's money was just . . . there."

"And you made that joke—'*My stepdad could lose 10K in a week and not even notice.*' And I don't know, Warren. I guess some part of me thought, what's the harm?"

"What's the harm?" His face twists, hurt flashing sharp and fast before he shuts it down. "Because you had *me*, Quinn. You had me, and you couldn't just ask?"

"I couldn't because it wasn't only about the money." I drag my fingers through the grass, pulling at the wildflowers until the stems snap. "It was about me. About feeling like I could take something—do something—for myself. Because I wanted something that wasn't about Wesley, or my family, or anyone else. Just me."

"I really wish you would have asked for help."

"I didn't know how to let you in," I say, voice breaking. "I didn't know how to let myself need you without being afraid you'd leave or that I'd screw it all up somehow." I laugh, bitter and brittle. "I guess I was halfway right about that part."

He exhales sharply, gaze drifting toward the horizon. "And now you . . ." He looks back, and for a second, there's a flicker of a smirk tugging at his mouth. "Now you want to come crawling back to me?"

I blink. I can't tell if he's serious. But then his smile grows, small and crooked, and—God—he's joking. He's actually joking with me right now, right here.

"Is that what you want?" I ask, all light and teasing. "Me on my knees?"

His eyes flash, throat bobbing as he swallows. "It would be a start."

"Warren."

The smile fades and the teasing slips away. He drags a hand down his jaw, the sound of it rough against the stubble lining his skin.

"It's not just the lying," he says, voice thick. "It's what you lied about. If it had been something else—if you'd flirted with someone or gotten drunk and said something cruel—maybe I could've let it go." He presses his fingers to his jaw, like he's trying to ground himself. "But stealing from my family? Quinn . . ."

"I know," I whisper. "I know what that means to you."

"No, I don't think you do."

He shifts, bending one knee so he's facing me more fully.

"You know what my dad used to do?" he asks, strained. "He'd wait until I was asleep—like dead asleep—and then he'd go through my stuff. My dresser, my gym bag, my backpack. I'd wake up, and twenty bucks would be gone from my wallet. Or my new tennis shoes would be missing because he pawned them."

He lets out a bitter breath. "One time, I saved up for a phone for months—like, extra shifts, tips, everything—and he still swiped it. Took it right off my desk while I was in the shower."

I wince. "Warren . . ."

"I used to think if I just kept my door locked, or kept stuff at school, or hid things better, it'd stop." He gives a short, humorless laugh. "But it didn't, not until my mom finally kicked him out. Because that's the thing about people like him—they always find a way. They always take what they want, no matter how much you try to keep it safe.

"And the thing is, Quinn? I never thought you were one of those people. I never thought I'd have to keep my shit locked up around you. Because I trusted you. And I know it wasn't the same thing—you weren't trying to hurt me; you weren't trying to screw me over. But it still hurt just the same."

I feel something crack open in my chest. I knew—vaguely—that Warren's dad had struggled. That their relationship was strained. But this? This weight he's been carrying—this pain that's been following him for years—I never really knew the depth of it.

That was my fault. I didn't ask enough questions.

I stare at the ground, my vision going blurry. "I can't say it enough. I'm sorry."

He's quiet for a long time. The kind of quiet that makes my ribs feel like they're closing in. Then, "I know," he says finally. "And I'm sorry, too."

My head darts up. "What do you have to be sorry for?"

"For not letting you in all the way when I thought I had. For not going after you. For letting it end right then and there, drawing a line in the sand when . . ." He trails off, rubbing his temple. "When maybe we could've figured it out. When maybe I should've given you more than one chance to explain."

I blink hard, my vision swimming. He's shouldering the blame, taking ownership for his part in the breakdown. And even though I know it wasn't his fault—that I made choices I can't take back—it's still nice to hear him say it.

"I kept telling myself you didn't want me to try," Warren continues. "That if you'd wanted me to understand, you would've said something. But . . . I know you were just scared." He swallows. "And I get that. Because I was scared, too."

His voice breaks a little on the last word, and something splinters inside me.

"You don't have to carry that. The burden of the blame."

"I should've tried harder. I should've fought for you, even when you didn't know how to ask."

My breath catches, raw and uneven. I look at him—really look at him—and wonder how we ever let it get this far. How we ever let each other go.

"I was really scared," I say quietly. "I still am."

He huffs out a laugh. "I am, too. I didn't expect to see you again this summer. Really didn't want to, actually. It threw me for a fucking loop."

"For someone who claims they didn't want to see me, you sure spent a lot of time watching my every move."

He snorts. "It's hard to look away when someone's constantly running their mouth."

"Yeah?" I tease. "And you've always been such a ray of sunshine."

"Don't act like you're any better."

His grin widens just a little, and it's like we're still those two sarcastic, stubborn teenagers who spent half their time bickering and the other half tumbling into a kind of love that didn't need explaining.

"I'm delightful," I say.

"Yeah, okay."

I don't see it coming. One second, he's shaking his head at me, and the next, he's pushing me back, his hands firm but careful as he rolls me over in the grass. His weight settles against me, broad and solid, all muscle and heat. Familiar in a way that makes my chest ache.

"Jesus, Warren!" I sputter, half laughing, half startled.

"What?" He braces himself over me, arms locked on either side of my head. "You're the one talking shit. Thought maybe you needed to be humbled."

"And what's your plan for that?"

His gaze drops to my mouth. "Haven't decided yet."

His breath ghosts against my skin. He's so close that his stubble scrapes along the side of my jaw. The weight of his hips pins me down, grounding me in place, and my pulse stumbles as his mouth dips closer, shy of my throat.

"Warren," I murmur.

His mouth brushes the curve of my neck, and my breath shudders out of me. "Tell me to stop. If you want me to stop . . . just say it."

I arch into him, my fingers sliding up the back of his neck, tangling in his hair. "Don't," I whisper. "Please don't stop."

And then he's kissing me with no hesitation. His mouth roughly slides against mine. He's been holding back for too long and can't anymore. Something inside him has snapped, and I'm the lucky recipient of all that pent-up want.

I gasp against him, fingers curling into his shirt before I can think better of it. He shifts, settling more of his weight against me. His hand slips beneath my shirt, fingers skating up the bare skin of my waist, and heat blooms low in my stomach.

I feel the press of his hips against mine, the hard, unmistakable evidence of just how badly he wants this—wants *me*—and it makes my head spin.

"Warren, baby," I mumble against his mouth.

He makes a low sound—half growl, half groan—and drags his lips down my jaw, his breath warm against my skin. His hand skims higher, thumb grazing the edge of my bra.

I swear my pulse trips over itself.

"Quinny," he mutters against my skin, voice frayed. "You're gonna kill me."

"I'll make it quick," I tease, but my voice is breathless, shaky.

My fingers are still tangled in his hair, my whole body pressed tight against his like I can't get close enough.

He laughs, breath warm against my throat, and it's different from before—softer, looser. It makes my chest tighten, the way he feels so close to the boy I used to know. The boy who used to look at me like I was something steady in his world. Something *good.*

"I missed you so much."

The bridge of his nose presses against my temple, dragging slowly enough to remind himself of every detail. The way I smell, the way I feel, the way I fit against him. I always have and I always will.

"God," he mutters, strained. "I've really fuckin' missed you, too."

Chapter Twenty-Six

WARREN

Quinn is soft and perfect and mine. I want her so fucking badly, and I don't care that I shouldn't. That we haven't fixed everything yet. That I still don't know what this means for us.

She screwed up. I screwed up. Maybe her explanation for stealing isn't enough. Maybe I'm a damned fool for letting her back in so easily. But against all reason, I get it. I accept it.

And right now, all I want to do is make up for lost time.

I'm not eighteen anymore. I've been with other women—enough to know that none of them were ever her. None of them felt like this. With them, it was just noise. Heat without purpose, connection without depth.

I kissed other women, fucked them, tried to forget the way Quinn felt in my arms. But no matter how many times I tried to move on, she never left me.

Because being with Quinn was never just about sex. It was her breath catching against my neck, her fingers curling against my skin like she was trying to mark me. It was her laughter against my chest when I said something annoying just to piss her off. It was the way I'd catch her watching me.

She always knew exactly what I was thinking before I even opened my mouth.

And now? Now, I can make her feel *good*, really fucking good. I can make her forget every second we spent apart. I can make her remember how good we were together. How good we can *still* be.

I unhook her bra, slowly undress her. Then I pull her hair out of its elastic and slip it around my wrist. Dark strands tumble loose, fanning out like spilled ink, with little glints of blueish silver catching in the sunlight.

Fuck, she's beautiful.

Her skin is warm and glowing in the afternoon light, her body soft in all the places I crave. Her breasts, full and flushed, rise and fall with each unsteady breath. My gaze traces the dip of her waist, the curve of her hips, the shadow between her thighs—already slick and glistening.

She's naked, back pressed into the grass, and I'm still fully dressed. Still in control. I drag my knuckles along her ribs, watch the way her stomach quivers. She's so soft, so fucking responsive. I think I could spend hours just memorizing the shape of her.

Her fingers twist into my shirt, tugging impatiently.

I grab her wrist, pinning it to the grass beside her head.

She gasps, her body arching beneath mine. There's a brief, instinctive struggle while she's trying to break free. But then she goes still, breath coming fast and shallow, her chest heaving beneath me. Her nipples pebble tight in the cool air, and her eyes—dark and glassy—flicker up to meet mine.

She likes this. She wants this. The weight of me holding her down, the tension hanging heavy in the air between us.

"You want my clothes off?"

"Yeah," she breathes.

"Then ask me nicely." I ease my thigh between her legs, press against the heat of her—hot and slick against my jeans.

She writhes, hips jerking forward. "Please," she gasps. "Warren, please."

I dip my head, brush my lips along her throat, desperate to feel the way she shivers. "You can do better than that, Quinny. Tell me what you want."

Her breath stutters, fingers flexing where I've still got her pinned. "I want you."

"Yeah?" I drag my thumb over her nipple, rolling it slowly until her breath stops. "You want me to fuck your pretty little cunt? Want me to make you come?"

"Yes," she chokes out. "Please."

"Please what?"

"Please fuck me," she says, voice breaking. "Please, Warren, I need you."

I groan—low and rough—because hearing her beg for it drives me fucking wild. I let go of her wrist, and her hands are on me instantly, fingers pushing at my shirt, fumbling at my belt.

"Easy," I mutter, catching her wrists again, pinning them just above her head. "You always did like your games," I say, dragging my mouth along the shell of her ear.

"You're the one playing games."

I grin against her skin. "And you love it."

I let her go, finally, and strip my shirt off over my head. Quinn's hands are everywhere—dragging down my chest, scraping against my abs, tugging at the waistband of my jeans. She's about to tear them off herself.

"Fuck," I mutter as I shove them down.

My cock is already hard, thick and pulsing, aching to be inside her.

I push my boxers down, too, and drag the head through her folds, coating myself in her slick. She's so fucking wet, and my mind spins with it—with the way she's trembling beneath me, her thighs twitching as I tease her.

"Warren," she gasps, hips jerking.

"You want it?"

"Yes," she chokes out. "God, yes."

I line myself up and press just the head inside her. "That what you want?" I taunt. "Just this?"

"Don't," she whines. "Don't tease me."

"You always liked it when I made you work for it."

I thrust forward another inch, her body clenching tight around me.

"Please," she begs. "Just fucking take me."

I almost break. Almost slam inside her and lose myself in the heat and the friction. But then I remember—no condom.

"Shit," I mutter, pulling back.

"No!" Her nails dig into my arms. "I'm on the pill. Please, I don't care—"

"I do," I cut her off, voice tight. "I'm not risking that."

She groans. "Then hurry the hell up."

"Do you need me to grab your inhaler?"

She huffs and glares. "I do not need my *inhaler* to have sex with you."

I raise a brow. "You sure about that?"

"Just fucking go already."

I force myself to roll off her, drag my boxers back up, and stumble toward my car. I'm still half-hard as I fumble in the glove box, digging through receipts and loose change until I find a few condoms.

Thank God.

Then I see it—the blanket in my back seat. I grab that too, drape it over my arm, and run back to her. When I get there, she's still on her back, flushed and breathless, her thighs pressed together. She's trying to ease the ache.

"You good?" I ask, half teasing.

Her glare is molten. "Get the fuck over here."

I grin, toss the blanket down, and crawl back on top of her. Then I shift us so we're on the blanket, my knees pressing into the soft fabric as I peel my boxers down and kick them aside. My cock is already hard and heavy in my hand as I roll the condom on, fingers slipping in my rush.

Quinn watches as I settle between her thighs and slide a hand down to guide myself against her. The tip of my cock drags through her wetness, and her hips lift greedily.

"P-please," she mumbles.

I push in—just a little—enough to stretch her open, to feel the wet heat of her pulse around me. Her nails scrape down my back, her legs winding around my waist.

"More," she demands.

"You're lucky I've forgiven you."

She huffs. "You're lucky I didn't leave when you went to your car."

I laugh—and then I'm kissing her once more with pressure.

If I stop, I'll lose her all over again.

"Yeah?" I rasp against her lips. "We're both lucky, huh?"

I can't get enough of her. Every gasp, every breathless moan. She's so warm, so fucking tight, and when I push fully inside of her —slow and deep—her whole body clenches around me. It's like she's trying to hold me there forever, like she's afraid I'll disappear if she doesn't hold on tight.

"Fuck," I mutter, my forehead dropping to her shoulder. "Even better than I remember."

Her hands slide up my back, nails dragging lightly down my spine.

"Harder," she whispers. "I need it."

I give her what she wants. Drive into her harder, faster—deep enough to make her gasp, deep enough that she's arching beneath me, clutching at my shoulders. She's panting now, her breath ragged against my ear, and I can't stop. Don't want to, either.

The sound of her—soft, desperate, so fucking sweet—just makes me want to bury myself to the hilt. To split her open. To make her take all of me.

I shift her legs up higher, one ankle over my shoulder, and fuck her like I mean it. Until her nails are biting into my skin. Until she's sobbing my name.

"Oh, God," she gasps. "Don't stop. Don't—"

"I won't," I growl, thrusting harder. "I won't. Fuck—Quinn—"

Her whole body tightens, legs squeezing tight around my waist as she shatters beneath me, her cunt pulsing and fluttering around my cock. I can barely breathe. Barely think. All I know is her—the heat of her, the way she's falling apart in my arms. The way she's mine again.

I spill into the condom with a strangled groan, muscles jerking as I ride out the last pulse of pleasure. But I don't move, not yet. I stay right there, pressed against her, panting into the crook of her neck.

Could I lose her, even after this?

Her hand comes up, fingers sliding lazily through my hair.

"Jesus," she says, wrecked.

I chuckle against her skin. "Yeah."

I should be done—I should be spent—but when I pull out and reach for the filled condom, I'm already half-hard again. My dick twitches in my hand, still slick from her.

"You've got to be kidding me," she says breathlessly.

I grin, reaching for her. "C'mere."

I pull her into my lap, fingers sliding between her legs, teasing her back open. "You're still really fucking wet."

"Yeah," she breathes, grinding down against my fingers. "You gonna do something about it?"

"Fuck yeah."

I reach for a fresh condom, barely able to roll it on before she's sinking down onto me. Slow at first, teasing me the way I teased her—grinding her hips in lazy circles, rolling her body.

My fingers dig into her hips, guiding her until she's bouncing on my cock, her tits flushed and full, her face twisted in pleasure.

"That's it," I growl, dragging my thumb over her clit. "Look at you."

Her breath stutters, her body finding its rhythm. It's slow at first because she's testing me, testing herself, rolling her hips in deep, deliberate circles that make my vision blur.

"Uh-huh," I mutter, head falling back. "Just like that."

She changes it up—leans forward, planting her hands against my chest as she grinds down. It's quick and dirty and greedy. Her nails bite into my skin, her breath coming fast and ragged as she moves.

"God, Quinn," I groan, digging my heels into the ground to thrust up and meet her. "Fucking perfect."

She gasps, back arching as she takes me even deeper, her body tightening like a fist. I can feel it—the way her muscles start to tremble, the way her breath turns shallow and sharp.

"C'mon," I rasp, circling her clit with my thumb again. "I know you're close. Give it to me."

She cries out, a choked little sound that makes my stomach tighten. Her whole body locks up, and then she's coming, her cunt squeezing me so tight I can barely think. Her face twists in pleasure, body shuddering as the orgasm crashes over her.

And fuck—I can't hold back anymore.

I thrust up one last time, spilling into the condom with a groan so loud I'm sure the whole damn forest hears it. I still need more.

I lay her back on the blanket, spread her thighs, and kiss my way down her body. Then I bury my face between her legs, tongue teasing her open, licking into her like I can't get close enough.

She's sensitive—still twitching and overstimulated, but she's pushing into me, riding the edge of it, chasing something more.

I suck her clit between my lips, flick my tongue until she's a trembling mess. She practically sobs through it. Tells me I'm the only one who gets her like this, and then her legs shake as she comes all over my face.

"Warren," she gasps, weak and breathless. "I can't. I can't—"

"You can," I mutter against her skin, kissing the inside of her thigh. "I'm not done with you yet."

I crawl back over her, kiss her until she's moaning into my mouth. Her fingers slide down between us, curling around my cock as it twitches back to life.

I groan into her mouth. My hips jerk forward.

"How is that even possible?"

I nip at her bottom lip. "It's been nearly a thousand days since I've had you, Quinny. I could fuck you for the rest of my life, and it still wouldn't be enough."

She looks up at me, dark brown eyes gone soft, fingers tracing slowly along my skin.

"Yeah? Then prove it."

Chapter Twenty-Seven

WARREN

When I wake up alone the next morning, tangled in my sheets, I find Quinn's hair tie sitting on my nightstand. It's black and stretched out, the elastic fraying at the edges. Hers. Definitely hers.

I took it off after I came home last night. Set it carefully beside my bed in the little tray I keep for my antidepressants, like I needed proof our time together wasn't just some fever dream. Holding on to that worn-out scrap of elastic somehow anchored me to the truth of it.

Only now, I'm fucking grinning again.

I drag a hand down my face, catch my reflection in the mirror across the room, only to find that ridiculous smile still sitting there. I wipe it off with the back of my hand. It's not enough to erase whatever this feeling is, though.

Giddiness, I assume.

It lingers—warm and impossible to shake—the kind of feeling that settles somewhere deep in your chest and refuses to budge. I think something cracked open inside me last night, and no matter how hard I try to patch it up, there's no going back.

I get up, pull on a pair of sweats, and head for my dresser. The top drawer sticks like always, and I have to jerk it twice before it gives.

I'm looking for a dingy chain necklace.

It has thin, silver curb links. Quinn gave it to me our first week at Dayton. She'd told me it was sexy. That I should wear it whenever I'm not swimming. So, I did—for months. Slipped it on after practice like I was putting on armor. It meant something to me then, to carry around a tangible piece of her.

After the breakup, I shoved it away in this drawer, buried it under socks and T-shirts and all the other things I didn't know what to do with anymore. Out of sight, out of mind.

Now, I'm holding it again. The metal's cool against my palm, and I rub my thumb absently over the chain links. I contemplate putting it back. Forgetting her hands around me, hooking it there the first time. But then I fasten the clasp and let it rest against my skin.

Feels good. Feels right.

I get dressed—jeans, an old Dayton soccer hoodie—and head out to the kitchen. It's unnaturally quiet in here. The cereal box is still half-open from yesterday, and I pour myself a bowl of good ol' Raisin Bran.

It's a normal day. Nothing special. But everything feels different. Something has shifted, tectonic plates or the very fabric of the universe, and the rest of humanity just hasn't caught on yet. A cataclysmic ripple in the ordinary.

I sit at the table, spoon in hand, and stare down at the cereal like it's gonna offer me some kind of answer.

Quinn and I didn't talk much after we had sex. The two of us lay there in the field, tangled up in each other until the sky started to darken. There's still so much we both have to say—so much to figure out—but for now? I think we're . . . enough.

We've done enough, said enough, in order to move forward. To start again and trust the rest will come when it's ready.

On my last bite of Bran, Liam appears in the doorway, hair still damp from a shower, earbuds dangling from his collar.

"Morning, sunshine," he says, reaching into the fridge for a protein shake. "You look like you've seen God."

I snort. "Something like that."

He cracks the cap off his shake and leans against the counter. "Special night?"

I raise an eyebrow. "It was fine. Where's Birdie?"

"She has a big showcase coming up. Wanted to rest."

"No wonder I slept like a baby," I add. "House was weirdly quiet."

Liam grins, all sharp and easy. "Yeah, bud, must've been real quiet." He takes a swig of his shake, then tilts his head like he's noticing something for the first time. "Are you wearing a necklace?"

"It's a *chain*," I mutter, fingers curling around the thin silver links as I tuck it back under my shirt.

"Right," Liam deadpans. "So . . . a necklace, then?"

I shoot him a look, but he's still smiling all big. Trust fund baby thinks he knows something, doesn't he?

I focus back on my cereal, shoveling another spoonful into my mouth.

"You're not gonna explain that one?" he presses.

I chew. Swallow. Sigh. "It was a gift from my ex. We . . . recently reconnected."

He blinks. "*You* had a girlfriend?"

"Once upon a time."

"Wow." He taps his chin, mock thinks. Smirks. "And in this magical fairy-tale land, did you smile like that, too?"

I laugh despite myself. "I think so. Probably, yeah."

"Your eyes were twinkling when I walked in here, just so you know."

"They were?"

I shouldn't be surprised because I feel . . . good. Lighter, somehow. Which doesn't make sense because none of this is simple.

Quinn and I are still a mess. Too much history, too many questions left hanging. We didn't fix anything last night. We barely even got started. And still, I woke up so goddamned pleased. Steady in a way I haven't felt in a long time.

But smiling to myself? That's some far-gone shit.

"Yeah." He sips his shake, eyeing me. "So . . . you two are back together, then?"

I shake my head slowly. "We're figuring things out."

"But you *are* sleeping together?"

I choke on my cereal, coughing hard enough that Liam has to smack my back.

"Annnd," I croak, "that's enough of that."

He sighs. "But we were just getting to the good part. No one ever wants to talk about the good part."

That's the thing about Liam. He's always throwing out a litany of oddly specific questions, even though we both hate small talk. It's like he gets a kick out of testing limits, seeing how far he can push before I react.

Maybe that's why he does it. For fun. For curiosity.

The strange thing is, I don't really mind.

Liam isn't easy to get close to. Letting people in doesn't come naturally to him. But when he does, he's loyal. He's the kind of person who'd drive two hours to pick you up off the side of the road or sit beside you in silence for as long as it takes.

When I agreed to move in with him, I didn't expect we'd get along like this. But we do. There's no pressure. No pretending or posturing. Liam isn't afraid of being exactly who he is. He's blunt, with no filter to speak of, but there's no guesswork, either.

I always know where I stand.

I don't think many people really get him the way I've come to. Except Birdie. She sees him in a way most people don't. The sharp edges, the quiet spells, the way he sometimes says too much or not enough. She just rolls with it.

And I get why he holds on to her the way he does.

"Except for Birdie, right?"

He scoffs, like I'm a dipshit for even questioning it. "Well, that goes without saying."

I glance at my bowl of leftover milk, stirring the spoon in slow circles. I should probably tell Liam about my plans for later. Make a bit more of an effort. We're family, even if it doesn't always feel that way.

And since we're living together, it makes sense to at least try.

"I was gonna watch the Bobcats game later."

"Okay," Liam says, cracking his knuckles like I'd just informed him of the weather. "Cool."

I wait a beat. "Yeah. So . . . I was thinking maybe you'd wanna watch it with me."

He frowns. "Why?"

I blink at him. "Because . . . I don't know, man. Thought you might be interested."

"In football? No, thanks. I'm not really a fan of sports."

My brows shoot up. "You're the captain of a D1 soccer team. You've been playing since you were two."

"Right," he says simply. "I like to *play* sports. Particularly ones where you run fast. But I don't like to watch them."

I let out a breathless chuckle. "Alright. Whatever, man."

He shrugs and takes another swig of his shake.

I go back to stirring, vaguely annoyed that I even asked.

It's not a big deal—just a game—but for some reason, the idea of sitting here alone in front of the TV doesn't sit right. Maybe I should just text Quinn, see if she wants to come over later. Or maybe that's too much, too soon.

"Ah shit," Liam mutters. "You were trying to hang out with me just now."

My ears heat. "I mean . . . I just thought I'd offer."

He's quiet for a second, tilting his head, sizing me up. "I'll order us some wings."

"So, you *do* want to watch it?"

He shrugs again. "Eh, why not? One of my friends plays for the team."

I rear back. "For the Bobcats?"

"Well . . . more of a friend of a friend. My buddy's girlfriend is best friends with *his* girlfriend. You know what, that's actually a hard train to follow." He waves a hand, clearing the thought. "Just . . . yeah, he's an acquaintance. Though I did go bowling with him not too long ago."

I snort. "Who?"

"Westman-Cooke."

I sit back in my chair. Theodore Westman-Cooke is in his second season with the Bobcats—a solid running back who put up some impressive yardage last season. Fast as hell, always dodging defenders like he's playing tag.

He's a fellow Dayton alum.

"He's a beast."

"Yeah," Liam says, "I beat him in bowling."

I stare at him, deadpan. "Well, shit. Someone call ESPN."

A COUPLE OF HOURS LATER, the game's on, and we're parked on the couch with a box of wings between us. The place smells like buffalo sauce and grease, and Liam's sitting half sideways with one knee tucked under him.

I think he might be getting ready for a nap, actually.

He's not really watching the game—not the way I am, anyway. Between bouts of nodding off, he's also reading player bios out loud like he's narrating a documentary.

"Did you know the quarterback has a pet tortoise that's thirty-six years old?" he says around a mouthful of fries. "Pretty tough."

"Yeah," I mutter, eyes still on the screen. "That's wild."

"I have a little turtle, too. His name is Otis."

I pause mid-bite. "I've never seen him."

"No, you wouldn't. He lives in the fountain between the engineering buildings."

"And he's *yours*?"

"Mine and Birdie's. We claimed him."

I laugh, squint, then blink at him like that'll somehow make it make more sense. "Alright, man."

By halftime, the Bobcats are down by ten. Their defense can't seem to stop a run play to save their lives, and the offense keeps choking on third down. It's legitimately painful to watch, but I've sat through worse.

"Gonna call Birdie," Liam says, standing and disappearing down the hall.

I sit there absently for a while, nursing a lukewarm beer and picking at the bones in the wing box. My phone's face down on the armrest, screen dark. I flip it over, thumb hovering over Quinn's name before I finally type out a text.

WARREN

you wanna come over tonight? after the game?

I stare at the message for a second, debating whether to hit Send. Things felt . . . right between us last night. Effortless and fucking perfect. Like maybe we were still *us* underneath all the wreckage. But maybe it was just that—one night. One good thing before she panics and runs again.

I send it anyway, and my phone buzzes less than a minute later.

QUINN

Busy, sorry! Talk later.

I frown. The message feels off—automatic and robotic. A preprogrammed response you hit when you're driving or stuck in a meeting. What a fucking cop-out.

I toss my phone back onto the armrest and lean back against the couch, tension crawling under my skin.

Is she gonna do what she always does? Pull away, build her walls back up, decide that whatever this thing is between us isn't worth the mess?

Maybe I should've kept my distance. Maybe I'm a fool for thinking we could patch this up so easily. I take another swig of beer, barely tasting it.

A few minutes later, Liam comes back, still grinning. Birdie must've just told him the meaning of life or something.

"She good?" I ask gruffly.

"Yeah. I told her about your little chain." He flops back onto the couch, grabs a wing, and waggles his eyebrows. "She thinks it's cute."

"Glad my love life's keeping you both entertained."

The rest of the game blurs by, the tension coiling tight in my chest. I can't focus. Not on the game, not on the wings, not on the occasional joke Liam throws out about the commentators. All I can think about is Quinn and that forced, too-perfect brush-off.

Busy, sorry! Talk later.

She's already halfway out the damn door, isn't she? I should've known better than to believe things could be simple.

I sink deeper into the couch, jaw tight, stomach sour.

Yeah. I should've fucking known better.

Chapter Twenty-Eight

QUINN

Monday feels . . . normal. Good, even. Everything is back to business as usual. I'm chatting with Professor Lang before class, casually leaning against the desk while she thumbs through her notes.

"You ready for this round of eager young minds? Or are you planning to fake your own death by mid-semester?"

I grin. "I think I can hold off until fall break."

Lang is a strict professor, but she's always been fair. She demands a lot of her students without making them miserable in the process. She's been in my corner since I joined her class as a freshman—pushing me, challenging me, even encouraging me to apply for journal submissions and writing contests.

She suggested The Silverleaf Emerging Voices Prize, the national debut fiction contest I used the stolen money to apply for. I don't blame her for what I did to cover the three-hundred-dollar submission fee, obviously. But it still lingers.

I gambled everything and then didn't even place in the contest. But I did torch my relationship, so something extraordinary came out of it in the end. Extraordinarily awful.

I wasn't good enough. Not for Silverleaf, not for Warren.

"Today should be good," she says, glancing toward the door as a few students start filing in. "It's one of my favorite topics."

"Symbolism?"

Lang's lips curve, dry and knowing. "Close."

Warren's near the back of the crowd, shoulder brushing the edge of the doorway.

HE's in dark jeans and a black T-shirt, hair still damp from his post-practice shower. His gaze scans the room—casual but searching—and then it lands on me. His grey-blue eyes flicker.

He's either carefully deliberating something or waiting for me to acknowledge him first.

I don't. I immediately look away, chest tight.

I focus on Lang—on her voice, her smile, her casual stance against the podium like nothing's out of place. Because nothing *is* out of place. It's the second week of classes, and Warren's been here since day one. Yet, every cell in my body feels like it's on high alert.

Deep breath. Relax. Don't overthink it.

I flip open my notebook, scanning the lines I've already memorized just to give myself something to do. Out of the corner of my eye, I watch Warren heading for his usual spot. Second row from the back.

He drops down and pulls out his laptop. There's an unmistakable scowl on his face, and I'm not even sure if it's meant for me. At this point, that might just be a permanent feature. I hope it is.

I keep my gaze glued to the page in front of me, nodding along as Lang keeps talking.

I don't look at him again.

I'm not supposed to. A TA hooking up with one of her students? That's the kind of thing that gets you fired. Not that I'd ever let our relationship—past or present—impact my job. I wouldn't.

Still, rules are rules for a reason. And if anyone found out, it wouldn't matter what explanation I gave. I'd be out of a job, and everything I've worked for would unravel in seconds.

The room fills steadily, students chatting as they settle in. Someone bumps my elbow on the way past, and I flinch. I'm too jumpy, too aware of the way Warren's presence is pulling my focus.

Lang clears her throat, and the room quiets.

"Alright," she starts, "Today, we're talking about the role of memory and perspective in fiction."

I remember this lesson from my own freshman seminar—how captivated I was by the idea that memory could be more narrative than fact. That truth wasn't always a fixed thing but something pliable. Slippery.

"Memory," Lang continues, "is never perfect. It's distorted by perspective, by emotion, by what we want to believe is true. In literature, that's what makes memory such a powerful tool—because two people can remember the same event completely differently, and neither one is necessarily wrong."

I jot down a few notes, not really reading them. My gaze flickers up and lands on Warren, slouched and unreadable. He's not looking at me at this time. He's staring down at his laptop screen like he's trying not to be here at all.

"A lot of authors play with this idea," Lang continues. "Kazuo Ishiguro's *The Remains of the Day*, for example, tells the story of a butler who convinces himself that his entire life—his choices, his sacrifices—were noble and right. And only later, looking back, does he realize how much he missed, how many moments slipped past him because he was so convinced he was doing what was best."

Something sharp twists in my chest.

You thought it'd be easier if I hated you.

Warren's words flash through my mind, clear as anything, and suddenly, it feels like my lungs are full of static. Like I'm breathing, but nothing's landing. Because that's exactly what I did. Told myself what I needed to hear—what I could live with—so I wouldn't have to face what I'd done.

That I didn't deserve his forgiveness.

I glance to the back of the room, and this time, Warren's looking right at me. His jaw's tight, his eyes sharp. And yeah, he's pissed. I can see it clear as day.

I drop my gaze and refocus on Lang's voice.

"The thing about memory," she says, "is that it's rarely about the facts. It's about the feeling. The version of the story you tell yourself to make it make sense."

The rest of class drags, each minute stretching longer than the last. Lang keeps talking, touching on narrative distance and how unreliable memory creates unreliable narrators. I try to focus, scribbling notes I barely register. But the whole time, my mind keeps circling back to Warren.

He's still stiff in his seat, shoulders tight, foot bouncing. He's counting down the seconds until he can leave and escape my presence. Every so often, I catch his hand flexing against the notebook on his desk, gripping his pen so hard I half expect it to snap in two.

Finally, Lang wraps up, dismissing the class with a wave of her notebook. Chairs scrape against the floor, bags zip shut, and students start filing toward the door in loose clusters.

Warren's up in a blink, shoving his notebook into his bag and charging out the door before I can even register it.

My head jerks up.

"What the hell?" I mutter under my breath.

Lang turns toward me, expecting our usual post-class debrief.

"Sorry, I need to catch one of my lit seminar professors," I say, voice rushed but steady. "There was a mix-up with a deadline, and she said she could talk if I caught her after class."

Lang raises a brow but nods. "Go ahead. We can touch base tomorrow."

"Thanks," I say, already halfway out the door.

Warren's almost at the end of the hall, moving like he's got blinders on.

"Warren!" I whisper-shout, weaving through the slow walkers.

He doesn't slow.

"Warren, wait!"

He stops just before the exit, one hand braced against the door. He's debating whether or not to keep going, and if he does, I might just scream.

His head turns just enough for me to catch the sharp angle of his jaw. "What is it, Quinn?"

I frown. "Why are you running from me?"

He lets out a humorless snort. "I'm busy. Places to be."

"You're . . . busy?"

It takes a beat, but then it clicks. The clipped tone, the look on his face.

That's my line.

"You're mad at me because I said I was busy yesterday?"

"Not mad."

"Warren."

He turns fully, his face hard. "I mean, what was that? An auto-response? Seriously? After Saturday, that's all I get?"

"So, we slept together," I say, folding my arms tight across my chest. "And I'm just supposed to drop everything the second you text me?"

He shakes his head, incredulous. "That's not what I want. I just . . . I wanted to see you." His voice drops on the last part, like saying it out loud costs him something. "And I'm not gonna be treated like an afterthought."

"I wanted to see you, too," I say quietly. "But I was busy."

He stares at me like he's still trying to decide if he believes me.

"I was at the boxing gym," I tell him. "The new one by my apartment. I knew it would be empty because of the game, so I wanted to take advantage of it. I was gonna stay for a while, then go home and work on my assignments."

His eyebrows draw together. "You're boxing now?"

"Yeah. I've been going a few times a week. There's this trainer —or almost trainer, whatever—who's been helping me out."

"You've got a trainer?"

"Kind of. He's not official or anything, but he knows his stuff."

Warren scrubs a hand down his face, and when he looks at me again, there's something sheepish in his expression. "I shouldn't have gotten so worked up," he mutters. "I'm just . . . on edge."

I tilt my head. "I put you on edge?"

"You know you do."

"Mmm," I say, smiling a little. "And I happen to like when you're *on edge*."

He laughs under his breath, but it's short and stilted. "*Fuck*. You really mess with my head, Quinn."

"And your dick," I say sweetly.

That gets a full, rough chuckle out of him. The tension in his shoulders eases, and when he looks at me again, it's softer somehow. Less guarded. We linger there for a while, neither of us quite moving. We're both waiting for the other to say something more.

"I'll text you later," he says finally.

"Promise?"

He smirks. "Yeah, promise."

Instead of letting him walk away, I grab his arm, tugging him back into the quiet stretch of hallway behind me. It's empty here, tucked away from the steady flow of students still lingering near the exit.

No one can see us or hear us. No one can catch the way my fingers tighten around his sleeve or the way he looks at me like he's still trying to convince himself I'm not running.

"What—?" he starts, but I'm already closing the gap between us, fingers curling under the cool metal chain at his neck.

His eyes flicker, something sharp and heated sparking there, but he doesn't pull away. He lets me guide him closer, lets me fist the chain in my hand and tilt his face down to mine.

"You're wearing it again?"

His gaze drops to my hand—my fingers looped through the silver links—and he swallows hard. "Yeah," he says roughly.

I don't know what to say next, so I don't say anything at all. I just tug the chain a little harder, drawing him down, and then I kiss him. Slow and deep and just this side of desperate.

Warren groans low in his throat, and then his hand is at my waist, fingers flexing like he's trying not to drag me closer but can't help himself. He leans in, pressing me back against the wall.

His mouth moves with a sharp, hungry edge. He's still angry, still strung tight—but now he's turning all of that into something else. Something that makes my skin burn and my pulse race wildly in my throat.

His tongue flicks against mine, his hand sliding under my shirt, warm and rough and insistent. I gasp, fingers curling tighter around the chain, and Warren groans again—deeper this time, like I've knocked the breath from his lungs.

"God," he mutters, breaking away just long enough to press his mouth to my jaw, my neck, my collarbone. "This is what I needed."

His kiss turns messier, more desperate. He's losing whatever grip he had on control, and I love that. His fingers dig into my waist, his knee presses between my legs, and I can't help it—my body arches, chasing the friction.

Finally, finally, he pulls back—just barely—and swipes his thumb across my bottom lip. His pupils are blown wide, chest rising and falling fast like he's just run a mile in the Carolina heat.

"What was that for?"

"You're sexy when you're worked up," I murmur. "Plus, you're wearing my chain."

He exhales hard, shakes his head, and mutters, "Jesus Christ, Quinny."

"I know."

He steps back, dragging his thumb down the curve of my hip.

He's not quite ready to let go and neither am I. I want this moment to last forever.

When he finally turns to leave, I watch him go—still catching my breath, feeling warm and reckless and entirely too pleased with myself.

Just before he pushes the door open, I call after him. "Hey!"

He glances back, brow raised.

"I won't auto-respond to you again," I say. "Even though I *was* busy, and it's way more convenient."

He rolls his eyes. "Yeah, well, you know how I feel about being left in the dark. Not a good habit, Rose."

I give him a mock salute, then, "Consider me reformed."

Chapter Twenty-Nine

WARREN

I'M HALFWAY to the training center when I spot Quinn sitting on the bench just outside the entrance. Her legs are crossed, her hair curled and twisted into two little buns. She's scrolling her phone like she belongs there. Like she does this all the time.

I gulp. Then grin.

What the hell?

Before I can say anything, she looks up and smiles at me. It's a small, easy sort of smile. The kind that tells me she's been waiting for me for a while. That she was intentional about being here and even more intentional about letting me know I matter.

She's not keeping me in the dark; she's showing up.

"Thought I'd come say hi before practice," she says, tucking her phone away. "I was in the neighborhood."

I snort. "The neighborhood of my practice pool?"

"That's right."

I shake my head. "You're a terrible liar."

"Yeah?" She stands, stepping closer, her fingers curling around the chain at my neck. "I don't know. Once upon a time, I remember you saying the opposite."

I snort again. She's half-amused, half-self-deprecating. The joke shouldn't land like this. It's too much, too soon. But it's Quinn, so of course it does.

I dip my head, letting my mouth brush hers. "I'm not always right the first time."

"Oh, no?" She kisses me —slow and sweet. When she pulls back, her eyes flicker with something sharp. "I cleared my schedule for tomorrow night, by the way. If you're interested."

"Interested?" I drag my thumb along her bottom lip. "Yeah, I might be into that."

She gives a low laugh. "Might?"

"Depends. What's in it for me?"

She rolls her eyes, steps back, and grabs her bag off the bench. "Guess you'll have to find out."

"Guess so."

We hover there a moment, caught in the in-between, neither of us quite ready to leave. Her fingers graze mine before she turns, and I'm still grinning like a fool when I hear a sharp voice call out behind me.

"Jesus, Mercer," Hawkins sneers. "You planning on skipping practice or just sucking face until Coach drags your ass inside?"

I bite back a sigh and reluctantly glance over.

Reed Hawkins leans against the wall with his arms crossed. He's got that cocky, know-it-all energy that makes you want to wipe the smirk off his face with a kickboard.

"Relax," I mutter. "I've got time."

"Just wouldn't want you distracted again."

His gaze flicks toward Quinn like she's the reason I've been off. Like she's some shiny object I can't stop chasing instead of the good-luck charm I know her to be. When we were together the first time, I swam cleaner, slept better, felt steadier.

My shoulders tense, heat crawling up my neck. It's not that I'm ashamed to be with her out loud. But there's something about Hawkins that makes everything feel like a performance. PDA just gives him more ammo.

"I'll see you later," I tell Quinn quietly.

She gives Hawkins a cool once-over before turning back to me. "Don't let him get to you."

"I don't care what he thinks."

The guy's been on my case for the last couple of weeks. It's obvious he resents the medley switch-up, thinks he should've been bumped into the lead-off spot instead of me. He's the backstroke alternate, and I'm the wild card with something to prove. Just trying to relearn my start, relearn my rhythm.

But he's wrong. I'm not choking. I'm adapting. I'm fighting for it; I just haven't nailed the first 50 yet.

And it's not like Omar, our captain, hasn't had to adjust, too. Voss has him covering anchor just in case Gaines doesn't make it back in time for the meets. Omar's been solid so far. He's a strong freestyle swimmer and a calm finisher, which helps.

But Dayton's always been a relay-heavy team. We had a stacked medley squad, and then we lost a few top guys last season—some graduated, others took time off to focus on Olympic training—and the rest of us have been filling in ever since.

The pressure's on both of us, and the last thing we need is Hawkins running his mouth.

"Yeah?" Quinn quirks a brow. "Tell that to the tension in your shoulders."

I give her a quick kiss, just enough to shut her up and let it linger.

Hawkins is smirking like he's won something.

I don't give him the satisfaction of a glance, just shoulder past him and keep walking.

Inside, the pool deck's a blur of motion and noise. Voices ricochet off the tile walls. The sharp slap of water echoes from every lane.

A few guys are still stretching on the benches, working resistance bands or rolling out their shoulders. Others are already in the water, arms slicing through the surface in smooth, practiced strokes.

Coach Voss stands by the whiteboard, scrawling down split

goals for the A relay. Omar leans nearby with his arms crossed, talking quietly with Lyle and Christian, freestyle swimmers who've been grinding out pace sets with me all week.

Tonight's practice is self-led, and somehow, that always makes us go harder. Voss isn't the micromanaging type, but he expects accountability. This early in the season, no one's slacking.

I strip off my shirt, grab my cap and goggles, and head to the blocks. The water shocks my system when I slide in, cold enough to make every muscle clench before I force myself to move.

Warm-up's standard. I fall into the rhythm: four laps freestyle, then four backstroke, followed by a few rounds of kickboard drills. My arms cut through the water in steady rotations, breath syncing up on autopilot.

Today's focus is pacing. Lately, it's been nonstop technique work. Relaxing my muscles for a smooth breakout. Stop overworking my pull. Stop forcing the rhythm, start following the glide.

Voss wants my backstroke clean, controlled, and fast. He wants me hitting rhythm the second I surface which is easier said than done.

I've got to explode off the block, settle into pace fast, and nail every turn. One mistimed breath or crooked entry, and the whole rep's off. I'm getting better, but I'm still not fast enough.

Frustrated but locked in, I launch into a 50 at race pace. Arms driving. Legs burning. Lungs tight. The cold rushes past me as I break the surface and power forward. When I hit the wall, my muscles are on fire, but the split feels close.

Again, it's better than last week, but still not quite fully there.

I'm barely gripping the ledge to catch my breath when I hear Hawkins' grating voice again. "Mercer! Looks like you're a lot more relaxed this week." He laughs to himself. "Guess that's what happens when you're finally getting laid."

I snap my goggles off the second I'm out of the pool. Water drips down my face as I glare at him. "You wanna repeat that?"

"I'm just saying . . . you seem real loose, but you're barely hitting pace."

"Cut the shit," I mutter. "I'm not in the mood."

"Clearly." He grins wider. "But hey, I'm glad you've found an outlet. Lord knows you need one. Though I do wonder what she sees in you. Do you even let yourself crack a smile when she's sucking you off?"

I'm moving before I can stop myself. I climb out of the pool, water streaming off my arms. My fingers curl tight, nails digging into my palms.

I glance toward Voss, but he's pacing near the diving well, too far to catch any of this. Our assistant coach, Finley, is across the pool, clipboard in hand, deep in conversation with Lyle.

And Hawkins? He's still standing there, head tilted like he knows exactly what button he's just pushed.

It's not just what he said about Quinn. It's all of it.

All the shit she deals with. The constant flirting at the club from guys who always take it too far. The way they crowd her space, stare too long, push too hard. They act like she's nothing more than something pretty to look at.

And Preston Beckett? He laid hands on her like she owed him something.

These degenerates think they can say whatever they want. Do whatever they want. No consequences. No respect.

It's fucking disgusting.

"Dude." Our captain rushes over, cutting through the tension before I can even say a word. He plants a hand on Hawkins' shoulder, firm and warning. "Knock it off."

Hawkins' smile falters just a little. "Just making conversation."

"You're making an ass of yourself," Omar says, voice flat. "Get in the pool."

For a second, Hawkins doesn't move. He stares me down like he's waiting for me to snap. And God, I'm close—too fucking close

—but Omar steps between us, and it's enough to keep me from losing it.

"Don't push your luck," Omar mutters.

Hawkins scoffs under his breath, but he doesn't say another word as he heads for his lane. Of course he doesn't. He only talks big when the coaches are distracted. When he knows no one's watching close enough to catch the way he winds people up.

And if he applies enough pressure? He can make it look like it's all my fault when things explode. The grumpy guy. The mean guy. The not-a-team-player who's always one breath away from losing it.

Of course I'd snap. That's what he's banking on.

I drag a hand down my face, breathing hard. My pulse is still hammering, my whole body wired like someone forgot to cut the fuse.

"You good?" Omar asks.

"Yeah." I exhale, slow and unsteady. "I'm good."

"You need to chill out."

He's right, obviously. He's always right. Omar's built for this. Confident. Unshakable. The kind of guy who keeps his head when everyone else is losing theirs. Exactly the captain you want when the water starts to boil.

Which is why it still doesn't make sense that Voss offered the role to me first.

Omar never said a word about it. Never made it awkward. But sometimes I feel it anyway—like a current running just beneath the surface. He's still waiting for me to explain why I passed it up, and I have nothing concrete to give him.

Maybe he thinks I didn't want the pressure. Or the politics. Or the weight of carrying everyone else. Or maybe, like the rest of the team, he thinks I couldn't be bothered. That I thought I was too good for it.

But if he was really paying attention, he'd realize I didn't take the role because I wasn't sure I could live up to it.

I adjust my goggles and slip back into the water, chest still tight. The next set is brutal. Hundreds on the clock with barely a breath between. I start strong, but by the third rep, I feel it. That drag in my shoulders, the way my arms tense too soon and fight the water instead of flowing through it. My jaw locks. My breath shortens.

I know better, but I can't seem to stop muscling through it. I'm not swimming smart. I'm swimming mad.

Omar notices, too.

After the set, he waves me over during the break, lifting his goggles to his forehead. "You're overworking the pull," he says. "You're forcing it."

"I'm fine."

"You're tense. I can see it from halfway down the lane." He gestures for me to follow. "C'mon. You've got to learn how to work with the speed, not against it."

He runs me through a few slow recovery drills—sculling, fingertip drag, exaggerated underwater pull. Stuff I've done a thousand times, but today, it feels like unlearning everything just to get back to neutral. He has me focus on the long exhale off the wall, too, forcing the breath to flow even when my brain's screaming for more air.

It helps. A little.

I hate that I need the help. But I hate how tight my chest feels more.

"Try to stay loose through the shoulders," Omar adds before I push off again. "You keep clenching up you're gonna burn out by mid-season."

By the time Voss calls for cooldown, my arms are burning, my legs shaking.

"Nice work today," Omar says as we're toweling off. His voice is casual, but there's an edge to it. He's waiting, I think, for me to lose my shit.

"Thanks."

I'm still keyed up. Still rattled and wondering why I let Hawkins get to me in the first place. He's a loudmouth, a try-hard, all bark and no bite.

But Quinn is my hot button. Always has been. Doesn't matter how good things are between us or how much we're trying to move forward. One wrong word, one cheap shot, and suddenly, I'm standing there like some hotheaded dipshit, ready to take someone's head off.

Omar waits a beat. "Look, man . . . I get it. Hawkins is a dick. But you're better than that."

"Am I?"

"Yeah, Mercer. You are. Besides"—his voice dips in volume—"you can't let a back alternate throw you off your game. You're naturally tense enough."

He says it like he means it. I guess he believes in me a little more than I believe in myself. It's good to know that at least someone on this team feels that way.

Because Voss hasn't let it go. Not the captaincy, not me. He keeps circling, nudging, making these quiet suggestions. Not outright asking me to take the role from Omar but floating ideas. Co-captaincy. Shared leadership.

There could be room for both of us at the helm.

But I don't think that's what he's really worried about.

I think he's afraid I'm going to walk away after this season. That once it's over, I'll be done with swimming for good. And maybe the captain talk, the extra work, all of it—it's his way of trying to keep me tethered to the sport. To give me something bigger than just the clock to chase.

Voss isn't loud or performative. He never wastes words, never raises his voice unless it counts. He doesn't tell you what to do. He expects you to figure it out and get it done.

He's blunt, sometimes to the point of brutal. But he gets

results. And I think he sees something in me that reminds him of himself. The way I push too hard. The way I overthink everything. The way I come off cold, even when I'm not trying to be.

He respects that. Respects *me*, period.

That's probably why he keeps pushing on the captain thing. The extra drills. The cross-training he insists I need. I think he's trying to shape me into someone who won't quit when the season ends. Someone who's meant to swim long after college.

I'm just not so sure I am that person.

Chapter Thirty

QUINN

There's a knock at my door. Three short raps, then silence.

I hesitate, my pulse picking up. Warren. He said seven, but it's six thirty on the dot. Being on time isn't unusual for him, but showing up early? That's not exactly his thing. Not unless something else is weighing on him.

If he's here to berate me for texting him the wrong way again, I'm going to lose my shit.

I wipe my hands on my sweatpants and head down the hall, pausing to double-check my reflection in the mirror by the entryway. Hair's good. Shirt's clean. Mostly. I straighten out my collar, then smooth a wrinkle near the hem.

When I open the door, Warren's standing there with his hands in his pockets. His shoulders are tense, weight shifted. He's not sure if he's supposed to smile or apologize for showing up at all.

His hair's damp, curling slightly at the ends, and he smells like crisp, piney shampoo. I adore that smell on him.

He rushed to get here, I think, and that's kind of adorable.

"Hey," he says quietly. "I know I'm early. I showered after practice and figured . . . I don't know. I just didn't feel like sitting around at home."

"Hey," I echo, leaning against the frame. "No worries. I wasn't busy."

I want to let him in and pretend that nothing's weird between us. That us sleeping together and then casually hanging out afterward is normal. But things are still a little uncertain.

We've had sex. We've kissed. We've shared space again. A few quiet moments that felt comfortable in a way they probably shouldn't have. Yet, we haven't had the *real talk* yet. The messy part. The part that either clears the air or burns everything down.

"So," I say, clearing my throat. "First time here, huh?"

I step back to let him inside, and he hesitates—just briefly—before crossing the threshold. I wonder if he's panicking about which version of my life he's stepped inside.

"Yeah." He glances around like he's taking mental notes. "It's . . . nice."

He grins, but it doesn't quite reach his eyes. It's not that he's uncomfortable, or at least not obviously so, but we're both still trying to figure out what this is. Where we stand and what we're supposed to be now.

"You wanna sit?"

"Yeah." He nods once and then lowers himself onto the far end of the couch.

I sit, too, tucking my legs beneath me, and for a second, I can't think of a single thing to say. That's not the norm for me. I'm usually rife with snark or softness when it comes to him.

"When did you move out of the dorms?" he asks suddenly.

I jolt a little. "Right after freshman year. Jordan and Alyssa were looking for a third to split costs, and it just kind of worked out."

His eyebrows lift. "Huh. Seems like something I should've known."

I smile—small, tight. "There's a two-year gap in your memory."

His face twitches, a flicker of something sharp behind his eyes, and I regret saying it that way. It's not a jab at my own choices or his absence, not really. It's just the truth.

"Right," he says quietly.

I pick at a loose thread on the hem of my sleeve, twisting it between my fingers. "They're good girls," I offer, filling the silence. "I like them. I just . . ." I trail off, my fingers stilling.

"You haven't really let them in," he finishes.

I glance up, surprised—but I shouldn't be. Of course he'd read me like that. He always could. Warren doesn't ask unless he already knows the answer. He sees through me like the glass isn't even there.

"Yeah," I say softly. "I haven't."

His fingers tug on the drawstrings of his sweatshirt. I shift, curling tighter into the corner of the couch, trying to keep my voice light, even though my chest feels anything but.

"It's just easier that way, I guess."

"Yeah," he says again, this time with the smallest tug of a smile. "I know the feeling. You should try, though. Give things a chance, Quinny."

I snort, trying to shake off the weight of it. "Like you try with your cousin?"

His mouth twitches. "We watched the Bobcats game together last weekend."

"And you said it was weird."

"Yeah, well," he mutters. "Liam's weird."

"You're weird."

"I know."

I laugh, and suddenly, everything feels easier, like we're slipping back into something familiar. I can sleep with Warren. Kiss him. Tease him. Flirt with him. But this casual talk about our lives, about our days, it's a new sort of game. One I'm eager to learn how to play.

"Hey," he says after a beat. "I've got a mock meet tomorrow. Was gonna swing by Sycamore before to grab my last paycheck. You want me to pick yours up, too?"

"Oh." I blink, thrown off-balance. "Yeah, that'd be great."

"Cool."

More than cool, it would save me a trip back to that place. I don't want to risk seeing Beckett again, and he obviously wants to protect me from that, too.

Though, he said that like it's nothing to him. Like this—being here, doing something small and considerate for me—is normal again.

I'd forgotten this part about Warren. How thoughtful he could be without making a big deal of it. How he'd pick up the slack before I even realized there was slack to pick up.

When I was sick, he'd grab my assignments without me asking. When I got a flat tire on my bike, he patched it up before I'd even noticed. When I spent days wallowing in my room after a shitty voicemail from my parents, Warren showed up with greasy fries and a six-pack and never asked why I wasn't leaving my bed.

He just . . . handled things.

And now, he's back to doing that. Back to taking care of me, even when I'm not sure I deserve it. For all intents and purposes, it seems he's forgiven me. Maybe even trusts me again. But I can't seem to extend that same grace to myself.

"This feels strange," I blurt. "Us, I mean."

"Strange how?"

I shift in my seat. "Like . . . I don't know." I shake my head, frustrated with myself. "Are we just pretending everything's normal now? Like nothing happened? Like we didn't break each other and then pretend the cracks weren't still showing."

He leans back against the couch, stretching one arm across the back of it. It's like he's giving me space but still wants to be close. For once, he's listening without trying to fix it.

"Does it feel normal to you?"

"No," I admit. "But I don't know what it's supposed to feel like."

His gaze softens, and I can't bear to look at him. Because this is

Warren—*my* Warren—and I'm still not sure what he sees when he looks at me now. If he's still angry. If he still resents me.

Am I still his Quinn? Or am I the girl who stole from him that he can't help but miss anyway?

"I didn't . . ." I swallow hard, my voice quieter now. "God, Warren, I didn't ruin your life, did I?"

His breath leaves him in a rush—half sigh, half laugh—and when I finally meet his eyes, there's something softer there. Open and unguarded. Like an ember that's been smoldering all this time, just waiting for me to give it air.

"No," he says, and his hand finds my knee, curling there. "You sure as hell haunted me, but you didn't ruin me."

I blink hard. "I still feel like I should be apologizing every five minutes."

"You don't have to." His fingers squeeze gently. "I mean, yeah, you pissed me off. Broke my heart a little." He smiles wryly, teasing, but there's an edge of truth there too. "But if I was still pissed at you, I wouldn't be here."

"Yeah," I murmur, swallowing past the lump in my throat. "I guess that makes sense."

"C'mere."

He tugs on my knee. I shift closer, and suddenly, his arm is around me, pulling me into his side. His body is warm, solid. Familiar in a way that makes my breath catch. This time, when he holds me, it's not about sex, or regret, or overthinking everything we've done wrong. It's just him, *us*, the steady rhythm of his heart against my ear.

"I missed this," I whisper. "You holding me like this."

He stills, his breath catching against my skin.

I know I'm usually prickly Quinn, guarded Quinn. The girl who keeps people at arm's length because it's easier than letting them see the parts of me I don't know how to explain. But with

Warren, I can soften. Let my guard down without it feeling like a risk.

With him, I never have to over explain. He just got it. Got *me*.

The bridge of his nose presses against my temple, dragging slowly and absently. Muscle memory. His body remembers even if his mind is still catching up. It's like he's trying to reorganize it all in his mind—the way I smell, the way I feel, the way I settle against him.

"Yeah," he says, low and strained. "Me too."

WARREN WENT HOME LATE last night. We didn't have sex. Didn't even kiss after that first lingering one on the couch. We just talked—filled each other in on the last two years—until my words started to slur and my eyes grew heavy.

I barely remember him easing me deeper into the cushions, pulling a blanket over me before he let himself out. I woke up warm and comfortable. My bones, I think, finally remembered what it was like to feel safe.

Jordan and Alyssa must've gotten home sometime after that. Hours later, from the sound of it. I heard them giggling in the hallway, keys jingling as they fumbled to unlock the door. I don't know how they do it, balancing endless social plans and still dragging themselves out of bed in time for brunch.

They're always going, always busy. Partying, networking, filling their calendar with more events than I'd ever have the stamina for. I swear they thrive on it. I can barely manage one night out without feeling like I need a day to recover.

Now, it's the next morning—well, technically early afternoon—and I'm at a corner table at the Bluebell with Jordan and Alyssa, staring down a mimosa I haven't touched yet. The table's cluttered with half-eaten plates of avocado toast and french toast sticks, syrup dribbling down the side of a bowl.

Jordan's on her third round of boozy orange juice, talking a mile a minute. Alyssa's sipping hers slower, half listening as she scrolls through her phone.

I'd almost bailed when they knocked on my door this morning. My hair was all wet from the shower, a towel wrapped around my head. I didn't want to face the small talk, the forced laughter, the effort it takes to be around people when I'm not sure I belong.

But then I remembered what Warren said. *You should try. Give things a chance.*

So here I am. Trying.

Jordan's telling some wild story about a guy she met last weekend. Some bartender at Lucky's who supposedly did a backflip off the bar and landed it, completely hammered. She's miming the whole thing, arms flailing as she half stands from her chair.

"And then," she says between laughs, "he popped up like nothing happened and started pouring shots for everyone. I swear to God."

"That's ridiculous," I say because I can't think of anything else.

"It was," Alyssa says, finally looking up from her phone. "But she left out the part where she went home with him."

Jordan gasps, smacking Alyssa's arm. "Excuse you! That's irrelevant."

"You let him make you a grilled cheese at two in the morning," Alyssa adds, grinning.

"And it was a damn good grilled cheese," Jordan says with a shrug, tossing back the rest of her mimosa.

I genuinely laugh, surprising myself. "So . . . a gymnast and a chef? The full package."

Jordan beams at me. "You get it."

I snort and finally take a slow sip of my drink. "I didn't know you were into the showy type."

"I'm into the fun type," Jordan says.

"And the red flag type," Alyssa deadpans.

Jordan cackles at that, and I smile, too. I can't help it. This—the casual jokes, the warmth of easy conversation—it's just nice. Maybe trying isn't such a bad thing.

"At least it's better than the year I tried dating musicians."

Alyssa groans. "Oh God, we were just eighteen and absolutely feral."

"What happened?" I ask.

Jordan props her chin on her hand, sighing dramatically. "Let's just say I learned three things that year. One, never trust a man with a guitar. Two, 'I'm working on new material' means he wants to sleep with your roommate. And three, if a guy tells you he's 'emotionally unavailable,' believe him."

"Yikes," I say, wincing.

"You're telling me." Jordan tips her glass toward me. "This is why I'm a bartender-only kind of girl now."

"Better career stability," I murmur.

"Exactly."

We fall into another round of laughter, and I feel strangely present in a way I haven't felt with them before. I'm not hovering on the edges of something. Not guarding myself in case they decide I'm not worth the effort.

I'm just here, being a girl.

Alyssa tilts her head. "So, what's going on with you, Quinn? You've been different lately. Is it the boxing? We knew you'd like punching things."

"That helps, yeah. But I guess there's a little more to it than that."

Jordan waggles her brows. "Is it a boy?"

I blink. "What makes you think that?"

"Oh my God, it is!" Jordan gasps. "Who is he?"

"No one," I lie automatically. "I mean . . . not *no one*. Just . . ."

"You're blushing," Alyssa points out.

I groan and cover my face with both hands. "I hate this."

"Is he hot?" Jordan presses.

"I'm not answering that."

"Oh my God, he is," she crows, clapping her hands. "I knew it. Quinn's finally got herself a man."

"He's not—I mean . . . he's just my ex, and we've been figuring things out," I stammer. "It's complicated."

"Please, do go on," Alyssa urges.

I hesitate, unsure how much I want to put into words. How do you explain Warren Mercer? The boy who once knew me better than anyone. Who saw through every wall I built and made me feel understood in a way no one else ever has.

And now? He's the one I'm still trying to rebuild something with, piece by careful piece.

"It's just a bit messy," I say finally. "But I think it's good. I think . . . I don't know." I exhale slowly. "I really want it to be good."

Jordan's smile softens. "Sounds like you've got it bad."

"Yeah, I guess I do."

Weirdly? That doesn't scare me as much as it should.

By the time the check comes, I'm still smiling. A real smile, the kind that lingers even when no one's paying attention. I'm glad I came out with them. Glad Warren told me to try. If this is what letting people in feels like, I think I could learn to like it.

Chapter Thirty-One

WARREN

The mock meet wasn't my best, but it wasn't bad, either. I hit my marks, mostly. Five events: 100 backstroke, 200 freestyle, 50 free, and the freestyle and medley relays. The former is still where I'm strongest, obviously, but my lead-off was solid.

It's not as sharp as Voss wants it, but it's getting there. Progress, definitely. A lock-in point that's just a good practice or two away from clicking. Tension that's slowly but surely fading.

I'm still damp, hair pushed back as I rap my knuckles against Robbie's office door. There's the familiar creak of a chair, then heavy footsteps before he swings it open.

Robbie's all broad-shouldered and smiling, his Sycamore visor sitting crooked on his head. He's always been the type of manager who knows how to keep things running without taking himself too seriously.

"Well, if it isn't my favorite lifeguard," he says, stepping back to let me inside. "Figured you'd be by soon enough."

Papers are stacked high on his desk, half-crumpled, some marked up with Sharpie. It's an organized mess, but it works for him. I always did kind of admire that.

"Came to grab my last check," I say, shoving my hands into my hoodie pockets. "And Quinn's, too, if that's cool."

"Sure thing," he says, heading to his desk. He pulls out two envelopes and hands them over.

"Thanks," I say, tucking them into my back pocket.

I'd like to leave without too much fanfare. Head back to the car, maybe grab a sandwich on the way home. But Robbie's still watching me, arms crossed, that satisfied grin tugging at the corner of his mouth.

"You know," he says slowly, "I'm glad you came back this summer. After everything."

"Yeah, well. Needed the cash."

"Sure." He waves off my nonchalance. "But I think you needed something else, too."

I scratch the back of my neck. "What, like a stress headache?"

Robbie laughs, the kind of loud, belly-deep sound that rattles the walls. "Nah," he says. "I just mean . . . you're a good kid, Mercer. Hardworking. Reliable. If you ever need a job—during breaks, after graduation—you've got one."

I blink. "Oh. Uh, thanks. I appreciate it."

"Don't mention it." He pauses, leaning one arm against the doorframe. "And hey," he adds, grinning wider now, "I hope things go better with Quinn this time around. You two were good together."

The words hit softly, landing somewhere I haven't fully let myself acknowledge yet. I know we were good together. Can we be that way again?

"Yeah," I mutter. "Me too."

I shove my hands into my pockets as I slip back down the hall and push through the side exit. I'm halfway to my car when I spot Preston Beckett in one of those ridiculous golfer outfits—a neon pink polo, blinding turquoise pants, and a belt that probably costs more than my car.

He's standing just a few rows down, leaning against his silver Maserati like it's some kind of throne. The passenger door's open, and Davis and Mancini are there, too, the three of them just as buddy-buddy as ever.

And that damned tire is patched now, looking brand-new and smug about it.

It rankles me, seeing those two with him again. Quinn told me they stuck up for her after the incident. Kept Beckett from escalating after the assault and got him to drop the investigation with the club. But now here they are, all chummy again.

I grit my teeth, walking faster. I could ignore them. Should ignore them.

But then Beckett laughs. It's one of those smug, self-satisfied laughs that makes my skin crawl, and I can't stop from turning toward him.

"Feeling pretty proud of yourself, huh?"

Beckett's head snaps toward me, his mouth twisting into a sneer. "What'd you say, kid?"

"I said," I repeat, slowly and clearly this time, "you seem pretty fucking proud of yourself. Did you manage to get dressed on your own this morning or what?"

Davis and Mancini smile, but they hide it behind their hands like cowards. The kind of laughter that doesn't belong to either side. Just floats there, waiting to shift with the wind.

Beckett shoots me an incredulous look. "You wanna try that again?"

He takes a step forward, and I almost want him to try and hit me. Because I'm still pissed off, still too keyed up to think straight. But before he can get any closer, Mancini grabs his arm, reeling him back.

He leans in close, murmuring something low in his ear, and whatever he says makes Beckett hesitate. He shifts his weight, rolls his shoulders. But when he smirks, it's colder now. More calculated. Another slow, greasy grin that makes my stomach turn.

"Might need to have a little talk with Daniel later on," he says. "Let him know his son's got a bit of a chip on his shoulder. He'll get things under control, I'm sure."

My jaw locks. The words are right there on the tip of my tongue. I'm not Daniel's son, so maybe he should take that up with my mother—or, better yet, shut the hell up altogether.

But I don't say it. Because Beckett's the kind of guy who feeds off explanations and overreactions, who thrives on getting under your skin. And dragging my family into this? Not worth the energy.

So, I turn and head straight for my car. I'm already gripping the door handle when I call back over my shoulder, "Oh, and Preston. One more thing—you might want to watch out for sharp objects. I heard some people were popping tires around here."

His face twitches. Not much, but enough. I found a way under his skin. And for now, that's all I need.

I slam my door shut, crank the engine, and peel out of the lot, tension coiled tight in my chest.

I should've let it go and ignored his presence. But I can still hear Quinn's voice in my head, quiet and strained when she told me what happened that day. How Beckett crossed a line and then painted her as the one who couldn't take rejection.

My grip tightens on the steering wheel.

I need to let it go. But the longer I drive, the harder it gets to shake the knot in my chest. That slimy smirk won't leave my head. Those fighting words are still rattling around by the time I pull into my driveway.

Daniel will get things under control.

Like I'm some stray dog his influence can leash. Like I couldn't possibly stand on my own two feet without someone else's name to prop me up. And what's worse is that, for a second, I almost wished it were true. Almost wished I *was* Daniel's son. That I had that kind of buffer between me and the mess I've had to carry on my own.

It makes me think of the man I actually belong to. The one I haven't seen in weeks. My dad's been convinced there's some larger conspiracy ever since he landed at Oakview. First, it was that the nurses were drugging him to keep him quiet. Now, it's that they're trying to steal his fifteen-dollar watch.

I need to visit again soon. Something that doesn't feel like crisis control. I need to be there without the pressure of money or mood management, even if it changes nothing.

I kill the engine and stew, gripping the steering wheel. My knuckles are white, my breathing still uneven. I tell myself to let it go, that Beckett's not worth the headspace, but the knot in my chest isn't budging.

I unlock my phone, half a mind to text Quinn. She'd calm me down or at least distract me long enough to forget. But before I can type out anything coherent, my phone buzzes with a text.

QUINN

boxing. late class. but I want to see you after?

My pulse kicks up, something tight easing in my chest. She's communicating. She's letting me in again, even if just a little.

I type out a quick *yeah, of course* and lean back against the seat. Try to breathe. Try to settle.

But five minutes later, I'm still sitting there, staring at my screen, restless and strung out. The last thing I feel like doing is stewing in my own head for the next couple of hours. I need to see her—now.

I turn the key and drive toward her apartment. It's easy to find the gym, just down the street, like she said. Emberline Boxing Co. A squat brick building with fogged-over windows and an old neon sign still buzzing overhead.

I park, kill the engine, and head inside.

The place smells like sweat and rubber mats, the air humid and thick. It's late enough that the place isn't packed, but the ring's still occupied, and a few guys are working the bags along the far wall.

I spot Quinn near the back. She's dressed in tiny black shorts and a sports bra, her dark hair piled into a slick ponytail. Her face is pink from exertion, her arms flexing with every jab.

She looks good—really fuckin' good—but it's the way she moves that gets me. Sharp and focused, like she's siphoning off every last bit of frustration into her fists.

I didn't realize she was this serious about it. She's not just hitting the bag to blow off steam. She's training. Every movement's clean and controlled. She already looks like a pro.

I hang back near the wall, watching her for a few minutes. I guess I should've waited for her to text. Should've given her the space to finish up without me hovering.

But I couldn't help myself.

I'm already moving toward her, full steam ahead, when I notice a man standing there, too. Probably the trainer she mentioned, though he doesn't look the part. Dark curls, piercings, tattoos. He's got that smug, try-hard look about him.

He probably spends more time posing in front of a mirror than actually hitting the bag.

And now he's not just standing beside her. He has one hand on her hip, adjusting her stance, the other lightly tracing down her arm. His fingers flex just a little too long, his thumb grazing her waist.

"Keep your guard up," he says roughly. "But relax your shoulders. You're too tight."

Quinn snorts. "*You're* too tight."

He chuckles, and I nearly roll my eyes hard enough to see stars. "Yeah? We might need to loosen up together."

She snorts as she adjusts her stance. She's not flirting back. Not really. But she's not shutting him down, either, and that . . . twists something inside me.

"Hey," I call sharply.

Quinn's head snaps up, her face breaking into a smile. "Warren, hi! What're you doing here?"

I flick my gaze toward the tattooed man, who's still got his hand on her waist. He doesn't move or acknowledge me at first. I'm invisible.

"Thought I'd pick you up," I say, pointedly eyeing the guy's hand.

He finally drops it, flashing me a tight, forced smile. I wish I could knock it off his face.

"Didn't know you invited a friend," he says.

"Yeah," I mutter, eyes narrowing. "Not her friend."

"This is Gage," she says, like that explains anything. "He's cool."

"Yeah? Seems like it," I say flatly.

She gives me a look, something between warning and exasperation. "Gage, this is Warren."

He barely glances at me before flashing a wide grin at Quinn. "I'll see you Tuesday?"

"Sure," she says easily. "See ya."

I wait for him to disappear around the corner before I turn back to her. I'm still wound tight, but she just lifts a brow, calm as ever.

"You didn't have to come all the way here. I would've just popped over to your place when I was done."

"Figured I'd save you the drive."

"Well, thanks." She smiles again—bright and warm, like she didn't just spend the last hour sparring—and heads for the locker room. "Give me five?"

"Sure thing."

Her hair is still damp from the shower when we head back to my place. She's quiet at first, scrolling her phone and sipping the protein shake she grabbed on the way out, but her gaze flicks toward me more than once.

"You're brooding," she says finally. "Why?"

"I'm not."

"Okay," she drawls. "You're simmering, then."

I snort. "I'm fine."

"Sure." She sets her shake in the cup holder, turning in her seat to face me. "So . . . what's up? Is this about your mock meet?"

"No."

"Then what?"

I pull into the driveway, kill the engine, and sit there a minute, fingers flexing on the wheel. I know I'm being annoying, but that doesn't make it easier to shake. The knot's still there, coiled tight in my chest.

Gage's hand on her waist—the way he looked at her, talked to her—like he was just waiting for a green light. Would she have given it to him? Would that even have been a thought that would ever cross her mind?

"Gage is kind of a dick," I say finally.

Quinn barks out a laugh. "Oh my God. Are you really that jealous?"

"No."

"You totally are."

"I'm not." I pause. Scratch my ear, shift in my seat like the pleather's suddenly too hot. "I just don't like the guy."

She grins, that smug little smile that makes me want to kiss her just to shut her up. "You sure about that?"

"Positive."

"Riiight. So, you're not jealous . . . but you turned up at the gym unannounced, nearly stabbed Gage with your eyes, and now you're sulking in the driver's seat."

"He had his fucking hands on you."

"He was fixing my stance," she says. "That's what trainers do."

"Yeah, well, I didn't like it."

"You know what?" she says, voice low and playful now. "Maybe I should text him, let him know I'm suddenly available for one-on-one sessions."

I shoot her a look. "Don't mess with me right now."

"Oh no, I'm serious." She grins wider. "I mean . . . now you mention it, Gage *is* kinda cute. He's got that bad boy thing going on. I wonder if he's single?"

"Quinn," I warn.

"I mean, maybe I should—"

I'm on her before she can finish, hand sliding to the back of her neck, practically hauling her over the center console for a kiss. She's still grinning when I meet her mouth, smug and amused, but I don't care. Because she's mine. And no one else—not Gage, not the guys at the club, not anyone—is touching her ever again.

"Still not jealous?" she teases when I finally pull back.

I drag my thumb along her bottom lip. Her breath hitches, and I feel it everywhere. "I don't share well."

"Good," she murmurs. "Because I wasn't offering."

Chapter Thirty-Two

QUINN

WARREN'S PLACE is much more chaotic than I expected.

If he lived alone, I'm sure the place would be spotless. But it's obvious he has roommates that aren't as put together as him. The living room's cluttered with soccer gear, cleats piled by the door, a couple of half-empty Gatorade bottles sweating on the coffee table.

His cousin, Liam, is sprawled across the couch, one sock on, one sock missing, scrolling through his phone. He's got that rangy, golden boy look about him. Messy blond hair, broad shoulders.

I know he's an athlete, too, and he looks it. Strong and confident.

I remember him from the summer before college started. We met briefly, just once, at an event hosted by Warren's parents. I was freshly eighteen then, and he was a little shorter, a little softer around the edges. Now, he's sharper, more defined.

But still just as clueless, apparently, because he barely looks up when Warren and I walk inside the room.

His girlfriend's curled up beside him, legs tucked under her, a sketchbook balanced on her knees. She's on the taller side and sharp-featured, with a cute, cropped bob and an artsy, mean-looking edge that I respect on sight.

Her eyes flick up from her drawing, landing on me first. From the slight tilt of her head, I'm pretty sure she knows exactly what I'm doing here.

"Hey, you two," she says, all curious and friendly. "This is the ex, huh?"

Warren drops his keys on the counter with a clatter. "Yeah, now don't scare her off."

She just shrugs. "I don't know. It looks like she can handle herself."

"She can," Warren says, his voice a low rumble. "Quinn, you remember Liam. This is his girlfriend, Birdie. They're . . . a lot when they're together."

Birdie's already closing her sketchbook and shoving it into her bag. "Yeah, we'd love to stick around and get to know you better. But sadly, I was just telling Liam we should head out."

Liam looks up, confused. "You were?"

"Yeah, we've been here for hours," she says. "And you still haven't shown me that thing you were talking about."

"What thing?"

"You know." She widens her eyes, tilting her head, hoping he'll catch on. "The thing," she says more firmly. "The—" She pauses, then blurts out, "The pasta thing."

Liam frowns. "I don't know what you're—"

Birdie grabs his arm, hauling him off the couch. "The pasta thing! Come on!"

"Oh." Realization finally clicks. "The pasta thing."

Warren stares after them. Birdie being Birdie and Liam trailing right after her.

The door clicks shut behind them, and I laugh. It was sweet, in a weird, chaotic way—her attempt to give us some space. Thoughtful, even if the delivery needed work.

Warren snorts. "She's real subtle."

"I think I like her."

"You would, actually. She's pretty grumpy, too. A bit of a loner. She's close with her roommate now, but Liam said she barely had any friends when they met."

I scoff. "I have friends."

He raises an eyebrow, clearly unconvinced. We both know he's right, but I'm not about to self-deprecate when we're finally alone together.

He nudges me gently, then tips his head toward the hallway, guiding me down toward his room. It's a quiet little corner at the end of the hall. Clean and well organized. He has a few textbooks stacked on his desk, mostly sports physiology and biomechanics.

His Dayton swim cap dangles from the lamp, and a battered paperback with a folded receipt marking the page sits on his nightstand. The walls are bare except for a corkboard cluttered with ticket stubs, old meet schedules, and Polaroids—Warren on the pool deck, arms around his teammates. A few of just him as a kid. One with his mom, grinning wide with a medal around his neck.

And the bed, though clearly well-used, is simple. White sheets, a soft blue duvet, and a worn-in blanket folded neatly at the end. A true picture of Warren in quiet, unshowy form.

I drop onto it without asking, stretching out. "You're very tidy, Mercer."

"I'm averagely tidy," he mutters, tugging his hoodie off and tossing it toward his desk chair. "But I do like my own space."

I grab the chain on the nightstand, letting it dangle between my fingers. "Why aren't you wearing it?"

He shrugs. "Took it off for practice. Haven't been back to the house yet."

"You should put it on."

He hovers at the edge of the bed. "Now?"

"Yeah." I sit up, looping the chain over his head and letting it fall against his chest. My fingers linger on the links, brushing his collarbone. "I like it on you. I want you to be wearing it when we have sex."

"Oh," he says, like he wasn't expecting that. "Is that what we're doing tonight?"

"If you're lucky."

He laughs under his breath. "Maybe I should make you wait. Punish you a little."

I lean back against his pillows. "Mmm. Afraid my little trainer friend's got something you don't?"

His smile falters. "Don't start with me."

I grin, tipping my head back. "Huh? Didn't realize you were so needy and insecure. That's a new feature."

His eyes narrow. "You trying to push me, Rose?"

"What?" I drag my fingers up my thigh, letting my shirt ride higher. "You don't want me to?"

"Depends. Is me being possessive a turn-off?"

"Undecided." I lick my lips. Really take my time, watching his jaw tense. "Maybe you should ask me if I fucked him to help me figure it out."

He blinks down at me. "Sorry?"

I wave a flippant hand. "Go on."

His gaze sharpens. "Did you fuck your trainer, Quinn?"

"What's it matter to you?"

"It matters," he says darkly, "because if you did, I'm gonna have to go back and break the fucking hands he put on you." He pauses, voice dropping to something low and lethal. "And then I'm gonna have to spend the rest of the night showing you what he could never do to you—what only I can give you."

The heat hits me like a punch to the ribs, curling low in my stomach. I want him more than air, more than reason demands.

"Mm-hmm," I murmur, grabbing his chain again and tugging him closer. "Yeah. I think that works for me."

I barely get the words out before he's on me. His hands are in my hair, mouth rough against my throat. There's nothing soft about it, nothing hesitant.

His teeth scrape my bottom lip, his fingers digging into my waist, and I meet every kiss with one of my own. I'm just as hungry for it, just as demanding and desperate to feel something that isn't doubt.

I hook my leg over his hip, dragging him closer. His hand slips beneath my shirt, rough palm skating over my ribs. That cold chain brushes my throat, a chill against heated skin, and I shiver beneath him, wanting more, wanting everything.

"Tell me you're mine," he whispers against my mouth.

I grab his face, fingers curling hard against his jaw. "I'm yours."

His breath stutters, and then he kisses me again, deeper and rougher. I don't stop him. I wouldn't even know how. I want to drown in it, to let it wash away whatever resentment might still be tangled up between us.

When his lips trail down my neck, dragging heat across my skin, I roll over and reach for his nightstand, fingers fumbling with the drawer until I find the box of condoms. It's half-crushed in the corner, with only one or two left inside.

My stomach twists. A sharp, ugly pang that I know I have no right to feel.

What did I expect? That he'd been waiting around for me? Celibate for two years, frozen in time?

I wasn't. I know I wasn't.

But still, the sight of it sticks, wedging itself beneath my ribs. A jealous, possessive knot that winds tighter with every breath. I made fun of him for being insecure, yet here I am, seething over something I can't even blame him for.

"Looks like you've been busy," I say sharply, flicking a condom at him.

He winces. It's a fractured sort of look, like he's almost ashamed of it. It obviously unsettles him, too.

I should back off. It would give me a second to breathe and let the bitterness pass. But all I can do is kiss him harder.

I don't know if it's because I want to stake my claim or because I'm trying to erase everyone else from his skin. But whatever came before this, whatever happened in the space between then and now, all I know for certain is that he's mine again.

His hand tightens at my waist, fingers pressing bruises into my skin. I pull him closer, teeth catching on his bottom lip, dragging him in until there's no room left for anything else.

We strip down fast, clothes hitting the floor in messy piles. The condom gets tucked aside for now as I push him back against the pillows and climb on top, sliding down his body and settling between his legs.

His cock is thick and flushed, the skin stretched tight, a bead of precum glistening at the tip. My mouth hovers just above him, practically salivating, tongue flicking over my bottom lip as I concentrate.

"I want you to look at me," he says. "When your lips are around my cock, I need you to keep your pretty eyes on mine."

He brushes my hair back and holds it out of my face, fingers curling at the nape of my neck. Our eyes stay locked, dark and heated, as I take him in. Just the head, then a slow, deliberate glide down the full length of him.

His stomach flexes tight, abs clenching with restraint. A sharp inhale breaks between his teeth. Then a ragged sound escapes him, breath hitching when I take him deeper, dragging my tongue so deliberately it borders on cruel.

I remember exactly what he likes—the way he gets tight and still, muscles locking up like he's bracing for impact when I hollow my cheeks, how his fingers tighten when I trace my tongue along the ridge beneath the head.

Now, I pitch forward, swallowing around him, letting my hand follow where my mouth can't reach.

I've thought about this so many times over the years. The way he'd groan, unraveling one breath at a time. The way his hand would tighten in my hair, not to push, but to keep himself from pulling me closer.

And now? He's everything I remembered and so much more. His hips stutter, and then he's gone in an instant. He comes hard down my throat in a broken, helpless release.

"Jesus Christ," he mutters, breathless. "You were always so fucking good at that."

"I know," I say, voice smug as I wipe my lips and grab the condom, tearing it open and rolling it on for him.

He's still breathing hard, but I know him. I know what he can take. He's stubborn like that, all muscle and stamina. His body's built to outlast anything.

"You're not done," I tell him softly.

His smile is lazy and crooked. "You really think I'd tap out now?"

I move to climb on top, but Warren catches my wrist and pulls me down beside him.

"Not yet," he says, slipping his hand between my legs. "Give me a minute to recover."

"Warren, baby," I murmur, twisting toward him. "I want you inside me."

His fingers stroke me first, teasing and slow, deliberately dragging it out. He watches my face the whole time—every shaky breath, every sharp hitch of my chest. Every flutter of my lashes when I can't keep my eyes open any longer.

"This is my pussy, isn't it?" he asks, thumb brushing just right until my legs go weak.

I barely manage a nod. Normally, I'd argue. Tell him not to get cocky, make him work for it. But now, with his fingers on my clit, his mouth hot against the shell of my ear, I can't bother to think of a comeback.

"Then I'll do what I want with it."

His fingers slip lower, sliding through the slick heat of me, moving slowly, savoring it. He presses a middle finger in, stretching me open before adding an index, twisting just enough to make my hips jerk.

"You're dripping," he murmurs, voice rough with satisfaction.

His fingers press deeper, curling until heat sparks sharp and fast behind my ribs. My hips lift to meet him, breath tumbling out in short, uneven gasps. My toes are curling, body tensing, but his fingers just keep working me through it, rough and perfect.

He knows exactly how to pull me under, and I let him. Every time.

When he flips me over and pushes his cock inside me, I'm already wrecked, clinging to him, breathless as he fucks me slow and deep, determined to make me feel it everywhere. And I do.

My legs shake with it, heat simmering beneath my skin, the ache lingering in places only he's ever known how to reach. He was right when he said only *he* could do this to me. Only *he* could touch me like this, leave me unraveling from the inside out.

The feeling settles low and deep, a throb that pulses with every shaky breath. It's like he's left something behind, something I can't shake.

I know I'll still feel him tomorrow. Not just physically but in the way he's worked his entire soul has been left beneath my skin. Threaded in deep, right where I've always kept him. He's made sure of it.

Chapter Thirty-Three

WARREN

I WAKE BEFORE MY ALARM.

It's barely 5:00 a.m., and Quinn probably shouldn't have stayed the night. We both knew that when her eyes started drifting closed, but neither of us could bring ourselves to untangle.

My arm is numb beneath her weight, her hair fanned across my chest, warm breath curling against my skin. I let myself stay like this, breathing her in. The soft scent of her cherry almond shampoo, the warmth of her pressed against me. Maybe if I stay still enough, I can make the moment last a little longer.

But practice is in less than an hour, and I need to move. Carefully, I brush her hair back from her face, fingers skimming her cheek.

"Hey," I whisper. "Gotta wake up."

She stirs, mumbling something I can't make out before shifting deeper into the blankets. I try again, fingers trailing down her arm this time.

"C'mon, Quinny. I've gotta go."

Her eyes blink open slowly, still heavy with sleep. She stares at me like she's not sure where she is. Then her gaze sharpens, and she pushes herself upright, dragging the blankets up with her.

I grab my shirt from the floor, pull it on, and start gathering my bag for the pool. Quinn sits on the edge of the bed, tucking her legs under herself, watching me.

Finally, she speaks.

"Look, I think we should address the gap," she says quietly. "Not let it linger."

I stop at the foot of the bed, tossing my bag over my shoulder.

"The gap?"

"The dark period," she clarifies, pulling her hair into a messy knot on top of her head. "Between our breakup and now?"

I snort. "Is that what we're calling it?"

"I'm not naive, Warren." Her voice is steady, but there's something tight in her expression. "I know you didn't just . . . wait around for me. I wouldn't have expected you to."

I exhale hard, running a hand through my hair. "Yeah, there were some girls."

There were a lot of girls, especially in the beginning. Hookups that felt more like distractions than anything else. I'd go out alone, drink too much, and find someone willing to let me burn off whatever I was trying not to feel. It never stuck. It never helped.

Eventually, I slowed down. I couldn't keep pretending it didn't leave me feeling worse afterward, emptier, like I was just proving to myself how much I didn't care. Because deep down, I knew it wasn't true.

I wouldn't tell Quinn that. Just like I wouldn't ask her for details about who she might have been with herself. Knowing that would hurt—too much, too fast—and I don't think I could sit still and listen to it, anyway.

She doesn't flinch, but I see something flicker across her face, something sharp and quiet. She's trying to swallow down the sting, but she's failing. Miserably.

"Nothing serious," I add. "No one I cared about."

I barely remember their faces, their names. I couldn't tell you what half of them even looked like. Because no matter how hard I tried, none of them ever came close to what we had back then. They were never her, and I was never fully present with them.

"Why not?" Her voice is small, like she's not sure she even wants the answer.

I shrug, shifting my bag higher on my shoulder. "I didn't know what I was feeling. I just knew I couldn't . . . feel like *that* again."

She swallows hard, her fingers curling into the blankets. "I tried, too," she says after a beat. "There was this one guy. Someone from one of my lit classes. But it felt wrong." Her voice dips lower. "I kept waiting for it to feel like . . . *you*. It never did."

My chest tightens.

I assumed it would feel like shit to hear it, and it does. She tried to move on, tried to forget me with some guy in her lit class. Someone who got to be close to her, even for a little while.

I wonder if he made her laugh. If she ever looked at him and thought, *maybe this could be something*.

I swallow hard, pushing the thought down before it festers.

"Even when I was with other people," I say quietly, "none of it mattered. I could've had a hundred hookups, and it wouldn't have changed a thing. I never forgot the way you made me feel. The way you looked at me . . . like I was something good."

"You are good." She laughs, soft and sad. "But I sort of hate it, you know. Hate *you*. For being with other people. And I know it's unfair because I tried too, but . . . it still hurts."

"I get it. Part of the reason I . . . did what I did was because I assumed you'd move on without looking back. Like you didn't care or that I never mattered enough for you to try."

"That's not true," she urges. "I cared. I always cared."

Silence stretches between us, heavy and lingering. There's no dramatic resolution, no perfect words to make it better. All we can do is sit in the fallout, letting it exist instead of pretending it never happened.

"I should go," I say, breaking the quiet. "I've got practice."

Quinn nods. "Yeah. Okay."

I start to move, and she reaches for my hand. Her fingers are cold, but her grip is firm.

"We'll figure it out," she says softly. "Right?"

I squeeze her hand in return. "Yeah. We will."

I HEAD onto the pool deck still feeling the dull ache in my shoulders from Saturday. Partly from the mock meet, partly from Quinn. My muscles are stretched and overworked. But I did spend the whole weekend getting wrung out, and I'd do it again.

Having sex with Quinn will never be a regret of mine.

Coach Voss stands near the bleachers, clipboard in hand, already flipping through splits and stroke counts. The rest of the guys mill around, half-dressed in sweats or pulling gear from their bags.

"Mercer," Voss calls, motioning me over. "Come talk to me."

I drop my bag near the bench and make my way over, trying to school my expression. I know what's coming. My times on Saturday weren't terrible, but they weren't what they should've been.

I hit my marks in the freestyle, but my lead-off wasn't sharp enough. My turns were clean but not aggressive. My breakout felt like I was fighting through syrup. It's enough for me to brace myself for the talk.

"So," Voss starts, his eyes still fixed on his clipboard. "I looked over your times again. I think you're capable of better."

"Yeah, I know," I say.

No point pretending otherwise.

"I know you've been working hard," Voss goes on, lowering the clipboard to meet my eyes. "But Gaines is back this week. Shoulder's healed faster than expected. We're gonna switch things around for the dual meets coming up."

I blink. "That's good."

"Yeah," Voss says, scratching something onto his clipboard. "So, we'll have you back on anchor for the medley and middle leg in the 400 free."

I nod. "Okay."

I'm not bothered by swapping back. Gaines is stronger in backstroke; I know that. But still, part of me can't help but wonder if I should've been better at cross-training. If I'd worked harder, if I'd pushed myself more, then maybe Voss wouldn't have even considered the switch in the first place.

I'm a freestyle swimmer, always have been. But I want to be well-rounded, too.

"Why not anchor in the free?" I ask.

Voss exhales through his nose. "Because you're not as sharp as you should be," he says, reading my mind. "You've got the stamina, no question. But you're overgripping the catch, shortening your stroke, rushing your recovery. You need to loosen up. Focus on clean extensions, smooth pull-throughs. Your underwaters could be faster, too. We'll drill those next week."

I nod, jaw tight. That was exactly what I was afraid of.

"And your hips are sinking," he adds. "Could be mobility. Start hitting the resistance bands, work on ankle flexibility. You want to swim at your full potential? You've got to stop muscling through everything and let the water work with you. No slack."

"I'm not slacking," I say, maybe too fast.

"I know you're not," Voss says evenly. "But you're still holding back. Get uncomfortable. Push yourself."

"I will."

"Good." He claps my shoulder, and I try not to wince at the sore muscles beneath his hand. "Now, get in the water."

I do as Coach commands.

The first lap feels like I'm swimming through cement. My strokes are too shallow, my body too tight. I tell myself it's just the morning stiffness working itself out, but the longer I push through, the more Coach's pestering nags at me.

I touch the wall and surface, chest heaving.

"Looks a little sloppy, bud," Hawkins calls from a few lanes over.

"Must be hard watching me swim faster than you all the time," I shoot back.

"Right. Just fast enough to get bumped again?"

The heat's already building under my skin. "What's your fuckin' problem with me?"

"My problem?" He pushes off the wall and swims over to meet me. "You think you're better than you are."

"Better than *you*. That's for damn sure."

His smile disappears. "Yeah? Funny you say that because you're the one Coach keeps moving around like a spare part."

I clench my jaw, my hand tightening on the gutter. "Why don't you line up and we can see who actually belongs here?"

Hawkins lets out a low chuckle, and I'm already mentally prepping for the race. If we do a 100 IM, then it's an even matchup.

"Easy, boys," Omar calls from the lane beside us. "You both swim like fish with anxiety disorders. No need to prove it."

"Whatever you say, Cap," Hawkins says, voice light but his gaze still sharp. "But if your boy is so solid, why's he the one Voss keeps second-guessing?"

"Voss is figuring out where I can make the biggest impact," I interject. "That's what happens when you're actually versatile."

Although I hardly believe it myself, I hold his stare and keep my voice even.

"Yeah," Hawkins drawls. "Or maybe you're just not good enough to own your spot."

I don't answer. Not because I don't have a comeback but because the annoyance is already settled in my chest, thick and tight, and I know if I keep talking, I'll say something I'll regret.

This is pointless, anyway. I should stick to ignoring my teammates like usual and focus on the only thing I can actually control. My success in the lane.

I push off the wall, cutting through the water fast and hard, turning every set into a race against myself. Frustration fuels every stroke, driving my legs harder, keeping my form tight. The burn in my shoulders flares, but I lean into it.

Even if I hate to admit it, Hawkins is right. Coach is right. If I want to qualify for Nationals, I need to stop coasting on what I'm already good at and start grinding where I'm not.

I'm not chasing titles or bragging rights. I don't care about being the fastest guy in the pool. But if I could hit a B-cut in my 200 free or shave enough time off my 50 to make it count—that sticks. That's something I can point to and say, *I did that.*

Now that I'm back in my anchor spot, I'll be stronger in the relays. My finish in the 200 medley helps, and the 400 free keeps me sharp. But if I can hit the mark on my own, that's different. That's mine.

I'll keep working on backstroke like Coach suggested. I probably won't race it again this season, but that's not the point. It's about pushing myself outside my comfort zone, finding the gaps and filling them.

If I can make it there—if I can push hard enough to earn that spot—maybe it means I haven't just been treading water this whole time. Maybe it means the early mornings, the late-night lifts, the moments where I thought I couldn't take another lap actually meant something.

Maybe it means I'm capable of more than just staying afloat.

Chapter Thirty-Four

QUINN

I'm in Lang's office before class, front row, grading papers on the tiny tablet desk and half listening as she rattles on about some new writing contest she thinks I should enter.

"The Blackthorn Prize is highly coveted," she tells me. "Big-name judges. Good prize money. And it's right up your alley. A little darker and gutsier than the usual lit mag fluff."

I make a noncommittal noise and keep my eyes on the essay in front of me. Something *darker and gutsier*. Sounds like me, sure. But the thought of putting my work out there like that again makes my stomach knot up.

It's one thing to write because I have to. To bleed out onto the page before it festers inside of me. It's another thing entirely to hold my work up in front of people and then wait for them to tell me if it's any good.

"Quinn," Lang presses, planting her coffee on the desk. "Seriously. You should do it."

I set my pen down and lean back in my chair. "It costs money to submit, doesn't it?"

"I think the early bird deadline is sometime in late October," she says. "You'll have to check into the details."

"Details," I echo.

I've been careful about money lately. The TA position pays enough to keep me afloat, and I've been trying to stash most of it away. Same with what I earned in the last month of summer. My savings took a serious hit before that.

I'd been traveling alone, worn thin from too many weeks on the move. Met a girl in a hostel. She was sweet, young, wide-eyed in a way that made me want to befriend her. I let my guard down for once. Told myself to stop being the suspicious girl who never lets anyone get close.

She was gone the next morning. So was the rest of my money.

Lang grins. "This would be a great resume builder. And you have a real shot at placing."

Maybe I do. I want to believe I do.

After I stole from Daniel, lost Warren and the contest to boot, I let myself believe in some kind of karmic balance. Like when I lost, I was paying my price. I didn't enter another writing contest after that. For a long time, I didn't think I deserved to.

But now, things are good again, and it feels like something's finally realigned. Maybe I've done the work, and maybe that matters. Maybe I can let myself want something without thinking I have to pay for it afterward.

"I'll think about it," I say.

Lang looks pleased. "Good. Any gems in the pile there?"

I wince and stare down at my stack of essays, red pen poised and ready. This group of students isn't the most inventive, but we're still early in the semester. Maybe they just need time to surprise me.

"One or two," I say. "Though I'm not holding my breath."

There are about ten minutes left until class begins. The room is filling slowly, students dragging their feet as they shuffle to their seats. I keep my head down, still flipping through the stack when Warren walks in.

I feel him before I see him. That quiet, steady presence of his, like gravity shifting slightly in his direction. He doesn't say anything as he makes his way down the aisle, his fingers brushing my desk when he passes. Something small and folded slips beneath my elbow.

I unfold the paper, a crooked smile tugging at my mouth.

> *I'm terrified by this dark thing*
> *That sleeps in Quinn;*
> *All day I feel her restless turnings,*
> *Her sharp edges and quiet claws.*

I bite down a laugh and tuck the note into my pocket. A warped rendition of Plath's *Elm*. Claws instead of feathers, my name dropped in like a dare.

It's a nod to something old, something ours. Back at Sycamore, Warren used to mess with me through poetry. He'd rattled off lines half-wrong and half-serious, rewriting the classics just to piss me off. But there was one night, after hours in the pool, where he recited them quite perfectly.

A Dickinson poem that, at the time, felt a lot like a confession.

"For Occupation—This
The spreading wide my narrow Hands
To gather Paradise."

He spoke slowly, carefully. He knew exactly what he was doing then, and I knew, too.

It was before we'd even kissed, before the idea of him and me and *us* was anything more than a fairy tale. Some dream I'd only ever dared to imagine in the quietest corners of my mind.

But after that night, he kept up with the lines. He'd whisper them in my ear when no one was around. Shoot them across the break room when we were meant to be folding towels or cleaning up.

When we got to Dayton, he started writing them down, too. Scribbled notes tucked in my pockets, slipped between the pages of my textbooks. Little reminders, like breadcrumbs leading me back to him.

Now, Lang's voice pulls me back to the front of the room. I shift in my seat, the paper crinkling in my pocket. When I stand and head to the front of the class, I glance behind me.

Warren watches, waiting to see if I'll smile at him.

And I do. Of course I do.

THE NEXT NIGHT, I'm at Emberline again. Three times a week now, sometimes more if I can swing it. I haven't been reading or writing as much, but I think the trade-off is worth it. My body feels stronger, but so does my mind. I'm gaining something solid after years of feeling a bit frayed.

It's easier to push myself now, too. To drown out whatever's still rattling around in my head with the sound of my fists hitting the bag. Easier to burn off the tension instead of letting it knot up inside me.

I've already made a mental note to shut down any unnecessary flirting or touching from Gage's end. Even if I find it harmless, Warren doesn't, and I want to respect that. Jealousy can be fun in the short term, but I know it can eat at a person if they let if fester.

Turns out, though I don't have to bother fending off his advances because Gage isn't here. No sharp smile, no easy swagger as he circles the floor, running drills. I pace by the heavy bags, scanning the room once, then again.

He said he'd see me Tuesday night. I know I didn't imagine that.

Still, the floor is quiet. There's no sign of him.

I tape my hands and get to work alone, running through my

warm-ups. I hit each rep harder than usual. Sweat gathers at the base of my neck and trickles down my spine, but I keep going until my arms burn and my chest aches, until the frustration starts to bleed out of me.

It's cathartic, I guess, but it's also exhausting in a way that feels more emotional than physical.

"You alright?"

I blink up to find the owner, Marcus, watching me from the side. He's got his towel slung over one shoulder, hands braced on his hips.

"Fine," I say, breathless.

"You sure?"

"Yeah." I shake out my arms and tighten the tape around my wrist. "Hey, you know when Gage is working next?"

"He's not."

I frown. "Why?"

"Fired him just yesterday," Marcus responds. "Caught him skimming money off me. Tried to lie and say it wasn't him, but I had two witnesses."

A sharp, familiar pang cuts through me. It's a tug behind my ribs that isn't quite anger. There's something colder threaded through it—disappointment, maybe.

When I was robbed this summer, I was gutted. At first, I felt violated, exposed. But after that? I just felt tired. Because anger never lasts forever. Eventually, it burns out, and you're left with whatever's underneath.

For me, it was the hollow ache of knowing I should've seen it coming. That deep down, I probably did. I know how these things unravel. How they start with excuses and end in damage.

Of course, I know what stealing feels like. I know the rush of it, the warped logic that tells you it's survival, not betrayal. But more than that, I know the aftermath. The shame. The part where you can't look anyone in the eye without wondering what they see when they look back at you.

That doesn't mean it's right. It doesn't mean it doesn't leave a mark.

But it would be hypocritical to sit here and act like I'm above Gage because I've been there myself. I know what it's like to convince yourself you're justified. To believe no one's really getting hurt. To think you're owed something just for surviving the grind.

I strip off my tape, tossing it into the trash, then lean against the wall.

"That really fucking sucks."

Marcus exhales through his nose. "Yeah. It does."

"How much did he take?"

"Couple grand," he says, sounding more disappointed than angry. "Kid was working his way up there, too. I had him on track for more hours. Could've taken over some of my morning clients. What a bullshit way to ruin a good thing."

"Yeah," I murmur. "Bullshit."

He pats my shoulder. "He's got no one to blame but himself."

I gather my things, feeling heavy in my own skin. Tired, achy, and hollow in a way that has nothing to do with muscle fatigue. I liked Gage. He was a good trainer. More than that, maybe he could've been a friend, too.

Back at my apartment, I unlock the door, kick off my shoes, and drop my bag just inside. I don't bother with the lights. The living room is still, faintly lit by the streetlamp outside. I sink onto the couch, muscles tight, mind tighter.

Warren wanted me to check in, so I pull out my phone.

QUINN

just back to my apartment now. safe and sound

WARREN

thanks for checking in. how was the gym?

QUINN

weird, kind of. Gage got fired

My phone starts ringing, and I answer on the second buzz.

"Yeah?"

"Tell me it didn't have anything to do with you. He didn't put his hands on you or—"

"Calm down, Mr. Vigilante. The owner caught him stealing, that's all."

"Oh." He exhales, the tension draining from his voice. "Ah."

"Ah is right."

The silence that follows is thick and unsure, stretched out between us like something neither of us wants to name. I shift, curling my free hand into the edge of the couch cushion.

"Warren," I say carefully, "do you ever think there's some part of me that's just . . . stuck?"

"Stuck?"

"Like I'm waiting for the next thing to go wrong." I hesitate, pressing my fingers to my temple. "Or worse—like I'm the one who will inevitably screw it up myself. And even if I try to fix it, even if I've done everything I can to atone . . . sometimes it feels like it doesn't matter. Like my life's still off-kilter somehow, like I'll never quite get it back on track. And I'm just waiting for the next bad thing to hit."

"I know what you mean, but no, Quinn," he says firmly. "That's not you. I know you're good. You're a good person, and good things are meant to happen to you."

I smile, but it's faint and doesn't quite stick. "I don't know about all that."

"Quinny," he says softly.

"Fine," I murmur. "Thank you for the reassurance."

"Anytime."

"Good night, baby."

"Are you sure you don't want to talk more?"

"Yeah," I say, rubbing my eyes. "I just need to pass out in bed and forget I'm a person for a while. I'll see you in class tomorrow."

"Alright," he says quietly. "Good night, then."

I hang up, feeling that familiar hollow space open up inside me again. I know I'll wake up tomorrow and fill it with something else —work, school, the gym. More soft, steady check-ins from Warren. Small things that keep me anchored when I start to drift.

It's not perfect. Some days, those old feelings creep back in. The way my parents used to diminish me without even trying. I had to work hard to be noticed and even harder to be valued. I spent so long chasing their approval that now, I don't always know how to let myself be cared for. How to let myself be fully seen.

Half the time, I'm not even sure I want to be.

But at least I know I'm not alone, and that's what keeps me steady. Because I have Warren, I have Wesley, and they see me—really see me—for exactly who I am.

Chapter Thirty-Five

WARREN

THE LOCKER ROOM's buzzing before warm-ups. The guys are joking around, slapping shoulders, and running through pre-race routines. I tune most of it out, dragging my fingers down the knots in my shoulder blades and stretching through my lower back.

It's the last weekend in September and our first dual meet of the season. We're swimming against Coastal University, a team that's practically made of fish. They train year-round by the beach, which means they're used to open water, longer swims, and rougher conditions.

Rumor has it their coach throws them in the open ocean when they slack off.

Today's meet is here at Dayton, though. We have home pool advantage. Our natatorium's warm and humid. The ceiling lights flicker sometimes. And I know every corner of this place—the scuffed tiles by the starting blocks, the crack in the wall by lane five.

But familiar or not, Coastal's still good. None of us can afford to let our guard down.

Coach Voss went over my lineup earlier: 200. 50. Medley anchor. Middle of the 400. Four chances to prove I can step up when it matters. Four chances to be solid.

I sit on the bench and start rolling out my calves, working through the tension that's been building all week. I meant to visit

Dad again on Wednesday. Thought about it the whole drive home from practice.

But then Quinn called, asking if I wanted to meet her for coffee. And then I had a paper due. And swim practice. And . . . everything. Now it's been a week, and I've run out of excuses.

As I shift to stretch my hamstrings, my phone vibrates inside my locker. I ignore it at first. Then it buzzes again. And again. I grab it, figuring it's Quinn or maybe my mom checking in before the meet.

It's my dad.

Seventeen missed calls.

I sit back hard against the locker, phone clutched in my hand. He's generally overzealous, but he's never called this many times back-to-back before.

Another call flashes across the screen. I don't answer. I can't speak to him before an event. It will rattle me and throw me off game. Of that, I'm sure.

So, I hit Decline and shove my phone under my towel, dragging my hand down my face.

Maybe he's just restless or lonely. Maybe Oakview's got him frustrated again and he wants to complain to his one and only son.

Then the texts start rolling in. More buzzing, more vibrating against the metal bench, each one louder in my head than the last. I try to ignore it. I try to focus on my breathing, on the sound of guys joking around across the room, but the buzzing won't stop.

I shove the towel aside and grab my phone again. The screen's flooded with messages, little text bubbles stacking higher and higher. I scroll through, pulse kicking up as I take in the mess of words.

It's strings of garbled nonsense. Whole paragraphs repeating themselves like he's stuck on a loop. Half sentences that cut off and start over again.

DAD

Warren where r u

They say im not allowed

Need u t come get me out

Get me OUT GET ME OUT GETMEOUT

My stomach knots up.

He's at Oakview. He's been at Oakview for years now. He shouldn't be able to get his hands on anything. He shouldn't be able to . . .

I power the phone off, stuff my phone into my locker, and slam the door. I don't have time for his bullshit right now. No distractions today. If I allow the noise to get in my head, I'll only be focused on drowning it out rather than winning.

That's not a good place for me to be.

The stands are busy when we walk out. Family members lean over the railings, teammates slap each other's backs, the whole place humming with nervous energy. But when I scan the crowd, it's Quinn I find first.

She's sitting on her own, hands tucked beneath her knees, chin lifted just enough to make it clear she's watching me. She's wearing all black with a tiny DU painted on her cheek in gold.

Something shifts in my chest. It's a quiet swell, like a muscle remembering how to move.

She used to come to a few of my meets during freshman year. She never told me when she was showing up, either. She just appeared in the stands.

Back then, I remember feeling electrified by it. A rush filled with pride and something more fragile and hopeful. Seeing her up there was like stepping into cold water. My pulse would spike, my breath would catch, and then slowly, my body would learn how to hold it.

That feeling's still there now, only warmer. Like sunlight on my back after an ice plunge.

I shake it off and roll out my shoulders, narrowing in on my first event.

The 200 free is all rhythm and patience. I stay controlled through the first hundred, matching pace with the guy in the next lane. He's taller—longer reach—but I'm sharper off the walls, four tight dolphin kicks carrying me past the flags before I even take a stroke.

When I flip into the third lap, I shift gears. Switch to a two-stroke breathing pattern, let the tempo build. My stroke rate ticks up, heart pounding harder as I fight to stay clean through the turn.

I lock in for the final fifty, holding form, legs burning, driving through the water like it owes me something. The last stretch is all grit. I edge half a stroke ahead just as my fingers slam into the touchpad.

Second place. An okay start.

I pull myself out of the water, and then it's over. I earned second place, but my time still isn't fast enough to turn heads. No PR, no B-cut, nothing that gets me noticed. It's just . . . fine.

The 50 free comes next. There are barely ten minutes between events, which gives me enough time to cool down, reset, and get back behind the blocks. For this sprint, I know I'll have to claw for every inch in the water.

It's all power with no pacing, no room to settle in. I need to explode off the block and go.

I snap forward on the start, driving hard through the breakout. Water surges past my ears, my arms digging fast and deep. My legs are still heavy from the last event, the quick turnaround leaving them sluggish, but I hammer each kick from the hips, forcing every ounce of power I can find.

I hit the wall first. A clean finish. But I barely register the win before I'm hauling myself out of the pool, heart thudding.

Still solid. Still sharp.

I glance up at the scoreboard overhead, catching my time. It's a low twenty-one. Not a personal best, but close. Clean enough to hold my spot, and more than enough to keep Coach off my back.

After I shake out my arms and catch my breath, I spot Quinn again in the stands. She's on her feet this time, clapping with that wide, full smile of hers. It looks a little crooked, like she's halfway through laughing.

I don't smile back—can't yet—but something settles inside me.

The next few heats blur past. I've still got the relays to go, but my head's clearer now. I just need to keep my pace and not overthink it. Let my body take over.

At the break, I towel off quickly and shrug into my parka, the fleece lining warm against my back. I grab my water, still riding the adrenaline. It's a good kind of buzz, the kind that leaves my skin tight and my pulse running for the next beat.

But then I hear a crash, followed by a few loud, slurred words. They rise over the chatter and the splash of the pool, ringing in my ears until everything else fades.

"Warren! Warren, you in here?"

I freeze, water bottle halfway to my mouth. *You can't be fucking serious.*

I turn, and there he is. My dad, leaning hard on his walker as he limps along the pool deck. He's hunched forward, mouth slack, face blotchy and red. His shirt's half-tucked, one shoe untied.

My gut twists.

"Warren!"

Laughter rings out from the bleachers. Someone points. My stomach bottoms out.

Coach Voss steps forward, already heading toward him.

But I'm moving, too, faster than I can even think. "Coach," I say, catching him by the arm. "It's okay. He's—that's my dad. Let me handle it, please?"

I jog across the rest of the deck, heart pounding in my ears. I don't normally like to be the center of attention, and now, every set of eyes is on me. Every stare on my back. Every breath loud in my throat.

"Dad," I say under my breath, grabbing his arm. "What are you doing here?"

"Had to see you," he slurs. "They're keeping me locked up in that place—said I can't even have a goddamn beer! Bullshit, Warren." His fingers grip my wrist too tight. "I needed to see you. You're my son, damn it."

I gulp. His breath is sharp and sour, cutting through the chlorine-heavy air. "How did—how did you know I'd be here?"

"Got your meet schedule from the school's website. Why?" He squints at me, swaying slightly. "You embarrassed?"

I pull back, trying to ease my arm free without making a scene. "Let's just—let's get you outside, okay? How did you get here?"

"I'm fine," he snaps. "I just needed to—"

"Dad, please. Come on."

"Don't you pull that crap," he barks. "Actin' like you're too good for me now? Too busy with your little girlfriend and your fancy school?"

He wrenches away from me, stumbling back a step. And his slurred, too-loud voice? It echoes off the tile walls, loud enough that the crowd noise quiets, people starting to turn their heads.

"Dad. Let's go."

"You're just like your mother," he sneers. "Think you're smarter than me, better than me."

"Stop." My pulse jumps. My voice is low, pleading. "Please. Don't do this."

"You know what your problem is?" His arm flies up, finger jabbing too close to my face. "You're too goddamn proud. Think you don't need me? I'm the reason you're even here. I'm the one who kept you in the water! Taught you to swim, damn it! And you just—just—"

"Fuckin' hell," someone mutters from the crowd.

An opposing swimmer whistles low under their breath, and I wince.

"Dad," I try again. "Please."

It seems someone's already called security. Probably a pearl-clutching mom from the stands who thinks she's witnessing a domestic crisis.

Two guys in bright blue polos push their way toward us from the back of the pool deck. My dad doesn't see them at first, but the second they reach him, he jerks away from me like I'm the one dragging him off.

"Don't touch me!" His shout cuts sharp and ragged across the air. "I'm talkin' to my son!"

They try to keep calm, murmuring something in hushed tones. My dad swats them away, stumbling sideways into a row of chairs. Metal screeches against the tile. People pull their bags closer, some standing, some whispering.

"Get off me!" he yells.

His face is red now, twisted with anger. He stumbles again, almost trips over his own feet. One of the security guys grabs his arm, trying to steady him, but my dad shoves him off so hard he nearly loses his balance.

"Jesus Christ," I mutter under my breath.

I step forward, but one of the security guys shakes his head, blocking me off.

"Sir," the other says, voice sharper now. "You need to come with us."

"You leave me the hell alone!" My dad's voice cracks. "I came here to see my son!"

"You're gonna hurt yourself."

They each grab an arm, gripping him tightly as he fights to shake them off.

"Let me go!"

I watch, helpless, as they drag him away. He's still swearing, still twisting against their grip, his voice echoing down the hall even after they've disappeared from sight. Once he's gone for good, the whole place stays silent.

The meet's officially been paused. I'm standing in the middle of it all, mouth agape, which is just about the most embarrassing kind of spotlight I can think of.

Some of my teammates are shifting awkwardly, others frozen just off the blocks. Parents are staring at me like they're wondering if I'm about to go off, too. And I'm not nearly brave enough to search out Quinn.

I exhale hard and drag a shaky hand down my face.

Voss appears beside me. "You good?"

I don't answer right away. My pulse is still, my lungs locked up tight.

"I need a minute," I finally manage.

"Go," he says. "Take your time."

I quietly slip into the hallway behind the bleachers, then lean hard against the wall and try to breathe. But the air catches halfway down, sharp and useless. Eyes fixed on the floor, I start counting down.

Five. Four. Three.

My dad's voice is in my head before I can finish, all loud and jumbled. His face, pale and blotchy. Those glassy eyes blinking at me. It's all I can focus on. All I can see.

His fingers locked around my wrist, too tight. The heat of his breath slurring my name. How thin he looked, like something hollowed him out from the inside. Drugs, maybe? Alcohol, definitely.

I bite the inside of my cheek, and blood instantly fills my

mouth. A sharp, metallic tang that cuts through the panic. It grounds me, but only for a fleeting second.

He shouldn't have been able to leave Oakview. He's supposed to be safe there, supposed to be somewhere they can watch him. He's not meant to have access to substances that make him spiral or wander off to crash my meets.

To stumble onto the pool deck and turn the whole thing upside down.

My pulse jumps like my heart's forgotten how to pace itself. My breaths come quick and shallow now, and no matter how hard I try, I can't seem to get enough air.

It's one of the worst panic attacks I've ever had.

I don't know how long I lean there, dizzy and barely holding it together, before I feel Quinn's hand on my arm.

My first instinct should be to push her away. To tell her I'm fine, that I need to deal with this the way I always have. Alone. But I can't summon the energy to push her off. Or maybe I just don't want to.

Maybe I know that if I let go of this—of her—I'll unravel completely.

I need her, and I think maybe that's okay.

"Hey," she says softly. "It's okay. You're okay."

I'm not, but I let her say it anyway.

I squeeze my eyes shut, chest still heaving. My fingers dig into the wall behind me, knuckles tight and white.

Quinn's hand slides down my arm, and then she laces her fingers with mine. "You're alright, baby. You're okay."

I shake my head. "I can't—" I gulp a breath. "I can't get enough air."

"You can. I'm right here."

I can feel her now, her knee brushing against mine, her words anchoring me. She lifts my hand, presses my palm flat against my chest, grounding me with her touch.

"Breathe with me," she says. "You can do it."

I try. It's shaky at first, but she keeps her hand over mine, and I follow her lead. My heart's still racing, but not as bad. My ribs don't feel like they're caving in anymore.

We slide down the wall together, legs stretched out on the cold tile. Quinn doesn't say anything for a while. She stays close, her arm pressed to mine.

I lean my head back, eyes closed, trying to gather what's left of myself.

"Was that a panic attack?" she asks eventually.

I swallow, my throat still tight. "More of an . . . anxious spiral."

"Right," she says dryly. "A panic attack, then?"

I half smile, breath still uneven. "Now's not the time to piss me off, Quinn."

"It might be exactly the time." Her thumb brushes the side of my hand. "You're still here, though. That's what matters."

I don't respond right away. My thoughts are still tangled, too sharp around the edges.

"Has this been happening a lot?" she asks.

"Last one was the night after we broke up."

"I knew you had anxiety," she says, fingers curling gently against mine. "And depression. But you never had panic attacks when we were together. Not that I knew of."

"Didn't have many before that," I tell her. "Had a few when I was younger, but . . . not like this." I shake my head, staring at a scuff mark on the tile. "Then, after we ended things, I guess."

"That's heavy. I'm sorry you've been dealing with that."

"My meds keep me steady most of the time," I tell her. "And I was good for a while."

"Yeah, and you will be good again. Do you want to finish the meet, or should I go talk to Voss for you?"

"No," I say. "I'm good."

"You sure?"

I drag in another ragged breath. "I just want to swim. I'll figure out the rest later."

"Alright." She reaches out a hand, helping me to my feet. "We can talk more about your dad later. Maybe we could even go to Oakview together."

"You'd come with me?"

"Of course I would. Unless you don't want to see him, then I'll support you in that, too."

I swallow hard. "I don't know what I want yet."

"That's okay. We'll figure it out."

I let her words sink in, something loosening in my chest. It's nice to know that she can help lead me back to solid ground. That when push comes to shove, I'm not the only one carrying it anymore.

"I'll be out there, baby," she adds, ruffling my damp hair. "Rooting for you."

I close my eyes, holding on to that warmth. I have Quinn again, and she's more than enough to get me through this.

Chapter Thirty-Six

WARREN

The pool deck is almost unrecognizable. Faint underwater lights shimmer against the surface, reflections scattering across the walls in broken, restless patterns. Everywhere else, it's fully dark.

The meet is long over. I swam hard and pushed through the weight in my chest. In the water, it was easier to bury the panic scraping at the edges of my ribs.

Somehow, I swam better than I expected. The relays were sharp. I was clean off the blocks with strong finishes. We were fast enough to hold our lead as a collective. It wasn't enough to drown everything else out, but better than I thought I had in me.

Maybe the panic actually helped.

That sick rush of adrenaline hit me harder than usual, dragging me through each lap. My strokes were sharper, my turns tighter. My body, I think, was too wired to crash, and too wound up to give in to it.

Normally, a spiral like that would leave me spent, wrung out and empty for days. But this time, I worked through it to my advantage.

During the debrief with Voss, I barely absorbed a word he said. I stood there with damp hair plastered to my forehead, nodding along while he talked. There was something about my start being stronger than last week, something else about maintaining pace in the back half of the 200 free.

I couldn't focus because all I wanted to do was decompress, and then find my way back to Quinn.

The guys trickled out after that, some heading for their cars, others off to celebrate. Hawkins didn't even look my way, which felt like a mercy. Most of the parents were gone before that. The last of the noise faded almost an hour ago.

Now, I'm alone again, standing under the hot spray of the shower.

I can't stop thinking about my dad. How thin he looked and how glassy his eyes were. The way his fingers locked too tight around my wrist.

I haven't seen him strung out like that in years—not since before he went to Oakview. The sight of that kind of despair shook something loose inside me.

I get that Oakview isn't a prison. Residents are allowed to leave. But I never thought he'd want to—not badly enough to drag himself here, all the way to Dayton, just to interrupt my meet. He hasn't been to one since I was seven years old.

I've been sitting with that fact for hours. Letting it loop inside my head until it's worn paper-thin, standing in the shower for what feels like half the night. The heat has scalded my skin, and I was hoping it might burn away the memories, too.

But it hasn't. It never does.

I shut the water's off, and the locker room goes silent. I've done a few late swims before, usually in the practice pool. Twenty-four-hour gym access has its perks. But I've never been in the natatorium this late, and certainly not alone.

When I finally head out, still damp from the shower, hair curling against my temples, I don't expect anyone to still be here.

But, to my delighted surprise, I'm quickly proven wrong. I see an unmistakable flash of dark hair and the sleeves of Quinn's black hoodie. She's tucked into one of the middle rows of the bleachers, notebook propped against her knees, pen flicking steadily across the page. Her head's down.

I stop halfway across the deck to watch her.

She actually stayed here for me.

And more than that, she's been here all fucking day. Showed up before the first race and didn't leave. Not even after I rallied to finish my events. After the chaos and silence and sideways glances, she just . . . waited. Sat here alone in the quiet, scribbling away in her notebook.

To her, I was worth sticking around for.

Something twists inside me, low and tight. It shouldn't hit me this hard. Shouldn't feel like this—a sudden, swelling ache in my chest. Relief and regret tangled up in one.

I step closer, feet scuffing the tile.

She finally looks up. "Hey, you," she says quietly. "Everything okay?"

"Not really."

She closes her notebook, tucking her pen inside before setting it aside. "Didn't think so."

"You've been here for hours."

She shrugs. "Figured you might need someone to lean on."

I should say something else to her. Give her something honest, something that explains the mess I'm still wading through. But I can't. Not yet. Not tonight.

"I don't really wanna talk," I say gruffly.

She watches me with that calm, steady look of hers and decides not to push. I'm grateful for it now more than ever.

I don't know what I expected. For her to sigh and pack up her things, maybe, or offer some quiet reassurance before waving me off. Instead, she stands and steps down the bleachers, cutting across the empty pool deck until she's standing right in front of me.

She's close enough that I can feel the heat coming off her skin.

Close enough that I could lean forward and press my face into her hair.

I grab for her waist, curling my fingers beneath the hem of her shirt.

She breathes in sharply. Her hands lift, palms warm against my chest. "Warren?"

I kiss her before I can second-guess the part of me that's still scared to need her.

Her breath stumbles, but then she's kissing me back, her fingers sliding up to my shoulders. I drag her closer, pressing her back against the wall, one hand catching her jaw while the other slips lower, fingers digging into the curve of her hip.

The sound she makes—low and breathless—sinks into my skin.

I know how this should go. It should be slower. Sweeter. We're still wading through too much. My dad. Our past. All the things we've barely started to untangle.

But I need her in a way that feels desperate, quietly breaking open beneath the surface.

She's my something solid to hang on to. The steady point that grounds me when my thoughts won't stop spinning.

She must know, must feel it, too, because she doesn't hold back. Her fingers hook into the waistband of my sweats, pulling me flush against her. Her lips brush my throat, then lower, tracing a slow path across my neck.

I slide my hands beneath her shirt, palms dragging over her ribs, and she arches into my touch, pressing closer still, chasing the heat.

"Here?" she murmurs, breathless. "On the deck?"

"Yeah. I just . . . I need you."

Her gaze flicks past me, toward the locker room doors. "Are you sure everyone's gone?"

"Yeah, Quinny. I'm sure."

"Good."

Her fingers knot in my shirt, pulling me closer. It's like she's trying to hold me together, like she's stitching all the jagged little pieces back into place.

I press my mouth to her throat, feeling her shiver beneath me. Her skin's still warm from the natatorium air, her pulse racing against my lips.

"Warren, baby."

I push her shirt higher, fingers dragging across her stomach, and she exhales shakily, her head tipping back against the wall. She's letting me take whatever I need—her warmth, her steadiness —and God, do I need it.

Her hand slides down my arm, fingers curling into my wrist. Then she drags my hand to her thigh, nails digging faintly into my skin, guiding me exactly where she wants me.

When I finally slip my hand beneath the hem of her shorts, she makes this soft, breathless sound that goes straight to my head. And I kiss her again, rougher this time.

Her fingers hook into my waistband, knuckles pressing hard against my stomach. We're moving without thinking now—shirts tugged up, skin pressed together, each touch a little harder, a little more desperate.

I push her shorts down her thighs, fingers curling around her bare hip.

Her breath hitches, and her hand catches the back of my neck, dragging my mouth back to hers.

"*Quinn.*"

"I know," she whispers. "I know."

I press into her, hips rocking slow and steady, and her whole body melts against mine. She clings to me like I'm something safe, like I'm something worth holding onto. I want to be that for her.

I let myself drown in the feeling. The warmth of her skin, the sound of her breath, the faint hum of the pool filters humming in the background. Everything else—my dad, the way my chest still feels too tight, the sharp edge of tonight's panic—all of it blurs and quiets until there's only her.

Only us.

She arches beneath me, and when I sink into her, I swear I feel her everywhere. She's under my skin, wrapped around my ribs, filling every breath. Her body fits mine like it was made for this, made for me. Every thrust leaves her gasping, fingers clutching, hips rising to meet mine.

"God," she breathes, voice ragged.

"I've got you," I rasp.

I catch her jaw, kiss her hard and deep, swallowing the sounds she makes. She digs her fingers into my back. Maybe she's afraid I'll disappear. I move faster, harder, chasing the sharp edge that's been scraping at my ribs all night.

I bury myself in her, lost in the way she tightens around me, in the pressure and heat and the way she pulls me in like she can't get enough.

When I come, it hits me like a wave. A sudden and overwhelming release, pulling me under until I'm weightless. She follows a second later, her body tightening, her breath shattering in my ear.

We collapse, clinging together, slick with sweat, skin pressed to skin. Her thigh is draped over mine, my hand still wrapped around her hip because I can't quite let go. Her hair sticks to my neck. My heartbeat thuds against her chest.

"You okay?" she murmurs.

I swallow hard. "Yeah. I am now."

There's a pause. I can hear the soft echo of water lapping against the pool's edge, her breath still a little uneven against my chest.

Then she shifts slightly. "We didn't use anything."

I blink at the ceiling. "Yeah. I know."

"You always make sure."

"I usually do," I say quietly. "I wasn't thinking."

She lifts her head a little, searching my face. "Are you freaking out?"

"Not freaking out," I tell her. "Just . . . registering it. We'll be more careful next time."

We stay like that for a while, entangled, until the tile beneath us starts to cool. Once the adrenaline fades and the warmth begins to slip from our skin, Quinn sits up slowly, brushing her hair back from her face.

"Come on," she says. "Let's go in there."

I glance toward the pool. The water is lit by the soft overhead glow, shades of blue and silver and deep green. The surface still shimmers like fractured glass.

"Like this?" I ask, motioning to our bare skin.

She gives me a wicked smile. "Like this."

She stands, walks to the edge, and holds out her hand. I take it, threading our fingers together. We jump at the same time, crashing into the water in one smooth, reckless motion.

The cold hits hard, stealing my breath, but when I break the surface, I'm laughing.

So is she, her head tipped back, eyes closed, hair slicked against her cheeks.

Despite scrubbing myself under the hot spray of the shower for hours on end, only now do I feel clean. Renewed. Maybe I can let it all go, as long as she's here with me.

I swim over and pull her into my arms.

Her legs wrap around my waist, arms locking around my neck.

"Quinn," I murmur. "Promise me you'll stay?"

We both know I'm not just talking about tonight. Not just this weightless moment, the quiet hush of the water holding us steady. I mean all of it. What comes next. Whatever rough waters may still be ahead for us.

I need to know I won't lose this, won't lose *her*.

"I think," she whispers, "I made you up inside my head."

I blink, turning the words over in my mind. *Mad Girl's Love Song.*

"You're quoting Plath to me right now?" I ask, half a laugh caught in my throat.

She smiles and ducks her head.

"Though I appreciate the sentiment, it's probably not the time to hit me with existential despair. I'm a little too fragile for that."

"I'm here, Warren." She swallows hard, her fingers curling tighter around my shoulders. It's like she's trying to make me believe it, like she's trying to believe it herself. "I'm not going anywhere. I'll always be here."

I close my eyes. "Thank you, Quinny. That's all I need."

Chapter Thirty-Seven

QUINN

I STARE at myself in my bathroom mirror, twisting this way and that, trying to decide if I look . . . good. Good enough, I suppose. Appropriate, whatever that means.

My dress clings in all the right places. It's fitted through the waist, but there's a little movement at the hem that could read casual. The color's deep blue, almost black in this light, and I thought it looked elegant when I pulled it from my closet.

Now, I'm not so sure.

The neckline dips a little too low. My collarbone feels too sharp, my shoulders too narrow. The bruised shadow of an old pimple lingers stubbornly near my chin.

I press my hands down the front of the dress, trying to smooth the doubt away.

I want to look good. I want to look right. Most of all, I want to look like someone who belongs at Warren's side, someone his family won't immediately question.

I turn again, checking the back. The fabric skims my hips, clinging to the curve of my waist. My hair's loose in soft waves, but I can't tell if it looks styled or just messy. My makeup's fine—maybe too light. I should've done more with my eyes. Or my lips. Or . . . something.

I blow out a breath and slump against the edge of the sink.

God, this is ridiculous.

I'm overthinking again. Spiraling because this isn't just a

dinner to me. It's dinner with Warren's mother and stepfather. A dinner I was invited to at the last minute to get to know the family better after all this time.

They heard Warren's been seeing me again through the grapevine. Apparently, Liam's mom blabbed after she ran into Mrs. Mercer at Sycamore last week, and now, here we are.

I groan softly and drag a hand through my hair.

Alyssa's voice floats down the hall, laughing at some rom-com she's watching. I hesitate, then push away from the sink. Screw it. I need backup.

I find her in her room, stretched across her bed with her laptop propped on her knees.

"Hey," I say, hovering in the doorway. "Got a sec?"

"Always. What's up?"

I step inside and gesture helplessly at my dress. "I'm supposed to look like a person who has their life together. I feel like . . . this isn't it."

She narrows her eyes, assessing the damage. "I think you're half a bad shoe choice away from panic spiral. But we can fix this."

Fifteen minutes later, I'm standing in front of her full-length mirror, hair half pinned back in a way that softens my face. She's layered a cream cashmere wrap over my dress, and somehow, it pulls the whole look together.

"You look amazing."

I squint at my reflection. "I look . . . fine."

"You look hot, but in a respectable way," she insists, planting her hands on her hips. "Seriously, your ex is gonna forget how to speak when he sees you."

I smile faintly. "Not really my ex anymore, is he?"

"You nervous?"

I shrug. "I don't know. Maybe a little."

"It's understandable. Meeting the parents is kind of a big deal."

I hesitate, chewing my lip. There's so much I haven't told her.

About the whole history, about how I wasn't just some girl Warren dated—I was the girl who stole from his family. The one who lied. The one whose mistake made everything fall apart. And Warren's stepdad blamed him for it.

But I don't want to ruin this whole roommate slash friend thing. Not when they're just starting to really like me. Not when I'm just now letting myself believe I might actually deserve it.

"I've met them before," I admit. "A few times, actually."

"I guess that makes sense."

"Yeah." I exhale shakily. "But . . . the last time I was really in Warren's life, I made a mistake. And if they knew . . . I mean, if they found out, they wouldn't exactly be thrilled that we're back together."

She's quiet for a second. "Are you gonna tell them about it tonight?"

"I don't think I can."

"Hey," she says softly. "Whatever happens, you're still you. And they'd be lucky to have you in Warren's life. Try and remember that. You're a catch."

I let the words settle. I'm starting to believe them, little by little. Being back with Warren, opening up again—to new friends, new chances, new versions of myself—it's made something shift. I feel more like a person. More like I belong.

"Thank you for saying that."

She grins and squeezes my arm. "Jordan and I will be here when you get back if you want to debrief. You know, in case it's a whole thing."

"It's probably gonna be a whole thing," I mutter.

"Then we'll have wine," she says brightly. "But really, Quinn, good luck out there."

Two short knocks at the door jolt me upright. I glance at myself one last time in the mirror, adjusting my hair and smoothing the cashmere wrap over my shoulders. Then I blow Alyssa a kiss, grab my purse, and head for the door.

Warren stands on the other side in a black short-sleeved button-up, the top few buttons left undone just enough to reveal the silver chain against his chest. He's wearing light linen pants that hang low on his hips.

It shouldn't work. The shirt is a little too unbuttoned, the pants a little too laid-back. But somehow, he pulls it off. He looks unfairly good. If I didn't know better, I'd think he just stepped out of an upscale bar where he'd been laughing with friends over whiskey and soft lighting. All casual confidence, all heat and ease.

And then there's the way those stormy eyes move over me. They drag slowly down my frame before returning to my face, lingering there with a quiet steadiness.

"You look . . ." He trails off, mouth curving like he's searching for the right word. "Fucking perfect."

My face heats. "Yeah?"

"More than," he says softly, eyes still fixed on me.

"You look really sexy all dressed up, too."

His smile curves higher at the corner. "Don't get used to it."

"I wouldn't dare."

We're still standing in the doorway, not moving as we watch each other. There's a confession, I'd wager, waiting on the tip of our tongues. Three words. Eight letters. A truth we haven't spoken aloud in years.

I reach for my purse, and Warren steps back, waiting while I lock the door. When I turn, he's still watching me like I'm something precious, afraid I might bolt if he looks away too long. He should know by now he has me for good.

"You ready?" he asks quietly.

"Let's go."

We head down to the parking lot together. Warren doesn't say anything as he unlocks the car and steps ahead to open the passenger door for me.

"Such a gentleman," I tease, sliding in.

"Only 'cause you're worth it," he says, flashing a crooked smile.

He leans in to buckle my seatbelt, his fingers brushing my side. Then, before pulling back, he presses a soft, lingering kiss to the curve of my neck. The kind of kiss that says he doesn't want to rush a single second of this.

The quiet lingers as we pull out of the lot, the world slipping by in shadow and streetlights. As soon as we hit the main road, his hand finds mine.

I trace my thumb along his knuckles, following the faint calluses and lines. "So, tonight," I start. "Should I expect to be served a salad course by that weird man who always tried to talk me into playing pickleball?"

Warren huffs a laugh. "You mean Mr. Jennings? Who swore he had a 'mean forehand and an even meaner backhand'?"

"That's the one." I cringe, already imagining it. "God, I can't wait to rub elbows with all my old caddy clients. Nothing like eating a filet while pretending I didn't once haul their golf bag uphill in ninety-degree heat."

"We both know you greased the fuck out of those guys."

"I had to," I mutter. "Tips weren't gonna earn themselves."

He laughs, but the sound falters too fast. It drops into silence, and something sharp presses at the back of my mind. Something I think we've both been trying not to linger on.

"You think Preston Beckett's gonna be around?"

His jaw flexes. "For your sake, I hope not. But honestly, I wouldn't be surprised." His voice darkens. "I wonder if he talked to Daniel after I told him off. I never heard anything."

I blink, turning to look at him. "What do you mean?"

His fingers tense, thumb tapping idly against the steering

wheel. "When I picked up our paychecks, I sort of . . . snapped at him."

My brow furrows. "Sort of?"

"I heavily implied I was the one who popped the fucker's tire."

I let out a sharp breath. "Warren."

"Wasn't my best moment, but I hate the sleazebag. Seeing his face again made me see red."

I should be mad at him for stirring things up, but all I feel is this tight, aching gratitude. Warren's always been like this—fiercely loyal, always ready to fight for me, even when I've tried to handle things myself.

I shake my head. "You don't have to do that, you know. Stick your neck out for me like that."

"Yeah, actually," Warren says quietly. "I do."

I can't speak. The words get stuck somewhere in my throat, tangled up with everything else I don't know how to say. I'm grateful, of course I am. But I don't want him to get in trouble while protecting me, not again.

"Was he . . . alone?" I ask carefully.

Warren shrugs, eyes still on the road. "His same old buddies were there with him."

My stomach twists. I slouch lower in my seat, arms curling tighter across my chest.

Of course Davis and Mancini would still be hanging around. They told me they'd "take care of it," that they'd talk to Preston. And in a way, they had. He backed off, dropped the complaint with the club.

But that didn't mean they dropped him.

"Right," I say bitterly. "Of course they were."

For a second—one foolish, fleeting second—I thought maybe they'd actually cared. Thought maybe I mattered enough for them to draw a line somewhere. But that's not how it works. There's always a divide between the people wealthy enough to belong to the club and the ones who were only ever allowed near it to serve.

I should've known better than to mistake their fleeting attention for loyalty.

Dinner's been . . . nice. Better than I expected, at least.

Daniel and Willow are warm, relaxed in a way that makes the whole thing feel less like an intimidating family dinner and more like an overdue catch-up. There's a bottle of wine on the table, Willow's hand curled loosely around her glass as she tells a story about their latest trip to Charleston.

Daniel chuckles along, adding the occasional detail or dry commentary. It's easy to see where Warren learned how to read a room. He knows when to chime in with a sharp one-liner and when to sit back and let everyone else take the lead.

I've always liked his mom. She's kind and joyful, grateful for the small things. I forgot how easy she makes it to relax. Around her, there's never this sense of being evaluated or measured. I don't have to watch what I say.

I think it comes from having lived many different lives. From having an unworthy, unhealthy partner and scraping by to make ends meet. That kind of thing gives you character, but it also makes you understand that people aren't perfect.

"So, Quinn," Willow says, turning her attention to me. "What's been keeping you busy this semester?"

I take a small sip of wine and smile. "Mostly drowning in essays. I'm in a really tough lit seminar this term."

Willow laughs. "You're an English major?"

"Guilty as charged."

"Careful," Daniel says with a teasing look in Warren's direction. "Writers are always trouble."

Warren's hand finds my knee beneath the table. "I know. That's why I like her."

We talk about the past a little after that. Stories about Sycamore and old memories from the so-called glory days. Daniel mentions his twin daughters, who are in the middle of their sophomore year of high school.

I never did have the chance to meet Chloe and Claire, but the way he talks about them is so sweet. I'm sure they're lovely girls.

"Miracle they've stayed out of trouble so far," Daniel says. It's loving but laced with that particular exasperation only a father can get away with. "We were sure they'd give us hell. Two teen girls under one roof? We braced for chaos."

"We've been very lucky with all three of our kids," Willow adds, shooting Warren a pointed, teasing look. "You've always been a stickler for following the rules. Aside from a minor blip here and there. Freshman year really threw us for a loop."

I freeze, my fingers tightening around my fork. Freshman year. Eighteen and taking the fall for his girlfriend without ever once telling them the truth.

Warren just laughs under his breath. "Yeah, well. We all make mistakes."

"Some of us more spectacularly than others," Daniel jokes.

I force a smile, but my chest feels tight. The air feels too warm, the room suddenly too small. I know his parents don't expect perfection, but maybe they do expect their son's girlfriend not to be a lying, stealing, no-good thief.

"Excuse me," I murmur, already rising from my chair. "I'll be right back."

Without waiting for a response, I slip out of the dining room and down the hall, barely registering the framed pictures lining the walls—vacation shots and old family photos. I keep walking until I find one of the break rooms near the back.

I sink into an old leather armchair and press my palms to my face, forcing a breath.

God, I should've said something to them years ago. I could've come back and told Daniel the truth before Warren ever had to take the blame for me.

"Quinn?"

I look up and find Warren in the doorway. He looks panic-stricken, and I wonder, briefly, if he assumed I was having an asthma attack. But it's not the tightening in my lungs that's stopping the air; it's guilt. Old and heavy, the kind that never quite lets go.

He steps inside and closes the door softly behind him. "You okay?"

"I'm fine," I lie, my hands still covering most of my face. "Just needed a second."

He doesn't believe me. I can see it in the way his eyes narrow, sharp with concern. He crosses the room, crouching down in front of me so we're at eye level.

"What's going on with you?"

"I should tell them, shouldn't I?" I ask quietly. "About what I did."

Warren places a firm hand on my knee. He doesn't flinch or look away.

"I know they've forgiven you, but I can't just sit there like nothing happened. I stole from Daniel, and they blamed you for it. They still do. That's not fair. They should know the truth."

"They don't need to know," he says softly. "Not anymore."

"But—"

"Quinn." His voice sharpens with certainty. "That's not going to fix anything. It'll only dig up something they already let go of." His fingers tighten slightly around my knee. "Besides, I have everything I want right here. I have you. I'm not losing that just so you can carry the guilt instead."

"I should be carrying it," I whisper.

"It's done now." His hand slips up to my face, fingers curling gently at my jaw. "Let's leave the bad where it belongs and take the good with us. Okay?"

I lean into his touch, pressing my cheek against his palm. His thumb traces along my skin, light and slow, and I let my eyes close. I let myself believe what he's saying.

"Okay," I murmur.

His forehead touches mine, his breath warm against my face.

"I can't let the girl that I love worry about something that's already behind us."

My eyes snap open. "What did you say?"

His fingers flex gently along my jaw. "I said I love you. You know that, right?"

I blink hard, my breath catching somewhere between my ribs and my throat. "I thought . . ." I shake my head. "I mean, yeah. I hoped."

"Always," Warren says, like it's a truth he never had to question. "I've loved you since I was eighteen, Quinn. Since you let me read your notebook in the break room and tried to act like it wasn't a big deal. Since you kissed me in the cart garage and laughed when I nearly tripped trying to leave."

"I love you, too. I never stopped."

"I know." His thumb brushes softly across my cheek. "I know."

It feels good, knowing that we both held on. That even after everything, we're still here. Still choosing this. Still choosing each other. If we hadn't come back together, I think I could have gone my whole life missing him.

Now, I don't know how I'm supposed to step back into that dining room without my heart trying to climb out of my chest.

"You ready to go back out there?"

"Not really," I mumble.

He laughs quietly and presses a kiss to my hair. "Yeah, me neither."

I close my eyes for a moment longer, breathing him in. Then I sit up, and his hand finds mine again. It's the steady, grounding force I need to get me through this.

"We've got this," he says, and somehow, I know we do.

Chapter Thirty-Eight

QUINN

Warren's room is calmer than mine. No chaotic piles of books or scattered notes threatening to avalanche at any moment. That's why I'm here now, trying to work instead of getting buried under my own mess.

My papers are spread in loose clusters across his desk, laptop blinking at me from the corner, waiting for me to get my act together. The coffee I brought over more than an hour ago sits untouched by the window, long gone cold.

I'm slumped in his desk chair, chin resting in my hand, pen tapping an uneven rhythm against my notebook. Every so often, I manage to write a word, stare at it like it betrayed me, then scratch it out until the page looks worse than when I started.

"You know," Warren says lazily from his bed, one arm thrown over his head as he scrolls his phone. "You could just submit that one about the train."

I exhale sharply, flick my pen across the page once more, and toss it aside. "I'm not submitting that one."

"Why not?"

"Because it's depressing as hell, for one."

"That's what makes it good," he argues. "I mean, your main character dies at the end, and it still felt . . . strangely hopeful. Bittersweet, at the very least."

"Right," I say dryly. "Totally what the judges are looking for."

"You're just overthinking it." He rolls off his bed, crossing the room until he's standing behind my chair. "You put too much pressure on yourself."

"I just want it to be good."

"It is good." His hands settle on my shoulders, his thumbs brushing along the curve of my neck. "You're not the same writer you were when you lost that first contest."

I let out a breathy laugh. "Wow. Thanks for the reminder."

He squeezes my shoulders. "I'm serious. You're better now. Besides, you had bad luck last time. Or karmic intervention. I mean, you were up against some kid who wrote about . . . what was it again?"

"Her mom's garden." I huff. "The whole thing was a metaphor for grief. And the pacing was perfect. And her prose—God, Warren, she made me want to quit writing altogether."

"Yeah, well," he says lightly, "she probably peaked in middle school."

I snort. "I can't believe you're talking shit about a little girl."

"I'm just saying, I know a thing or two about burning bright too early. Junior champ and all."

"You did not burn out. You still have your best years ahead of you."

He grins and drops a kiss to the side of my head.

I hum softly, letting my eyes close, relishing it. His hands are still on my shoulders, warmth soaking through the fabric of my shirt. The tension that's been riding my muscles all morning finally starts to ease.

"You have to submit *something*," Warren says quietly.

"I don't know."

"I do."

"What if I lose again?"

"Then you lose again." He steps around the chair until he's facing me. "But at least you'll know you tried."

I study him, my eyes narrowing. He's serious about this. No

teasing grin or smart remark. He's looking at me like I'm capable of more than I believe I am. Like I'm someone worth betting on, and he'd wager it all so long as I bet on myself, too.

"I'll think about it," I say finally.

"Mmm-hmm."

His gaze flicks up toward the shelf above my head, and something shifts in his face.

Curious, I turn and reach for the book he's looking at. It's thick, the cover soft with wear and the corners bent in enough to suggest it's been read again and again. The spine is cracked and sun-faded, the title stamped in silver foil worn down to a soft shimmer: *Selected Poems of Emily Dickinson*.

Something about it stops me. Not just the name of the author, though obviously, I know her well. It's the book itself. I've seen this exact copy before. Propped in the corner of his desk. Page-side down beside his glove box. Once, half tucked into his gym bag, the edge of a dog-eared page peeking out.

"Hey," Warren says quickly, stepping closer. "Don't—"

I flip it open, skimming past the table of contents. The pages are worn, too, corners bent, almost every poem marked up with underlines and notes in that sharp, slanted handwriting of his. Some are so full of scribbled comments I can barely make out the text.

"You . . . you've actually been studying this? Like, full-on annotating?"

He snatches the book from my hands. "Don't make a thing of it."

"Warren, baby," I say softly, still staring at the pages. "You didn't just search up these quotes. You memorized them. You . . . you did all this for me?"

His fingers flex. "I just wanted to get it right," he mutters.

And he did. He got it right every single time. Not just the words but the feeling. The delivery. He always knew when I needed to hear those lines—when I needed to be reminded that hope was a thing with feathers or that paradise could fit inside my palm.

He always knew when to soften his voice, when to make me laugh. And I thought it was instinct or something. I thought he was winging it, that he just had some uncanny sense of what I needed to hear.

But no. He worked for it. He cared enough to sit down with this book, to underline the parts that made him think of me, to scribble thoughts in the margins. He was trying to crack some impossible code, and he managed it.

He's always been like that. Intentional. Always thinking two steps ahead. Even when I was too stubborn or scared to see it.

God, I love him. I love him so much I can't even breathe for a second.

I step forward and press my mouth to his. He kisses me back, his arm curling tight around my waist, hand curling into my hair. When we break apart, I can still feel his breath against my lips.

"Okay, I'll submit something for the contest," I tell him. "If you do something brave for me, too."

"You mean like visiting my dad at Oakview after he embarrassed the shit out of me?" he deadpans. "Shouted incoherent nonsense at a meet in front of my entire team, our rivals, and my coach."

I laugh because I know he's half joking. But I also know he's right. That *is* brave.

We're heading to Oakview in an hour, and Warren's been quietly gearing up for it all day, bracing for whatever version of his dad is waiting on the other side of that visit. And that's more than just brave—it's generous. It's gutsy. It's Warren.

"Something else," I say. "Something more for me."

"You want me to come train at Emberline?"

"Ugh, no." I wrinkle my nose. "Boxing's my thing, and you wouldn't be any good at it anyway."

I love it there. The rhythm, the focus it demands. The sport has become part of my routine in a way I never saw coming. It's one of the only places that quiets my mind. Along with the anxiety medication I started last month, Emberline gives me mental clarity.

I never pictured myself as the kind of person who enjoys sweating through drills or pushing past exhaustion, but here I am. I've gotten stronger. I *feel* stronger. And after everything, that matters more than I can explain.

When Gage got fired, it rattled things for a bit. Sometimes I still wonder what happened to him. If he found a new gym, if he's still running his mouth somewhere. But not enough to go looking.

Marcus has stepped in here and there, offering advice when he can. He's got his hands full running the place, so most days, I'm on my own. But I'm figuring it out, getting better bit by bit.

And honestly, I like it that way. I like knowing this space is mine. Something I've built that grounds me. Not for anyone else's approval or for attention. It's something I'm doing solely for myself.

"You want me to track down Gage?"

I glance up, surprised. Despite his jealousy, his misplaced distaste, he's offering to help anyway. That feels generous in a way I didn't expect. But more than that, it feels like trust. He's trying—really trying—to show me he believes in what we have.

"You'd do that? I thought you didn't like him."

He shrugs. "I don't. But I know he was helping you."

"That's oddly sweet, but no." I spin around, planting my hands on my hips. "And enough with the guessing games. My actual proposal is that you get a tattoo, and I want to pick it out for you."

"Oh God, what are you thinking?" he asks dryly. "A butterfly on my lower back?"

"As hot as you'd look with a tramp stamp, I was actually thinking about something more basic. Like . . . a quote." I trace the skin of his forearm, just above his wrist. "How about, '*I dwell in Possibility*.'"

"Done," he says. Not even a second of hesitation. "I'll get the tattoo if you submit for the contest."

"Wait . . . seriously?"

"Seriously."

Something flutters low in my chest—shock, maybe, but something warmer, too. I didn't expect him to agree so fast, but God, I think I'm a little giddy about it. A tattoo would mean something lasting. Something permanent.

We'd be tied together forever in this quiet, certain way.

"Deal," I say, smiling against his mouth as he kisses me again.

There are a few scattered cars and a woman pacing by the entrance of Oakview.

Warren parks at the far end, engine idling much longer than necessary. He taps his fingers on the steering wheel, staring straight ahead. I can feel the tension rolling off him in harsh, unrelenting waves.

They told him his dad was still agitated but starting to settle again. Apparently, it takes time for him to float back down to earth after a binge. The staff wasn't sure how he'd gotten his hands on anything—alcohol, maybe something stronger—but once he left the facility, it was out of their control.

He must've slipped past them during quiet hours, ducked by the front desk when no one was watching closely enough. According to Warren, he's always been good at finding his way through the cracks.

When they called to say his dad was back in their care, Warren didn't ask them for details. He didn't press for answers. He listened closely, then let the phone drop to the mattress beside him and stared at the ceiling. I think he was waiting for something else to drop.

For the Big Bad to come next and claim up everything good in his life.

He figured his dad had relapsed. But when the staff ran tests, they didn't find anything in his system. No drugs, anyway. Just alcohol, exhaustion, and a string of impulsive choices that spiraled faster than anyone could catch.

"I can go in alone," he says finally, voice low. "If you want to wait out here."

I reach across the console to find his hand. "Nope, I'm coming in with you."

He exhales, eyes still on the building. "I don't know how this is gonna go."

"Doesn't matter. I'm still coming with you."

He finally looks at me, and I don't know what he sees, but something in his expression shifts. Strengthens a little. His fingers tighten, his shoulders pull back. He's deemed himself prepared.

"Okay," he murmurs.

We step out of the car and cross the lot together. Warren's hand stays in mine, his grip never faltering, and I match his pace. The doors slide open for us. Inside, the air is stale and cold.

We pause past the entryway and wait. I squeeze his hand once. He squeezes back.

He's learned to lean on me, to trust that I won't let go when things get hard. And I've learned to lean back, to trust him just the same. We're not perfect, but we're better now. We know how to stay when things get messy, and we know how to savor it when things are good.

"I'm right here," I whisper.

"I know," Warren says.

And then we step forward, hand in hand, into whatever comes next.

Epilogue

WARREN

Maggie's Diner is mostly empty tonight. There are a few scattered tables and a jukebox in the corner that's humming faintly. The dinner rush is over, but the faint scent of grilled chicken still lingers in the air.

I reach for my glass, turning it slowly in my hand. The ice clinks, water tracing lazy lines down the sides. Across from me, Quinn's twirling her fork in what's left of her pasta, barely eating.

I presume it's because she's too busy being happy. Beaming with the kind of smile that starts slow and stretches wide until her whole face is glowing. It's radiant.

I can't seem to stop staring at her.

"You're still floating a little," I say. "Still grinning, too."

"Am I?"

"Yeah, like a little weirdo."

"I'm just happy," she says with a half-shrug. "I think I've earned it."

She has. Quinn doesn't just look lighter; she *feels* it. The weight she used to carry around, the tension that clung to her like armor, it's . . . softer now. She's figured out how to breathe easily again.

"You should be happy," I say. "Winning the Blackthorn Prize is a big deal."

She worked for it. Bled for it, in her own quiet way. I know because I watched her do it.

She stretched herself thin to finish a brand-new short story. Wrote a perfect, tight ten thousand words about a girl who returns to her coastal hometown to clean out her grandmother's house, only to find a salt-stained journal filled with entries she doesn't remember writing—entries dated weeks after she supposedly left.

It was a story with teeth, a little bit horror-edged and aching.

On top of the writing, the rewrites, and the gnawing self-doubt, she also picked up a few weekend shifts at Sycamore to cover the submission fee. Bar backing, not caddying, so she could avoid running into the three stooges entirely.

I offered to spot her, but she waved me off, said she wanted to pay for it herself. That it mattered more that way.

After the contest, she finally plucked up the courage to talk to her parents about the issues she's been having her whole life. About how it felt growing up a little off-center, the third wheel in her own family.

And for once, they listened. They asked questions. They even framed the letter she got from the contest committee—her first-place award—and hung it up in the living room beside the many, many pictures of Wesley.

"I'm not just happy because of the contest or because my parents finally saw me as more than background noise. I mean, yeah, it's all great stuff. But I'm also just so happy because you made it."

What she means is that I made it to Nationals. Placed ninth in the prelims. The kind of finish that didn't just mark the end of the season; it rewrote how I'll remember it entirely.

"You're proud of me?" I ask, half-joking.

"Of course I am." She leans forward, elbows on the table. "You were incredible out there, Warren. B-class cut or not, you swam your ass off this season. You earned it."

I huff a laugh, staring down at my glass. "I barely scraped by. Qualified last-minute."

"And then placed ninth," she points out. "Ninth, Warren. Out of everyone."

"I still didn't make the finals."

"You made it to Nationals, though," she counters, voice firm. "And you didn't just make it, you held your own. That's huge."

I let the words sink in. She's right, of course. That last B-class cut came late in the season, later than it should have. I hit my time at the conference championship meet and pulled my fastest 200 free split all year.

I made it just in time to sneak into Nationals. Just in time to squeak by with a finish that fell just short of the final heat.

It wasn't enough to qualify for finals, but it did help me believe I belonged there. It was proof to myself that I was good enough. I swam among the best collegiate swimmers in the country, and that's worth something.

I'm not going pro. I know that. No offers came afterward, and honestly, I'm okay with it. I'm heading into grad school next year. I'll stick with kinesiology and pursue a career in sports performance and rehab.

I've already accepted a spot in Dayton's program, and I'll be working with the swim team, too. It's an assistant position that pays modestly but keeps me in the pool. Voss is excited to have me on board, and I'm grateful for the trust.

It feels right. The right way to stay close to the water and everything I've worked so hard for.

"I'm proud of you too, you know," I say.

Quinn's smile falters, but she can't hide from me. I know she's proud of herself, too. She carries herself differently now. She's someone who finally stopped apologizing for taking up space, and I love that I've been there to witness that.

"I still can't believe you're writing a novel," I say.

"I can't believe it, either. But I figured . . . why not? After the last contest, I finally remembered what it felt like to love writing again." She pauses, tucking her hair behind her ear. "And I don't know . . . I think I'm ready to try for something bigger."

"You should be," I say. "You're the best writer I know."

She snorts. "How many writers do you know?"

"Just one," I admit. "But she's still the fucking best."

Quinn rolls her eyes, but she's smiling again. She reaches across the table, her fingers finding my arm and tracing the ink just above my wrist. Her thumb glides over the words—*I dwell in Possibility*—soft and lingering, reading them through her fingertips.

"I can't believe you actually went through with it."

I turn my wrist under her hand and catch her fingers in mine. "You knew what you were doing when you made the suggestion."

She laughs quietly, then leans down and presses her mouth to my wrist, her lips brushing the ink. To her, it's something sacred. The thought makes me ache in that deep, quiet way that feels like being cracked open and put back together all at once.

I don't know what I expected when we found our way back to each other. I don't know if I thought it would feel like this. So steady and certain and full of soft, stubborn hope.

"I love you, Quinny."

She lifts her head, her eyes warm and sure. "I know," she says. "I love you, too."

God, if it doesn't feel just as good to hear it now as it did the very first time. Back when we were eighteen, when we were still figuring ourselves out. Just two headstrong kids fumbling through something almost too big to name.

And now, it feels inevitable, like a path we mapped out in the dark and still found our way back to. We just turned a corner, I think, kept walking, and then realized we were already home.

Acknowledgments

Thank you to my husband for the support, the toddler wrangling, and the quiet understanding of how this all works. And to my daughter, who somehow makes me laugh even when I'm running on fumes.

Mom, I appreciate you more than I say. Thanks for always showing up.

To my swim beta readers, Ana and Arley, thank you for fact-checking the technical stuff and keeping Warren honest in the water. Megan, my forever beta, thank you for your sharp eye, thoughtful notes, and steady encouragement across every book.

To my writer friends and real-life friends, thanks for the check-ins, the brainstorms, and for always keeping it honest.

Sandra, thank you for editing seven books and a novelette with me now. Your feedback always makes the work sharper.

To Books and Moods, thank you for nailing another gorgeous cover. And to my character artists, I'm so grateful for your talent and vision.

To the bloggers, influencers, and early readers who started hyping this book long before it released, thank you for the posts, the comments, and the endless enthusiasm.

And to the readers who've followed the Coastal Rivals series all the way here, thank you for sticking with it. I'm lucky to tell these stories, and even luckier that you're still reading.

BYTE

BLACKWINGS
CROFTRIDGE

TEAGAN
BROOKS

BYTE

BLACKWINGS MC - CROFTRIDGE
BOOK ONE

TEAGAN BROOKS

Adult Content Warning: For ages 18 years old and older due to graphic sexual content, explicit language, and violence.

ISBN: 978-1-951704-25-4

BLURB

Gabby

When my sister and brother-in-law agreed to chaperone a school trip to another country for my niece and nephew, I assured them I'd be okay while they were gone. I'd been living on my own in a different city since I started college several years ago. I was in the middle of my last semester of school and couldn't take the time off to go with them. My sister gave me her friend's phone number and told me to call him if I needed anything while they were gone. I agreed to her request and took his number, thinking I'd never need to use it. A few days later, when I heard someone's footsteps in my house, I hid in my closet and called him immediately.

Byte

When Keegan asked me to listen out for her younger sister while she and Shaker were out of town, I happily

agreed. Gabby had never been a problem. She worked as a nurse at the hospital in Cedar Valley and was in school to become a nurse practitioner. She was too busy to get into trouble. I assumed I wouldn't hear from her at all during the two weeks they would be gone. When Gabby called me to tell me she was hiding in her bedroom because someone was in her house, I couldn't get to her fast enough. Neither one of us knew that one phone call would bring secrets to light and change both of our lives forever.

ACKNOWLEDGMENTS

Cover Designer: CT Cover Creations

Proofreading and Editing: Tina Workman at Romance Revisions

CHARACTER LIST

- Phoenix Black - Blackwings MC President
- Badger Marshall - Aaron - Blackwings MC Vice President
- Duke Jackson - John - Blackwings MC Sergeant at Arms
- Carbon Walker - Chase - Blackwings MC Enforcer
- Shaker Marks - Jacob - Blackwings MC Road Captain
- Dash Lawson - Reed - Blackwings MC Treasurer
- Byte Fuller - Michael - Blackwings MC Tech Support
- Patch Vaughn - Blackwings MC Member and Physician
- Ranger Norris - Noah - Blackwings MC Original Member
- Edge - Jamie - Blackwings MC Member

- Ink - Isaac - Blackwings MC Member
- Dice - Grady - Blackwings MC Member
- Diesel Jackson - James - Blackwings MC Member - Son of Duke and Reese
- Flint Black - Blackwings MC Member - Son of Phoenix and Annabelle; Twin brother of Blaze Black
- Blaze Black - Daughter of Phoenix and Annabelle; Twin sister of Flint Black
- Annabelle Black - Phoenix's wife; Mother of Ember, Coal, Nathan, Flint, and Blaze
- Ember Lawson - Dash's wife; Daughter of Phoenix and Annabelle
- Raven Lawson - Daughter of Dash and Ember
- Harper Walker - Carbon's wife; Duke's sister; Mother of Harlow Walker; Licensed Clinical Therapist
- Harlow Walker - Daughter of Carbon and Harper
- Jake Marks - Son of Shaker and Keegan
- Quincy Marks - Daughter of Shaker and Keegan
- Gabriella Marks - Keegan's half sister; adopted by Keegan and Shaker
- Jacquelyn Marks - Shaker's mother
- Ronan Pierce - Jacquelyn's husband; Shaker's stepfather
- Irene - Byte's friend; Owns diner in Cedar Valley

- Luke Johnson - FBI Agent
- Tina Rivera - Attorney for the Blackwings MC
- Lawrence Hastings - Keegan's stepfather; Gabby's father

CONTENTS

PROLOGUE

BYTE

My mother and her husband were fighting again. It wasn't surprising. They argued all the time, but it was always worse on the weekends. As soon as they got home from work on Fridays, they started drinking, and then they would spend the next few hours arguing until one or both of them passed out.

I'd gotten used to it and knew to stay in my room and out of their way. I didn't like it, but I tried to make the best of the situation by drowning them out with headphones and using the time to learn everything I could about computers. It took me several months to save up enough money to buy a laptop, and I had every intention of using it to get as far away from my toxic environment as possible.

It didn't take me long to learn how to utilize my skills to make money. I started out with small jobs, like hacking into the school's computer system and changing a few grades for paying students. Next, I discovered the

art of forging IDs, which proved to be a more lucrative endeavor.

I was in the middle of creating a new ID for my most recent customer when I heard a loud noise, despite the music blaring in my ears. I removed my headphones and listened for another sound, but the house was eerily silent. I assumed I had been working longer than I thought and my parents had crashed for the night, but after a quick glance at the time, I realized it was far too early for that.

I started to put my headphones back on and resume my work, but something told me to go see what was going on. I pushed back from my desk and opened the door to my room, completely unprepared for what I saw when I looked into the hallway. My stepfather was standing at the top of the stairs, staring down at something with a look of disbelief on his face. I opened my mouth to ask what he was doing, but quickly shut it when I noticed the large knife he was grasping in his hand.

I took a few steps closer and saw my mother lying haphazardly at the bottom of the stairs. I inadvertently gasped at the sight, alerting my stepfather to my presence. He turned toward me with an evil smile on his face and raised the knife. "Your turn."

I didn't stop to think; I just reacted. With one fluid movement, I kicked my leg out and swept his feet out from under him, causing him to fall backward and tumble down the stairs.

After he reached the bottom, I continued to stand at

the top, staring down at him in disbelief, exactly like he'd been doing only moments earlier.

I'm not sure how long I stood there watching for any signs of life before I snapped out of my shock. Quickly descending the stairs, I glanced between the two of them, unsure of which one to check first. The decision was made for me when Glenn let out a weak groan. He was clearly still alive, and I couldn't let that be.

A flicker of light reflecting off the metal caught my attention when he tried to move his arm. He was still holding the knife. Once again, I didn't hesitate or stop to consider the possible ramifications of my actions. I carefully lifted the hand holding the knife and plunged it into the center of his abdomen. His eyes shot open, and he opened his mouth to speak, but the words died on his lips as his body went slack.

I wasn't one hundred percent sure he was dead, so I stepped over my mother's body and crouched down on the far side of her to check for a pulse. Given the way her body was unnaturally twisted, I wasn't surprised when I didn't feel one.

I stood and stared at Glenn. I really didn't want to check him, but I couldn't leave the job unfinished. He never liked me, and he destroyed my mother by turning her into an abusive alcoholic, just like him. There was no way I was going to let him live and risk going to prison for attempted murder. While my initial actions were in self-defense, I doubted anyone would believe me. Especially if Glenn survived. He was good at manipulating situations to his advantage.

Inhaling deeply, I squatted beside him and gently

pressed my fingers against the pulse point in his neck. The relief I felt at the absence of his heartbeat was almost overwhelming. I'd done it. I was finally free.

Even though I was planning on leaving and had been preparing for that eventuality for months, I never anticipated it happening the way it did. My original plans didn't involve death and murder, but I couldn't undo what was done and had to move forward with the hand I was dealt.

Adrenaline soon kicked in, and I had to remind myself frequently that there was no need to rush. No one would start looking for either of my parents until Monday morning, when they would expect them to show up for work. I had plenty of time to gather what I needed and disappear without a trace.

I didn't take much from the house—the cash my mother kept hidden from her husband, a few pieces of jewelry I could pawn if needed, my laptop, the money I'd saved, several changes of clothes, and most importantly, my new ID.

With my backpack stuffed so full it almost wouldn't zip, I walked to the bus station the next morning and used the ID I was working on to buy a ticket to the closest large city. From there, I used my new ID to purchase a ticket to a place I'd randomly chosen—Cedar Valley, TN.

It took almost twenty-four hours to get there, and I was exhausted once I arrived. The first thing I did was find somewhere to have breakfast, which ended up being a locally-owned diner right down the street from the bus station. I ordered enough food to feed three people and

drank more coffee in one sitting than I ever had before. I'm not sure if it was my ravenous appetite or my disheveled appearance, but the waitress, who happened to be the owner, offered me a job. I took it but explained that I had just arrived in town and needed a day or two to get my affairs in order. Once again, she saved me a lot of time and trouble by telling me about a trailer she had available for rent. She said I could move in immediately. I jumped on the opportunity and moved in that same day. Even though I slept on the floor using my backpack as a pillow, that first night in my new place was the happiest I'd been in a long time.

1

GABBY

"I really wish you could go with us," my sister said into the phone.

"I do, too, but there was no way I could miss two weeks of school." I was in the middle of my last semester of school to become a nurse practitioner. Between classes, clinicals, and work, I had little to no free time.

"I know, and I understand. I just hate leaving you here when we're going to be so far away."

I laughed. "Keegan, I'll be fine. We don't even live in the same city."

"Cedar Valley is only thirty minutes away. Scotland is a different story," she reminded me. My niece and nephew were going on a school trip to Scotland for two weeks, and my sister, her husband, and my grandfather were attending as chaperones. While it was going to be the first time they went on a trip without me, I think she was more worried about it than I was. Sure, I was

disappointed about not being able to go, but it couldn't be helped.

"I know, but it's not like you're leaving me here all alone. The club's here. I can call any one of them for help if something happens."

"Promise you will?"

"Of course," I promised. "But nothing's going to happen. Between school and work, I don't have time to get into trouble."

"I can't wait for you to be finished."

"Me, too, Sissy," I said honestly. I was more than ready to start the next phase of my life. I was so close, but it felt like time was crawling at a snail's pace.

"It'll be here before you know it," she reassured me.

"So will your flight. Have you finished packing?" I asked, hoping to take the focus off of me.

"Are you kidding?" she asked with a laugh. "I still have a load of clothes waiting to be dried. Meanwhile, I don't think Jake has even started packing, and Quincy has repacked three times trying to get everything in one suitcase while also meeting the weight requirements."

"What about Jacob and Papa?"

She snorted. "They've been ready to go since this morning. And they've been getting in the way ever since."

I laughed. "Sounds like them."

"Oh, I need to go; I just heard the dryer. I'll call you once we get to the hotel. It will take us around twenty-four hours to get there."

"Okay. Be careful and enjoy your trip."

"I'll try. You be careful, too. Love you."

"I will. Love you, too, Sissy."

Even though Keegan was my sister, technically my half sister, she'd adopted me when I was five years old and had always been more like a mother to me. Our mother died while giving birth to me. Keegan was in college at the time, leaving me to be raised by my father, a corrupt politician. I don't remember the first few years of my life, which I count as a blessing, but I have a few memories of life with my biological father, and none of them are warm and fuzzy. He was a cold and calculating man whose only use for me was to boost his political career.

I vaguely remembered being sent away to a boarding school for a brief period before a woman showed up claiming to be my grandmother and whisked me away to live with Keegan. At the time, I didn't know that my father had been arrested for several crimes, including human trafficking, and Keegan worked with the FBI to put him behind bars for life in exchange for custody of me. I was just happy to be with her, her husband, Jacob, and my two new grandparents—Keegan's grandfather, Papa, and Jacob's mother, Gigi. A few years later, my family grew when Gigi married her bodyguard, who became Papa Ronan, and then again when Keegan and Jacob had children—Jake and Quincy.

The sound of a text message pulled me back to the present.

Byte: Your sister asked me to text you so my contact info would be handy in case you need anything. I'll be around. Don't hesitate to call if something comes up.

I shook my head and smiled. My sister was a worrier, but it didn't bother me. She had gone out of her way to make sure I had a happy life, and I would be forever grateful for her.

Gabby: Thanks, Byte. I appreciate it, but I'm sure I'll be fine.

Even though Byte was a member of the Blackwings MC like Jacob and Papa, I always considered him more Keegan's friend than Jacob's. I didn't know him very well since I only saw him at club functions, but he seemed like a nice guy. Then again, all the Blackwings members were nice guys.

I glanced at the time and sighed. I had just enough time to shower and eat dinner before I needed to be in bed. I had to work a twelve-hour shift at the hospital the next day, and I learned early on that a good night's sleep was the key to making it through such a long day.

* * *

I WAS EXHAUSTED WHEN I GOT HOME AFTER ALMOST fourteen hours on my feet. It was nothing new. Twelve-hour shifts were rarely, if ever, twelve hours. I don't know why, but it seemed like most emergencies happened right before or during shift change. I was

doing my final round on my patients when a family member stepped out into the hallway screaming for help. The patient wasn't one of mine, but I was there, so I went to help. I walked into the room to find the patient completely non-responsive. I called a code, started resuscitation efforts, and waited for the code team to arrive. Forty-five minutes later, the patient had been transferred to the ICU, and I had thirty minutes of paperwork to complete before I could leave.

The thing that really pissed me off was that the patient's primary nurse clocked out and went home while all of this was happening. It was those kinds of moments that really made me yearn for the day I finished school. Or, more specifically, the day I passed the exam to become a nurse practitioner.

It wasn't that I hated my job, per se. I just didn't like a few of the people I worked with. And since a lot of us worked a set schedule, I frequently worked with the handful I didn't care for. But I wouldn't have to be there much longer. I reminded myself of that every day.

I trudged to my room and dropped my bags on the floor beside my bed. I gave it a longing look before I turned and forced myself to walk to the bathroom. I desperately needed a shower, but I really wanted to fall face-first into my mattress and go to sleep.

"Your clothes are covered in germs and who knows what else," I told myself. Working at the hospital often left me feeling like a walking biohazard by the end of my shift. So, I begrudgingly stripped off my clothes and took a quick shower.

While I was getting dressed, I heard the sound of a

floorboard creaking in the living room. My heart began to race as adrenaline rushed through me. Someone was in the house, and no one should have been in the house except me.

As quickly and as quietly as I could, I picked up my cell phone and tiptoed to my closet. Carefully opening the secret door, I stepped inside the small space and slid the door back into place before securing the locks. It wasn't exactly a panic room. It was more of a top-of-the-line hiding spot. When my brother-in-law insisted on adding it to my closet when I first moved into the house, I thought he was being his usual overprotective self. As I used it to hide from an intruder, I'd never been more grateful.

With shaking hands, I made sure my phone was silenced and placed a call to Byte.

"Hey Gab—" he started.

I cut him off with a harsh whisper. "Someone's in my house."

"Are you in the safe room?" he asked.

"Yes."

"Stay quiet, but stay on the phone with me," he instructed and moved the phone away from his mouth. "Hey, man! Gotta run. This should cover it."

"Can you still hear them?" he asked.

"Yes." I could hear someone moving around the house. They were no longer trying to be quiet, and I hoped that was because they thought no one was home.

"I'm on my way," Byte said. "It'll be okay. I'll be there soon."

The sounds got progressively louder, and I knew the

intruder was in my bedroom. I jumped and almost let out a scream when something thumped against one of the walls surrounding me. My heart was beating against my chest faster than it ever had before while I was trying to breathe and not breathe at the same time.

And then it felt like my heart stopped when I heard someone softly say, "Gabby girl, where are you?"

It was a man. And he said my name. At least, I thought he did.

Please don't let him find me.

Please don't let him find me.

Please don't let him find me.

My internal chant was interrupted by the sound of motorcycle pipes, which did little to comfort me. There hadn't been enough time for Byte, or any of the Blackwings, to get to me.

"Fuck!" I heard from a male voice I didn't recognize, followed by the sound of someone running through the house.

"Hey!" another voice yelled. "Stop right there!"

Then more running.

A gunshot.

A GUNSHOT!

Footsteps pounded through the house, right into my bedroom.

Someone knocked on the secret door hiding me.

Before I could drop dead on the spot, he spoke. "Gabby, it's Byte. Open up."

2

BYTE

I wasn't prepared for her to open the door and launch herself into my arms. I wasn't prepared for her to cling to me with such great relief and sob into the crook of my neck. I wasn't prepared for her to beg me not to let her go. I wasn't prepared for any of it.

I was sitting at a bar in Cedar Valley talking to a woman I had absolutely no interest in. Well, I did at first, but not after talking to her for a few minutes. As I was trying to come up with a polite way to ditch her, my phone rang.

I glanced at the screen, surprised to see Gabby's name. "Excuse me, I have to take this," I told the annoying woman and answered without waiting for her response. "Hey, Gab—"

"Someone's in my house," she whispered harshly.

"Are you in the safe room?" I asked and waved my hand to get the bartender's attention.

I shoved a wad of bills in his hand and turned to the woman beside me. "Gotta go. Family emergency."

"Wait! Let me get your number," she said to my back because I was already headed for the door. I pretended not to hear her and all but ran for my bike.

I didn't need directions to Gabby's house. I'd helped when she moved in and remembered exactly how to get there. Thankfully, she wasn't far from the downtown area of Cedar Valley.

I darted in and out of traffic, rode between cars, and drove as fast as I could, but it still felt like it took forever to get there. Once I arrived, I jumped off my bike, pulled my gun from my holster, and entered her house through the open front door without hesitation.

No one was in the living room or kitchen. I started down the hallway and stopped dead in my tracks when a man stepped out of Gabby's bedroom.

"Hey! Stop right there!" I ordered.

He turned his head to look at me for one second before he sprinted out the back door. I ran after him and chased him through Gabby's back yard.

He glanced over his shoulder and saw me running after him. That's when he produced his own gun and blindly fired at me while he continued to run.

I took a shot at him, and I was fairly certain I hit him, but he continued to run into the wooded area behind Gabby's house. The fucker was fast. It didn't take long for me to lose sight of him once we were no longer out in the open. Instead of wasting time trying to find him, I turned around and ran back to the house to check on Gabby.

I knew exactly where the makeshift panic room was

in her closet and hoped she was still in there. I knocked on the fake wall. "Gabby, it's Byte. Open up."

The door opened, and Gabby launched herself at me. Her legs went around my waist while her arms wrapped around my shoulders, and she buried her face in the crook of my neck.

"Are you okay?"

She answered by nodding her head against me.

"I need to hear the words."

"I think so," she said shakily. "Are you okay? I thought I heard gunshots."

"Yeah, he took a shot at me," I said and felt her tense in my arms. "But he missed. I'm fine."

I moved to the kitchen and attempted to place her on the counter so I could look her over and make sure she was okay for myself, but she refused to release her hold on me.

"Gabby," I said slowly.

"Please don't let go of me," she whispered. "Not yet."

"Okay," I promised and tightened my hold on her. "Are you sure you're okay?"

She nodded again, and that time, I felt the wetness from her tears. "Just scared," she said softly.

"You're safe now," I promised and moved to the living room to take a seat on her couch. "We need to call the club. And your sister."

"No!" she insisted. "They just left for their trip. You won't be able to get in touch with her until they land, and I don't want her to turn around and come home as soon as they get there."

"Okay, okay," I said and held my hands up in a placating manner. "But I can't keep this from the club."

"You have to!" she yelled.

"Why?"

"Because they'll want me to come back to Croftridge until Keegan gets back, and I can't do that. I have to work, and I can't miss school."

"Fucking hell," I grumbled and tried to think of a solution that would satisfy both of us.

"Should we report it to the police?" she asked quietly.

I sighed. When I agreed to listen out for Gabby while Shaker and Keegan were gone, I never once thought anything would actually happen. And for some reason unbeknownst to me, I was completely blanking on how to handle the situation.

"Listen, I understand where you're coming from, but I need to give Phoenix a call." She opened her mouth to argue, but I held my hand up to stop her. "He's reasonable. He knows how hard you've worked to get where you are. I'm sure he'll have a solution that won't compromise your education or your safety."

"Fine," she huffed and crossed her arms over her chest. "Call Phoenix."

He answered on the first ring. "I don't usually see your name flashing on my screen on a Friday night. What's going on?"

"Gabby's house was broken into tonight. She called me while she was hiding. I got here and chased the intruder outside. Shots were exchanged, but he got away.

She doesn't want Keegan and Shaker to know until they get back. She can't come back to Croftridge while they're gone because of school and work. Police have not been notified. What would you like our next move to be?"

He inhaled deeply. "You said shots were exchanged. Was anybody hit?"

"He missed me. I might've gotten him in the shoulder. Not sure, Prez."

"Okay, here's what we're going to do. I'm going to send Edge your way. He'll call when he's about ten minutes out. That's when you call the police. Report everything as it happened, with the exception of who fired the shots. Wipe your gun down and give it to Edge when he gets there so it'll have his prints on it. Once the cops are finished doing their thing, bring Gabby back to Croftridge with you for the night. You two stay at your place and come see me after lunch tomorrow," he ordered. And that's why he was the president—problem solved in a matter of minutes.

"Thanks, Prez," I said before he ended the call.

"What'd he say?" Gabby asked anxiously.

I explained the plan to her and waited for the inevitable question.

"Why do we need to say it was Edge who shot at the guy?"

"Uh," I shifted uncomfortably. "That's something I can't tell you." When she narrowed her eyes, I felt compelled to give her a little more of an explanation. "Let's just say it won't be problematic for Edge, but it could be for me."

"If this is one of those times that it's better for me to know as little as possible, I'm okay with that."

"It absolutely is," I admitted. Truthfully, I'd managed to avoid any major run-ins with the police for the entirety of my life. I didn't know what would happen if I did, and I didn't want to find out. All it would take was one fingerprint to turn my world upside down. Thankfully, I'd been wearing gloves when I arrived and was careful not to touch anything once I'd taken them off.

"Should I go ahead and pack a bag for the night?"

"No, wait until after the police come and go. This is technically a crime scene, and we don't want to disturb any evidence."

A few minutes later, Edge called to let me know he was almost at Gabby's house. I waited another minute or two and placed the call to the police.

Edge knocked on the door twice before letting himself in. "Hey, brother," he said and held his hand out for my gun. Then he turned to Gabby. "You doing okay, sweetheart?"

"Yeah, I think so. I'm a little rattled, but I'm not hurt."

"Good. When the cops get here, you called Byte, like your sister told you to, and I arrived with him. He found you in the safe room while I chased the guy out of the house."

Gabby nodded her head vigorously. "Got it."

"What bar were we at?" he asked me.

"The Watering Hole. We stopped there after having dinner with Irene," I explained.

"I doubt they'll check, but she'll say I was with you?"

"She'll say whatever I ask her to," I told him. Irene had been looking out for me since the day I arrived in Cedar Valley all those years ago. And I knew she always would, even if that meant lying to the police on my behalf.

"Who's Irene?" Gabby asked as three sharp knocks sounded on the front door.

"Show time," Edge said quietly.

I opened the front door to greet the two officers and invited them inside.

"So, tell us what happened," they started.

They spent the next hour asking us questions and looking through Gabby's house. Somewhere in the midst of that, another crew showed up to dust for fingerprints. It felt like it took forever before they were finished. As they were heading out the door, one of the officers pointed to the alarm panel on the wall beside Gabby's front door. "It'd be a good idea to keep your alarm on whenever you're home, not just before bed."

"Uh, yeah, I will," Gabby stammered. "Thanks."

I waited until I heard their cars pulling out of the driveway before I asked, "What was that about with the alarm?"

"It was on. I know it was. I get home, turn it off, and reset it in stay mode immediately. Without fail. But it didn't go off," she explained.

"You're sure?" I asked, even though I knew she was. Shaker and Keegan would have drilled that into her head. They were no slouches when it came to safety.

"Yes! Look," she said and handed me her phone. On

the screen, her security app showed the alarm being disarmed by her, reset in stay mode, and disarmed again minutes before she called me.

"I'll be damned," I mumbled to myself.

"How is that possible?" she asked. "I use my fingerprint to turn it off and on."

"Do you also have a numeric code you can use?"

"Yes, but I never do."

"Okay, so one possibility is someone hacked into your system and disarmed it using a numeric code. The other possibility is someone made a copy of your fingerprint and used it to get into your house," I explained.

"What are you saying?"

"I'm saying whoever did this is likely someone you know."

Her eyes widened in shock. "Are you serious?"

"Yes, but we can figure out who that might be once we're back in Croftridge. Do you want to go and grab your things?"

"Sure. I'll be just a few minutes," she said and took a few steps toward the hallway. She stopped and turned back to me with a terrified look on her face. Without a word, I got to my feet and followed her to her bedroom.

"Thank you," she whispered.

I nodded in acknowledgment. She was scared, and rightfully so. Her sense of security had been abruptly stolen from her, and it would take a while for her to get it back.

3

GABBY

I didn't argue when Byte told me Phoenix wanted us to return to Croftridge for the weekend. Any other time, I would have protested, or at least insisted that they ask me instead of telling me. But I was terrified and wanted nothing more than to feel the safety and security I knew the club could provide.

Their protection was something I'd taken for granted. In Croftridge, no one messed with anyone affiliated with the club. Women and children were off limits, and everyone knew it. Apparently, the same wasn't true for Cedar Valley.

I quickly packed a bag for the weekend, with Byte standing guard at my bedroom door. I don't know how he knew, but I was too scared to enter my room alone. When my steps faltered, he wordlessly rose to his feet and followed me. I'd felt so safe in his arms, and I desperately wanted to feel that safety again. To be curled up against him where nothing could hurt me. It was odd. I'd been around him for most of my life and had

never thought of him as anything other than Jacob's club brother and my sister's friend. But suddenly, I didn't want to be more than a few feet away from him. It was silly, and I knew it, but that didn't change anything.

Once my bag was packed, I followed Byte back to the living room on autopilot.

"Are y'all ready to go?" Edge asked.

"I think so," I said and readjusted the backpack I was carrying.

"Do you have a helmet?" Byte asked.

"Of course," I said and reached into the closet by the front door to retrieve mine. With that, I locked the front door, set the alarm, and climbed on the back of Byte's bike.

My mind was a whirlwind of activity the entire ride to Byte's house. I kept replaying the events of the night over and over, and one part stood out to me more than anything else. I wasn't sure, but I thought I heard the person say my name, and Byte said it was probably someone I knew. That couldn't be a coincidence, could it?

Before I knew it, Byte turned off the road onto a long, winding driveway that led to a house hidden by the surrounding trees. I couldn't see a lot because it was dark, but from what I could tell, it looked to be a modern two-story log cabin.

Once inside, Byte showed me to the room I'd be staying in and told me to make myself comfortable. I dropped onto the bed and covered my eyes with my arm, inhaling deeply. I intended to enjoy a few minutes

of peace before going out to talk to Byte. Instead, I promptly fell asleep.

* * *

I WOKE TO THE SMELL OF FRESHLY BREWED COFFEE AND cooked bacon. After a quick trip to the bathroom, I made my way to the kitchen and found Byte standing in front of the stove wearing a pair of gray drawstring pants and no shirt. He was tall and lean, with his well-defined muscles on full display.

"Good morning," I said awkwardly. I'd known Byte for the majority of my life, but I'd never spent any time alone with him. And I'd never seen him with so little clothes on.

"Morning," he replied without turning around. "Help yourself to coffee. Eggs and bacon are almost done, but there's cereal in the pantry if you'd prefer that."

"I'm good with eggs and bacon. Where do you keep your mugs?"

"Top cabinet to the right of the sink."

"Thanks," I replied and set about making a cup for myself. Thankfully, the sugar was already out on the counter so I didn't have to ask where it was. I had no idea why I felt so uncomfortable, but I was hyperaware of every move I made, and I couldn't seem to shake it.

"Is there anything I can do to help?"

"Nope. Just make yourself comfortable," he said and started plating the food. I almost snorted at his choice of

words. I was so far from comfortable it was almost funny.

Moments later, he placed a plate in front of me with more food than I could possibly eat. Well, I could handle the few strips of bacon, but the mountain of eggs was another story.

"Um, at the risk of sounding rude, there's no way I'll be able to eat all of this."

He laughed. "I made extra for the chickens. Eat what you want, and I'll give the leftovers to them."

"You have chickens?" I asked in surprise.

"Yes. Why?"

I shrugged. "You don't seem like a chicken person."

He eyed me curiously. "Really? Should I be offended? I feel like I should be offended."

"What? No! I didn't mean—"

"Relax," he laughed. "I'm just messing with you."

"In my defense, I don't know any bikers with farm animals," I said and shoved a forkful of eggs into my mouth.

"Are you forgetting about the dairy farm? And your sister has so many horses, I've lost count."

"My sister isn't a biker. And the dairy farm is a business. I don't know any bikers who have farm animals at home," I countered.

"To be honest, it wasn't exactly my idea to have chickens. They showed up in my back yard one day. When I didn't have any luck finding out who they belonged to, I decided to keep them," he explained.

"Are these eggs from them?" I asked between bites.

"Yes," he nodded. "I haven't had to buy eggs from the store since they showed up. And I never will again."

"I can see why. These are really good."

"I never understood the hype about fresh eggs until I had them for myself," he admitted.

"So, you feed the chickens their own eggs? Isn't that weird?" I asked.

He shrugged. "Not really. A lot of animals eat their own kind, including their offspring—fish, for example. But I don't have a rooster, so these eggs aren't fertilized. I guess it's kind of like recycling."

I started to ask more about the chickens, but he changed the subject before I had the chance. "We need to talk about what happened last night."

"I know," I said and reached for my cup of coffee to take a big sip. I knew it was coming, but I'd hoped to avoid the subject for a bit longer.

"Is there anything you haven't told me?" he asked.

"Why do you ask?" I returned, trying to stall.

"When I said the perpetrator was likely someone you knew, you opened your mouth like you were going to say something but didn't. It seemed like you made some sort of mental connection."

"Well, aren't you observant," I muttered.

"Start talking, Gabby," he said sternly.

I sighed and clasped my hands together. "When I was hiding and waiting for you, I thought I heard him say my name."

"Like he was calling your name?"

"Not exactly. He was in my closet, and I thought he said, 'Gabby girl, where are you?' But I'm not sure.

Everything was happening so fast, and I was really trying not to make a sound."

"Do you have any idea who it could have been?" he asked.

"Maybe," I admitted. I didn't really think it was him, but I couldn't come up with any other possibilities. "I met a guy a couple of weeks ago, and we went out a few times. We weren't hitting it off, so I told him I didn't think we should keep seeing each other after our last date. He agreed, and that was that. Or so I thought. A few days later, I was pulled over on my way home from work for having a taillight out. When I looked at it, the light wasn't just out, it had been smashed. The next week, I had a flat tire. Then, last night, I heard someone say my name. I can't say for sure that he's the one doing these things, but this unprecedented string of bad luck started shortly after I broke up with him."

Byte stopped pacing and turned to look at me. "What's this prick's name?"

"You can't kill him," I blurted.

"Why the hell not?"

"Because I don't want you to get in trouble because of me. And I don't even know if it's him."

"If you tell me his name, I'll find out if it's him."

"What if it is?"

He sighed in frustration. "Gabby, it sounds like someone is terrorizing you. We need to figure out who it is, and then we'll come up with a way to put a stop to it. I'm not opposed to killing someone who deserves it, but it isn't my go-to response."

"His name is Chad Higgins," I confessed.

"What else do you know about him?"

"He said he was twenty-nine and works as a correctional officer at the prison."

"Anything else?" he asked.

"Not really. He was very closed off and never wanted to talk about himself, which is one of the things that unnerved me."

"Wait. I thought you said you broke it off because you two didn't hit it off?"

"We didn't, but there was something about him that creeped me out. I feel bad saying that because I can't tell you why exactly. It was just a feeling," I admitted.

"I'm going to grab my laptop and see what I can find out about creepy Chad."

He returned to the kitchen moments later with his computer and started searching. I wasn't sure what to do while he worked, so I busied myself with cleaning the kitchen and loading the dishwasher. I berated myself the whole time for not checking into Chad myself. I was nowhere near as skilled as Byte when it came to technology, but I was capable of performing a basic internet search.

The sound of the laptop closing and Byte's chair sliding back from the table brought me out of my thoughts. "What did you find?"

"What makes you think I found something?"

"Because you're you. You always find something."

"I can't argue with that," he said with a slight smile that quickly disappeared. "I'm afraid I don't have great news."

"Well, let's hear it," I said and tried to brace myself for whatever news he was going to share.

"I need to do some more digging, but from what I can tell, he's not a correctional officer at the prison."

"What do you mean?"

"I checked the prison's current employees. He's not one of them. Like I said, I need to do some more digging, but I can already tell you he's not who he said he was."

"I'm so fucking stupid," I mumbled to myself.

"Don't say that. You had no way of knowing. And you ended things because he made you uncomfortable. There's nothing stupid about that," he corrected.

"Thanks." I appreciated his words, though they didn't make me feel any better. Thankfully, I trusted my intuition and ended things when I did. Before I could continue thinking about what could have happened, another thought occurred to me. "Did you see a picture of him online? Was he the one who broke into my house?"

"I'm not sure. A few pictures came up, but none of them are very clear. I didn't get a good look at him because it was dark, and he was wearing a hat. I also didn't notice anything distinctive or identifying about him."

"Let me see the pictures."

He opened up his laptop and turned the screen toward me. I scrolled through the few images and shook my head. "None of those are him."

"I had a feeling that was the case," he admitted.

"So, what do you think I should do now?" I asked.

He exhaled audibly and leaned back in his chair. "Phoenix wants us to come to the clubhouse after lunch. We'll talk to him and go from there."

I glanced at the time and exhaled heavily. "That's still a few hours away, and this is going to drive me crazy until then. I don't like not having a plan."

"He'll likely agree to not notifying Keegan and Shaker as long as the club knows what's going on and you're safe."

"Right, but how is the club going to ensure my safety? I can't come back to Croftridge until Keegan and Shaker get back. Between school and work, I'm barely home as it is," I explained.

"Well, what's your schedule like for the next two weeks?"

"I have to work Monday. I'm at the doctor's office from eight to five on Tuesday, Wednesday, and Thursday for my clinical hours. I'm off Friday, work Saturday and Sunday, and off Monday. The next three days are clinical hours again. I work on Friday, and I'm off for the weekend. Then, it repeats every two weeks until the end of the semester."

"That's intense."

"Don't I know it," I commiserated.

He was quiet for a few moments before he made a suggestion. "Okay, how about this? I'll stay at your place and be your shadow for the next two weeks."

"I, um," I stammered. "Can you do that?"

He shrugged. "I don't see why not. I can work from anywhere as long as I have a computer and an internet connection."

"What about your chickens?" I blurted. I wasn't necessarily trying to find a reason why he couldn't stay with me, but I wasn't completely comfortable with the idea. Truthfully, I was uncomfortable with it for reasons I didn't want to acknowledge, like how safe I felt in his presence or how my stomach fluttered when he smiled.

He waved his hand dismissively. "One of the prospects or club kids can take care of them while I'm gone."

"Well, I guess we have a plan," I conceded.

"Once again, I feel like I should be offended," he teased and placed his hand over his heart.

Suddenly, I felt like an asshole. He came to my rescue the moment I called, risked his life chasing away the intruder, and offered to spend the next two weeks of his life being my bodyguard. "Crap. I'm sorry, Byte. I'm truly grateful for everything. I'm just upset about the whole situation. It has nothing to do with you personally."

"It's fine, Gabby," he said and stood from his seat. "You want to help me feed the chickens?"

"I'd love to," I said. "Do you have any other animals?"

"Why? Are you hoping I have a pig?" he laughed.

"Do you?" I asked hopefully. I loved pigs and had begged Keegan for one when I was little.

He shook his head. "No. Just the chickens. But who knows? One may wander into my yard one day."

4

BYTE

As I expected, Phoenix agreed to my plan with one added condition. "If you find anything of concern about this Chad guy or anyone else, you let me know immediately, and we'll reevaluate."

"Understood, Prez."

"Ranger's going to be pissed," he added.

"Oh, I know, but I have a plan for that."

"Yeah?"

I nodded. "Yep. It was Gabby's idea, so she can deal with her grandfather."

Phoenix laughed. "You're going to throw her under the bus?"

"Shamelessly," I confirmed.

"All right, when are you two heading back to her place?" he asked.

"Probably tomorrow afternoon, but I'll let you know if that changes."

"Sounds good. Keep me updated," he ordered.

"Will do, Prez. And tell Flint not to throw any parties at my house while I'm gone."

Phoenix chuckled. "You don't have to worry about anything like that with Flint. Now, Blaze and Raven are a different story." He shook his head and rubbed his hand over his beard. "I swear those girls are responsible for every gray hair I have."

"I don't doubt it." Even though Blaze and Raven were aunt and niece, Blaze was only a few weeks older than Raven. They grew up more like sisters or close cousins and had been giving their parents a run for their money ever since they learned to walk and talk. I had a feeling Flint kept them out of more trouble than any of us knew. He was a good kid and was well on his way to making a fine club brother.

I made my way back to my room to collect Gabby and head back to my house. She opted to hide out in my room at the clubhouse while I spoke with Phoenix to keep the club chatter to a minimum. We both knew it would get back to Keegan if anyone spotted her at the clubhouse.

She sat up and clicked off the television when I entered the room. "How did it go?"

"Fine. He agreed with our plan," I said and paused for dramatic effect. "But you have to handle your grandfather when he finds out someone broke into your house and no one told him for two weeks."

She laughed. "I don't have a problem with that."

"Really?"

"Really. It won't be *me* that Papa's mad at after I explain."

"Fucking hell," I grumbled. For as long as I'd known him, Ranger always had a rifle within arm's reach, no matter where he was. And I also knew he did not mind using it. "If he shoots me, I'm blaming you."

"He won't shoot you," she countered.

"That's what you think. You get the teddy bear version of him while the rest of us get the grizzly." And that grizzly became an entirely different beast when it came to someone messing with his grandchildren. I vividly remembered him pointing his rifle at an FBI agent when Keegan had gone missing years ago.

I flinched when Gabby placed her hand on my shoulder. I hoped it wasn't noticeable, but she quickly pulled her hand back. Before I could comment, she continued as if nothing had happened. "Just make sure you stand behind me or my sister. He can't shoot you if we're in the way."

"Aw, it's cute that you think I'm going to be anywhere in the vicinity when you tell him what happened."

"Yeah, that's probably a better plan," she conceded.

"You ready to go?"

"I'm ready if you are."

Somehow, we managed to make it back out to my truck without running into anyone. The clubhouse was never empty, especially on the weekends.

"That was weird, right?" Gabby asked as soon as I pulled out onto the road.

"Shhh! Don't say anything else. I don't want to jinx it."

"Really? You believe in jinxes?" she asked.

I shrugged. "I'm not overly superstitious, but I don't see any reason to push my luck when I don't have to."

"Yeah, that's pretty much how I am, too. Do I really think spilling salt will bring me bad luck? No. But tossing a pinch over my left shoulder is super easy, so why not do it?"

"Oh, that reminds me. We should probably pick up something for dinner on the way home," I suggested.

"That works for me."

"Where do you want to go?"

"Anywhere's fine."

"Oh, no. You're the picky eater, not me."

"I'm not a picky eater," she insisted.

"Maybe not now, but you used to be. You wouldn't even eat macaroni and cheese. All kids eat mac and cheese."

"I still won't eat it if it came out of a box. I don't care what anybody says. Cheese is not supposed to be that color. No thanks," she said and crossed her arms over her chest. "I can't believe you remember that."

"It's hard to forget almost getting your ass kicked over macaroni and cheese," I grumbled.

"Say what now?"

I sighed. "You'd been living with Keegan for a few months when this happened. One weekend, I walked into the kitchen at the clubhouse to get something to eat and found your sister staring into the pantry with tears running down her face. I put my hand on her shoulder and asked if she was okay. She started sobbing, so I hugged her. She was steadily soaking my shirt and telling me all about how she was afraid you were going to

starve because you wouldn't eat anything, not even macaroni and cheese, and she didn't know what to do. I leaned back to tell her everything would be okay, and that's when Shaker walked in."

Gabby threw her head back and laughed. "Oh, I can only imagine," she said and lowered her voice to imitate Shaker. "Get your hands off my wifey."

I grinned. "Yeah, that's exactly what he said. Then Keegan threw the box of macaroni at him and told him to stop being an asshole. That's when I grabbed a box of Little Debbie's and bolted."

"Did that happen often?" Gabby asked quietly.

"What? Shaker wanting to kick my ass?"

"No, Keegan crying about me," she clarified.

"Oh," I said, suddenly realizing I may have inadvertently upset her. "No, I don't think so. It had more to do with her own insecurities than you. She went from being a single woman working toward a business goal to a married woman with a newly adopted five-year-old in a matter of months. Back then, James was the only other kid around, and he was still a baby compared to you. So, she felt like she didn't know what she was doing and didn't have anyone in the same boat to talk to. I do remember your grandmother coming for an extended visit after the mac attack day, and I'm sure the reason was to help her get things figured out."

"I never knew any of that."

"Good. You weren't supposed to. And if anyone brings it up, you still don't know," I added.

"Oh, come on. I was looking forward to giving Shaky Jakey shit about his mac attack," she teased.

"Shaky Jakey," I laughed. "I haven't heard that in years."

"It's an oldie but a goodie."

"All right, food. What are we getting?" I asked.

"Pizza?" she suggested.

"Pizza sounds good. What kind do you want?"

"Personally, I like cheese, but get whatever you want. I can pick the toppings off."

Instead of agreeing or disagreeing with her, I placed a call to my favorite pizza restaurant and ordered a pizza for her and a pizza for me.

"Byte, I can't eat an entire pizza by myself," she said as soon as I ended the call.

"Well, I can," I told her. "And they don't sell by the slice."

* * *

"MMM," SHE GROANED AFTER TAKING A BITE OF PIZZA. "I forgot how good this is."

"They don't have good pizza in Cedar Valley?"

She shook her head. "Not like this."

"I guess we won't be having pizza while I'm hanging out with you next week."

"Can I ask you something?"

"You can, but I reserve the right to not answer," I teased.

"How did you get to my house so fast?"

"Oh, that's easy. I was in Cedar Valley when you called." I had no idea what she was going to ask me, but I was definitely relieved it was something simple.

"Crap. I hope I didn't interrupt a date or something important."

"You didn't," I assured her. "I had dinner with an old friend who lives in the area, and then I stopped by a bar to have a drink before heading home. Actually, I should thank you. You called at the perfect time."

"How so?"

"I'd been trying to shake this barfly for a while. I was trying to be nice about it, but she just wouldn't take the hint. Then you called," I explained.

"Does that happen often?"

I nodded. "More than you'd think. There are a lot of women out there who seek out members because they want to be a part of the club. Sort of like the women who try to get pregnant by military men for the benefits."

"Does the club have a premium healthcare plan I don't know about?"

"I think it has more to do with the family aspect. Sometimes, people who don't have any family will do anything to be a part of one."

"Speaking of family, what's the deal with yours? I don't think I've heard you mention them."

I swallowed thickly. No one had asked me about my family in years. In fact, it had been so long that it took me a moment to decide what to tell her. "That's because I don't have one. My father disappeared before I was old enough to remember him, and my mother died when I was eighteen. I didn't have an extended family, so once she was gone, it was just me."

"Oh, Byte, that's terrible. Is that why you joined the club? To have a family?"

"Pretty much," I lied. While the Blackwings did become the family I never had, I joined the club because I wanted their protection and a safe place to hide.

I'm not sure if it was my short answer or something else, but she seemed to pick up on my unease about the topic and changed the subject.

After dinner, she excused herself to the guest room to study for an upcoming exam while I spent the evening searching for information on Chad Higgins. As much as I hated to admit it, I found very little on Chad, and what I did find wasn't helpful. And that wasn't good. Because I could find almost anything. In my experience, there was only one reason for someone's digital footprint to be virtually nonexistent—because it was intentionally hidden.

5

GABBY

Despite the events of Friday night, I felt well rested and ready for the week when I woke up Monday morning. Though, I did feel a little bad for Byte. I was in the middle of my last semester of school and my schedule was brutal. I had to remind myself frequently that it was almost over.

I found Byte sitting at my kitchen table, intently focused on his laptop screen while he typed. "Morning," I said and made a beeline for the coffee machine. "Did you sleep okay?"

"Yeah," he said distractedly and kept his attention on the screen in front of him.

Assuming he wasn't a morning person, I continued getting ready for the day in silence. Once I finished, I felt awkward and unsure of how to interrupt him. Finally, I cleared my throat and announced, "I'm ready if you are."

Without a single word, he rose from his seat, grabbed his keys, and headed for the front door.

I spent the first half of the ride to the hospital going over every interaction we'd had, trying to figure out what could have caused his sudden change in demeanor, but I couldn't come up with anything. I also didn't want to spend the whole day thinking about it. I had enough to stress about without adding more. So, I mustered up some courage and asked, "Did I do something to piss you off?"

"What?" he asked in surprise. "Of course not. Why would you even think that?"

"Because you've only said one word to me this morning."

"Shit. Sorry," he said and adjusted his grip on the steering wheel. "I haven't been able to find much on this Chad guy, and it's frustrating the hell out of me."

"Oh, well, I guess that's good. I mean good for me, not for you," I rambled. "Not that it's bad for you. Oh, hell, you know what I mean."

He chuckled. "I really got under your skin, huh?"

"I don't like it when someone's upset with me, especially when I don't know why," I admitted.

"Since we're going to be spending a lot of time together over the next two weeks, how about this? I promise to tell you if you do anything that bothers me."

I exhaled in relief. "That'll work for me."

"But you have to promise to do the same," he added.

"Oh, I don't know if I can do that."

"Come on, Gabby. You can't ask me to do something you're not willing to do yourself."

"Of course I can. Let's say there was a spider in the

kitchen. I'd have no problem asking you to get rid of it, and that is definitely something I wouldn't be willing to do," I said as he pulled into the parking lot. "But for the sake of time, fine. I'll tell you if you do something that bothers me."

"Great," he smiled. "Now, what time do I need to pick you up?"

"Can I text you this afternoon and let you know? Technically, my shift is over at quarter after seven, but I can't leave if something's going on or if I haven't finished my work. Most of the time, I'm finished by seven thirty, but there have been times I was there until nine."

"That's fine, and I'll text you when I get here. Make sure you stay inside and in an area with people around until you hear from me."

"I will," I promised. "I'll see you later. Thanks again."

"You're welcome. Have a good day."

"Thanks. You, too," I said and got out of his truck. Then I stopped at the front door and turned to wave goodbye before I walked into hell.

* * *

"Rough day?" Byte asked when he picked me up from work.

"If I never hear my name again, it'll be too soon."

"What happened?"

"Today, I had a patient who's bedridden, blind, and

has some dementia. As I always do, I started the day by going to each room and introducing myself. 'Hi, my name's Gabby, and I'll be your nurse for the day.' From the moment I said my name, the man started saying it. On repeat. He called for me all day. Do you know what it's like to hear someone calling your name nonstop for twelve hours? Let me tell you. It is a special kind of nerve-wracking, anxiety-inducing, maddening torture."

Byte grimaced. "That sounds awful. There wasn't anything you could do?"

"I gave him the medicines his doctor had ordered for anxiety and agitation, hoping they would make him sleepy like they do every other person on the planet. But, no, not this guy. He sounded like a bird with the way he would draw out my name in his croaky little voice. 'Gaaabby. Gaaabby. Gaaabby.' And it's not like I could ignore a patient calling for me. So, I pretty much spent my entire day hovering around his room."

"I can't say I've ever experienced anything like that."

"Enough about me. How was your day?"

He sighed. "Uneventful."

"Really?" I asked in surprise.

He shrugged. "Well, I guess that's not completely true. I did figure out the guy you were seeing was using a fake name. I don't know what his real name is, but it's not Chad Higgins."

"Well, that's great," I muttered.

He shrugged. "It's not a big deal. I was kind of expecting it."

"Really? Why?"

"When I initially searched his name, I should've

found a lot more than I did. It's nearly impossible to not have some presence online. Think about it. Public records like traffic violations, judicial records, property taxes, and marriage licenses are all available online."

"Right, but what if he'd never been married, rented instead of owned, and hadn't been to court for anything?"

"Even if that was the case, I find it hard to believe that a twenty-nine-year-old has never been cited for a traffic violation."

"Touché," I admitted.

When we arrived at my house, I waited in the truck while Byte made sure the house was clear. He waved me inside a few moments later, and I went straight for the bathroom. I made quick work of showering and returned to the kitchen, only to realize I had very little to eat in the house.

"Byte," I gasped. "I'm so sorry. I completely forgot about groceries."

"Not a problem. I stopped by Irene's for dinner," he said and reached into the fridge. "I wasn't sure what you'd like, but I figured I couldn't go wrong with a cheeseburger."

"You're the best," I said and happily took the container of food from him. "Thank you."

"You're welcome."

After reheating the food, I sat down at the table and took a huge bite. "Mmm," I moaned. "This is delicious."

"Glad you like it."

"You mentioned her before. Who's Irene?" I asked and continued to inhale the cheeseburger.

"She's a good friend. She owns the diner on Main Street," he explained.

"Oh," I said, feeling slightly deflated with his response. Whatever, or whomever, he did in his free time was none of my business. Suddenly, the burger I had been devouring didn't taste as good as it initially had.

"You've obviously never been to the diner," he mused.

I cocked my head to the side. "What makes you say that?"

"Because if you had, you'd know Irene is in her sixties. She was the first person I met when I moved to Cedar Valley, and she's been like a mother to me ever since. Well, maybe a crazy aunt is a better way to describe her," he explained.

He was far more observant than I thought. I felt seen, and I didn't like it. I had no right to be jealous of anyone in his life. Then I silently laughed at myself. I wasn't jealous. I was under a lot of stress and tired. It was nothing more than that.

I swallowed the last bite of my burger and smiled. "Please thank her for dinner. It was wonderful. And thank you for thinking of me."

"Gabby," he started.

"Byte, I'm beyond tired. I'm going to bed."

"All right. I'll see you in the morning."

"Good night," I said and headed for the sanctity of my bedroom.

* * *

"DID YOU CHANGE CLOTHES?" BYTE ASKED WHEN HE picked me up from the doctor's office the following evening.

"Yes, I did. Twice, actually," I huffed.

"Do I want to know why?"

"Probably not, but I'll tell you. The first time was because a patient vomited all over me. An adult patient who couldn't be bothered to turn her head away from me or attempt to cover her mouth. And she didn't apologize. Seriously, if you spray your stomach juice all over someone else, the least you can do is say you're sorry."

Byte tried to stifle his laughter, but he failed miserably. "I'm sorry. It's not funny, but the way you told it is." He cleared his throat and tried to regain some composure. "So, what caused the second change of clothes?"

"After lunch, we were seeing a patient who had her infant with her. She'd been holding the baby and put her in her carrier for the exam. Little Miss did not want to be put down and started screaming her head off. The patient was having sutures removed from her chest, so she couldn't hold her. I'm telling you, this baby was crying so hard her entire head was damn near purple. I was genuinely concerned for the child, so I offered to hold her while the doctor removed the stitches. The kid calmed down as soon as I picked her up. And two minutes later, she turned into a geyser of shit. Literally. It sprayed out of the leg holes of her diaper while

simultaneously shooting up her back and out the neck of her onesie. I'm not sure how, but I managed to not drop the baby and keep a straight face while baby shit seeped into my clothing. The mother was apologetic, but I didn't care. I handed that kid off and bolted for the bathroom as soon as I could."

"Sounds like you had a pretty shitty day," Byte laughed.

"Ha. Ha. Ha," I sniped.

"I'm sure you'll be able to laugh about it later."

"Maybe, but right now, I feel disgusting, and I'm starving. And let me tell you why I'm starving. Because my lunch 'mysteriously' disappeared."

"What do you mean by 'mysteriously'?"

"I mean someone other than me ate it," I griped.

"Are you serious?"

"Yep. And it's not the first time it's happened."

"Someone's stealing your lunch?" he asked in disbelief. "Do you know who it is?"

"I have no idea, and I don't know how to catch them without hanging around the break room all morning, which I can't do."

"Oh, that's easy. Add some really hot peppers to something in your lunch. If your food doesn't get stolen that day, don't eat whatever has the peppers in it. If it does get stolen, you'll know without a doubt who took it," he said.

"That's brilliant!" I said excitedly.

"Do you want to stop by the grocery store on the way home?" he asked.

"Normally, I'd say yes, but I really, really want to

take a shower. I rinsed off in the staff shower at the office, but I still don't feel clean. Can we go to the store after? And pick up something for dinner while we're out?"

"Sure, if that's what it takes to get you out of your crappy mood," he teased.

6

BYTE

After I dropped Gabby off at the doctor's office Wednesday morning, I spent the rest of the day searching for information about the man posing as Chad Higgins. To say I was frustrated would be an understatement. Every path I went down led me to a dead end. He only had two social media accounts associated with his alias, and neither of those had a clear picture of his face. The phone he was using to communicate with Gabby was a pay-as-you-go phone and appeared to be no longer active. Usually, I could find anything I set my mind to, but I needed a starting point. This time, I had nothing to go on, and I was at a loss on how to proceed.

I don't know how long I'd been staring at the computer screen when the sound of a text message caught my attention.

Gabby: Can you pick me up at 5:15 today?

Byte: I'll be there.

I glanced at the time and realized it was much later in the day than I thought. I only had an hour and a half before I needed to be at the doctor's office. Since I had made no progress, I decided to get out of the house for a bit and clear my head.

When I walked into the diner, Irene spotted me immediately and made a beeline for me with a huge smile on her face. "I didn't expect to see you again so soon."

"I had some time to kill, and I couldn't think of a better way to spend it than having a cup of coffee with one of my favorite people."

"Is that so?" she asked and stepped behind the counter to pour me a cup of coffee.

I exhaled heavily. She knew me better than most and could obviously tell something was bothering me.

"You want to talk about it?" she asked and placed the steaming mug in front of me.

"I'm searching for someone, and it's like looking for a needle in a haystack."

"That saying has always puzzled me."

"How so?"

"A needle is metal. Use a magnet. Problem solved," she said and gave me a knowing look.

While she tended to her other customers, I sat there and mulled over her words. In theory, her idea would work, but Gabby was the only proverbial magnet I had, and I wasn't willing to use her to find Chad.

"I can see I've given you something to think about," she said when she returned.

"You certainly have. I'm just not sure if I can make it work," I admitted.

"Give it some time. You'll think of something," she assured me.

"I hope you're right," I mumbled.

"I know I am," she said and patted my hand. "I'm going to make you something to eat before you go."

"Oh, you don't have to do that."

"I know," she winked. "But I want to, so I'm going to. Shall I make something for your friend as well?"

I grinned. "She asked me to thank you for the cheeseburger and wanted me to tell you it was the best one she'd ever had."

Irene nodded with a smile. "All right. A cheeseburger for her and a surprise for you."

She returned with two bags of food and a cup of coffee to go. "You should bring your friend by the diner sometime. I'd like to meet the girl who's making your forehead wrinkle."

"Oh, this isn't because of her," I corrected.

"My mistake," she said and smiled.

* * *

"YOU'RE WEARING THE SAME CLOTHES YOU WERE THIS morning. Does that mean today was better than yesterday?" I asked when Gabby got into the truck.

"I made it through the day without getting anyone's body fluids on me, so I'll say yes."

"How was lunch?"

She sighed. "Of course, the one time I want someone to steal my lunch, they don't."

I laughed. "Well, there's always tomorrow."

"Speaking of food," she said, and inhaled deeply. "What's that smell?"

"I stopped by the diner, and Irene sent me home with food," I said and gestured to the back seat with my thumb.

"I hope she sent another burger," she said excitedly.

"She did. I told her how much you loved the one you had the other day. She said she'd love to meet you and asked me to bring you by the diner sometime."

"Maybe we can go on one of my days off," she suggested.

Once we were back at Gabby's house, she changed clothes before we sat down to eat. I noticed she always changed as soon as she got home and never walked through the house with her work shoes on.

"I have to ask. Is that something they taught you in school or something you do on your own?"

"Um, I'm not sure what you're talking about," she said in confusion.

"Changing clothes as soon as you get home," I clarified.

"It's something I do, but they probably should teach it in school."

"Sounds like there's a story behind your reasoning."

She nodded and swallowed the food in her mouth. "One day, I came home from work, had dinner, and watched a few shows before heading to the shower.

When I walked into the bathroom, I looked into the mirror and noticed something on my upper arm. Upon closer inspection, I realized it was a big wad of sputum. I've changed immediately ever since."

"A wad of what?"

"Sputum. Phlegm. Lung butter. Throat snot," she explained.

I scrunched my face in disgust. "Gross."

"I'm sorry," she said and covered her mouth. "I should've waited until we weren't eating to tell you that story. I live and breathe nursing. It's easy to forget that not everyone wants to hear about medical stuff over dinner."

I waved my hand dismissively. "It doesn't bother me. I was just agreeing with you."

"Oh, good. Because it's more than likely going to happen again."

I laughed. "I enjoy hearing your stories. They're quite—"

I was interrupted by someone knocking on her front door. "Are you expecting company?"

Gabby vigorously shook her head. "No."

"Stay here. I'll go see who it is," I said and got to my feet.

I peeked through the window at the top of the front door to see a girl around Gabby's age standing on the front porch with a book bag on her back and a basket of muffins in her hand. I quickly dismissed her as a threat and opened the door. "Can I help you?"

Her eyes widened in surprise. "Um, is Gabby home?"

"Who wants to know?"

"L-Lauren," she stammered.

"Just a moment," I said and closed the door.

"Who was it?" Gabby asked as soon as I returned to the kitchen.

"She said her name is Lauren. Do you know her?"

Gabby jumped to her feet. "Shit! I completely forgot we had plans to study tonight."

I followed Gabby through the house as she hurried to the front door. "Hey, Lauren. Come on in."

"I brought muffins," Lauren said and leaned around Gabby to look at me. "Is this a bad time?"

"No, not at all," Gabby said and ushered Lauren into the living room. "This is Byte. He's a family friend and is staying with me this week while he's in town for work. Byte, this is my friend from school, Lauren."

"Byte?" Lauren asked.

"Nickname," Gabby explained. "He works with computers."

"Oh, that's clever," Lauren said and took a seat on the couch.

"I'll just finish up in the kitchen and get out of your hair," I said.

"I'm sorry, Byte. This totally slipped my mind."

"Don't worry about it. I have some work I need to catch up on anyway," I told her. I didn't, but it gave me an excuse to be close by so I could eavesdrop without looking like a creep. I opened up my laptop and pretended to work while Gabby went back to the living room to study with Lauren.

"What's going on, Gabby? It's been days since I've

heard from you, and then I show up here to find you with some super hot guy being all protective."

"Oh, stop. It's nothing like that. I told you my sister and her family were going on a trip to Scotland. I went home for the weekend to help her pack and see them off. Monday was hell at work, and Tuesday at the office wasn't much better," Gabby explained.

"If you say so."

"I do. Can we study now?" Gabby asked, sounding irritated.

Throughout the evening, Lauren strayed off topic several times, mostly to ask Gabby about me. How she met me. How long she'd known me. How old I was. If I was seeing anybody. Each time, Gabby gave her a vague answer and redirected her attention back to whatever they were studying.

When Lauren finally left, I could tell Gabby was relieved to have her gone. "That was exhausting."

"Why'd you lie to her?" I asked.

"I may not be a member of the club, but I've been around long enough to know to keep things to myself when something's going on," she explained.

"Yeah, you're right about that."

7

BYTE

"What the hell?" I shouted when we walked out to my truck the following morning. All four tires were flat.

"Did someone slash them?" Gabby asked.

"Yeah, that's exactly what happened."

She glanced at the time on her phone and back to me. She didn't have to say anything. Her thoughts were written all over her face. She didn't want to be late, but she didn't want to leave me to deal with the tires.

"Come on," I said and guided her back to the house. "We'll take your car, and I'll deal with this when I get back." Thankfully, her car had been safely parked in the garage.

Gabby was unusually quiet on the ride to the office. I had a feeling she was blaming herself for what happened to my truck, and I couldn't let her continue to do so for the whole day. Before she got out of the car, I reached over and grabbed her hand. "This isn't your fault."

"Yes, it is," she said quietly.

"No, it isn't," I insisted. "I get why you think it is, but trust me on this. It's actually kind of a good thing."

"How in the hell is having your tires slashed a good thing?"

"Typically, tire slashing is an act of rage. Angry people are sloppy, and sloppy people are easy to catch," I explained, and gently squeezed her hand. "Go do your thing, and don't worry about this. I'll have it all taken care of before I come back to get you."

"I'll try," she said and gave me a weak smile. "Thanks, Byte."

I called Phoenix as soon as I pulled out of the parking lot and filled him in on the new developments.

"He slashed your tires? What a bitch move," Phoenix said.

I chuckled. "That's exactly what I thought."

"How'd Gabby handle it?"

"I think she's blaming herself, but otherwise, she took it in stride."

"She's a sweet girl, but she's strong, too. You said she's off tomorrow, right?" he asked.

"Right. She's off Friday and Monday and works the weekend."

"Okay, here's what we're going to do. I'll send one of the guys with a tow truck to get your truck. When you pick Gabby up this afternoon, I want the two of you to come back to Croftridge. In the meantime, I want you to pick up a couple of cameras and get them hooked up to her system. Try to keep them as inconspicuous as possible."

"You got it, Prez."

* * *

Gabby looked absolutely drained when I picked her up. "Are you okay?"

"Yeah, I'm just tired," she said and changed the subject. "Did you get your truck fixed?"

"Phoenix sent a tow truck to pick it up and take it back to the garage. He also wants us to come back to Croftridge for the night."

"Do we need to leave right away or can we stop by the house first?" she asked.

"We can go back to your house first. There's no rush," I said and opened my mouth to say more but decided against it.

"What were you going to say?" Gabby asked.

"Now, who's the observant one?" I teased.

"Me. Now, what was it?"

"I was going to say something about how nice it is that you go with the flow instead of arguing with whatever plan we've come up with."

"It would be stupid of me to argue. You guys have dealt with plenty of crazy-ass people over the years. I haven't. Besides, I promised my sister I'd go to the club if anything happened. This is me keeping that promise," she explained.

"You're a good person, Gabriella Marks," I said sincerely.

"Thank you," she started and paused. "What's your real name?"

Every part of me wanted to tell her my real name, the one I was born with, not the one I gave myself when I left my old life behind at the age of fourteen. But I couldn't. So, I swallowed thickly and told her the lie that had become my truth. "Michael. Michael Fuller."

"Michael," she said slowly. "That doesn't seem right."

I laughed. It didn't seem right because it wasn't, but I couldn't tell her that. "It's because you're used to calling me Byte, like everyone else."

"I guess I'll stick with Byte then," she said as I parked her car in the garage and closed the door. "I need to shower and pack a bag. It'll probably take me thirty minutes to be ready to go."

"Take your time. We can leave whenever you're ready."

She was ready almost exactly thirty minutes later, and she didn't look any better than she did when I picked her up. In fact, I thought she looked worse. Her skin was pale with some darkness underneath her eyes. Then she fell asleep as soon as we hit the highway.

"Gabby, we're here," I said softly and reached over to gently shake her shoulder.

"Yeah, okay," she mumbled.

"Gabby, wake up," I said a bit louder.

Her head shot up, and she looked around in confusion. "What? What's going on?"

I chuckled. "You fell asleep."

"Oh, I'm sorry," she said and wiped her hand over her face.

"You don't need to apologize for being tired. Come on, let's go inside. I'll get your bag for you."

"Is that Flint's truck?" she asked as we walked to the front door.

"Yeah. He's been staying here taking care of the chickens."

I opened the door and started to step inside but halted in my tracks when a large black and white dog appeared in front of me. It wasn't barking or growling, but it wasn't giving off friendly vibes either.

Gabby peeked around me. "Aw, look at the pretty little doggy," she cooed. Before I could stop her, she moved around me and went straight for the dog.

"Gabby, stop!" I shouted. She wasn't wrong. The dog was beautiful. It was also huge and unfamiliar. I didn't know if it would roll over for a belly rub or rip her to shreds.

At the sound of my raised voice, the dog placed itself between the two of us and started growling. At me.

"You scared him," Gabby scolded.

Flint rounded the corner and took in the scene. "It's okay, boy," he said and snapped his fingers. The dog growled once more before dutifully retreating to Flint's side.

"When did you get a dog?" I asked.

Flint shifted uncomfortably. "I noticed him hanging around the edge of your property a few days ago. He looked pretty rough when I first saw him, so I brought him inside, gave him a bath, and fed him. I've posted about him everywhere, but I haven't been able to find his owners."

"Can I pet him?" Gabby asked excitedly.

"Yes, he's friendly," Flint said.

"He didn't seem very friendly just now," I grumbled.

"Maybe he doesn't like you," Gabby said and stuck out her tongue.

Flint laughed. "I think he was just defending what he considers his territory. He's shown no signs of aggression, even with food."

"He's a big baby," Gabby said. I couldn't help but laugh. She was sitting in the middle of my kitchen floor with what appeared to be a giant pit bull in her lap. She had both arms wrapped around him while her head rested on his back. "Are you going to keep him?"

Flint shrugged. "I hadn't planned on it."

"What are you going to do with him?"

"I was hoping I'd find his owners. I haven't thought about it beyond that."

She turned her attention to me. "What about you? You took in stray chickens. How do you feel about a dog?"

"Hold that thought. Flint, come with me," I said and motioned for him to follow me outside.

"What are we doing?" he asked.

"I want to try something," I said and walked around to my back door. I waited a few minutes before I loudly knocked on the door. The dog started barking and appeared at the door moments later.

I grinned. "Yeah, I think I'm okay with him hanging around for a while."

"So, you want me to leave him here?" Flint asked.

"What do you mean?"

"Well, I was going to head out since you're home," he said.

"You don't have to leave unless you want to. We're only here for the night."

"Stay and hang out," Gabby added. "It's been a while since I've seen you."

Flint laughed. "You don't have to ask me twice. The beds here are much more comfortable than the one I have at home."

Gabby nodded with a grin. "Yes, they are. I fell asleep as soon as I sat down the last time I was here."

"You can thank Keegan. She picked them out."

"My sister picked out your beds?" Gabby asked in surprise.

"Actually, I think your grandmother helped, too."

"How did that happen?"

I shrugged. "Right after I bought this place, I realized I had no idea how to furnish it, so I asked Keegan for help." Truthfully, I'd lived with the bare minimum for years, so when I finally bought a house, I wanted it to feel like a home. Keegan and Shaker's place had always felt like a home, so I thought she was the perfect person to ask.

For some strange reason, the fact that I hadn't known how to decorate my house on my own made me feel vulnerable, so I changed the subject. "Who's hungry?"

"Me!" Gabby and Flint said at the same time.

We ordered pizza and started watching a movie after we ate, but Gabby fell asleep within the first fifteen minutes. I knew she was tired, so I carried her to

bed and went back downstairs to finish the movie with Flint.

* * *

"Does Gabby usually sleep this late?" Flint asked.

I glanced at the time and realized it was close to eleven. "I'm not sure, but based on the few days I've spent with her, I'm going to say no. I'll go check on her."

I knocked on the door a few times, but she didn't answer. I slowly opened the door and stepped inside to find her asleep in bed. "Gabby," I called. She didn't budge. "Gabby," I said again and walked to the side of the bed. Placing my hand on her shoulder, I gently jostled her. "Gabby, wake up."

She blinked her eyes open and looked at me in confusion. "Byte?" she croaked and started coughing.

"Sorry. It's after eleven, and I didn't know if you wanted to sleep this late. Are you okay?"

She started to sit up and quickly dropped back onto the pillow. "I'm not sure. I don't feel very good."

I placed my hand on her forehead and was shocked at how warm she felt. "I think you might be running a fever."

She sniffled and coughed again. "Do you have a thermometer?"

"Yeah, just a minute," I said, then hurried to my bathroom to retrieve it.

When I returned, Gabby had propped herself up in bed, and she looked awful. Her pale skin, coupled with

the darkness under her glassy eyes, had my concern growing.

"Maybe we should call Patch," I suggested.

"It's probably just a cold," she said, and placed the thermometer under her tongue.

I was by no means an expert, but I was pretty sure she had more than the common cold. My suspicion was confirmed when the thermometer beeped. "One hundred and four point two."

"What?" Gabby gasped. "No, that can't be right."

"It is," I said and showed her the number displayed on the digital screen. "I'm calling Patch."

"Fine," she said and covered her mouth when she started coughing again.

Her response surprised me. I expected her to refuse and was ready to argue my point. Instead, I nodded once and stepped out of the room to call Patch.

After explaining the situation and sharing Gabby's symptoms, he asked me to bring her to his office so he could examine her. She didn't want to go, but I told her she didn't have a choice. She could go willingly, or she could be carried to the truck and driven there, but she was going.

"Fine," she huffed and got out of bed to get dressed. She took two steps and started to sway. I reached out to steady her and guided her back to the bed.

"You don't need to change. You're sick and going to the doctor. No one cares what you're wearing."

"I care," she grumbled. "Will you get my brush out of my bag? I'm at least going to brush my hair. And I'd like to brush my teeth, too."

I helped her brush her hair and get it pulled back into a low ponytail. Then I brought her a cup of water, an empty cup, her toothbrush, and toothpaste so she could brush her teeth without having to get out of bed.

"Anything else?" I asked.

"I guess not," she sighed and moved to stand.

"Let me help you," I insisted and looped my arm under hers.

Flint gasped at the sight of her when we made it to the bottom of the stairs. "What's going on?"

"She's sick. I'm taking her to Patch's place."

"Anything I can do to help?" he offered.

"Yeah, get the doors for me," I said and scooped Gabby into my arms. She had enough trouble walking down the stairs. I didn't want to push it by having her walk to the truck when I was perfectly capable of carrying her.

I had to wake her when we reached Patch's office. I offered to carry her, but she insisted on walking inside. Thankfully, he was waiting for us and took us back to a room right away.

"Well, kiddo, you look like hell," he said as soon as she was situated on the exam table.

"I feel like it," she admitted.

He held up a tube with a long cotton swab. "Let's see if my suspicions are correct. You know the drill."

Gabby frowned but tilted her head back so Patch could swab her nose. He handed the specimen to a nurse I hadn't seen enter the room and told her to run it immediately. While she was gone, he listened to Gabby's lungs and checked her ears, eyes, nose, and throat.

He'd just finished when the nurse knocked on the door. She stepped inside to whisper something to Patch and quickly left the room.

"Congratulations, sweetheart. You have the flu," Patch said.

"But I had the flu shot," Gabby argued weakly.

Patch chuckled. "You know as well as I do that it only covers a few strains. Besides, we're almost at the end of flu season. If you got the vaccine at the beginning, it's probably worn off by now."

"I don't have time for this," Gabby said, sounding as if she was on the verge of tears. "I have school and work."

"I'll write you some prescriptions to start today. You're young and healthy, so you should only be down for a few days," Patch told her. "Do you need a note for school and work?"

"Yes, for work. I don't have school until Tuesday, so maybe."

"I'll give you one for both, just in case," Patch said.

"Thank you."

"You're welcome. Go home and get into bed. Rest and drink plenty of fluids."

"I'll take you back to my house and then go pick up your prescriptions," I told her once we were back in the truck. "Do you want anything particular from the store? Like drinks and snacks?"

"Will you get me some berry Propel, ginger ale, and Cheez-Its?"

"I'll get whatever you need," I told her sincerely. I'd felt helpless all morning. Being able to fulfill a simple

request made me feel like I was helping, even if it was minimal.

"Do you have acetaminophen? If not, I'll need that, too."

"If I do, it's probably old, so I'll get a new bottle while I'm at the store."

"Thank you," she said softly.

Flint opened the front door and stepped out onto the porch when he heard us in the driveway. "What did Patch say?"

"She has the flu," I told him as I helped Gabby out of the truck and into the house.

"I can go to the store if you need anything," he offered.

"Actually, that'd be great. Her prescriptions need to be picked up, as well as a few other things. I'll text you a list as soon as I get her in bed." It was a relief when Flint volunteered to go to the store for me. I hadn't realized how much I didn't want to leave Gabby's side until he did.

I also hadn't noticed the dog following along closely behind us until he jumped onto the bed and laid down beside Gabby. She placed her hand on his head and smiled weakly. "Maybe being sick won't be so bad if I get to cuddle with you."

As if he understood her words, the dog scooted closer and rested his head on her stomach. "Is it wrong of me to hope we don't find his owners?"

"Your intentions aren't malicious, so no, I don't think it's wrong."

"Okay," she whispered and closed her eyes.

"You should probably call your boss before you fall asleep," I reminded her.

"Right," she grimaced. "I hate calling in sick to work."

"Why? Will they give you a hard time?"

"No, nothing like that. I hate knowing they'll have to search for a nurse to replace me and might have to work short-staffed if they can't find someone," she admitted.

"That's better than you going to work sick, not providing your patients with proper care, and exposing everyone there to the flu."

"I hadn't thought of it that way," she said, and reached for her phone to make the call.

"Do you need to notify anyone from school?" I asked when she was finished.

She shook her head. "Not yet. I'll wait until Monday and email my instructor if I'm still sick."

I didn't think she would be well enough by Tuesday to go to her clinical, but I kept my opinion to myself.

When she yawned and closed her eyes, I got up to leave the room, intending to wake her when Flint returned with her medicine. She reached out and managed to grab my hand without opening her eyes. "Will you stay?"

"If you want me to."

"I do," she almost whispered. Then she scooted herself and the dog over to make room for me. So, like a complete idiot, I climbed into bed beside her and wrapped my arm around her when she snuggled against my chest. Then she let out a contented sigh. And as

hard as I tried, I couldn't ignore how right it felt having her in my arms.

* * *

I JOLTED AWAKE AND LOOKED AROUND IN CONFUSION FOR a few seconds before I realized I had fallen asleep in my guest room with Gabby. She rolled to her side, mumbled something I couldn't make out, rolled back, and groaned as if she was in pain. The dog was still on the bed, but he was sitting up, watching every move she made. She continued to roll around, and I tried to decide if I should let her be or wake her. We'd been asleep for over two hours, but Patch did say she needed to rest. The decision was made for me when I placed my hand on her forehead. She was burning up and needed to take her medicine.

I slipped out of bed and went downstairs to find Flint watching television in the living room. "Everything you asked for is on the kitchen table. How's she doing?" he asked.

"Not good. She's tossing and turning, and I think her fever's gone up. I'll wake her up and get some of this medicine in her."

"Anything I can do?"

"Yes, but let me get her situated first," I said and grabbed all the bags from the table and took them upstairs with me.

Gabby wasn't easy to wake, but I managed to rouse her long enough to take her temperature and give her the medications Patch prescribed, as well as

acetaminophen for her fever. I got her to drink half a bottle of the Propel she requested before she refused to have any more.

"I just want to sleep," she mumbled and closed her eyes.

"Go ahead. I'll come back and check on you in a little bit."

She patted the bed beside her. "Where's my dog?"

Once again, the dog seemed to understand her and snuggled up beside her.

Before I knew what I was doing, I leaned over and kissed her forehead. Realization dawned as my lips brushed across her skin, and I flew out of the room like my ass was on fire.

"So, what do you need me to do?" Flint asked when I returned to the living room.

"I need you to go to Gabby's house and get her a few changes of clothes. She's going to be here for a few days at least."

"No problem. Do you have her keys?"

"Yes, but there are some things you need to know first," I said, and proceeded to fill him in on everything going on with Gabby.

Flint wasn't gone long, maybe an hour and a half at most. I spent the entire time pacing around the house and trying to find things to keep myself occupied. I knew Flint could handle himself if something happened, but I didn't want him to have to.

When he walked through the back door carrying two large bags, I breathed a sigh of relief. "Did everything go okay?"

"Yeah, it was fine. Nothing seemed out of place. As I was leaving, a girl named Lauren pulled into the driveway. She said she'd been trying to get in touch with Gabby for a few days and wanted to know where she was."

"Shit. What did you tell her?"

"I told her Gabby was in Croftridge for the weekend. She wanted to know why and what I was doing at her house. I told her I didn't know why Gabby was in Croftridge and that I was sent to pick up a few things for her," he explained. "When I asked who she was, she said she was a friend from school."

"Yeah, I met her when she came over to Gabby's house a few days ago to study."

"She gave me her phone number," he said.

"She did?"

"Yeah," Flint chuckled. "She asked if I was seeing anyone. When I said no, she handed me a piece of paper with her phone number on it and told me to call her. Then she winked at me before she got into her car and drove away."

"Are you going to call her?"

"Hell no," he laughed. "I could tell from the few minutes I talked to her that she wasn't my type. She's too pushy and seemed to lack boundaries."

"Yeah," I agreed. "I got the same feeling from her."

8

BYTE

I spent the rest of the weekend taking care of Gabby and searching for information regarding her situation. Despite my efforts, I still had found nothing on the man pretending to be Chad Higgins. I needed a good photo of him or a piece of legit information to use. Hitting a dead end was rare for me, and it was frustrating as hell.

The sound of a door opening upstairs broke me out of my thoughts. Since Gabby was the only person up there, I hurried up the stairs to see what she was doing out of bed.

"What are you doing?" I asked.

"I'm feeling better, so I thought I'd go downstairs and get something to eat."

"Nope. Get back in bed, and I'll bring you something," I insisted.

"You've been waiting on me hand and foot all weekend."

"And I'm going to keep doing it for a little while

longer. You might be feeling better right now, but you don't want to overdo it."

"Yeah, you're probably right," she admitted and leaned against the wall.

"Come on, let me help you back to bed, and then I'll bring you some soup."

"Thanks, Byte."

When I returned with a bowl of ramen noodle soup and a sleeve of saltine crackers, I watched in horror as she crumbled the entire package of crackers and dumped them into her soup. "What are you doing?"

"Having soup and crackers."

"No, you're having crackers with a little bit of soup."

"I like it this way," she said and took a bite. "I don't tell you how to eat your soup."

I laughed. "You mean you don't tell me how to eat my crackers."

"If I felt better, I'd throw something at you."

"I thought you said you were feeling better."

"I am, and I'm not. I think my fever finally broke, because I woke up covered in sweat. But I still feel like crap."

"Have you talked to your instructor?"

"Not yet. I'll see how I feel Monday."

"Gabby," I said slowly. "It is Monday."

"What?" she gasped and reached for her phone on the nightstand. "I can't believe it. I've been asleep for three days?"

"Yes, and no. You woke up long enough to take your medicine or make a trip to the bathroom," I explained.

"I don't remember any of that."

"Well, you were pretty out of it. Patch said that was because of the fever."

"How high was it?"

"Anywhere between one hundred and three and one hundred and five."

"That explains all the sweat," she grumbled. "I really need to take a shower."

"Why don't you finish eating first?" I suggested.

She looked down at the half-eaten bowl of soup and frowned. "I don't think I can eat any more."

"Are you sure?" I asked, hoping she'd reconsider.

"Yeah, I'm sure," she said and picked up her phone. "I need to let my instructor know what's going on." Her eyes widened as she read something on the screen.

"What's wrong?"

"Lauren has been blowing up my phone. I have twelve missed calls and seventeen text messages from her."

"Is that unusual for her?" I asked.

"Hold on, let me send this to my instructor before I forget," she said and quickly typed out a message. "I don't know Lauren that well, but I'm going to say this isn't normal behavior for anyone. What do you think?" she asked and handed me her phone.

I read over the text messages and had to agree with Gabby. The first couple of messages were fine, but they became increasingly insistent and demanding.

"Yeah, these messages sound like they're from a controlling parent or a jealous girlfriend, not from a concerned friend."

"I guess I should text her back and tell her I'm sick."

"Before you do, there's something you should know. I asked Flint to go to your house and pick up a few things for you on Friday. She showed up at your place when he was headed back out to his truck and grilled him about where you were."

"What the hell?"

"Yeah," I said. "He told her you were in Croftridge for the weekend. Then she asked him if he was single and gave him her phone number."

Gabby covered her face with her hands. "I can't believe she did that. What did Flint do?"

"He took her number and left, but he has no intention of calling her."

"This is unbelievable. We've studied together a few times this semester. Before that, we'd had lunch together the handful of times we had a break between classes. We're acquaintances, not friends, so I don't know why she's acting like I owe her explanations of my whereabouts."

Gabby's phone dinged with a text.

"Is it Lauren again?"

"No, it's from my instructor. She said three people at the office are out with the flu, including the physician I've been shadowing. He's out for the rest of the week, which means I am, too," she explained.

"Is that going to be a problem?"

"Not unless something else happens. I had some extra hours worked into my schedule to cover for emergencies, but this is going to use up all of them."

Gabby's phone dinged again.

"It's Lauren," she sighed. "I'm not sure what to say

to her. I don't exactly want her to know I'm still in Croftridge or that my clinical hours have been canceled for the week."

"Tell her you're sick and have been sleeping a lot. If she pushes for more info, don't respond."

Seconds after Gabby sent the message, Lauren responded with multiple texts. I could tell Gabby was overwhelmed. I held out my hand. "Give me your phone."

She handed it over without hesitation.

Lauren: Are you okay?

Lauren: Where are you?

Lauren: Do you want me to stop by?

Lauren: Do you need anything?

I typed out a response and turned Gabby's phone off.

"What did you say?" she asked.

"I told her you had the flu and there was no need for her to stop by because your family friend was taking care of you. Then I said you were going back to bed and would text her in a few days when you were feeling better."

"Thank you."

"No problem," I said and got to my feet. "I'll let you get some rest. Do you need anything before I go?"

"I'm good, but I'm going to take a shower first," she said.

"I don't think so."

"You're telling me I can't take a shower?"

"I'm telling you I don't think standing in a hot, steamy shower is a good idea. You could barely walk down the hall," I pointed out.

"Byte, I haven't showered since Thursday, and quite frankly, I stink."

"I think you should wait until you have more strength. Maybe tomorrow."

"No," she said firmly. "If you want to hang out in the bathroom while I'm in there, fine. But I'm taking a shower."

"All right. Let's go," I said, hoping to call her bluff. Unbeknownst to me, she wasn't bluffing.

I got the water started for her while she gathered her clothes and toiletries. When she was ready, I waited outside while she undressed and stepped into the shower. "You can come in," she called out.

She'd only been in there for a few minutes when her hand shot out from behind the curtain. "Towel, now," she demanded as the water shut off.

"What's wrong?" I asked as I placed a towel in her hand.

"You were right," she admitted and shoved the shower curtain to the side. Seconds later, her towel-clad body fell against mine. I wrapped my arms around her to hold her up as her head rested against my chest.

"Are you okay?" I asked.

Instead of answering me, her big blue eyes filled

with tears. "Gabby," I said quietly. "Tell me what's wrong."

"I feel awful," she cried. "I thought a shower would make me feel better, but I can't even wash my hair."

I helped her walk to the edge of the bed and sit down. "Don't move. I'll be right back."

I rushed out of the room before she could argue and returned with a bathrobe I'd received as a Christmas gift and had never worn. "Put this on."

"What are you doing?"

"Making you feel better," I said cryptically.

Once she had the robe on, I scooped her into my arms and carried her downstairs to the kitchen, where I placed her on the countertop by the sink.

"Seriously, Byte, what are you doing?"

"You'll see. Do you think you can stay there without falling off?"

She narrowed her eyes. "Yes, I think I can manage that."

I ran back upstairs to get a couple of towels as well as her shampoo and conditioner. Her eyes widened in surprise when she saw what I was carrying.

"Byte—" she started.

"If washing your hair will make you feel better, that's what we're going to do," I said and helped her lie back so her hair was in the sink. "Let me know if the water's too hot."

"It's perfect," she said and sighed when I started to work the shampoo through her long, dark hair. I was surprised by how thick it was and even more surprised at how long it took to rinse all the suds out.

Once I finished rinsing the conditioner, I wrapped her hair in a towel and nudged her to sit up. She jolted, and her eyes shot open. I couldn't help but laugh. "Did you fall asleep?"

"What? No, of course not," she lied.

"Yes, you did," I said and helped her sit up.

"You can't hold it against me. I'm sick," she said and wrapped her arms around me. With her head resting on my shoulder, I felt it more than I heard it when she whispered, "Thank you."

9

GABBY

By Thursday, I was much better. I still had a nasty cough, but my fever was completely gone, and I could move around without feeling like I was going to collapse. I had even managed to take a shower and wash my hair by myself.

"When do we need to head back to your place?" Byte asked over breakfast.

"Maybe around noon?" I suggested. "I have to go by Employee Health and get clearance so I can work tomorrow. Then I need to do laundry and probably make a grocery run."

"We can leave whenever you're ready. Just let me know."

I showered and made myself look as presentable as possible. I was still paler than usual, but I no longer looked like I was knocking on death's door. Once I was ready, I made my way downstairs, carrying the two bags with my belongings.

Byte immediately took the bags from me. "You should've let me bring these down for you."

"I'm not helpless."

"I didn't say you were. But you have been sick, and there's no sense in wasting energy if you don't have to."

"Fine," I huffed. "Would you like to carry me to my car as well?"

"We're taking my truck."

"What about my car?" I asked. I didn't necessarily need it since he drove me everywhere, but I didn't want to leave it in Croftridge in case something happened to his truck again.

"Flint is going to drive it to your place later. Diesel will follow and drive him back to Croftridge."

It took me a moment to realize he was referring to James. I wasn't used to his road name because he'd always been James to me.

While he placed my bags in the truck, I squatted down and hugged the dog who'd been by my side for the last week. "I'm going to miss you," I said and struggled to hold back my tears.

"He's coming with us," Byte announced.

"What?"

"He's coming with us. We haven't found his owners, and he barks whenever someone approaches the house. I think he'll be good to have around," he said, and opened the back passenger door. "Come on, boy. Let's go."

I laughed when the dog didn't budge. "I bet you'll get in if I do," I said and patted his head. Then I got

into the front seat while my new best friend dutifully hopped into the back seat.

"You should probably name him," I said once we were on the road.

"Me? He's your dog."

"What?" I asked in surprise. "I can't have a dog. I'm hardly ever home. It wouldn't be fair to him."

"Relax," Byte laughed. "I was kidding. Well, sort of. He obviously likes you more than me."

"I mean, I would love to keep him, but I can't leave him inside for twelve to fourteen hours on the days I work. And even if I did have a fenced yard, I don't think I could leave him outside for that long either."

"What about when you're finished with school? Could you have a dog then?" he asked.

"Probably. It'll really depend on where I end up working."

"How about this? He can stay with me for now. Then after you graduate and start working, if you want him, you can have him," he offered.

"You'd do that for me?"

"Sure," he said, like it wasn't a big deal. "He hasn't been any trouble, and I kind of like him. Besides, I was planning on keeping him before I knew you might want him."

"What a lucky dog. He went from having no one to having two people love him."

"You're not naming him Lucky," Byte grumbled.

"I wasn't going to," I laughed, followed by a fit of coughing.

"Are you okay?"

"Yeah, it's just a residual cough. It should go away in a week or two," I explained.

We spent the rest of the drive trying to come up with a name for the dog, but nothing we thought of seemed to fit him. Before I knew it, Byte was pulling into the parking lot at the hospital.

"This shouldn't take long," I told him.

I was right. It didn't take long. I was walking back to the truck and trying not to cry less than ten minutes later.

"What's wrong?" Byte asked immediately.

"They didn't clear me to return to work," I huffed.

"What? Why not?"

"Because of this fucking cough. I even gave them the note from Patch saying I could return to work, but they didn't care."

"What happens now?"

"She said they'd recheck me in five days. Which means I can't work tomorrow or Monday. Since I'll be at the doctor's office on Tuesday, Wednesday, and Thursday, I won't be able to get rechecked until Friday. I don't know what in the hell they're thinking. Residual coughs can last for weeks!"

"Are you just upset about letting your coworkers down, or is there more to it?" Byte asked carefully.

"What do you mean?"

He cleared his throat. "Is this about money?"

"Oh, no, it's nothing like that. I have a trust fund from my mother. Well, it's really from Keegan. Our mother set up a trust fund for Keegan, but she died before she set one up for me. Because Keegan is

Keegan, she put half of hers into an account for me. Somewhere along the way, Gigi added to it. I don't actually have to work. Well, that's not entirely true. I needed the clinical experience to get into grad school. Once I'd worked enough to fulfill the requirement, I kept working part-time for the experience. I've learned much more at the hospital than I ever did from textbooks."

"So what's got you so upset?"

I sighed. "I'm just frustrated, I guess. Because of a protocol created by someone behind a desk, I can't work, even though a practicing physician says I can. Hospital politics are bullshit."

"There's nothing you can do about it, so you might as well enjoy your days off," he said.

I shook my head. "I'm not sure I even know how to do that. Since I only have one or two days off at a time, I usually spend them running errands, doing laundry, or studying."

"Now you have four. Think of something fun to do, and we'll do it," he said.

"There's a place not too far from here where they teach you how to weave your own basket. Then you can fill it full of berries you pick yourself from their farm. I've always thought that would be fun. What do you think?"

Byte audibly swallowed and nodded once. "Sure. I mean, if that's what you want to do," he said and failed to hide his reluctance.

I wanted to keep going, but I couldn't hold back my laughter. "I'm just fucking with you."

"You're going to pay for that," he teased.

"Were you seriously going to go basket weaving and berry picking with me?"

"Yes, I was, but I really didn't want to," he admitted.

"You weren't going to try to talk me out of it?"

He shook his head. "You seemed like you wanted to go. If it was going to make you happy, why would I try to talk you out of it?"

I placed my hand on his arm and gave it a gentle squeeze. "You're a good man, Byte."

"I do what I can."

He did a lot more than he could. He'd gone out of his way to watch over me while my family was out of town, after he came to my rescue and chased a burglar out of my house. Then he took excellent care of me while I was sick. He offered to take care of a dog for me until I finished school. And he was willing to spend a whole day doing things he had no interest in to make me happy. I was beginning to realize he was more than a good man. He was a great man. Maybe even a perfect man.

My thoughts were interrupted when Byte abruptly put the truck in park and turned to me. "Stay here," he said and pulled his gun from the holster at his back.

"Wait! What's going on?" I demanded and grabbed his arm to stop him from getting out of the truck.

He pointed toward my house. "Your front door is open."

"I don't think you should go in there."

"I'll be fine, but you need to stay here," he insisted.

"Lock the doors, and if something happens, drive away."

"No! Please don't go," I begged.

"Gabby, I'll be fine. I doubt anyone's still in there."

"Then why can't I go with you?" I argued.

"Because you need to stay safe in case someone is in there."

"So do you!"

"Gabby, this is what I do. I'll be okay."

"Fine," I huffed. Then I grabbed his shirt and pulled him toward me until my lips met his in a bruising kiss. I wasn't sure what kind of reaction to expect, but him grabbing my hair and returning my kiss was more than I could have hoped for.

He broke the kiss before I was ready to let him go. "We're going to talk about that when I get back. Stay here," he said and got out of the truck before I could try to stop him.

While he cleared my house, I sat there for what felt like forever. I coaxed the dog into the front seat with me and wrapped my arms around him while I waited. I was debating on whether to break my promise and go inside when Byte finally appeared at the front door and motioned for me to come inside.

When I got out, the dog trailed behind me like a shadow. "Shadow," I said and looked at Byte. "His name is Shadow."

Byte nodded. "It suits him."

"I take it no one's in there."

"No, but someone was," he said and stopped me

before I could go inside. "You need to brace yourself. It's pretty bad in there."

Pretty bad was an understatement. My house had been trashed. Every shelf had been cleared. Every cabinet had been emptied. Basically, everything I owned was on the floor. Even the contents of my refrigerator had been dumped on the floor.

After walking around the house with Byte and taking in the scene, we returned to the living room. I stood there, staring blankly at the floor. I didn't know what to do, and I couldn't think of any words to say. I wanted to cry, but I couldn't manage to do that either. I couldn't do anything.

"Gabby!" Byte shouted in a way that made me think he'd said my name more than once.

I lifted my head to meet his eyes but couldn't make myself speak. "It's going to be okay," he said.

I turned my gaze back to the floor and waited for him to tell me what to do. I couldn't think. I couldn't function. I needed him to take charge because I had completely checked out.

10

BYTE

"I'm getting you out of here," I said and scooped Gabby into my arms.

Once I had her safely in the truck with Shadow, I closed the door and called Phoenix.

"Prez, I need help," I said as soon as he answered.

"Tell me what's going on."

"I drove Gabby back to Cedar Valley today. We just got to her house, and the place is trashed. Almost everything she owns has been destroyed. And I think she's in shock. She hasn't said a single word since we went inside, and she's got this blank look on her face that is freaking me the hell out. I don't know what to do."

"Bring her to the clubhouse. I'll round up the brothers while you're on your way, and I'll get Harper to come over so she can stay with her while we have church."

"Thanks, Prez. Oh, Flint and Diesel were going to drive her car back to her place. They may have

already left, but can you call them and let them know to leave it at my house or drop it off at the clubhouse?"

"Yeah, I'll take care of that. You take care of Gabby and drive safe."

"Will do, Prez. See you soon."

When I got into my truck, Gabby was staring blankly out the window. Shadow was sitting on the floor in front of her with his head resting in her lap.

She didn't move or even acknowledge me when I placed my hand on her shoulder. "I talked to Phoenix. I'm taking you to the clubhouse, and we're going to take care of this." Then I moved closer and gently kissed her cheek. "I'm going to fix this for you. I promise," I whispered.

I didn't wait for her to respond. Instead, I took her hand in mine and drove us back to Croftridge.

It looked like Phoenix had called everyone in because the forecourt was packed when we arrived.

"Do you want to go in through the back?" I asked.

She didn't respond.

"Okay, we'll go through the back, and I'll take you to my room," I said, as if she had answered me. I had no idea how I should respond to her, but I thought acting like everything was okay was better than letting her know how much she was scaring me. And she was. I was fucking terrified. I'd never seen anyone shut down the way she did.

I walked around the truck and opened her door. "Do you want to walk?" I asked, unsure if she even could, or would. She didn't answer verbally, but she got out of the

truck on her own accord. Shadow jumped down behind her and waited by her side.

"Come on," I said softly and took her hand to lead her inside.

Once we reached my room, I led her to the bed and had to tell her to sit down. Then I took both of her hands in mine and squatted in front of her. "I'm not sure what's going on in your head. I know you're scared. And what happened today was very upsetting. I guess what I'm saying is it's okay to feel however you feel. And while I'd love to have some kind of response from you, I'm not going to pressure you for one. Take all the time you need, and I'll be right here when you're ready. In the meantime, you're safe, and we're going to take care of this for you."

I leaned forward and kissed her forehead right as someone knocked twice on the door, causing Shadow to bark.

I quickly stood and opened the door to find Phoenix standing there with a look of surprise on his face. "When did you get a dog?"

"Flint found him hanging around my property last week, and he's since taken a liking to Gabby. She named him Shadow, and well, now we have a dog."

"How's she doing?" he asked.

"See for yourself," I said quietly and gestured for him to come in.

Phoenix took one look at her and exhaled heavily. "Are you okay with Harper staying with her while we have church?"

"I can't think of anyone better." Harper and Keegan

had always been close, so I knew Gabby was comfortable with her. Plus, Harper was an excellent therapist, and it was clear that Gabby needed help.

"I'll send her in," Phoenix said and left the room.

Harper must have been waiting right outside the door because she was in my room mere seconds after Phoenix left. She bypassed me and sat down beside Gabby, wrapping her arms around her. "Oh, sweet girl, you're going to be okay."

Harper looked at me over Gabby's head. "I'll stay right here until you get back. Lock the door on your way out. I don't want anyone coming in here except you."

"Thanks, Harper."

"Hold on," she said suddenly. "Who's that?"

"Shadow. He's friendly, and he adores Gabby."

"Perfect," she said, and patted the bed. "Come here, Shadow."

Shadow jumped onto the bed and situated himself beside Gabby. Harper smiled. "Sometimes dogs are the best therapy. Go on. We'll take care of her until you get back."

With that, I locked the door behind me and headed to church.

Phoenix filled the officers in on everything that had happened with Gabby.

"The cameras didn't catch anything?" Carbon asked.

"I haven't had a chance to check, but I'm going to assume they didn't since I didn't get any notifications of activity," I said and opened up my laptop. It only took a

few moments to confirm my suspicions. "The cameras were disabled two days after I installed them."

"How was that possible?" Badger asked.

"Someone accessed her account remotely and made changes," I explained.

"So, her security system is useless?" Dash asked.

"In this instance, yes. Whoever is behind this knows how to hack security systems. Ironically, disabling residential alarms is fairly easy."

"This is exactly why I'm going to have at least two brothers stationed at Gabby's house. They can hide their bikes in her garage. If we want it to look like she's there, we can park her car in the driveway. This person has already entered her house twice. I have no doubt they'll try again," Phoenix said.

"Her house is a mess, Prez," I added.

"We'll have the cops come out so she'll have a report for her insurance company. Once that's done, we'll get her place cleaned up and put back in order. When does she have to go back to work or school?"

"Tuesday morning."

"All right. Let's have her stay in Croftridge through Monday. She can stay at the clubhouse or your place. Shaker and Keegan will be back on Sunday. We'll reconvene then and come up with a plan for next week if there are no developments between now and then. Any objections?" Phoenix asked.

When everyone agreed with the plan, Phoenix asked if I had any updates.

"Nothing, Prez. I haven't been able to find anything on Chad Higgins, or who he really is."

"Are we sure he's the one behind this?" Phoenix asked.

"No, not completely. But the timing, the lies he told Gabby, and his lack of an online presence strongly suggest he is," I said.

"Are there any other potential suspects?" Duke asked.

I shook my head. "No, just Chad. Gabby said he was the only new person in her life, and her troubles started right after she broke things off with him."

"Sounds like Chad knows a thing or two about computers," Carbon said.

"Yeah," I agreed. "And it's pissing me right the hell off."

"He'll fuck up sooner or later," Badger said. "And we'll be ready for him."

"Okay, I'll send Edge, Diesel, and Ink to Gabby's house. Once the police have come and gone, Edge can disconnect the cameras while the other two get started on clean up," Phoenix said.

"Wait. Why would he disconnect the cameras?" Duke asked.

"So the little wanna-be hacker can't turn them on remotely and see that Gabby's house is being occupied by a bunch of pissed-off bikers," I said.

"All right, I think that's everything. Are you two staying here or going back to your place?" Phoenix asked.

"I guess we'll stay here unless she says otherwise, which I doubt will happen since she's not talking."

"What do you mean she's not talking?" Carbon demanded.

"She hasn't said a word since she saw her house. She'll respond to directions, like 'get out of the truck' or 'let's go inside,' but that's it. Harper's with her now," I explained.

"Reese used to do that," he said quietly. "After we lost our family, sometimes she'd just shut down. She was like a damn robot."

"What did you do to bring her out of it?" I asked eagerly. I was willing to do anything to bring Gabby back from wherever her mind had gone.

"I held her and talked to her like I always did. I never acknowledged her zombie-like state. I carried on like everything was normal," he explained.

"And that worked?"

He shrugged. "I really don't know. Sometimes it was only minutes, while other times it took days, but she always came back around."

"I don't mean to sound like an asshole, but Gabby's reaction seems a bit extreme. Reese lost the majority of her family. That's far more traumatic than having your house broken into," Duke said.

"Not if the break-in has triggered something from Gabby's past we don't know about," Dash said.

"What do you mean?" I asked.

"Keegan and Shaker adopted Gabby when she was five. We don't know what her life was like before they got her," Phoenix said.

"Fucking hell," I mumbled.

"She'll be okay," Phoenix assured me. "She's got one

hell of a support system. Make sure someone is always with her while she's working through this."

"And don't hesitate to call Harper if you need her," Carbon added. "If y'all are staying at the clubhouse tonight, we can crash here, too."

"Thanks, brother. I'll see how she is and let you know."

"All right. Church dismissed," Phoenix announced and banged his gavel on the table.

* * *

I RETURNED TO MY ROOM TO FIND HARPER, GABBY, AND Shadow in my bed. Harper had her arms wrapped around Gabby, who was resting against Harper's side. Shadow was wedged in between Gabby's legs with his head resting on her stomach. He barely lifted his head to look at me when I opened the door to the room. Apparently, I'd earned his seal of approval.

"How was church?" Harper asked.

"You know I can't tell you. Club business."

Harper rolled her eyes. "That line didn't work twenty years ago, and it's not going to work today. Besides, I think Gabby wants to know the plan," she said and widened her eyes, as if willing me to understand what she wasn't saying.

I took a seat on the edge of the bed and placed my hand on Gabby's foot. "Well, Phoenix wants us to stay in Croftridge for the weekend. He said we can stay at the clubhouse or my house, whichever you prefer. He's going to send Edge, Diesel, and Ink to your house.

They're going to have the police come out and make a report for your insurance company. Then they'll get the place cleaned up. He also wants them to stay there for a few days to see if anybody tries to break in again. If someone does, the boys will be waiting for them."

When Gabby didn't respond, Harper chimed in. "That sounds like a good plan. Do you want to stay at the clubhouse tonight? Harlow and I can spend the night, too, and we can have a movie night like we used to when you were little."

I was at a loss. So, I followed the advice Carbon gave me and carried on like everything was normal. It seemed like that's what Harper was doing, too. "Hold on. Before anyone agrees to a movie marathon, I need to know what we're watching. I have no interest in watching anything that's going to end with all the girls crying."

"If you're referring to the night we watched *The Notebook*, I believe your eyes were rather shiny, too," Harper teased.

"Lies! It's all lies!" I protested.

"How about a comedy?" Harper suggested. "Though I wouldn't mind trying to make the brothers cry again. I won so much money that night."

"You're an evil little woman."

Harper raised her hands in mock surrender. "It was Keegan's idea. I'm only guilty of placing wise bets."

"Keegan and her bets," I chuckled. "She loves to make them, yet rarely wins them."

Harper snapped her fingers. "Didn't you two make a robot or something like that?"

"Yeah, we did," I laughed. "And we placed bets on who would be the first to shoot it. I won fifty bucks off her."

"It was Carbon, wasn't it?" Harper asked.

"Carbon and Savior," I confirmed.

"I can't believe y'all didn't get in trouble for that."

"We probably would have if it weren't for everything else going on with Keegan at the time. Phoenix knew she needed to have a little fun. I think that's why he let it slide," I explained.

"Why is it that whenever we find our women in another brother's bed, it's always your bed?" Carbon asked as he entered my room.

"What can I say? The ladies love me."

"I don't know what you're talking about, but this is the first time I've ever been in Byte's bed," Harper said.

"He's referring to Keegan. Shaker found her in here a few times. His freak-outs were so epic she did it a couple of times just to piss him off," I laughed. "It would've been nice if she'd let me know that's what she was doing."

"Where's the fun in that?" Carbon chuckled.

"So, what's the plan for tonight?" Harper asked.

"I thought I'd go get Harlow and pick up pizza on the way back," Carbon said. "Do you want to stay here?"

"No, I'll go with you," she said and turned her attention to Gabby. "We'll be back soon, sweet girl."

Once they were gone, I took Harper's spot on the bed beside Gabby. I wrapped my arm around her shoulders and kissed the top of her head. "I know you've

been through a lot over the last two weeks, but we're going to get you through this."

Unfortunately, movie night wasn't the magic cure I hoped it would be. Gabby barely ate and never uttered a word. She sat between me and Harlow and fell asleep before the movie was over. I carried her to my room and tucked her into bed, hoping things would be better in the morning.

11

GABBY

I hugged my knees to my chest and cried as the little boy destroyed my room. He pushed over my dollhouse, knocked over the cart with my LEGOs, and threw everything in my toy box onto the floor.

"Stop!" I cried.

"I hate you!" he screamed and threw my favorite doll against the wall.

"What is going on in here?" my father demanded.

"He's breaking my toys," I whimpered.

"Come with me," my father said and grabbed the little boy's hand. "Gabriella, get this mess cleaned up. Now."

* * *

I WOKE WITH A START.

"What's wrong?" Byte asked and was immediately at my side.

"I don't know," I said and rubbed my hands over my

face, feeling confused. “I had a dream, but I don’t think it was a dream.”

“What do you mean?”

“I think it was a memory.”

“Tell me about it,” he encouraged.

“I was little, maybe three or four, and I was in my bedroom at my father’s house. A little boy was there, and he was destroying my room. My father came in and took him away, but he made me clean up the mess.”

“Do you know who he was?”

“No,” I said and shook my head. “I’d completely forgotten about him, but now I can remember him coming over to our house a few times. He was always so mean to me.”

“Well, I think the events of yesterday are responsible for triggering the memory.”

“Yeah,” I agreed. “And I think the events from my childhood are responsible for my reaction to the events of yesterday. I’m sorry about that. I don’t know what happened. I just couldn’t make myself respond to anything.”

“You don’t need to apologize. Like I said, you’ve been through a lot in a short amount of time. I’m just glad you’re talking to me now,” he said, sounding relieved.

“It was weird. I felt like I was going to get in trouble, which is ridiculous because I’m an adult. But that’s how it was when I was a child. If my father was upset, it was best to be quiet and, if possible, unseen. I guess the similarity between what happened yesterday and what happened when I was little triggered some childhood

trauma response I was unaware of," I said and covered my face with my hands.

Byte gently tugged my hands away from my face. "There's nothing to be embarrassed about. Almost everyone in this club has something from their past that haunts them."

"Do you?"

"Yes, but it's—" he started, but was interrupted by someone knocking on the door, followed by Shadow barking.

He opened the door to reveal a smiling Harper. "I thought I heard talking in here. Are you feeling better?"

"Yes," I nodded. "Sorry if I scared you."

She waved her hand dismissively. "I was a little worried, but I knew you'd come around. There's breakfast in the common room if you're hungry."

I was hungry. I had barely eaten the day before and was ready to make up for it. "I am. I'll be there in a few minutes."

I wasn't sure what to expect when I entered the common room. Part of me thought I would be bombarded with people hugging me and asking if I was okay. To my surprise, everyone carried on as if it was business as usual.

I'd been pushing a piece of French toast around on my plate for a few minutes when Byte asked, "What are you thinking about?"

I exhaled heavily. "As much as I don't want to, I really should go back to my house to help clean up and sort through things. I need to know what needs to be

replaced, and I'm the only one who will know if something's missing."

"If you don't want to go, you don't have to," Byte said. "Edge can send pictures for you to look through."

"I appreciate the offer, but I'll be okay. I can't sit here doing nothing while they're at my house cleaning up a huge mess."

"Are you sure?" Byte asked carefully.

"There won't be a repeat of yesterday."

"If you want to leave, say the word, and we're out of there. I don't care if we've only been there for five minutes."

"I will," I promised.

* * *

When we pulled into my driveway, Byte paused before getting out of the truck. I assumed he was going to ask me if I was okay again and was ready to assure him I was. However, that's not what happened. Instead, he picked up his phone and started typing.

"What are you doing?"

"Letting the guys know we're here. I didn't tell them we were coming, and I don't think surprising them is a good idea."

"Yeah, probably not," I agreed.

His phone buzzed with a message. "Okay, let's go."

Edge stepped out onto the front porch while we were letting Shadow out of the truck. "What are you guys doing here?"

"Gabby wanted to help with the cleanup so she

could get an idea of what she needs to replace and make note of anything missing," Byte explained.

Edge nodded. "We started with the kitchen. We threw out all the food that was ruined, as well as any broken dishes. Anything that isn't broken is being run through the dishwasher before we put it back in the cabinets. But it's good you're here, because we don't know where anything goes."

"Thanks, Edge. I really appreciate your help," I told him.

"I'm sorry someone did this to you, but I'm happy to help," he said and looked at Shadow. "You might want to watch where he goes in the house. We haven't gotten all the broken glass and ceramic off the floor. On that note, you both need to keep your shoes on."

"Crap," I mumbled. I hadn't even thought about the possibility of Shadow stepping on glass shards. "Is there anywhere that's safe for him?"

"The kitchen's clear."

"Okay, he'll have to stay in there until we make more progress," I said. Since Shadow had been with us, he hadn't been confined in a room or limited space. I wasn't sure how he'd react, but there wasn't much I could do about it.

"He'll be fine," Byte assured me.

"All right, where should I start? I asked.

Edge chuckled. "It's your house. Start wherever you'd like. Frankly, it'll be nice to have you here to provide some guidance."

"I guess I'll start in the living room and work my way through the rest of the house."

As it turned out, the damage wasn't as bad as I initially thought. It was still bad, just not as bad. Initially, I thought virtually everything was going to be a loss. While some items were broken beyond repair, most things were only knocked over or strewn about. The kitchen definitely bore the brunt of the assault, with my bedroom coming in second.

I was in my room sorting through my clothes covering the floor when Byte interrupted me. "Are you hungry?"

"Now that you mention it, I could eat."

"Diesel's going to pick up something from the Mexican restaurant beside the grocery store. Do you want something from there or somewhere else?"

"I love that place. I'll have a taco salad, no tomato and no guacamole," I told him and walked over to the bed to get my purse.

"I got it," he said and closed the door before I could argue.

I looked at Shadow, who was resting on my bed, and shrugged. "Well, okay then."

Despite the extensive mess, cleaning up my room was much easier than I thought. Every single item of clothing I owned had been removed from a drawer or hanger and thrown on the floor. Since there was no way I was going to wear anything until it had been washed, all I had to do was gather the clothes and stuff them into laundry baskets and boxes.

I'd worked my way to my closet when Byte returned to tell me the food had arrived. "One second," I said

and opened the hidden door in my closet. I'm not sure why I opened it, but it was a good thing I did.

"Byte," I gasped. "Look."

He quickly crossed the room and read the words spray-painted on the wall behind the false door. "I'll find you next time, bitch."

He pulled out his phone and snapped a few pictures. "We need to add this to the police report."

"Yeah," I agreed quietly. I tried not to let the words get to me, but I couldn't help it. The place that kept me safe had been discovered. It was the last semblance of security I had, and it was gone. What would I do if someone broke in again? Or when someone broke in again, according to the words written on the wall.

"Gabby," Byte said sternly. "They won't get to you."

"We don't even know who it is," I countered.

"Doesn't matter. You'll have someone with you at all times. No one will get to you," he assured me.

"I know," I said and swallowed thickly. "It was just a little jarring to see that my safe space has been discovered."

"Let's go eat," he said and gently led me out of the room, with Shadow following along behind us.

I stopped abruptly before entering the hall. "Is it okay for him to be out here?"

"It should be. We've gone over the floors at least twice with the vacuum."

We joined the guys in the kitchen for dinner. I looked around in awe. With the exception of the dishes waiting to be washed, my house looked almost normal.

"You guys are awesome. I can't believe how great this place looks."

"We were glad to help," Edge said. "Have you been able to figure out if anything's missing?"

"From what I can tell, they didn't take anything."

"But they did leave a message in the hiding space in her closet," Byte said and slid his phone over to Edge.

Edge looked at the picture and passed the phone to Diesel, then to Ink. "They're going to find a lot more than they bargained for if they show up here again."

After dinner, I finished up in the bedroom while Byte loaded my baskets and boxes of clothes into the truck. Then we said our goodbyes and headed back to Croftridge. I was exhausted and had a long day of laundry to look forward to.

12

GABBY

"Are you nervous?" Byte asked.

Keegan and Jacob were back from Scotland, and we were on our way over to their house with dinner.

"I'm not sure nervous is the word I'd use," I said. "But I'm definitely not looking forward to telling her about everything that happened while she was gone."

"I'm sure it'll be fine," he assured me.

"Well, we're about to find out," I said as he parked in the driveway.

I guess I was nervous. I picked up a few bags of food and went straight to the door without waiting for Byte.

Keegan engulfed me in a hug as soon as she opened the door. "Gabby! I missed you so much!"

"I missed you, too," I said and wiggled my way out of her arms so I could put the food on the table.

"Hey, Gabby," Jacob said and wrapped one arm around my shoulders. "It's good to see you."

Keegan started unpacking the food when Byte walked in, carrying a box of more food.

"Hey, Byte. What are you doing here?" Jacob asked.

Keegan looked up and froze. Her eyes moved from Byte to me. "Something happened," she said knowingly.

I nodded slowly. "Yeah, something happened. But everything's okay. Well, sort of."

"Just tell her," Byte encouraged.

I exhaled heavily. "Someone broke into my house the Friday after you left. I hid in my closet and called Byte. Byte chased after him, but he got away. We notified the police, but so far, nothing has come of it."

"Why didn't you tell me?" Keegan asked, sounding hurt.

"Because I knew you'd either come home or spend the entire trip worrying about me. Byte agreed to stay with me and play bodyguard until you got back, and Phoenix okayed it."

Keegan sighed. "Well, I can't say I'm happy about it, but I do understand."

"Did anything else happen?" Jacob asked.

"Yeah, a few more things," I said. "The following Thursday, we woke up to find Byte's tires slashed. We came back to Croftridge that afternoon. The next morning, I woke up with the flu, confirmed by Patch. We stayed in Croftridge all week and went back to Cedar Valley on Thursday since I had to work on Friday. However, Employee Health didn't clear me to return to work. I have to go back next week to be rechecked. We left the hospital and went back to my house to find that someone had broken in again and ransacked the place. After filing another police report, we came back to Croftridge, and here we are."

Keegan sat silently with a look of shock on her face.

"What about your alarm system?" Jacob asked.

"Whoever's doing this has been able to access her alarm and disable it. The same thing happened with the cameras I installed after my tires were slashed," Byte explained. "For the time being, Phoenix has Edge, Diesel, and Ink at Gabby's house in case anyone shows up."

"Do you have any idea who it might be?" Jacob asked.

"We think it might be a guy Gabby went out with a few times, but I haven't been able to track him down. From what I can tell, he was using a fake name, and everything he told Gabby was a lie. He obviously has some computer skills because he's been able to cover his tracks, as well as hack into her alarm system."

"I don't think you should stay at your house until we catch whoever's doing this," Jacob said.

"I agree," Keegan added. "Even with Byte staying with you, someone could get into the house when you're not there and plant a bomb or something."

"I'm not disagreeing with you, but I can't stay in Croftridge. Depending on traffic, I'd spend almost two hours each day commuting."

"I'm sure we can find a short-term rental in the area," Keegan said.

"I don't think that will work," Byte said. "If the rental property's in your name, or anyone's name associated with Gabby, it'll be easy to find her. There's also the possibility of her being followed."

"I think I have a solution," Jacob said and pulled out his phone.

"You can't just say that and not tell us what it is," Keegan said.

Jacob finished typing out his message and placed his phone on the table. "Luca Peccati has several guest houses on his gated and guarded estate. I can't think of a safer place for her in Cedar Valley."

"You want me to stay with a mafia boss?"

"His association with the mafia has never been confirmed," Jacob pointed out.

"I'm not sure how I feel about this," I admitted. I'd heard of Luca Peccati, but I'd never met him. And I wasn't buying what Jacob was selling. Confirmed or not, I wholeheartedly believed Luca was involved with the Mafia and was likely one of the top bosses.

"I'll be with you," Byte said.

"What?" I asked in surprise.

"You'll still need protection when you're traveling to and from work and school, and anywhere else you need to go," he explained.

I hoped no one noticed how relieved I was when Byte said he'd be going with me. The moment those words left his mouth, all of my reservations vanished.

"What about Shadow?"

"Who's Shadow?" Keegan asked.

"He's our dog."

"You two have a dog?"

"Sort of," I said. "He was a stray Flint found at Byte's house. I want to keep him, but my schedule isn't

exactly conducive to having a pet, so Byte agreed to help me with him until I finish school and get a new job."

"If he can't go with us, I'm sure Flint won't mind watching him," Byte said.

"Or we can take care of him," Keegan offered.

Jacob's phone buzzed on the table. He read the message and smiled. "Luca has a house available. When should he expect you?"

"I have clinical hours on Tuesday, so sometime tomorrow afternoon."

Jacob exchanged a few more texts while the rest of us continued on with dinner.

"Luca said the guard at the gate will be expecting you. He'll show you where you'll be staying and get you set up with keys and a gate code. And you're welcome to bring the dog."

"Great," I said. "Now, tell me all about Scotland."

13

BYTE

After dinner, Gabby and I went back to my house. Keegan asked if Gabby wanted to stay with them, but she declined, saying that her stuff was already at my place.

"I'm going to let Shadow out and put the chickens up for the night," I said.

"I'll come, too, and check for eggs," Gabby said.

I was throwing a ball for Shadow when I heard Gabby's footsteps crunching through the grass behind me. "Did they have any eggs?"

"Yes," she said, "but I found something else."

I turned to see Gabby holding a large black snake. For a brief moment, I didn't know what to say or do. Finding a snake in the chicken coop didn't surprise me, but the fact that Gabby picked it up and was holding it like a pet did. I opened my mouth to lecture her on the dangers of handling an unfamiliar snake, but she stopped me before I could utter a single word.

"I can identify all the venomous snakes in our area,

and this isn't one of them. While I can't always give you the exact species of the nonvenomous snakes in our area, I can tell you this one is a gray rat snake. They are one of the most common snakes in our state and usually feed on rodents, though this one obviously just had one of your eggs," she said and pointed to the prominent egg-shaped bulge on the snake's body.

"I take it you like snakes."

"I do," she smiled. "Even the venomous ones, but I know to admire those from a distance."

"Good," I said and gestured toward the water. "Lakefront property comes with snakes. I've seen my fair share of copperheads around here, and even a few timber rattlers."

"I'll let you in on a little secret. If you don't want to come across a snake, look for them. I'm always looking for them, and this is only the third one I've managed to catch."

"How did you catch it?"

"This one was a piece of cake. They move a lot slower after a large meal."

"What are you going to do with it?" I asked.

"I'm going to let it go. Will you take a picture first?"

"Sure," I chuckled and snapped a few pictures of her posing with the snake.

"Thank you," she said and walked over to the trees to let her snake friend go.

I couldn't take my eyes off of her. She was smiling, and it was the first time I'd seen her really smile since her whole ordeal began.

"I'm going to go inside and wash my hands," she said and pointed toward the house.

"We're right behind you," I said and followed her and Shadow inside.

"In case I haven't told you, you have a great place out here. It's exactly the kind of home I hope to have one day."

"Thank you," I said sincerely. I chose my house for me, but it was nice to know that Gabby liked it, too. "Where do you think you'll end up when you finish school?"

"It'll depend on where I can find a job. Hopefully, I'll be able to find something in Croftridge or nearby."

"What about Patch's place? I'm sure he'd hire you," I suggested.

"I can't say I haven't thought about it, but I'd never know if he hired me because of my skills or because I'm a club kid."

"You don't have to worry about that with Patch. Being a club kid might give you an advantage in getting an interview, but he wouldn't hire you if he didn't think you'd be a good fit, and he certainly wouldn't keep you around if you weren't doing a good job," I explained.

"I'll keep that in mind."

"You could also open your own practice in Croftridge," I suggested.

"Maybe one day," she said. "I need to get a few years of experience under my belt first."

* * *

A LOUD, ROLLING RUMBLE OF THUNDER WOKE ME. I started to go back to sleep when I heard footsteps on the stairs. I got up to investigate and found Gabby tiptoeing down the stairs with Shadow not so quietly following along behind her.

"Sorry, I didn't mean to wake you," she said.

"You didn't. The thunder did. Are you okay?"

"Yeah, I'm fine. I'm just going to sleep on the couch," she said.

"Because of the storm?"

"Uh, yeah. It's pretty loud up there. I thought I'd sleep better down here."

I grabbed her hand and gently tugged. "You can sleep in my room."

"Byte, I—" she started.

"It's not a big deal, Gabby. It's not the first time we've shared a bed."

"What?" she asked, sounding surprised.

"Where do you think I slept when you spent the night in my room at the clubhouse?"

"I didn't really think about it," she admitted.

"And we took a nap together when you were sick."

She climbed into bed beside me but seemed uncomfortable. I wasn't sure if it was me, the storm, or something else.

After several minutes of awkward silence, I decided to address the issue. "I can practically hear you thinking over there. Do you want to talk about it?"

"Not particularly," she said.

"Remember when we agreed to tell the other if something bothered us?" I reminded her.

"Fine," she huffed. "You kissed me, said we'd talk about it later, and haven't mentioned it once."

I rolled onto my side and propped myself up on my elbow. "Technically, you kissed me."

"Semantics," she said and made a dismissive motion with her hand.

"I haven't brought it up because I haven't had a chance to."

"You have a chance now. What did you want to talk about?" she asked.

I exhaled heavily. I knew I had to choose my words carefully. "I'm a lot older than you."

"Really?" she gasped and feigned surprise. "I had no idea."

"Seriously, Gabby. Have you thought about this?"

"I don't care how old you are, Byte. I care about what kind of person you are, and from what I've seen, you're a really good guy."

I wondered if she'd still think I was a good guy if she knew the truth about my past.

"But I understand if you have reservations about someone as young as me," she said.

"Gabby," I started. We weren't as far apart in age as she thought we were, but I couldn't tell her that. Instead, I said, "Your age isn't an issue for me."

"Good," she said and leaned forward to press her lips to mine. This kiss started off slowly and tentatively but quickly grew in intensity.

I rolled on top of her and struggled to keep myself under control. I hadn't realized how much I wanted her until I was so close to having her.

She reached between us, grabbed the hem of her tank top, and pulled it over her head. Her braless breasts bounced free, and I groaned at the sight. I took one nipple into my mouth while my hand went to the other.

Gabby threaded her fingers through my hair and moaned. "Please, Byte."

I grinned against her skin. She was as worked up as I was. "Please what?"

"More. I want more," she said and shoved her pajama pants and underwear down her legs. She tossed them to the side and reached for the waistband of my boxer briefs. Once my cock was free, she wrapped her hand around me and rubbed the head of my dick against her slick slit. She lined me up with her opening and wrapped her legs around me to urge me forward.

It took everything I had to refrain from granting her wish and pushing into her. "Wait," I managed to say. "Condom."

"I'm on birth control," she said and tightened her legs around me.

That was enough for me. My hips surged forward, and I entered her in one fluid movement. She felt better than anything I'd ever experienced, and I took a few seconds to relish in the feeling.

When I started to move, she dug her fingers into my back and groaned. Before long, I lost what little control I had and was pounding into her. I couldn't take my eyes off of her. Her eyes were closed, her mouth was open, and her tits were bouncing with each of my thrusts.

I sat back on my heels and draped her legs over my arms so I could get a better view. I almost lost it when

she cupped her breast with one hand and reached down to rub her clit with the other.

"Don't stop. Don't stop," she panted.

I didn't want to, but it wasn't going to be long. She felt too good.

I almost sighed in relief when I felt her body tense, and she came. I waited until she was finished before I picked up the pace and found my own release.

I dropped down beside her and tried to catch my breath. "That was," I said and trailed off when I couldn't think of the right words.

"Yeah," she agreed. "Again?"

Well, who was I to say no?

14

GABBY

When we arrived at Luca's estate, I was taken aback by how large the place was. The entire property was surrounded by a wrought iron fence, complete with a guarded gate. The main house was situated at the end of a long driveway with several guest houses on each side. A man named Piero met us at the gate and showed us to the house we would be staying in.

"The code to the door and alarm system is on the kitchen table, as well as my phone number. Please don't hesitate to call me if you have any issues," he said.

"Thank you so much," I said sincerely.

He smiled kindly. "We were happy to help. I'll be at the main house if you need anything."

Shadow went around sniffing every corner of the house while Byte and I checked out the place. It was a cute one-story house with two bedrooms and two bathrooms, and it had definitely been customized with the finer things in life. I flopped onto one of the beds to test out the mattress and sighed. "Oh yeah, this will do."

"Hey," Byte said, feigning offense. "I thought I had the best mattresses."

"Sorry to burst your bubble, but Gigi has the best mattresses."

"I have the same ones she does," he countered.

"Well, then, I guess it's a tie," I laughed.

We moved on to look at the other rooms and made our way back to the kitchen. "I guess we need to pick up something for dinner and make a stop at the grocery store."

Byte opened a few cabinet doors and looked inside the refrigerator. "No need," he said and gestured to the fully stocked fridge. "Unless there's something specific you want, it looks like we're all set."

I nudged him out of the way to see for myself. "There's more food here than I ever have in my house."

Byte laughed. "I was thinking the same thing."

"I feel like we should make dinner and invite him to join us to thank him."

"I think this is probably standard practice for him," Byte said.

I'd been around wealthy people my entire life. While Keegan and I had plenty of money, Gigi and Jacob were loaded. But Luca was on a completely different level. "Do you think he'll let us take our vacations here?"

Byte chuckled. "We can always ask."

* * *

I WAS IN THE MIDDLE OF MY LUNCH BREAK WHEN MY phone dinged with a text. I inwardly groaned when I saw who it was from.

Lauren: Just checking to see if we're still on for studying tonight.

Crap. Once again, I'd forgotten about my study sessions with Lauren. I really needed to get some study time in, but there was no way we could meet at my house. I wasn't sure what to do, so I texted Byte to see if he had any ideas.

Byte: What about the diner?

Gabby: Perfect.

I replied to Lauren and asked her if she could meet me at the diner to study.

Lauren: Why can't we study at your house?

Gabby: My house is being fumigated.

Lauren: Where are you staying? I can come there to study.

Gabby: I'm not staying anywhere else. I just can't go back home until later tonight.

Lauren: Fine. I'll meet you at the diner.

Gabby: Great. See you then.

She was a bit of a pain in the ass, but I tolerated it because I did get a lot done during our study sessions.

I let Byte know that she agreed to meet me at the diner and hurried to finish my lunch before my break was over.

Thankfully, I was able to leave the office on time. We barely had time to run back to Luca's place so I could change clothes and grab my books before we were supposed to meet Lauren at the diner.

When we arrived, I felt rushed and a little frazzled. Lauren was already seated at a booth with her books open on the table. I slid into the booth and scooted over to the side so Byte could join me.

"I'm going to sit at the counter," he said and knocked his knuckles on the table twice before leaving.

"Why's he here?" Lauren asked.

"He has to eat, too," I snapped. What was with all of her questions? She was really beginning to annoy me.

"I made you brownies," she said and pushed a container toward me. "You like those, right?"

"I do," I said and opened the container to take a peek. "Thank you. They smell delicious."

"Try one," she said.

"I should probably have dinner first," I said. I hadn't had anything since lunch, and I was starving.

We placed our orders and started going through notes while we waited for our food.

"What's the deal with this Byte guy?" Lauren asked.

"He's a friend of the family," I said, repeating what I'd already told her about him.

"Yeah, but how long's he staying with you? I thought you said it was only for two weeks."

"I'm not sure. He said the project he was working on was extended, but I didn't ask for how long. Can we get back to the notes?"

"Sure," she said, but she didn't sound like she was interested in studying.

When our food arrived, she took the opportunity to ask me more questions about Byte. She wanted to know how old he was, where he was from, how my family knew him—all the same questions she asked me the first time she met him. Once again, I tried to pacify her with vague answers and redirect her back to the task at hand, but she was relentless. And I couldn't leave early since I told her I had to stay away from my house until later that night. I was stuck, and it sucked. I found myself watching the clock instead of studying. The whole night was a bust.

Finally, it was time to leave, and I couldn't have been happier. Lauren took her time packing up her stuff while I was ready to go in seconds. I stood by the table and resisted the urge to yank her out of the booth and shove her out the front door.

"You seem irritated," Byte said once we were on the way back to Luca's estate.

"I am," I said and shoved a brownie into my mouth.

"Why?" he asked. "And where did you get those?"

"Because we got nothing done because Lauren wouldn't stop asking questions about you," I said and

reached for another brownie. "The brownies are from Lauren. She likes to bake and doesn't want the goodies to go to waste, so she brings the extras to me."

"Are you going to share?"

"Yes," I said and happily handed him a brownie. "Please, take some. Otherwise, I will eat all of these, and I really don't need to."

"Don't even go there," he said. "You look great."

"Because I don't eat containers full of brownies," I countered.

"You have to admit, they are good brownies," he said and held out his hand for another.

"I know," I grumbled. "It's like she's trying to fatten me up on purpose."

Byte laughed. "Why would she do that?"

I shrugged. "I don't know. Maybe she wants to take a shot at you since Flint was a resounding no."

"She can try, but she doesn't have a snowball's chance in Hell with me. I'm happily taken."

15

GABBY

"I hope this goes better than the last time," I said to Byte when he parked at the hospital.

"You barely have a cough. I'd be shocked if they don't give you clearance," he said.

"Me, too," I said and gave him a quick kiss before I got out of the truck.

I only had to wait a few minutes before they called me back to a room. The nurse asked me a few questions, one of which was if I still had a cough.

"Nope. No cough. No fever. No aches and pains," I said and immediately clamped my mouth shut. I didn't want her to suspect me of lying because I was too insistent about my lack of symptoms.

"Great. We just need to collect a urine sample from you, and you should be good to go."

"A urine sample?" I questioned.

"Yes. It's hospital policy to perform a urine drug screen on all employees who have been out of work for over seven days," she explained.

"Okay, show me where to go."

"Follow me," she said and led me to a bathroom down the hall. "Once you're finished, return to the room, and I'll be in shortly with your paperwork."

I did my business, returned to the room, and waited. After twenty minutes passed, I started to wonder if they had forgotten about me. I was considering stepping out into the hall and flagging down someone when the nurse entered the room.

"Sorry for the wait," she said and handed me a stack of papers. "You'll need to take these over to Human Resources so they can complete the process."

"Thank you."

When I arrived at Human Resources, I gave my paperwork to the receptionist. "Have a seat. Someone will be with you shortly."

While I was waiting, I sent a text to Byte to let him know what was going on and that I wouldn't be much longer.

"Gabriella Marks," a lady called. "Come with me."

I followed the woman back to a small conference room and was surprised to see my manager and a man I didn't recognize sitting at the table. "What's going on?" I asked. Suddenly, I had a bad feeling, but I had no idea why.

"Have a seat," the unfamiliar man said.

"Seriously. What is going on?" I asked again as I took a seat.

"Gabby," my manager started, "your drug screen came back positive for THC. Your termination is effective immediately."

“What?” I demanded. “There’s no way that’s possible.”

She pulled out a sheet of paper and placed it in front of me. “See for yourself.”

Even though the results were right in front of me, I couldn’t believe what I was seeing. “This isn’t right. I don’t smoke weed,” I insisted.

“Your test results say otherwise.”

“I don’t care what that paper says. It’s wrong!”

“Let’s not make this any harder than it needs to be,” my manager said.

“Oh, my apologies. Let me quietly cooperate and make things easier for you while you’re trying to ruin my life!” I yelled. “Why are you doing this? I’ve been an excellent employee. I don’t deserve this!”

“Miss Marks, please calm down so we can continue,” the man said.

“I’m not going to calm down. You’re firing me for something I didn’t do!”

“If you don’t get yourself under control, we’re going to call security to remove you.”

“There’s no need for that. I’ll happily remove myself,” I said and got to my feet.

“We need you to sign a few papers, and then you can leave,” my manager said.

I glared at her. “I’m not signing shit.”

“If you leave now, there’s nothing I can do,” she said.

“And if I sign whatever that is,” I said and pointed to the papers in front of her, “there’ll be nothing I can do.”

With that, I stormed out of Human Resources in a

state of disbelief. I managed to hold it together until I made it back to Byte's truck.

"What happened?" he demanded.

I held up one finger and tried to compose myself. My heart was pounding, and my mind was racing. I inhaled deeply and uttered the words I never thought I'd say. "They fired me."

"What? Why?"

I nodded and swallowed thickly. "They asked me to provide a urine specimen for a drug screen, and I tested positive for THC."

"Do you smoke weed?" he asked.

"No!"

He held his hands up in mock surrender. "I'm not passing judgment. I'm just trying to understand what happened."

"Yeah, me, too. There's no way that test should've been positive."

"Do you think they made a mistake?"

"That's the only explanation I can come up with. You've been around me for the last two weeks. When have you seen me do anything that would make me test positive for THC?"

"Do you use any CBD products? I've heard those can sometimes trigger a positive test," he said.

I was already shaking my head before he finished. "No. I've heard the same thing and didn't want to take the risk. What in the hell am I going to do?"

"If you think the test was wrong, there's an easy way to prove that."

"What? How?"

"Take a test at home. If the results are different, you'll know they made a mistake," he explained.

"What do you mean 'if'?" I asked defensively.

"Poor choice of words," he said. "I'm not questioning you. If you say the test should've been negative, I believe you."

"I'm sorry. I just can't believe this is happening."

He took my hand in his and gave it a reassuring squeeze. "Let's go get some drug tests."

* * *

"WHY ARE YOU TAKING ONE?" I ASKED WHEN BYTE headed toward the bathroom with a urine cup in his hand.

He shrugged. "Why not?"

Before I could respond, he stepped inside and closed the door.

When he returned, he placed his cup on the counter beside mine. "How long do we have to wait?"

"The instructions said five minutes."

"What do you want to do for the next five minutes?"

"Stare at the cup and make myself crazy," I said flatly.

"Let's take Shadow out. By the time he's finished, the tests will be done," he suggested.

Even though the entire estate was surrounded by a fence, I didn't want to let Shadow run free for his bathroom breaks, so we'd been taking him out on a leash. I tried not to continuously check the time as we walked from tree to tree, but it was a struggle.

"It's time!" I announced and almost ran for the door.

My jaw dropped open when I picked up my test and read the results. Everything was negative, except for THC. "What the hell?" I whispered in disbelief.

Byte was staring at his specimen with an equal look of disbelief on his face. "Mine's positive, too."

"And it shouldn't be?" I guessed.

"No, it shouldn't be. I haven't smoked weed or used anything with THC in well over a year," he explained.

"Then how in the hell are both of us testing positive?" I asked, as my eyes landed on the brownies Lauren had sent home with me. I gasped and pointed at the container. I felt bad for even thinking it, and could barely bring myself to even make the suggestion. "Do you think it could've been the brownies?"

Byte glanced at the container and back to me. "At this point, I'd say anything's possible."

"How can we find out?"

"There are kits to test food for different substances. They can be ordered, but let me see if Patch can help us get our hands on one today."

"Wait," I started.

"He won't say anything," Byte assured me before I could even ask.

"I'm not going to keep this from Keegan, but I don't want her to hear about it from anyone other than me," I explained.

"I know, and Patch will, too."

I couldn't sit still while he was on the phone with Patch. I had so many thoughts and questions running

through my mind. First and foremost was whether or not Lauren intentionally gave me brownies laced with THC. I really didn't see how it could have been an accident, but I also couldn't think of a reason why she'd do something like that.

"All right, he said they have them at the hospital. He's going to go by the ER and get some," Byte said and paused. "Since you don't have to be in Cedar Valley until Tuesday, do you want to spend the weekend in Croftridge? It's totally up to you."

"Yeah, I think I'd like that. This place is nice, but I kind of feel like I'm under a microscope when we're here," I admitted.

"I know what you mean. Gather up what you need, and we'll leave when you're ready."

"How did you meet Lauren?" Byte asked once we were on our way back to Croftridge.

"I met her at school. We were both in the library between classes. She asked me to help her with something she didn't understand. We continued to run into each other at the library and started studying together. She's a semester behind me in the program, but I still found the study sessions to be helpful."

"When did you start studying at your house instead of the library?"

"At the beginning of this semester. The last semester is basically all clinical hours, so I don't have a need to be on campus," I explained.

"Have you ever been to her place?"

"No. With the exception of this past Wednesday, we've always studied at my house."

"And does she always bring you something she baked?"

I slapped my hand over my mouth as realization dawned. "Yes! She's been doing that for months. She told me she loves to bake but can't eat everything she makes, so she gives it away. Do you think she's been drugging me the whole time?"

"We'll know for sure soon," he said and turned into Patch's neighborhood.

Instead of us getting out and going inside like I expected, Patch came out to the truck when we pulled into the driveway.

"Thanks, brother," Byte said.

"Yes, thank you!" I added.

"No problem," he said and focused his attention on me. "If you need my help with anything, let me know. I'll be happy to help in any way I can. In the meantime, be sure to document everything and get in touch with the club's lawyer sooner rather than later."

"Thanks, Patch. I really appreciate it," I said sincerely.

"I know it doesn't seem like it right now, but you'll get through this. Try to think of it as nothing more than an inconvenience. It might take some time to get it sorted out, but don't get discouraged."

"I'll do my best," I said.

"All right, Patch. We've got some brownies to test."

"Good luck," he said and waved goodbye.

"Do we have to wait until we get to your house?" I asked excitedly.

Byte chuckled. "Yes, we do. And not because drug

testing a potential pot brownie in a moving vehicle is a bad idea."

"Okay, then why?"

"Because I put the brownies in the toolbox in the bed of my truck."

"Fine, I'll read the instructions so I don't have to do it when we get there," I said and picked up one of the test kits.

"Well, that's incredibly simple," I sighed and dropped the test into my lap. "Swab the sample, then rub the swab on the test card in the designated area. If the sample turns red within ten seconds, the result is positive."

"On the bright side, ten seconds is a lot faster than five minutes," Byte pointed out.

"I don't know why I'm being so impatient. It doesn't matter how long the test takes. I'm not going to be able to do anything about it until Monday anyway."

"True," he agreed. "But at least you'll know."

"How could I not know? I mean, shouldn't I have felt different?"

"Not necessarily. If she used one of the other cannabis compounds like delta-eight, you likely wouldn't have noticed any impairment. Now that I'm thinking about it, that would also explain why the baked goods didn't have an unusual taste or smell," he explained.

"You seem to know a lot about this."

"When the bill was passed that made a lot of hemp-derived products legal, Ember asked me to do some research to see if growing the legal plants would be lucrative for the farm."

"Was it?" I asked curiously.

"Yes, and no. While it definitely would have turned a nice profit, there was still a lot of uncertainty with the legalities on a state level. Since our state isn't known for being progressive where marijuana is concerned, she decided against it."

He pulled into his driveway a few minutes later and put the truck in park. "You ready for round two of testing?"

"Yes!" I said excitedly. "But it's round three for me."

"I didn't know you guys were coming back tonight," Flint said from the front porch. "Is everything okay?"

"Everything is so far from okay it's not even funny," I said and let Shadow out of the truck. He jumped down and ran straight for Flint.

Flint leaned down to pet him. "So, what's going on?"

"In a nutshell, I got fired today because I tested positive for THC on a urine drug screen. We think my so-called friend from school has been feeding me homemade edibles without my knowledge."

"Are you serious?"

"Yep," I nodded. "No one besides Patch knows about this, so please keep it to yourself for the time being."

"Of course," he promised. "So, what are you going to do?"

"I still have some of the brownies she gave me on Wednesday. We're going to use the kits Patch gave us to test them for THC."

"Then what?"

"Either way, I need to contact a lawyer. I don't so much care about getting my job back, but I don't want my nursing license to be affected by something I didn't do."

"What about school?" Byte asked.

"I honestly don't know what to do about school. If I tell them, I'll definitely be kicked out of the program. If I don't tell them, I might be able to finish the program and graduate before anything comes up with the Board of Nursing. I won't be able to take the practitioner boards if my nursing license isn't in good standing, but at least I'll have my degree."

"Do you want to do the honors?" Byte asked and placed the container of brownies on his kitchen table.

"Sure," I said and picked up a test kit.

I rubbed the swab on the brownie as instructed and then rubbed it on the test panel. It turned red almost immediately. I stared at the result and tried to process my feelings. Part of me was happy to know why I tested positive, while another part of me was livid that Lauren had drugged me. And I wanted to know why.

"You okay?" Byte asked.

"Yes. No. I don't know," I said. "I want to know why she did this, but it's not like I can ask her."

"No, you definitely can't ask her. In fact, I don't think you should have any contact with her at all."

"That shouldn't be hard. I only saw her every other Wednesday to study."

"When do you want to tell Keegan?" Byte asked.

"I'll call her now," I said and headed for the stairs.

16

BYTE

While Gabby went upstairs to call her sister, I grabbed a beer from the fridge and dropped onto the couch in the living room.

"Why do you think this girl is trying to sabotage Gabby?" Flint asked.

"I've been thinking about that, and I honestly don't know. Initially, I thought it might be because of jealousy, but that doesn't make sense. They don't work together. They aren't in classes together. I'm Gabby's boyfriend, so it's not a jealous ex thing," I explained.

"Wait. You two are together?"

"Yeah," I grinned. "I'm surprised word hasn't gotten around. It's not a secret."

"What about the guy who broke into Gabby's house? Could he be connected to this Lauren chick?"

"At this point, I think anything's possible," I said and went to the kitchen to grab my laptop. Then I sent a quick text to Gabby.

Byte: What's Lauren's last name?

Gabby: Wiener

I tried not to laugh. I really did. But I failed miserably.

"What's so funny?" Flint asked.

"I asked Gabby for Lauren's last name," I said and tried to compose myself. "It's Wiener."

"Wiener? Like a hot dog?" Flint chuckled.

"Yep," I laughed. "And normally, I wouldn't make fun of a person's name, but she deserves it. So, from this point on, I will only refer to her as Wiener. Maybe Weenie, on occasion."

"No judgment here. She fucked with a member of our family. The rules no longer apply to her," he said seriously.

"Well," I said and opened up my laptop. "Let's see what we can find."

Finding information on Wiener was much easier than finding information on Chad. Within seconds of typing her name and pressing enter, I knew her full name, age, date of birth, and address. A few clicks later, I had her phone number, email address, a list of previous addresses, and a list of potential relatives.

Flint joined me on the couch and watched my screen intently. "Is there anything I can do to help?"

"You can take notes for me," I said and handed him a notebook and pen.

We spent the next hour digging into the life of

Lauren Wiener. And we uncovered quite a bit of pertinent information.

"What are you two doing?" Gabby asked when she came back downstairs.

"Checking into Wiener," I said, causing Flint to chuckle. "How did Keegan take the news?"

"Oh, she's pissed," Gabby said. "And I mean really pissed. She wanted to call Papa and tell him so he could 'put his rifle to good use.' Thankfully, Jacob and I were able to convince her otherwise."

"Oh, hell. I didn't even think about how Ranger would react. You, Keegan, and Quincy are the only ones he'll listen to. Seriously, you may have to ask him to stand down."

"What about Phoenix?"

"Do you know how many times I've heard Ranger say he was around when Phoenix was in diapers? He respects the hell out of Phoenix, but no one is going to stop that man if he thinks he's doing the right thing for his family. Remember when I told you he almost shot an FBI agent? It wasn't Phoenix that stopped him. It was Keegan."

"That was when my father kidnapped her, right?"

"Yeah," I nodded. "I don't think I ever told anyone how scared I was that day. I was a patched member, but I was still what I would consider new to the club. I'd been through a few situations with the club, but that one was different for me because Keegan and I were friends. I'm just glad it turned out the way it did."

"Yeah, me, too," she agreed.

"Um, could one of y'all give me the cliff notes version of this story?" Flint asked.

"My biological father was a wealthy senator in Kentucky. He and his business partner were pretending to sell horses when they were actually selling women. One woman escaped. Since she'd already been paid for, they needed to repay the money or replace the woman. They tried to arrange a marriage for Keegan to get access to her trust fund. When that didn't work, they kidnapped her. What they didn't know was that the buyer was an undercover FBI agent. Keegan was taken to a safe house, and they were arrested shortly after," Gabby explained.

Flint's jaw was practically on the floor by the time she finished. "Gabby, I had no idea. Where were you when all of this happened?"

"I was at boarding school. I wasn't there long before Gigi showed up," Gabby said and smiled wistfully. "She told me she was my long-lost fairy grandmother and was taking me to see my sister."

"Where's your father now?"

"He received a life sentence. So, if he's not dead, he's still in prison. I'm not sure which because I don't keep up with him."

"If you ever want to know, I can answer that question for you without any additional details," I offered.

"Thanks, but I truly don't care. Once I was with Keegan and Jacob, I never looked back."

"I hope I didn't upset you. I didn't know what I was asking," Flint said sincerely.

"Oh, no, you didn't," Gabby assured him. "It's really more Keegan's story than mine. I wasn't there for most of it, and I don't have many memories of what life was like before I moved in with Keegan and Jacob."

"Let me add one more shocking detail, and then I want to tell Gabby what we found on Wiener," I said to Flint.

"I'm not sure I want to know," he said hesitantly.

"You'll want to know why I didn't tell you if you find out later."

"That's true. Let's hear it."

"You've heard the story of how Ember and your dad found each other, right?" At his nod, I continued. "The man who was going to buy her was Gabby's father."

Flint jumped to his feet and started pacing. "Well," he huffed. "I'm not sure what I was expecting, but it certainly wasn't that."

"I didn't know that either," Gabby said with a look of utter shock on her face.

I reached for her hand. "I'm sorry, Gab. I assumed you knew."

She shook her head as if she was trying to clear the thoughts from her mind. "No, it's okay. The connection is surprising; his actions are not." She released my hand and got to her feet. "I think I need a drink. Flint, you want a drink?"

"Uh," he hesitated and looked at me.

I waved my hand dismissively. "I don't care if you drink. I mean, you're staying here if you do, but have a drink if you want one."

"You're not old enough to drink?" Gabby asked.

"I'm twenty," Flint told her.

"What the hell? Might as well add contributing to the delinquency of a minor to the list of laws I'm breaking today. Where's your liquor, Byte?"

I pointed across the room. "In that fancy-ass thing your sister said I needed."

Gabby bent at the waist and started laughing. "Has Jacob seen that?"

"I don't think so. Why?"

"Because he's wanted one for years, and she's always said no. But she bought one for your house," she cackled.

"I'm not even remotely surprised," I chuckled. That sounded exactly like something Keegan would do.

"All right, let's keep it simple. How do Crown and Gingers sound?" Gabby asked.

"Works for me."

"Sounds good."

Once the drinks were made, Gabby sat down and took a large sip. "Okay, what'd you find out about Lauren?"

"Have a few more sips first," I suggested.

Gabby tipped up her glass and emptied the contents in one go. "Okay, I'm ready."

I shook my head and laughed. I hoped she was as ready as she thought she was. "So far, I've come across two things I think are significant. One is that she works at the doctor's office where you do your clinical hours for school."

"No, she doesn't," Gabby said confidently.

"Yes, she does. You've never seen her there because

she only works on Mondays and Fridays," I explained.

"Okay, okay," Gabby said and nodded her head a few times. "I'm not going to ask why she didn't tell me. Even though she knew that's where I was assigned. And now that I'm thinking about it, she was the one who suggested I ask Dr. Gordon about doing my clinical hours with him. Nope, I'm not going to ask why. I'm just going to assume it's because the bitch is certifiable. Yep, that's what I'm going with. What else?"

"You okay?" I asked after her tirade.

"Not at all," she said and went back to the bar to make herself another drink.

"What else?" she asked again after she returned to her seat.

"I kind of wish I'd started with this one," I mumbled and inhaled deeply before I delivered what I knew would be a shocking revelation. "Lauren Wiener isn't in the nurse practitioner program at Cedar Valley University, or any other program."

"What?" Gabby gasped.

"She's not a student," I repeated.

"Was she ever?"

"No, she's never been enrolled at the university."

Gabby sucked in a sharp breath and clasped her hands together tightly. "You're telling me the girl I met at the library on campus, the girl with a stack of nursing books, the girl who asked for my help with a project, the girl I've been studying with for months isn't really a student?"

"Yes," I said carefully. "That's exactly what I'm telling you."

"Holy fucking shit," she breathed. "I thought we were friends, and she was stalking me the whole time. Who the hell is friends with their stalker? No, who the hell is friends with their stalkee? Is that even a word?" She picked up her glass and downed half the contents. "I think I'm having a panic attack. I feel like it's hard to breathe, and my chest kind of hurts. That's a panic attack, right? Because if it isn't, something else is really wrong. But that's how they work, right? You think you're dying when you're really just having a panic attack? Why do I keep saying panic attack? That's just making it worse. I've got to calm down. But I can't calm down. I don't like this at all," she rambled.

Shadow, who'd been quietly resting on the floor at her feet, jumped onto the couch and climbed into her lap before she could continue. She wrapped her arms around him and heaved in breath after breath.

"Flint, will you get a paper bag from the pantry in the kitchen?" I asked calmly.

He darted out of the room and returned seconds later with a bag in his outstretched hand.

"Breathe into this," I instructed. "You're hyperventilating. And yes, you're having a panic attack."

She took the bag from me and covered her mouth. After a few minutes of huffing and puffing, her breathing slowed to a manageable rate. I gently took the bag from her and smoothed my hand over her hair. I would have moved closer, but Shadow was in the way, and it was clear he was not moving. "Better?" I asked.

"Yeah, I think so," she said quietly, followed by a slight laugh. "Well, that sucked."

17

GABBY

I knocked on the wooden door and waited.

"Come in."

I took in a deep breath and opened the door. "Hi, Dr. Harmon. Thank you for meeting with me today."

She gestured to a chair in front of her desk. "Have a seat," she said with a kind smile. "What can I do for you today, Gabriella?"

I clasped my hands together tightly, hoping to hide my nerves. "First, I want to make sure that everything said during this meeting will remain confidential."

She peered at me over her glasses. "I'm sure you know there are some things I can't keep confidential, such as allegations against a teacher or student."

"It's nothing like that. This only involves me," I said.

"If it's something I can legally keep confidential, I assure you I will," she promised.

I nodded and swallowed thickly. "I'm dealing with a rather personal situation. My house has been broken into twice, and I'm being threatened and harassed. After

some investigation, it appears the person doing this to me is a woman who has been posing as a student at this university. I met her at the library and have been studying with her every other week for quite some time, but I recently learned she's not a student here. The reason I'm telling you this is because I would like to change my clinical location. I understand we're in the middle of the semester, but this is for my safety."

"Well, this is definitely an unusual request," she said. "I'd like to help you, but I'm not sure if we can find someone for you to work with on such short notice," she said.

"I've already found someone who's willing to let me start right away," I said. "The only issue is that his practice is located in Croftridge, not Cedar Valley."

"I'm sorry, Gabby. I'd love to help you, but we can only approve facilities located in this county," she said as her phone began to ring. She pressed a button to silence the phone and returned her attention to me, but her phone started ringing again. "Excuse me for just a moment. This appears to be urgent."

While she took her phone call, I tried to think of anything I could say to change her mind. I hadn't told her that Lauren worked at Dr. Gordon's practice, but I didn't want to share that information unless I had to.

Dr. Harmon cleared her throat and gave me a tight smile. "That was Dean Winston. I've been authorized to grant you special permission to finish your clinical hours at your desired location in Croftridge."

I couldn't mask the surprise on my face. "How is

that possible? I haven't spoken to the dean. I didn't go above your head," I blurted.

Her face softened. "It's okay, Gabriella. I didn't want to deny your request, and now I don't have to."

The amount of relief I felt was overwhelming. "Thank you," I said in a shaky voice. "The past few weeks have been difficult to say the least."

"I hope this change will make things better for you."

"It definitely will," I said, and took a moment to choose my next words carefully. "This is what I was referring to when I asked for confidentiality. I don't want anyone other than you and the dean to know where I'm finishing out my hours."

"You have my word," she promised. "I won't change anything in the computer system. Email your completed hours and sign-off sheets to me at the end of each week, and I'll manually enter them into the system."

"Thank you," I said. "I really appreciate your help."

"I'm glad this worked out for you," she said with a smile.

With that, I left her office and hurried back to Byte's truck. Being on campus made me feel uneasy, and I didn't want to be there any longer than I had to.

"How did it go?" he asked.

"It was kind of weird. She initially denied the transfer, but the dean called in the middle of her explanation and told her to approve my request."

"Really? So, you were approved?"

"Yes, but I don't understand why. How would the dean know about my situation?" I asked.

"Come on, Gabby," Byte laughed. "This has Jacquelyn written all over it."

I nodded in agreement. "Yeah, you're probably right. Do you think I should call and thank her, or pretend like I don't know?"

He shrugged. "You should probably ask Shaker about that one."

"I'll just send her a vague text," I said and reached for my phone.

Gabby: I'm not sure, but I think my fairy grandmother may have waved her magic wand in my direction today.

Gigi: She might have…

Gabby: Thank you.

Gigi: You're welcome. I love you, sweet girl.

Gabby: I love you, too.

"Oh yeah, it was her," I said. "And I'm totally okay with that, but I wonder who told her."

Byte shifted in his seat. "Shaker did, because I asked him to."

"You did?"

"Yes," he nodded. "When you mentioned they might not let you transfer locations, I had to do something. You're safer in Croftridge, and I knew if anyone could make that happen, it was Jacquelyn."

"Thank you," I said. "I didn't know what I was going to do if they denied my request."

"I'm glad it didn't come to that," he said.

"Me, too," I agreed.

He glanced at the clock. "Do you think we have enough time to get our stuff out of Luca's guest house before our next appointment?"

"Yes, but that means Shadow will have to come with us."

"If they won't let him come in, I can stay outside with him."

"But you have a part in this as well. And I really want you there with me," I admitted. It was hard enough to face Dr. Harmon by myself. I didn't want to talk to the lawyer alone if I didn't have to.

"Then we'll just have to convince them to let Shadow join us for the meeting."

* * *

As luck would have it, the lawyer was an animal lover and was happy to allow Shadow to accompany us. And Shadow soaked up all the attention he got from everyone in the office.

"He's such a ham," I said to Byte.

"He is, but it seems to be working in your favor."

"If I didn't know better, I'd think he was doing it on purpose."

Byte chuckled. "He probably is."

We followed Tina into her office and took a seat while she closed the door.

"Before we begin, let me formally introduce myself," she said, while she extended her hand to me. "I'm Tina Rivera. I've worked with the Blackwings MC, both chapters, for many years. Anything you say to me falls under attorney-client privilege, so please, speak freely."

"Thank you. I'm Gabriella Marks, and this is Byte. I mean Michael Fuller."

"Please call me Byte," he said and shook her hand. "And she goes by Gabby."

"It's nice to meet you both. So, what brings you in today?"

"I'm a registered nurse, and I'm in school to become a nurse practitioner. I was recently fired from my job at the hospital because I tested positive for THC on a urine drug screen. Since I don't use any products with THC, I assumed the test was wrong. As it turns out, an acquaintance from school has been giving me baked goods laced with THC. I'm not interested in trying to get my job back, but I don't want this to have a negative effect on my nursing license or my ability to become a nurse practitioner. I also don't want her to get away with this."

"How do you know the THC came from the baked goods?" Tina asked.

I removed the container of brownies from my bag as well as one of the test kits. "May I show you?"

"Please do," she said eagerly.

"This is a kit to test food and other substances for the presence of THC. We obtained the kit from a friend who's a physician," I explained and rubbed the swab on the brownie. "When I rub the sample on the test card, it

will turn red within ten seconds if it's positive for THC."

We all watched as the result turned red almost immediately.

"Can you prove the brownies were given to you?" she asked.

"Yes, we can," I said and gestured to Byte.

"I have video evidence. Can I email it to you?"

"Absolutely," Tina said and handed him a business card with her email address on it. After Byte emailed the videos, Tina pulled them up on her computer.

"The first video shows Lauren walking into the diner carrying the container of brownies. The second video shows Gabby joining her at the table where Lauren hands the brownies to her," Byte explained.

"I'm impressed. You two have really done your homework," Tina said.

"I've worked my butt off for the last five years, and I'm so close to being finished. I'm not going to let her ruin everything I've worked for."

"I completely understand," Tina said sincerely. "So, we have a couple of things to do. First, we need to file an official report with the police and submit the evidence. She'll likely be arrested and charged. Assuming she doesn't admit to the crime, it'll come down to her word against yours. She'll most likely claim you knew the brownies contained THC and consumed them anyway. But that'll be later down the line. What we're after is the police report and proof of her arrest to present to the Board of Nursing. We'll also ask for a restraining order against her. It will also be helpful to have some negative urine drug screens to

present to the Board. Wait two weeks and have a test done. It can be at your doctor's office or a third-party lab. Have the results sent to me. If you can afford to do so, continue having tests done every two weeks. We want to show the Board that your tests were consistently negative after you reported Lauren and cut ties with her."

"I can afford to have multiple tests done. I'll have them done every week if you think that'd be better."

"Every two weeks will be more than sufficient," she assured me. "In the meantime, we'll wait for the Board of Nursing to contact you. You'll receive a letter in the mail. It usually takes a month or two from the time the complaint was filed. When you receive the letter, give me a call, and we'll make the necessary arrangements."

"Do you think I'll be able to keep my license?" I asked.

"Absolutely," she said confidently. "Even if you admitted to being guilty, you'd be able to keep your license."

"That's good to hear," I said and exhaled in relief.

"I don't foresee any issues regarding your licensure. At most, they might want you to agree to random drug screens for the next year, but I honestly think they'll drop the case once they hear your story and review the evidence."

"Thank you. Thank you so much."

"You're welcome," she smiled. "Are you ready to make the police report?"

"Yes, I suppose so. How do we go about doing that?" I asked.

"Normally, you'd go down to the station, but I have a friend on the force who agreed to stop by and take the report."

I covered my face with my hands and sighed. "Did my grandmother call you?"

"No," Tina laughed. "I'm sorry. I don't mean to laugh, but I do know who your grandmother is. You can thank Phoenix's grandfather for this favor."

"Pop," I smiled. "I adore that man."

"Me, too," Tina agreed and opened the door to her office. "Detective Hayes, we're ready for you."

Detective Hayes came in and shook hands with us as we introduced ourselves. Then he reached down and rubbed Shadow's head before taking a seat. "Tina gave me a brief overview of what happened, but I'd like to hear it from you," he said.

I told him the same story I told Tina. Then we showed him the brownies, the test results, and the surveillance videos.

He opened the container of brownies and inhaled deeply. "These don't smell like marijuana."

"I have another test kit if you'd like to see for yourself." I must have sounded defensive, because his response was almost apologetic.

"Oh, I believe you. I just meant I can understand how you didn't know. There's no distinct smell. I'm assuming there was no distinct taste as well?"

"That's right. Nothing seemed off about the brownies. I can also say I didn't notice any impairment after eating them. They may have made me sleepy, but

between my work and school schedule, I'm sleepy by nine or ten o'clock regardless."

"All right, I think I have everything I need. If not, I'll give you a call," he said and got to his feet. "I'll get these down to the lab for testing, and we'll go from there."

"I'll be submitting a request for a restraining order. I'm hoping the timing will work out so that Lauren can be notified of the order during her arrest," Tina added.

"Let me know when it's approved. I'll see if I can coordinate with you," he said.

"Thank you, Detective Hayes," Tina said.

"Yes, thank you for coming to meet with us," I added.

"Thank you for doing the leg work for me," he said and raised the container of brownies. "It's not very often that I get a case handed to me with the evidence already collected."

With that, he left the office, and we said our goodbyes to Tina. I thanked her profusely for her help. I likely would have continued thanking her if Byte hadn't ushered me out of her office.

"I can't believe how well everything went today. I know it's not over yet, but I feel so much better after getting my transfer approved and talking to Tina," I said once we were on our way to Croftridge.

"I'm sure you do," he said. "It's a relief to know they approved your transfer. I'll feel better knowing you're with Patch all day."

"I think I'll enjoy working with him," I said.

"I'm sure you will. Everyone I've met who's worked with him seems to love him."

"Let's hope he feels the same way about me."

"I'm going to pretend like you didn't say that."

"What?" I asked innocently.

"You know as well as I do that everybody loves you. You're cute and sweet and kind. You're the kind of person that even people who want to hate you can't."

"So, I'm annoyingly sweet?"

"Nice try. I'm not falling into your trap."

"You will," I teased.

18

BYTE

After dropping Gabby off at Patch's office for her first day of clinicals with him, I went to the clubhouse and spent the first part of the day trying to find a connection between Lauren and Chad, or whoever the hell he was. Unfortunately, I couldn't find anything helpful, and I was beyond frustrated.

I was staring at my laptop and fighting the urge to throw it across the room when my phone rang with Irene's name on the screen. She rarely called, so I answered immediately.

"Hey, Irene. You okay?"

"I'm just fine, but I had an odd encounter I thought you should know about," she said. "The girl Gabby was studying with last week came in for lunch today. When I took her order, she asked about you and Gabby. I told her I hadn't talked to you since the night she met y'all here. She said she was worried because she hadn't been able to get in touch with Gabby. I told her I would give you a call after I tended to a few tables."

"Tell her you couldn't get in touch with me either and leave it at that," I said urgently. "I'll fill you in on the details later, but she's not well, and the police are looking for her."

"Ah, well, that might explain what happened next."

"What? What happened?"

"Some guy came in and they started arguing. They were getting pretty loud. I was about to ask them to quiet down or leave when he grabbed her arm and walked her out of the diner."

"How long ago was this?"

"They left about fifteen minutes ago," she said. "Maybe it was just me, but the whole thing seemed weird."

"It definitely wasn't you," I assured her. "If they come in again, act like you don't know anything's going on and call or text me."

"That won't be hard since I don't know what's going on."

"It's a long story, but the gist of it is Lauren has more or less been stalking Gabby and trying to sabotage her at work and school. We're not sure why, but Gabby filed an official complaint with the police yesterday. They should be arresting her and serving her with a restraining order in the near future," I explained.

"I wish I would've known before I served her," Irene said. "I would've given her soggy fries and spit in her drink."

"You're the best," I laughed.

"That's what I hear," she said. "I've got to get back to work. Behave yourself and take care of Gabby."

"I will," I promised.

As soon as we ended the call, I pulled up Irene's security camera feed and downloaded the clips with Lauren and the male who joined her. From what I could see, Lauren arrived at the diner in a vehicle that was different from what I'd seen her driving before. She parked, went inside, and placed an order. Ten minutes later, a male arrived on foot and entered the diner. He went straight to Lauren's table, where the two began arguing. As Irene said, he grabbed her arm and escorted her from the diner. They walked to her car, where he helped her into the passenger's seat. Then he got into the driver's seat and drove away.

I couldn't say for sure, but I was fairly certain the guy who joined her was the guy who had been posing as Chad. They appeared to be around the same height and weight. Once again, he was wearing a hat, so there wasn't a clear shot of his face. There was, however, a clear view of the license plate number.

My excitement was short-lived. The plates came back registered to a rental car, which had been rented to a John Smith. John Smith paid in cash and put down 123 Main Street as his address.

I sighed in frustration. I hit dead end after dead end when it came to Chad, and it was maddening. And I still couldn't say for sure if he was connected to Lauren. The guy from the diner could be a new player in the game. I had no idea.

I hated not being able to find the information I was looking for, but I hated not having a next step to take

even more. Once again, I was at a standstill, and there was nothing I could do about it.

* * *

"How was your first day?" I asked when I picked Gabby up.

"Great!" she said with a wide smile. "It's completely different than the office in Cedar Valley. The people are friendlier, and the overall environment is much more upbeat."

"So, you think you'll be happy there?"

"I know I will," she said. "How was your day?"

"Frustrating," I grumbled and told her about Irene's phone call.

"Let me see the videos. I can tell you if it's Chad," she said excitedly.

I handed her my phone. "Pull up the last two videos I saved."

She was quiet for a few beats before she gasped. "That's him."

"You're sure?"

"Completely," she said confidently. "It looks just like him, and that's his hat. Every time I saw him, he was wearing that hat. I've also seen him in that jacket before."

"Call Edge from my phone and put it on speaker."

It rang several times before he answered. "Hello," he said, sounding out of breath.

"Hey, brother. Everything okay?"

"Yeah. Sorry. I couldn't find my phone. What's up?"

"Earlier today, Lauren and an unknown male were in Irene's diner asking about me and Gabby. Gabby just identified him as Chad," I started.

"Got it. I'll head there now," he said.

"What?"

"You want me to have dinner at Irene's in case either one of them comes back, right?" he asked.

"Yeah, that's exactly right," I said.

He laughed. "Don't sound so surprised. I know how you feel about Irene. And honestly, it's not a hardship. She's hilarious, and her food is fantastic."

"Thanks, man. Let me know if anything happens."

"Will do," he said and ended the call.

Gabby was quiet for the rest of the drive to my house. It was a comfortable silence, so I didn't realize she had something on her mind until we sat down to have dinner.

"Will you tell me about Irene?" Gabby asked.

"I'm not sure what you mean," I hedged. I had a feeling I knew exactly what she meant, but there was only so much I could tell her. And I hated that. The lie I was living had never been an issue until I met Gabby. Lying to everyone else was easy, but I didn't want to lie to her.

"You said she was the first person you met when you moved to Cedar Valley, and she's like a crazy aunt. But she's more than that, isn't she?"

"She is," I said and blew out a slow breath. "I told you my mom died when I was eighteen. What I didn't tell you was that I left town the very next day. I had my laptop, a few changes of clothes, and very little money.

After spending almost an entire day on a bus, Irene's diner was the first place I went. She took one look at me and knew I needed help. Help I didn't even know to ask for. She gave me a job and a place to live. At first, I thought she felt sorry for me, but that wasn't the case at all. She'd recently lost her husband, and she didn't have any other family. She said her lonely soul recognized the loneliness in mine. Well, she didn't tell me that part until years later."

"So, she claimed you as her family?"

"That's exactly what she did. She made sure I had food and let me wash my clothes at her house. She taught me how to survive on my own, but stood by me so I didn't have to. Then she introduced me to the Blackwings."

"She knows the club?"

"Yes, and no. They stopped by the diner from time to time. One particular day, she overheard Phoenix talking about upgrading the computers at the clubhouse and switching to wireless internet access. She told him she knew someone who could help and pulled me from the kitchen to introduce me. I started prospecting two weeks later."

"Well," she said and got up to take my plate, "I'm glad you found her."

"Me, too."

* * *

Gabby found me in the living room with my feet on the coffee table and my laptop in my lap.

"Did they give you any trouble?" I asked.

"Henny and Penny? No. Lenny? Yes," she said.

"She was like that with me at first. I'm not sure what kind of situation they came from, but she takes longer to warm up to new people than the others do," I said and continued typing.

"What are you working on?"

"I'm emailing the video clips to Detective Hayes and making sure he knows about the other police reports we filed. I don't think we mentioned those during the meeting since we didn't realize there was a connection between Chad and Lauren," I said and clicked send before closing my laptop. "And now I'm finished."

"Have you heard from Edge?" she asked.

"No, but I can call him and check in if you want."

"Yeah, I'd like that."

I took a moment and studied her face. "Are you worried?"

"A little," she said shakily, and inhaled deeply. "I don't want to be the reason something happens to your family. I can't be."

"Gabby," I said and pulled her into my arms. "If something happens at the diner, it won't be your fault. You didn't ask for any of this, and you didn't do anything to cause any of this."

"That's what I keep telling myself," she said quietly.

"Let's see if we can put your mind at ease, at least for tonight," I said and picked up my phone to call Edge.

"Hey, man. How's it going?" I asked when he answered.

"No sign of either of them so far, but I'm going to hang around until she closes to be sure. I'll text you when I'm headed back to Gabby's house."

"Thanks, man."

"Any time."

I ended the call and placed my phone on the table. "Feel better?"

Gabby sighed, but the tension didn't completely leave her body. "Yes, and no. I feel better now, but what about tomorrow? And the next day?"

"We'll take the same precautions tomorrow, and the next day, and the day after that until we find them. I don't know how long it will take, but we have more to go on than we did, and the police are helping us," I told her.

"I can't wait for all of this to be over."

"Me, too," I agreed.

* * *

When my phone rang, I didn't recognize the number but answered anyway.

"Hi, this is Detective Hayes. Is this Byte?"

"Yes, this is Byte."

"I have a few updates on your case. I tried to call Gabby, but she didn't answer," he said.

"She's at school right now, but I can pass along any information."

"As expected, our lab confirmed the presence of THC in the brownies. I've already sent a copy of the results to Tina's office," he said.

"Thank you."

"As for Lauren, we issued a warrant for her arrest. When we went to the address on file to bring her in, we found someone else living there. I spoke to the landlord, and he confirmed Lauren moved out several months ago. Before you ask, she didn't leave a forwarding address."

I pinched the bridge of my nose and fought back the urge to throw my phone across the room. "So, what happens now?"

"Now, we keep looking for her," he said simply.

"Do you have any leads? Any direction to go in?" I asked.

He exhaled audibly. "We've got an APB out with her information, including the make and model of her car and her tag number, but I don't think it'll help much since the car from the video you sent was determined to be a rental that was returned early this morning."

"What about her phone?"

"It's been disconnected."

"Her job?"

"She didn't show up for work Monday, and they haven't been able to get in touch with her. They have the same contact info we do," he explained.

"What about an emergency contact? Don't most places of employment require an emergency contact?" I asked.

"She listed Chad Higgins with the phone number that has since been disconnected."

"Damn it," I cursed.

"My sentiments exactly," he said. "I know this is

frustrating, but I assure you, we're exhausting all avenues and doing everything we can."

"Thank you, Detective Hayes. I appreciate the update."

"I'll be in touch," he said. "Hopefully with better news than I had today."

I dropped my head into my hands and groaned. There was nothing I could do except sit and wait for Lauren to resurface. I hadn't felt so helpless since before that fateful day when my life changed at the age of fourteen.

* * *

"WHAT'S WRONG?" GABBY ASKED WHEN SHE GOT INTO my truck.

"What makes you think something's wrong?"

"I've been around you every day for weeks now. I can tell," she said.

"Detective Hayes called earlier today," I started and filled her in on what he told me.

"I don't understand how people can just disappear," she said.

I did, but I kept that to myself.

"So, what do we do now?" she asked.

"The same thing we've been doing. We stay vigilant and wait."

19

GABBY

Two weeks passed with no sign of Lauren or Chad, and I wasn't sure how I felt about that. Part of me was happy they weren't bothering me, but the other part of me wanted the whole ordeal to be done and over with.

I shook my head and tried to clear them from my thoughts. I had one more patient to see before I was off for the next four days. Byte and I were planning on going up to Badger's cabin for a long weekend, and I couldn't wait.

"The last patient of the day is ready in room three," Jan said.

"Thanks. I'll go ahead and get started. Will you let Dr. Vaughn know?" I asked and opened the patient's chart on my laptop.

"Sure. He'll be right behind you."

I knocked on the door and entered the room. "Hello, Ms. Watson. I'm Gabby, a nurse practitioner student working with Dr. Vaughn. What brings you in

today?" I asked and almost dropped my computer when my eyes landed on Lauren. She was sitting on the exam table with a devious smile on her face, and a large gun in her hand.

"Yes, Gabby, I know who you are," she said snidely.

I instinctively took a few steps away from her. "Don't even think about it. Unless you want me to kill everyone in this building, you'll keep your mouth shut and do as I say."

"What do you want?"

"I want what's rightfully mine," she said.

"I don't know what you're talking about."

Before she could respond, Patch knocked once on the door and entered the room. "Hello, Ms. Watson. I'm Dr. Vaughn. I see you've already met Gabby."

"Yes, I have," she gritted out.

At her tone, Patch looked up from the computer screen and noticed the gun in her hand. "What's going on here?"

Lauren rolled her eyes dramatically. "I thought doctors were supposed to be smart. Isn't it obvious?"

"Sorry. This is my first time being held at gunpoint at my place of business."

"I want you to send everyone home," she instructed. "And don't even think about trying to alert anyone."

Patch nodded and stuck his head out the door. "Jan, you guys can go ahead and go home. We're going to be a while longer."

"Are you sure? I can stay and help," she offered.

"Thanks, but I think we're good. I'll see you

tomorrow," he said and closed the door. Turning back to Lauren, he asked, "Now what?"

"Now we wait for everyone to leave," she said. "While we're doing that, both of you put your phones over there where I can see them."

I reluctantly removed my phone from my pocket and placed it on the counter beside Patch's. The only thing keeping me from completely freaking out was knowing Byte was in the parking lot, waiting to pick me up. When Patch and I didn't leave with the rest of the employees, he would realize something was wrong. I just needed to stall long enough for that to happen.

"All right, everyone should be gone by now," Lauren said and pulled out a roll of duct tape from the large purse beside her. She pointed the gun at Patch and gestured to the chair. "You, sit down. Gabby, you're going to secure him to the chair and cover his mouth with tape."

I couldn't tape Patch to the chair. If I did, I'd be completely on my own against her. "What? Why? Why are you doing this?"

"Oh, now you're interested in me?" Lauren spat.

"What are you talking about?"

"I shouldn't be surprised. You've always only cared about yourself," she said and laughed derisively. "You know, I actually thought you'd try to find me. For years, I waited for someone to show up, but they never did."

While Lauren was talking, Patch had been slowly inching his way closer to her. Unfortunately, Lauren noticed and angrily pointed the gun in his direction. "Not another step closer."

I completely ignored their interaction and tried to bring her attention back to me. "I'm sorry, but I'm really not following you. For years you thought I'd come for you? How would that have been possible? I just met you last year."

She narrowed her eyes, and the muscles in her jaw tightened. "No, you met me when we were children."

I remembered Byte telling me angry people were sloppy people, and I hoped that would be the case with Lauren. "You obviously knew I had no recollection of you. Why are you acting so upset about it now?"

"I'm not upset," she growled and emphasized her words by aiming the gun at me. "I'm pissed."

"Yes, I can see that," I said and gestured to the gun. I really didn't have a clue what I was doing, but I was determined not to let her win. I had to keep her talking until one of us could get the upper hand. "Will you at least tell me why you're so mad? What did I do to make you hate me so much?"

"Oh, Gabby. Dear sweet, stupid Gabby. I don't hate you. I'd have to feel something for you in order to hate you, and I have zero feelings for you."

I didn't point out that she'd just admitted to being angry. She was clearly in the middle of a psychotic break of some sort.

"Okay, I got it. No feelings for me. So, what's this all about?"

"I already told you!" she screamed. "I want what's rightfully mine!"

"And you think I have what's yours?" I asked. I truly had no idea what she was talking about.

She huffed in frustration. "How do you not know? Look at me!"

At that point, I was just as frustrated as she was, and I was tired of talking in circles. "I am looking at you! Just tell me!"

"I'm your fucking sister!"

"No, you're not," I uttered in disbelief. "You can't be."

"Why not? Because I didn't come from some hoity-toity rich bitch like you did? Because politicians are known for their fidelity? Tell me, Gabriella Hastings, why can't I be your sister?"

I gasped at the sound of my original surname. "I-I," I stammered while I tried to make sense of her words. My sister? There was only one way that was possible. "Are you saying Lawrence Hastings is your father?"

"You always had so much more than me, and you didn't even appreciate it. You had a room full of toys you never played with. Everything sat untouched on the shelves while your bedroom was in pristine condition," she sneered.

Suddenly, realization dawned. She was the kid from my dream. "I remember you," I breathed. "You used to come over to my house. You would break my toys and destroy my room. I got in trouble every time you came to visit."

"Oh, boo hoo. Poor little princess Gabby had to clean up after her slovenly sister," she spat.

"Okay, fine. You're my sister. What do you think I have that belongs to you?"

"My inheritance."

"Your what?"

"Our father was a senator. I know he was loaded. I want my half of the money you got from him."

My brows furrowed in confusion. "I didn't get any money from him."

"Don't lie to me!" she screamed.

"I'm not lying to you. He was convicted of numerous crimes. Everything he had was seized by the authorities," I explained.

"I know you're loaded," she insisted.

I swallowed thickly, knowing she wasn't going to like my response. "Yes, I have a substantial trust fund, but that came from my mother and my grandmother. I didn't inherit anything from Lawrence."

"You know what? I don't care. I want half of what you have. We'll call it compensation for my pain and suffering. Now, it's time to go." With that, she pointed the gun at Patch and fired.

I watched in horror as the bullet pierced his left upper chest. He stumbled backward and fell to the floor as blood appeared on his lab coat. I dropped down beside him and covered his wound with my hands. "Patch," I cried. "Are you okay?"

"Let's go, Gabby," Lauren insisted.

"I'm not going anywhere with you!" I yelled.

"Do what she says," Patch croaked. "Don't worry about me."

"Listen to the dying doctor," Lauren hissed.

"I'm not leaving you," I said to Patch. "She can't kill me and get her money."

Lauren sighed in exasperation. "You're right. I can't kill you, but I sure as hell can maim you."

As soon as the words left her mouth, another loud boom filled the room, and white-hot pain pierced my shoulder. And that was it. I'd had enough, and I couldn't take any more. My only explanation for what happened next was that I snapped.

I got to my feet and launched myself at Lauren, tackling her to the ground. We landed on the tile floor with a thud, but I didn't let the impact stop me. I raised my closed fist and plowed it into her face, followed by my other closed fist. Over and over. I didn't stop until someone touched my shoulder and shouted my name.

Patch was slumped in the chair, with Lauren's gun in his hand. "I've got her. Go get Byte."

Byte. The sound of his name filled me with overwhelming relief. He was right outside.

I ran to the back door and almost dropped to my knees when I saw him.

20

BYTE

I was beginning to get worried when Gabby and Patch still hadn't come out of the office. At least fifteen minutes had passed since the other employees left. I was reaching for my phone to text Gabby when movement at the back door caught my attention.

Gabby pushed open the door, and my heart stopped. She had blood all over her hands, arms, and chest. She even had some splattered on her face.

I opened the door and ran to her as fast as I could.

"Byte," she cried. "Lauren. Sh-she shot Patch. And I…I don't know what happened."

"Where are they?" I asked and pulled my gun from its holster.

"In exam room five."

When I started to move toward the room, she came with me. "No. You stay here."

She shook her head. "She's down, and Patch needs help." The urgency in her voice kept me from insisting she let me check it out first.

I entered the room to find Patch pointing a gun at an unconscious and almost unrecognizable Lauren on the floor. It looked like she'd been beaten within an inch of her life. "What happened?" I finally asked.

"She was posing as a patient and ambushed us," Patch explained. "She shot me, then Gabby. Gabby took her down. I picked up her gun, and here we are. I need you to call nine-one-one, call the club, and make sure she's okay."

"I'm okay," Gabby insisted. "Help me get him to the table so I can hold pressure on his wound. Then make the calls."

Gabby seemed to have snapped out of her shock and gone into nurse mode. I took that as a win and helped Patch onto the exam table. Then I called nine-one-one. They tried to keep me on the phone by asking questions, but I hung up after telling them everything I knew. My phone call to the club was much more efficient.

"Phoenix Black," he answered.

"I need the club at Patch's clinic. Patch and Gabby have been shot. Both are alert and talking. Shooter is secure. Cops and paramedics have been called. Come through the back."

"We're on the way, brother," he said and disconnected the call.

"I don't think she'll wake up, but there's duct tape on the floor you can use to restrain her," Patch said. He sounded weak, but I was glad to hear his voice.

"Found it," I said and started taping Lauren's hands together. "How are you doing, Gabs?"

"I'm using this adrenaline for everything it's worth," she said.

I wasn't at all surprised when I heard motorcycle pipes well before the sirens. Minutes later, Phoenix appeared in the doorway with a frantic Shaker right behind him.

"Gabby," he shouted and started toward her.

"Stop him, Byte," she insisted. "I'm barely holding it together. If he touches me, I'll lose it. And I can't lose it until EMS gets here."

I stepped in front of him, prepared to tackle him to the ground, but it wasn't necessary. He stopped on his own accord. "Gabby?" he asked carefully.

"I'm okay, Shaky Jakey," she said softly. "I just need to focus on Patch right now."

"Croftridge PD!" someone shouted from down the hall.

Phoenix stepped out of the room. "We're in here, officers. The shooter's restrained on the floor. Everyone else is with me, including the two with gunshot wounds who need medical attention."

As soon as the paramedics entered the room, Gabby started giving them a rundown of Patch's injuries and his status. They thanked her and took over.

I knew what was going to happen and had been anticipating it from the moment Gabby mentioned her adrenaline rush. She'd taken two steps away from Patch when her knees buckled. I swooped in behind her and eased her to the floor. "You're okay, baby. You're okay."

"Gabriella!" Shaker shouted and dropped to the floor beside her. He took one of her hands in his,

causing her to groan in pain. He quickly released it with a look of horror on his face. "What happened to your hand?"

"That," I said and tipped my head in Lauren's direction.

Shaker did a double-take before he turned back to Gabby with a proud smile on his face. "You did that?"

Gabby lifted one shoulder in a weak attempt to shrug. "She shot me," she said simply.

"Your papa is going to be so proud," he said.

"Papa," she gasped. "Where is he?"

"He's with Keegan. They're going to meet us at the hospital."

"Can they take her to a different hospital?" Gabby asked and gestured toward Lauren, who was still unconscious on the floor.

"I think that can be arranged," he said.

"Excuse me, sir, we need to take a look at her injuries," a paramedic said from behind Shaker.

He didn't look happy about it, but he got to his feet and stepped to the side. "Don't leave her," he said to me.

"I won't," I vowed.

"Hi, I'm Cam. Can you tell me where you're hurt?"

"I have a gunshot wound to my right shoulder. No exit wound. And I'm fairly certain both of my hands have multiple fractures."

Cam glanced down at her hands and grimaced. "Yeah, I think you're right about your hands. Let's have a look at your shoulder."

"You're going to have to cut my shirt off to get to it. I can't move this arm anymore."

Cam pulled out a pair of scissors and started cutting Gabby's top. I wanted to protest, but clamped my mouth shut before I said anything stupid.

Gabby turned her head to the side and whispered, "I have on a tank top."

I feigned ignorance. "What?"

"I felt you tense," she said knowingly.

"Well, the good news is you aren't bleeding excessively," Cam said.

"And the bad news?" she asked.

"It's not necessarily bad news, per se, but you were right. You don't have an exit wound."

Gabby sighed. "Okay, let's get this show on the road."

Cam motioned for his partner to bring the stretcher over.

"What's the issue?" I asked Gabby.

"The bullet is lodged somewhere in my shoulder. Depending on where it is, I might have to have surgery to remove it," she explained. "It's not really an issue. I just don't want to have surgery."

"I don't think anyone *wants* to have surgery."

"You're wrong about that. There are plenty of people who like having surgery, but I'm not one of them."

"Are you ready to roll?" Cam asked her.

"Almost," she said and turned her attention to me. "Where's Jacob?"

"Right here," he answered. He'd been hovering a few feet away the whole time.

"Please let Keegan and Papa know my injuries are

minor and that I'm okay for the most part. I know how Keegan worries. And will you see if you can get an update on Patch? He's probably in surgery, or will be soon, but I'd like to know how he's doing," she said.

"I'll call right now," he promised and leaned down to place a kiss on top of her head. "Love you, Gabby."

"Love you, too, Shaky Jakey."

Cam started to wheel her toward the door. "Wait! Make sure she's taken to a different facility please," she said and looked down at the woman on the floor.

"I'll see to that," one of the officers said.

"Thank you," Gabby said. "Okay, I'm ready."

* * *

Keegan and Ranger were waiting on the curb in the ambulance bay. They were by her side before the wheels of the stretcher touched the ground.

"Gabby!" they said at the same time.

"Fancy seeing you two here," Gabby said with a slight slur.

"She's had some pain medicine," I clarified.

"Tell me everything," Keegan insisted.

"I will," I promised. "Let's get her inside first."

Cam wheeled Gabby to a room and wished her a speedy recovery before he left. Then a doctor and two nurses came in to assess her. After a flurry of activity, Gabby was in a hospital gown, connected to an IV, and was resting in a hospital bed.

"I'm Dr. White. Are you the family?"

"Yes," the three of us said in unison.

"I'm going to order some X-rays for her shoulder and her hands. I won't know for sure until I see the films, but at this point, I'm more concerned about her hands than her shoulder. With the amount of swelling and bruising, I suspect multiple fractures. Her shoulder may require surgery to remove the bullet, but again, I won't know anything until I see the X-rays. She appears to be resting comfortably, but please let us know if that changes."

"Thank you, doctor," Keegan said. "My husband, Jacob Marks, will be arriving shortly. Do I need to give his name to someone at the front so he'll be allowed to come back and be with his daughter?"

"I'll make sure they know to let Ms. Marks's father back to her room."

"Nicely done, Mrs. Marks," I said once Dr. White was gone. It sounded weird to me to hear her refer to Gabby as Shaker's daughter, but, technically, she was from the moment they adopted her.

"I only name-drop when it's important," Keegan replied.

"No judgment here. I would've done it if you hadn't," I admitted.

"Welcome to Club Marks," she teased. "Now, tell me what happened."

I exhaled heavily and dropped into a chair in Gabby's room. "Lauren pretended to be a patient and pulled a gun on Patch and Gabby when they entered the room. She had Patch send the rest of the employees home so only the three of them were in the office. I don't know the details, but Lauren shot Patch first, then

Gabby. Gabby managed to take Lauren down while Patch got her gun."

"That crazy bitch. Where is she?" Keegan demanded.

"Gabby arranged for her to be taken to another facility. She didn't want anyone getting into any unnecessary trouble," I explained.

Keegan smiled and Ranger shook his head. "I don't have to kill her now. I can wait," he grumbled.

"Please don't, Papa," Gabby mumbled. "She's not worth it."

"She tried to kill you," he argued.

"But she didn't. I whooped her ass."

"Is that right?" Ranger asked.

"It is," I nodded. "She beat the piss out of her. Seriously, I didn't recognize her when I got there."

"That's my girl," Ranger said proudly.

"Do we know why this girl has been terrorizing my sister?" Keegan asked.

"No," I said at the same time Gabby said, "Yes."

"You do?" I asked.

"I didn't get a chance to tell you," she croaked. "Can I have some water?"

"They don't want you to have anything to eat or drink in case you need to have surgery," Keegan said.

"Give the girl a sip of water. Blame it on me," Ranger said and got up to hold the cup for Gabby.

She took a small sip and continued. "Sissy, you might want to sit."

Keegan situated herself at the end of Gabby's bed. "Okay, I'm sitting. Spill it."

Gabby sighed. "She said she wanted what was rightfully hers. Meaning the inheritance she thinks I got from Lawrence. Apparently, she's his daughter."

"What?" Keegan shouted and jumped to her feet. She took two steps and fell into a chair against the wall.

"Told ya to sit," Gabby said.

"Keegan!" Shaker yelled seconds before he burst into the room. "I heard you scream. What happened?"

"The bitch that's been harassing my grandbaby is Lawrence's bastard child," Ranger so eloquently summarized.

"Are you serious?" Shaker asked in disbelief.

"Congratulations," Gabby sang. "I have a crazy relative, and none of you are it."

"She's been medicated," I said quietly.

"I can still hear you," Gabby whispered.

"She obviously didn't seek out Gabby to have a relationship with her as a sister, so what was her end goal?" Shaker asked.

"Money," Gabby blurted. "She thought I had Lawrence's money and wanted half of it. What an idiot."

"Why would she think that?" Keegan asked.

"She knew about my trust fund. She thought it was from him," Gabby said sleepily.

"This is my fault?" Keegan asked in horror.

Gabby's head shot up, and her eyes were wide open. "No. Absolutely not. None of this is your fault. Or my fault. Or anyone's fault except hers. And maybe Lawrence's. But it's not ours. Now, I don't know what they gave me, but it's kicking my ass worse than I kicked Lauren's. Promise me

you won't blame yourself so I can let this glorious euphoria take over. My hands hurt, Sissy. I want to go to sleep."

Keegan reached for Gabby's hand but stopped herself before she made contact. She carefully placed her hand on Gabby's uninjured shoulder. "You're right. We can't control what other people do. Rest, Gabby. I won't blame anybody except the two of them."

"Good," she smiled as her eyes started to close. "Your turn, Papa."

"Fucking hell," Ranger grumbled. "I promise I won't kill her."

"Thank you," she grinned. "Any word on Patch?"

"He's in surgery, but he's expected to make a full recovery."

"Fantastic. I love you all. Thanks for coming. I hope you've enjoyed the show. And I'm out," she said and closed her eyes as her head slumped to the side.

"What in the hell did they give her?" Keegan asked.

"I'd guess it was one of the big boys," I said and gestured to her hands.

"How did she hurt them this bad?" Keegan asked.

"She was running on pure adrenaline when I got there. I'm sure she didn't even notice when it was happening," I explained.

"Knock, knock," Dr. White said as he entered the room. "How's our patient doing?"

"She just conked out, but she seemed to be feeling pretty good prior to that," I said.

"Good, I'm glad her pain is under control. So, I'll get right to it. We will need to remove the bullet in

surgery. It's very close to a large blood vessel, and we don't want to risk compromising the vessel by removing it manually at the bedside."

Keegan grimaced. "I wish Gabby was able to translate."

"The hospital has translators. Do you need one?" Dr. White asked.

"Oh, no, that's not what I meant. Gabby's a nurse and will soon be a nurse practitioner. She speaks medical, and I don't."

"Oh, my apologies," Dr. White said. "Let me try again. The bullet is very close to a large vein and a large artery in her shoulder. If we try to remove it at the bedside, we could easily hit one of those vessels and cause her to bleed excessively. There is still a risk of hitting one of those vessels during surgery, but they have the tools necessary to stop the bleeding right away if that were to occur. In Gabby's case, surgery is the safer option."

"Thank you, doctor," Keegan said sincerely. "What about her hands?"

"She has multiple fractures on each hand. I don't think any of them require surgical intervention, but I'm going to ask the orthopedic doctors to come by and see her. In the meantime, we'll wrap her hands to stabilize and protect them until Ortho makes their recommendations."

"When will she be going to surgery?" I asked.

"I don't have a solid answer to give you. I believe there's only one emergency surgery ahead of her, and

it's already in progress. If I had to guess, it'll probably be within the hour, but don't hold me to that," he said.

Keegan breathed a sigh of relief. "Oh, good. That means Patch will be out soon."

"The man currently in surgery is our friend. He and Gabby were shot by the same person," I clarified.

He gasped in surprise. "She's the one who helped Patch?"

"Yes, she is," I confirmed.

"She saved his life," he said seriously.

"She did?" Keegan asked. "I'm not doubting her by any means. I just didn't realize his injuries were life-threatening."

"Yes, she did. And she did a damn fine job. From what the paramedics said, she stopped him from bleeding to death by squeezing the vessel with her fingers until EMS arrived and clamped it with hemostats."

"That explains a lot," I said. "Thank you."

"Last I heard, the surgery was going better than expected. They should be finishing up soon. I'll be sure to keep you guys updated," he said and left the room.

"Why did you say, 'that explains a lot'?" Keegan asked.

"When I got there, she was laser-focused on Patch. She asked me to help him move to the exam table. Then she never left his side. They were quietly talking back and forth, but I couldn't make out what they were saying. She also had me busy securing Lauren and making phone calls. It didn't occur to me until just now that she was keeping me busy, while I'm sure her and

Patch knew exactly what was going on. Then when EMS arrived, she rattled off all kinds of medical jargon. I was watching her closely when they took over. It was almost seamless the way her hands moved out of the way and were replaced by a new set of hands. Seconds later, they rushed out the door with Patch. Then, Gabby collapsed. She really was running on pure adrenaline."

"That's why she keeps asking about him," Keegan said quietly. "She knew it was much worse than they let on. Why didn't she tell us?"

"He asked me not to," Gabby mumbled. "He didn't want anyone to worry if they didn't need to."

"They said you saved his life," Keegan told her.

"So he's okay?"

"He's still in surgery, but they said it was going better than expected and should be over soon. The doctor we spoke with said you did a damn fine job. The paramedics did, too."

"Will you let me know when he's out of surgery? Even if you have to wake me up?"

"About that. Once he's out of surgery, it's your turn," Keegan said gently.

"Damn it," Gabby cursed. "I knew it. I fucking knew I'd have to have surgery. Why? Is it lodged in the bone? Am I going to be able to predict the weather based on the way my shoulder aches?"

"The doctor said the bullet was near a large blood vessel, and they need to remove it during surgery in case they hit the vessel and cause it to bleed," Keegan explained. "And I don't know how to answer your question about the weather."

"Oh, well, that's not as bad as I thought. It must be near the axillary artery and vein. They're being cautious. I'm okay with that. What about my hands?"

"He said you have multiple fractures, so he's asking for an ortho consult, but he doesn't think you'll need surgery."

"Any update on Lauren?"

"No," Keegan said slowly. "Did you want one?"

"Yes," Gabby said as if Keegan should have known. "If I have broken bones in my hands, she better have broken bones in her face."

"I can already tell you that she does," I said. "But if you want to know specifics, I'll find out for you."

"I do. If I'm going to brag, I want to do it accurately."

"Who are you?" Keegan laughed.

"I'm a brawler," Gabby yawned.

There was a slight commotion somewhere nearby followed by a flurry of activity. When I looked up to see Shaker and Keegan grinning at each other, I knew exactly why.

Seconds later, my suspicions were confirmed when the door opened to reveal Shaker's mother, her husband, and their security detail. "Gabby!" Jacquelyn cried and rushed to the side of the bed.

"Gigi!" Gabby returned.

"Oh, my sweet girl! How are you feeling? Are you in pain?"

"I'm better now that you're here," she said.

"Hey," Keegan said in mock offense.

"You know you feel better now that she's here, too,"

Gabby quipped. "The same thing happens with Papa. It's the grandparent effect."

"You girls always know how to make me feel special," Jacquelyn said. "Now, what can I do?"

"Make sure Keegan doesn't worry herself silly while I'm in surgery. And make sure Papa is present and accounted for."

"I believe I can handle that. Anything else?"

"Yes, will you see if I can have a cheeseburger and fries after surgery? And a large Coke with the good ice?"

"Absolutely, sweetheart," Jacquelyn smiled.

"One last thing," Gabby said and closed her eyes. "Byte's my boyfriend. I know he's a little older than me, but he's become one of my rocks, and I love him. He chased a burglar out of my house, he took care of me when I was sick, he gave me a dog and helps me take care of him, and he let me play with his cannibal chickens."

"Sweetheart, you don't need my approval. I'm happy if you're happy."

"I'm happy," Gabby said and appeared to fall asleep.

"Cannibal chickens?" Jacquelyn asked.

"I have three chickens. Sometimes I feed them scrambled eggs, and Gabby finds that hilariously morbid," I explained.

Dr. White knocked on the door and stepped inside the room. "Patch's surgery went well, and he's in recovery now. He's asking about Gabby. Is it okay if I give him an update?"

"Yes, please do," Keegan said. "Is he by himself?"

"He is at the moment, but they literally just wheeled

him out of the OR. They'll allow a family member or two back once he's settled. I believe he has a group of people waiting to see him."

"Yeah, most of the club's probably here by now," Shaker said.

Dr. White's attention shifted to a physician walking toward us. "Hey, Butch, are you ready for my patient?"

"As soon as I speak to her and her family," he said.

"Here they are," Dr. White said. "Dr. Butcher will be performing Gabby's surgery. I'm going to go let Patch know how Gabby's doing."

Gabby's eyes opened as she started to giggle. "A Wiener shot me, and now a Butcher's going to cut me open. You can't make this shit up."

"Gabby," Keegan scolded.

"Relax, Sissy. He's a surgeon named Butcher. I'm sure he's heard it all before."

"She's right," Dr. Butcher said with a smile. "Except for the Wiener part."

"The last name of the person who shot her is Wiener," I explained.

"Ah," he said. "Well, as you've heard, I'm Dr. Butcher, and I'll be performing your surgery shortly. I wanted to come by to introduce myself, but I also want to personally thank you for saving Patch's life. He's a good friend of mine and a great physician. He was lucky you were there to help."

Gabby looked down at her lap. "Thank you, but I can't take all the credit. He talked me through most of it."

"He's alive because you were there, and you can take

credit for that," Dr. Butcher said sincerely. "Now, about your surgery. We're taking you to the OR as more of a precaution because of the bullet's location. Barring any complications, you should be in and out in less than an hour. Any questions?"

Gabby shook her head. "I don't think so."

"I have one," Keegan said and pointed to Gabby's hands. "Will you please make sure to take extra precautions with her hands? She hasn't been seen by orthopedics yet, and I'm not sure how much protection her current bandages will provide."

"She's a worrier," Gabby stage-whispered.

Dr. Butcher grinned. "I'll personally make sure her hands don't incur any further injuries while she's in my care."

"Thank you," Keegan said.

"All right, I'll let the team know we're ready. I'll see you in the OR soon."

"Thank you," Gabby said.

I waited until everyone else had their moment with her. Then I leaned down and gently kissed her lips. "I love you, Gabs. I'll see you soon."

"I love you, too. Keep an eye on Papa, and don't forget to verify my bragging rights," she said.

"You got it," I promised and gave her one more quick kiss before they wheeled her away.

21

BYTE

After they took Gabby back for surgery, we joined the other club members present in a private waiting room. Patch's status at the hospital, coupled with the Marks family name, had the hospital staff treating us like royalty.

Phoenix pulled Shaker and me off to the side shortly after we entered the room. "I'm not sure when, but the police will be stopping by to get a statement from Gabby. I told them what I could at the scene, but they'll want the details from her and Patch. Has she said anything that we didn't already know?"

Shaker and I nodded at the same time. "I haven't had a chance to verify it, but Lauren told Gabby she is Lawrence Hastings's daughter," I said.

Phoenix let out a low whistle. "I can't say I saw that coming. Where's she been all this time?"

"I don't know, but I can try to find out when I have some time," I said.

"Does Gabby know why she shot her and Patch?"

"Patch was collateral damage. She shot Gabby to try to make her cooperate, which obviously, for lack of a better word, backfired."

"Cooperate with what?" Phoenix asked.

"She thought Gabby inherited money from Lawrencc and wanted half of it," I explained.

"Why would she think that?"

"Gabby's trust fund," Shaker said quietly. "She thought the money came from Lawrence, not Keegan and Mom."

"What do you need to verify her story?" he asked.

"My laptop," I said. "Flint has a key to my house. I'll see if he can go by and get it."

"I'll call him. You two go get something to eat and sit down," he said and pointed to the bags of food that had just been delivered to the room. "You both look like hell."

"I'm guessing your mom had something to do with this," I said to Shaker as I picked up a deli sub and a bag of chips.

"She likes to feed people. It's her love language," he smiled.

Before I took a seat, I walked over to speak to Jacquelyn. "Thank you for dinner."

She immediately engulfed me in a hug. "No, thank you. You've been taking care of and protecting my granddaughter for weeks. I owe you a lot more than a sandwich."

"You don't have to thank me. I love her. I'll take care of her and protect her for as long as she'll have me," I said sincerely.

Jacquelyn smiled. "I'm glad she has you," she said and patted my cheek. "Go eat, and see if you can get Keegan to eat while you're at it."

"Yes, ma'am," I said and picked up another sandwich.

I dropped into the chair beside Keegan and held out the wrapped sub for her. "I promised your sister I wouldn't let you worry too much while she's in surgery, and I think I just promised your mother-in-law that I'd get you to eat. I'm not sure why they both think I'm the Keegan whisperer, but they do, and I'd rather not disappoint either of them."

Keegan took the sandwich from my outstretched hand. "Fine, but if I throw up, I'm blaming you."

"I'll take that blame if you promise to aim for Shaker," I said.

Keegan smiled. "You're wrong for that. He hates vomit."

"I know. But wouldn't it be fun to see him do the Shaky Jakey dance?" I asked.

Keegan snorted a laugh. "Yes, yes it would."

"What are you two laughing about over here?" Shaker asked.

"Nothing," we said at the same time.

He shook his head. Over the years, he'd gotten used to our antics. "Jake and Quincy are on their way," he said.

"Shit," Keegan cursed. "How'd they find out?"

Shaker grimaced. "They saw it on the news and put two and two together when they couldn't get ahold of

you, me, or Ranger. Jake called Flint in a bit of a panic, so Flint told him what happened."

"I'm not sure they should be driving," Keegan said worriedly.

"They're not. Flint's picking them up and driving them here," Shaker said.

"Were they mad?" Keegan asked.

"Why would they be mad?" I asked before Shaker could answer.

"Because we didn't call them right away, and they had to hear about it on the news."

"I think they're shocked and worried, not mad," Shaker said.

"Honestly, Keegan, when have you had a chance to call them? You literally just sat down a few minutes ago," I reminded her.

"I know," she conceded. "This whole situation is just awful."

"Tell me about it," I commiserated. "I don't think I'll ever be able to get the image of her appearing at the back door covered in blood out of my head. And then Patch," I paused and shook my head. "I knew he was hurt worse than Gabby, but I had no idea how bad it was."

"I hate that she was hurt, but I'm so damn proud of her," Keegan beamed.

"Me, too," I agreed and nudged Keegan with my elbow. "Eat your sandwich."

"Fine," she huffed and took an exaggerated bite. "Happy now?" she asked with a mouthful of food.

She'd almost finished the entire sub when Jake,

Quincy, and Flint arrived. "Mom," Quincy cried and rushed into Keegan's arms. "Are they going to be okay?"

"Yes," Keegan assured. "They're both going to be just fine. Patch is already out of surgery, and Gabby should be out soon."

Flint filled the empty chair beside me and handed me my laptop. "I'll swing back by your place on my way home to let Shadow out and put the chickens up for the night."

"Thanks, brother," I said. "I really appreciate it."

"No problem," he said. "I heard Gabby took down the shooter and saved Patch's life."

"She did," I said proudly. "Word travels fast around here."

He shrugged. "My dad's the president. I tend to hear things before the others do." He shifted in his seat and gestured toward my laptop. "You need any help with anything?"

Suddenly, I recalled all the times he'd asked me that same question and felt like an asshole for not asking sooner. "Are you interested in computers?"

"Not the shit they were teaching at school, but the stuff you do looks interesting," he said.

"If you want to learn, I'll be happy to teach you," I offered.

"You sure? Because I'm going to take you up on that offer."

"I'm sure," I said and handed my laptop back to him. "In fact, you can have your first lesson now."

"Really?" he asked excitedly and opened the computer. "What are we looking for?"

"We need to find out who Lauren Wiener's biological parents are," I said and started explaining how we were going to go about it.

Flint was able to follow my instructions with little to no difficulty. There were even a handful of times where he knew what to do next without direction from me. He definitely had a knack for information retrieval, or as some liked to call it, hacking.

"I've got it," he said. "Here are her birth records. Diana Wiener is listed as her mother. The father's information is blank."

"Yeah, I was kind of expecting that," I grumbled. "We'll come back to the father. Let's see if we can find out where the mother is."

Flint opened a new tab and started typing. "Is this her?" he asked moments later.

"I think so. Click on the details and see why she's incarcerated."

"Human trafficking and kidnapping," Flint said.

"Open a new page and type her name and Lawrence Hastings," I instructed.

Flint did as I said and brought up numerous articles listing Diana Wiener as an accomplice in Lawrence Hastings's and Harold Hensley's human trafficking operation.

"Of all the things you learn from me, what I'm about to tell you will be one of the most important. I've seen numerous hackers go down because they didn't follow this one rule. If you can get the information by another means, do it. I don't care if hacking will take less time. If you have another option, take it. Especially

if it involves anything with high-level security, like government websites," I explained.

"Is that what we need to do now?" Flint asked.

"Yes," I said and motioned for Phoenix to come over.

"Got something?" he asked.

"Yes, and no. I don't have information on Lauren's father, but her mother is currently in prison for human trafficking and kidnapping. She was working with Hastings and Hensley. Do you think Luke Johnson might be able to tell us anything about Diana Wiener and her daughter?" I asked.

"There's only one way to find out," Phoenix said and pulled out his phone.

"Luke is our go-to guy for anything FBI related. It just so happens that he was the lead agent on the case against Hastings and Hensley. So, while we could hack into the files and see for ourselves, it's safer for us, as well as the club, to ask for the information since we have a contact. If you're ever in a situation and you're not sure if you should proceed, just ask me or your dad."

"Got it," Flint said. "Is there anything else we can do while we wait to hear from Luke?"

"Actually, there is. And this is another example of asking for the information instead of getting it ourselves," I said and got to my feet. "Follow me."

I stepped out into the hallway and scanned the area for Dr. White. I spotted him at the nurses' station and waved him over when he noticed me.

"What can I help you with?"

"Well, it's a little unconventional, but I promised I'd

ask. Gabby and Patch have both asked about the status of the shooter. I'd call and ask myself, but I know they won't give that information to just anyone. Is there any way you could find out about her injuries for them? Even though she was defending herself, I think Gabby's worried that she may have caused permanent damage, and I'd like to put her mind at ease."

Dr. White smiled. "I have a friend who works in that ER. I'll call and ask. Give me a few minutes."

"Thank you. I really appreciate it."

"Gabby saved my friend's life. I'm happy to help," he said.

"Is Gabby really worried about Lauren's injuries?" Flint asked when Dr. White was out of earshot.

"No," I said and tried to stifle my laughter. "She wants to know how much damage she caused so she can brag accurately. Her words, not mine."

Flint chuckled. "That's hilarious."

Dr. White returned a few moments later. "Lauren Wiener has a grade four concussion. She has fractures to both eye sockets, her right cheek, nose, and left jaw. It will take some time, but she should recover without permanent damage, with the exception of her nose, but that really falls under cosmetic."

"Thank you, Dr. White," I said and extended my hand to shake his.

"What were you talking to the doctor about?" Keegan asked as soon as we returned to the waiting room.

"I was getting your sister's bragging rights like I promised."

"Really? What'd he say?" she asked.

"Gabby did a number on her," I said and relayed the list of Lauren's injuries.

"Damn. No wonder her hands are so bad," Keegan said.

"Byte," Phoenix called. "Patch wants to see you."

I followed Phoenix to the recovery area. "Go through there and stop at the sink to wash your hands. He can only have two visitors at a time, and Badger's back there with him now."

"Got it."

"Before you go, Luke got back to me. He said Diana's daughter, Lauren, was sent to live with Diana's parents in Idaho after her arrest. That's all the information he had."

"Thanks, Prez." The information didn't seem like it would be helpful, but it was more than we had.

After washing my hands, I went through a set of doors and easily found Patch, since he was the only patient in recovery.

"Hey, brother," I said and reached out for his hand. "You look a hell of a lot better than the last time I saw you." And he did. His color was much better, and his breaths were steady and even.

"Thanks, man. How's Gabby?"

"Still in surgery, but she was doing pretty well before they took her back."

"Good. Let me know how she is once she's out."

"I will," I promised.

"Tell her not to worry about school. We're both going to be out for a while, but we can do five or six

days a week to make up her hours if we need to," he said.

"Can I tell you not to worry about her school?"

Patch chuckled, followed by a groan. "Okay, fine. You made your point."

"She's asked about you constantly since she got here," I said quietly. "I'm pretty sure she would have refused to go to surgery if she didn't have an update on you."

"I figured as much," he admitted. "She's far more advanced than any other nurse practitioner student I've worked with. Hell, she knows more than ones I've worked with for years. There was no bullshitting her. She knew exactly how bad my injuries were, and she knew what to do until help arrived."

"She claims she was just following your orders," I said.

"She was already digging around in my chest to find the bleeder before I ever said a word. Don't let her sell herself short."

"I think modesty is in her nature."

"Yeah, I think you're right about that," he agreed.

22

BYTE

I waited until the day after Gabby was released from the hospital to go to the clubhouse and talk to Phoenix.

"That's the fifth time you've walked past my door in the last hour," Phoenix said. "Get in here and say whatever you need to say."

I hesitated for a brief moment before I inhaled deeply and entered his office.

"Well, what is it?" he asked.

"You know Gabby and I are together," I started.

"Yeah."

"I don't see that changing, and I don't want it to, but I don't think I can move forward unless I'm honest with her. Completely honest."

"You want to tell her about your past," he said knowingly.

"Yes," I admitted. "I want her to know my name. My real name."

He leaned back in his chair and rubbed his chin.

"Gabby was raised in the club. We're her family. I'm not concerned about her telling someone she shouldn't or trying to use the information against you. If you want to tell her, it's fine with me, on one condition. You have to tell Ranger, Shaker, and Keegan. You can't tell Gabby something of that magnitude and ask her to keep it from her family."

I exhaled in relief. "Thanks, Prez. I don't have a problem with her family knowing. Actually, I prefer it," I said and paused before I voiced my other concern.

"But?" he asked.

"I don't want Shaker and Ranger to think the club was keeping secrets from them."

"The club wasn't keeping secrets," he said firmly. "I was. And I'd do it again in a heartbeat. You were a scared fourteen-year-old boy who needed protection. The only way to help you and protect the club was to keep your secret to myself. My decision isn't something you should have to explain. How about you tell Gabby, and then we can tell Ranger and Shaker together?"

"I'm not scared of them," I blurted.

Phoenix laughed. "I know. If you were, you never would've started dating Gabby."

"Yeah, you're definitely right about that," I agreed.

"Think about it and let me know. I'm happy to explain my decisions and my line of thinking."

"Thanks, Prez."

"I don't think you'll need it, but good luck."

* * *

"I BROUGHT PIZZA," I ANNOUNCED WHEN I WALKED INTO my house.

"Yay! I'm starving," Gabby said from the living room.

"I'll bring it to you. How many slices do you want?"

"Two, please," she said.

I carried our plates into the living room to find her camped out on my couch, surrounded by textbooks and binders. "It looks like you've been busy."

She sighed. "I've been trying to study so I don't go crazy from boredom."

"You'll be back on your feet before you know it."

She held up her bandaged hands. "It's not my feet I'm worried about."

"Your hands are going to be fine," I reassured her.

"I know. I just wish bones healed faster. I hate sitting here when there are so many things I could be doing."

"Whenever you feel frustrated, think of Lauren drinking all of her meals through a straw."

Gabby laughed. "Yeah, that definitely helps. At least I can eat solid food." Gabby carefully lifted a slice of pizza to her mouth and awkwardly took a bite. "Well, sort of."

"Do you want me to cut it for you?" I offered.

A look of disgust appeared on her face. "No. It won't taste the same."

"What?" I laughed.

"If you cut it into bites, it won't taste the same," she explained. "Thanks, but no thanks. I'll make this work."

"Are you serious?"

"Yes, I am. If you don't believe me, cut yours and give it a try."

I looked down at the slice of pizza on my plate and imagined cutting it into bites. "You know, I'll take your word for it."

"Told you," she giggled.

Her laughter, her smiles, her love—they meant the world to me. And I hoped they'd still be there after I shared my truth with her.

"Gabby," I said and inhaled deeply, "I need to tell you something."

"Okay," she said slowly.

"It's big. And it's something you have to keep to yourself. But this thing between me and you is real. Like the forever kind of real. And I can't keep going until you know everything. It's not right, and it's not fair to you."

"Are you married?" she whispered with a look of horror on her face.

"No! It's nothing like that. It's about my past."

Her shoulders relaxed slightly, but her body was still tense. "What about it?"

"Most of what I told you about my past was true. I did move to Cedar Valley after my mother died. Irene helped me get on my feet, and I joined the club not long after. What I didn't tell you was that my stepfather killed my mother and tried to kill me. I pushed him down the stairs to keep him from stabbing me."

"Oh, Byte," she started.

"There's more," I interrupted. "He didn't die from the fall. He was hurt but not dead. I knew he would place the blame on me for what I did to him and what

he did to my mother. He was still holding the knife, so I lifted his arm and essentially made him stab himself. He was gone within a few seconds."

"It was self-defense," she said vehemently.

"Pushing him down the stairs was self-defense. Stabbing him after the fact wasn't."

"It was self-preservation then," she countered.

"Yes, it was, but it was also murder," I pointed out. "I didn't know if they would believe he killed my mother and fell on the knife, or if they would accuse me of killing them both. If they thought I did it, I would've gone to prison. If they thought he did it, I would've been put in foster care. Neither of those outcomes were okay with me, so I ran."

"You wouldn't have been put in foster care. You were eighteen."

I shook my head. "No, Gabby, I wasn't. I was fourteen."

"You were fourteen? When you came to Cedar Valley? When you joined the club?"

I nodded. "I'd already been making fake IDs for other kids. That night, I made one for myself and left town the next morning."

"So, you're four years younger than you told me?"

"Yes, and my name's not Michael Fuller."

"What is it?"

"Blake Williams," I said quietly.

"I knew Michael didn't sound right."

"I've wanted to tell you my *real* real name from the moment you asked. The lie I've been living has never bothered me. Until you."

"Why?"

"Because I love you," I said simply. "I love you in a way I didn't know was possible. And I couldn't keep lying to you. Even if telling you the truth meant losing you."

"You're not going to lose me," she whispered.

"I'm not?"

"None of what you told me changes who you are. If anything, it reinforces it."

I reached for her and carefully pulled her into my arms. "I love you so damn much."

"I love you, too, Blake."

I smoothed my hand over her hair and held her tightly. The relief I felt from sharing the deepest and darkest parts of my life with her was overwhelming. It felt like I could finally breathe freely without a massive weight on my chest.

"Does anyone besides me know?" she asked.

"Phoenix knows. He's always known. I told him the day he asked me to prospect."

"He agreed to let a fourteen-year-old prospect for the club?"

"He agreed to help me. There were rules and stipulations, but basically, I traded my computer skills for his protection," I explained. "I went to the clubhouse today to talk to him. To ask for permission to tell you, and to tell your family. My secret shouldn't be your burden."

"He obviously said yes."

I nodded. "Yes, he did."

"Does my family know?"

"Not yet. I wanted to tell you first."

"Well, when do you want to tell them?" she asked.

"Whenever you feel up to it." It had only been a few days since the shooting, and I honestly didn't know what would be too much for her.

She made a dismissive motion with her bandaged hand. "Don't worry about me. I'm fine."

"Gabby," I said slowly.

"I mean I'm fine for a family meeting. Why don't we have them over for dinner? They're over here every day to check on me anyway."

"When? Tonight?"

"Might as well," she said. "Unless you'd rather wait."

"It's not me I'm worried about."

She smiled triumphantly. "Great. Tonight it is."

* * *

Ranger, Keegan, and Shaker showed up at my house for dinner right on time. I wasn't nervous, but I wasn't exactly relaxed either. I had talked about my past more in the last week than I had in my entire life, and I hoped dinner with Gabby's family would be the last time.

"Come on in," I said and held the door open for them to enter. "I hope you're hungry."

Shaker cocked his head to the side while Keegan gave me a quizzical look. Thankfully, Gabby entered the room and stole their attention before either one of them said anything.

Ranger's big hand landed on my shoulder. "You okay?"

"Yeah. Why?" I blurted before I had a chance to think of a better response.

"You seem jumpy."

"I probably will be until this whole situation is completely resolved," I admitted. Even though Lauren was in police custody, Chad was still in the wind, and that wasn't sitting well with me.

"Let me know when you find him. I'll be happy to put an end to it once and for all," Ranger said as he made his way to the table.

We were just starting to dish out the food when there was a knock on the door. I opened it to find Phoenix standing there. He grinned. "Hope you have room for one more."

"Prez," I said slowly.

"I'm not letting you explain decisions I made without me. Now, invite me in for dinner."

I shook my head. I should have expected him to show up. I opened the door and gestured for him to come in.

"Prez," Shaker said. "What are you doing here?"

"Thought I'd join you guys for dinner," he said and took a seat.

Everyone continued passing the food and loading their plates. Everyone except Keegan. She sat frozen in place until Shaker nudged her with his elbow. The fork she was holding fell from her hand and landed on her empty plate with an echoing clank.

"Keegan?" Shaker asked.

She ignored him and glanced around the table. "What in the hell is going on?" she demanded.

I leaned back in my seat and exhaled slowly. "I have something to tell you guys. No one's hurt or anything like that. It's about my past."

"Okay," Shaker said and gestured for me to continue.

"Fucking hell! Are you married?" Keegan shouted.

"No! What is with you two? Gabby asked me the same thing."

Keegan shrugged. "Duke was."

"Duke's an asshole," I countered.

"Touché," she said with a slight smile.

"Well, let's hear it," Ranger said with a touch of impatience.

I took a deep breath and started telling them the whole story. Surprisingly, no one said a word until I was finished. Actually, there was a long period of awkward silence before Keegan finally broke it. She aimed her eyes directly at Phoenix. "Why are you here?"

"Because he knew," Shaker said.

Phoenix nodded. "That's right. And I didn't think he should have to explain or defend the decisions I made. He was fourteen years old and needed help. I had a feeling he would be an asset to the club, and I wasn't wrong. I was also willing to take sole responsibility if I was."

"How in the hell did none of us realize you were so young?" Shaker asked.

I shrugged. "I was always big for my age. Most

people assumed I was older than I actually was, even when I was in elementary school."

"There's a big difference between fourteen and eighteen," he said.

"The club was never in danger. I would've said I lied about my identity if anyone found out who I really was," I added.

"This is why you never went out with the club brothers or were involved in any club business for the first few years you were a member," Shaker said.

"That was my doing. I wasn't going to put a teenager in the middle of dangerous situations. I only allowed him to be involved in club business behind the scenes until he was truly an adult, regardless of what his ID said."

"And this is why you stay out of trouble," Ranger added.

"I wouldn't say that."

Shaker laughed. "Dude, you're squeaky clean for a biker."

I shrugged. "I wasn't sure what would happen if I was ever arrested, and I didn't want to chance it. I still don't. There's no statute of limitations for murder."

"Wait a minute. You didn't keep tabs on the situation with your parents?" Keegan asked.

I shook my head. "No, I didn't. I figured it was best not to know. If I knew they were looking for me, I would've been worried about it all the time. If it turned out I wasn't suspected of murder, I knew I wouldn't have been as careful to stay hidden and probably would have been found at some point. Like I said before, I wasn't

going down for murder, and I wasn't going to be put into foster care."

"Can't say I blame you," Ranger said.

"So, why now?" Keegan asked.

"What?"

"Why are you telling us now?" she clarified.

"Because I love your sister, and I wanted her to know the truth before things went any further," I explained.

"You could've told her without telling us."

I wanted to roll my eyes. "Seriously, Keegan? I wasn't going to ask her to lie to her family for me."

She grinned. "Just checking."

"You're such a little shit sometimes."

"That's why you love me."

"What are we doing about this Chad prick?" Ranger asked. When all heads turned to him, he looked slightly confused. "What? I thought we were finished with Byte's secret life. Is there more?"

"No, that's everything," I confirmed.

Ranger looked at Keegan and Shaker. "Do you guys need to have feelings about this new revelation?"

Shaker shook his head, and Keegan laughed. "No, Papa. We're good."

"Really?" I asked in surprise.

"Yes, really. Why?" Keegan asked.

"I don't know. I guess I thought there'd be more."

"I mean, it was a big secret to share, but it doesn't change anything," she said. "Well, except for your age."

"And even that doesn't matter," Shaker added. "Your name and age don't change who you are."

Gabby smiled and leaned closer to me. "Told you they wouldn't care."

I leaned over and kissed her forehead. "Yes, you did."

Ranger cleared his throat. "Now that we're one big happy family, let's talk about Chadprick?"

"Chadprick?" Keegan laughed.

"I assumed Chad was short for Chadwick and made my own improvements on his name," Ranger said.

I sighed. "Nothing new there. The police haven't found anything, and neither have I." I hated admitting defeat, but I hadn't been able to find anything on Chadprick.

"Then I think it's time someone had a chat with Lauren," Ranger said.

"Papa, we can't do that," Gabby said.

"Of course we can," he countered. "We just have to be creative."

"Something tells me you've already given this some thought," Phoenix said.

Ranger grinned. "Who? Me?"

"Yes, you, you old pain in the ass."

"I'll pretend to be offended later."

Surprisingly, it was Gabby who spoke next. "Can we skip to the part where Papa tells us his plan?"

"I don't really have a plan. I just think we should send someone in to talk to her while she's still in the hospital. It won't be as easy once she's discharged," Ranger said.

"Even if we manage to get someone in there, she can't talk. Her jaw's wired shut," Gabby pointed out.

"I've got a pair of wire cutters," Ranger said.

"Papa," Gabby admonished with a smile.

"What? They wired it once; they can wire it again."

"Not before she tells someone who cut the wire," Shaker said.

"That won't happen if she's threatened properly," Ranger argued.

"I think I have a better idea," Phoenix said. "Tina knows the detective working the case. Maybe he'd be willing to offer Lauren a chance at a reduced sentence in exchange for information on Chad."

Gabby shook her head. "I don't like it. She's already going to get off easier than she should. I'm more than grateful that Patch and I lived, but attempted murder doesn't receive the same sentencing as murder."

Phoenix grinned. "She won't get a lighter sentence. The detective doesn't have the authority to make an offer like that. Attorneys do, but detectives do not. That's also why I said 'a chance at a reduced sentence.' It's all in the wording."

"Do you think it'll work?" Gabby asked hopefully.

"There's only one way to find out," Phoenix said and pulled out his phone.

23

GABBY

"Well, that went better than I expected," Byte said after everyone had gone home.

"I told you it would be fine," I said and tried to carry a plate to the sink using my forearms.

Byte immediately took the plate from me. "What are you doing?"

"Trying to help," I huffed.

"While I appreciate the effort, I'd much rather you let me do it," he said. "I don't want you to get hurt, and I know you don't want to do anything to make your healing take longer."

He had a point. "Fine," I sighed and dropped into a chair. "This sucks."

"You're cute when you pout."

"I'm not pouting," I grumbled. I was totally pouting. "And I'm cute all the time," I said and stuck out my tongue for good measure.

He put down the dishes and turned to study me. "You're in pain." I opened my mouth to say otherwise,

but he raised his hand to stop me. "Don't deny it, Gabs."

"Fine," I conceded. "I am. How'd you know?"

"Because you're grumpy and trying to hide it with humor."

"Well, aren't you observant?"

"You should know that by now," he said and left the room to get my medicine. A few moments later, he placed the pills and a drink with a straw in front of me. I could manage a fork or a spoon, but we learned that I couldn't hold a drink in my hands on the first day home from the hospital.

I grimaced at the sight of the pills. "I hate the way they make me feel."

"I know you do," he soothed. "But it's better than hurting. And I hate seeing you in pain."

He was right, and I knew it. You would think the gunshot wound would be the most painful, but my hands hurt far worse than my shoulder did. I tried not to complain too much. Byte was doing everything for me. Well, almost everything. I drew the line at assisting me in the bathroom. Thankfully, my sister suggested installing a bidet so I could take care of my personal business by myself. Otherwise, I would've stayed with her. I don't care what he said; I'd rather have my sister wipe my butt than Byte.

"Do you want to go lay down?" he asked.

"Not yet. I'll keep you company while you finish the dishes. And maybe have a little snack." He immediately went to the cabinet, got a pack of miniature muffins and a granola bar, and opened both

before placing them in front of me. Since it took me so long to eat, I was usually tired before I was full, so it seemed like I was hungry all the time. "Thank you," I whispered.

"Hey," he said, and tilted my chin up with his fingers. "What's really going on?"

"I'm sorry you have to do everything for me."

"I'm not," he said vehemently. At my look of confusion, he reached out and gently cupped my face. "I could've lost you that day. If that bullet would've hit you a few millimeters over," he said and shook his head. "Taking care of you for a few weeks is a dream come true in comparison. I'm more than happy I have the opportunity to do it, so let me."

"Okay," I said softly and leaned into the hand cupping my cheek.

"The kitchen can wait. Let's go to bed."

By the time Byte finished helping me change clothes, wash my face, and brush my teeth, the pain medicine had kicked in, and it was all I could do to crawl into bed before closing my eyes.

"Love you," I mumbled.

"Love you, too."

* * *

I WAS FLIPPING THROUGH A TEXTBOOK AND READING over my notes when my phone rang with a number I didn't recognize. Normally, I would have let the call go to voicemail, but I decided to answer in case it was something regarding my case against Lauren.

I fumbled with the phone for a few seconds before I managed to answer it, and was met with silence.

"Hello," I repeated.

"This is Manchester Correctional Institution. Please hold for a collect call from an inmate," an automated voicc said.

I almost dropped the phone in my haste to end the call and resisted the urge to throw my phone across the room. I only knew one person in prison, and he had no business calling me. Why the hell would he be calling me? And how in the hell did he get my phone number?

I tried not to panic while I picked up my phone and called Byte, but I lost the battle when the same number appeared on the screen before I could navigate to Byte's name. He called five more times before finally giving up. By that time, I was barely holding myself together. To top things off, Byte unexpectedly walked through the front door and scared the shit out of me. I screamed and immediately burst into tears.

"Gabby!" he shouted and dropped to his knees in front of me. "What's wrong?"

"L-L-Lawrence," I stammered and motioned toward my phone. "He's been calling me."

"What? Why?"

"I don't know," I sniffled and looked around for something to wipe my nose. "I didn't answer."

Byte produced a tissue and proceeded to dry my tears and wipe my nose. "Did he leave a message?"

"I'm not sure. I didn't check. I was trying to call you, and he just kept calling," I cried. "I haven't spoken to

him in over twenty years. What could he possibly want now?"

Byte pressed his lips into a thin line. "It has to be about Lauren. I seriously doubt his timing is coincidental."

"I don't want to talk to him," I said.

"You don't have to," he assured me. "Do you want me to block the prison's number?"

"Yes," I answered immediately. I didn't need to think about it. There was nothing he could say that I would want to hear.

"Let me get my laptop. I'll be right back," he said.

A few minutes later, he was sitting beside me on the couch typing away on his computer.

"What are you doing?" I asked.

He grinned. "Solving your problems and answering your questions. Give me a few minutes."

Those few minutes felt like hours. Since there wasn't much I could do to distract myself while I waited, I basically sat there watching him type.

Finally, he looked up with a proud smile on his face. "First, I blocked the prison's number from your cell phone. Next, I took a look at Lawrence's visitation records. Lauren's been visiting him about once a month for the last year."

"What the fuck?" I breathed. "I'm not sure what to make of this."

"I'm not either," he admitted. "I think it's safe to assume she's the one who gave him your phone number."

"Do you think he knew what she was doing?" I asked.

"I really don't know," he said and paused for a few beats. "I can probably find out if you want."

"No, I don't think I do." It didn't matter if he knew or not. It wouldn't change anything as far as I was concerned. Maybe if he had warned me before she tried to kill me, and that was a big maybe, but definitely not after the fact.

Byte nodded in understanding. "Well, my afternoon's free. What about yours?"

"You're lucky I can't hit you right now."

"You know you love me," he grinned and gave me a quick kiss. "How about we spend the rest of the day watching movies and eating junk food?"

"Yes, please."

* * *

THE NEXT MORNING, I WAS WOKEN UP FAR EARLIER THAN was acceptable by my ringing phone. It took me longer than usual to answer due to my sleepiness coupled with my bandaged hands. "Hello," I finally croaked.

"Hey," my sister said. "Sorry for waking you."

I was wide awake at the sound of her voice. I knew she wouldn't call and risk waking me for something trivial. She reminded me frequently that I needed to rest. "What's wrong?"

"Nothing. Well, not exactly. I have news. It's not good news, but it might not be bad news either," she rambled.

"Just tell me," I said and waved away Byte's hand that was reaching for my phone.

She exhaled heavily. "Luke Johnson called a few minutes ago. Lawrence was stabbed by another inmate last night. He's in the hospital, but they're not sure if he's going to make it."

"He called me yesterday," I said quietly.

"What?" she yelled, causing me to move the phone away from my ear for a few seconds. "Why didn't you tell me?"

"I was going to mention it when I saw you later today, but there isn't much to tell. He called several times in a row. I didn't answer, and he didn't leave a message, so I don't know why he was calling."

"Do you want me to find out?" she offered.

"No, but thank you. Byte asked the same thing, but I don't want to know."

"Tell her about Lauren," Byte said.

"What about her?" Keegan asked.

"Byte checked Lawrence's visitation records. She's been visiting him about once a month for the last year," I told her.

"What the hell?"

"That's exactly what I said," I laughed. My sister and I were a lot alike and often said the same thing at the same time or had the same reactions.

"I don't like this," Keegan said.

"I don't think I care one way or the other."

"Come on, Gabby," she said. "You can't tell me these events aren't connected. Lauren tries to kill you. Lawrence calls you multiple times out of the blue, and

then he's stabbed by an inmate. Wait. How did he get your phone number?"

"That's actually why Byte decided to look at his visitation records. We're assuming Lauren gave it to him."

"Who else was visiting him?" she asked.

"Hang on," I said and moved the phone away from my mouth. "Who else was visiting Lawrence?" I asked Byte.

"No one. It was just Lauren," he said.

"Tell him to check it again," Keegan said urgently.

"She said you should check it again," I relayed.

"Why?" he asked.

"See if anyone visited him yesterday," Keegan said before I could pass the phone to Byte so the two of them could talk. "If the records aren't updated until the end of the day, you might've missed someone."

I'd barely finished repeating Keegan's words before he jumped out of bed and hurried down the hall. He returned moments later with his laptop balanced in one hand while he typed with the other.

"Son of a bitch!" he cursed.

"I think he found something," I told Keegan, who was now on speaker.

"What is it?" we asked in unison.

"Lawrence did have a visitor yesterday. About an hour before he called you."

"Who was it?" Keegan and I asked at the same time.

"The records have a Michael Fuller listed," Byte said.

I heard Keegan gasp through the phone. "That's not possible," I insisted.

"Obviously, it wasn't me," Byte said. "I'm guessing Chad created a fake ID using my name. I know they scan the IDs and keep a record of them. Give me a few minutes to find it, and we'll know for sure."

"If he knows your name, he knows where you live. I think y'all need to stay at the clubhouse until we find this prick," Keegan said.

I sighed. I knew she was right. There was little to nothing I could do to defend myself with two broken hands and a wounded shoulder, but I was also tired of living in a different place every other week. "Yeah, you're probably right," I conceded. "We'll get some stuff together and head that way."

"I'll meet you there," she said.

I had just ended the call when Byte sat down beside me and showed me his computer screen. "Is that Chad?"

"Yes," I confirmed as I stared at the driver's license displayed on the screen. It was Chad's picture, but with Byte's name and address.

"All right," he said and closed the laptop. "I'll start getting our things together."

Once he had our bags packed and loaded, he locked up the house and helped me into the truck. Shadow jumped into the back seat and looked around excitedly like we were going on a new adventure.

Keegan was waiting by the doors to the clubhouse when we arrived. She hurried over to Byte's truck and

opened the door for me. Yet another thing I couldn't do without help. "Thanks," I grumbled.

"Hang in there," she said. "It won't be for much longer."

"I know," I sighed. "I'm just frustrated with the whole thing. And I'm hungry. Someone woke me up and indirectly booted me from my home before I had a chance to have breakfast."

"You can have breakfast now," she said and led me inside with Shadow trailing along behind us.

Byte took our bags to his room before he joined us at a table in the common room. "I need to go talk to Phoenix. Do you need me to get you anything?"

Keegan answered before I could. "I've got her. Go do what you need to do."

"I'm not sure how long I'll be," he said.

"I'll be fine," I assured him and waved him away.

Once he was gone, Keegan leveled me with her serious look. "Are you really okay?"

I attempted to shrug and grimaced when a pain shot through my wounded shoulder. "If you're referring to the man who was in cahoots with the crazy bitch who tried to kill me posing as my boyfriend and visiting my birth father in prison the same day said birth father was stabbed, I think I'm appropriately disturbed by the situation. If you're referring to my inability to care for myself because of said crazy bitch, I'm frustrated and more irritable than usual," I said and inhaled sharply as a new issue occurred to me. "Byte doesn't have a bidet in his bathroom."

Keegan pulled out her phone and started typing.

"I'm ordering one for pickup right now. As long as you don't have to poop before noon, it shouldn't be a problem."

"I never thought pain pills causing constipation would be a plus, but here we are," I said flatly.

"Is it really that bad?" she asked.

"I guess not. It's only been a day or two."

"Not that. I meant everything else," she said.

"What do you think? I'm drinking coffee through a straw."

Her face scrunched in disgust. "Eww."

"Exactly."

24

BYTE

I left Gabby and Keegan in the common room and went to Phoenix's office. I wasn't surprised to find Shaker already there, filling him in. When Shaker got to the part about Lawrence's visitor using an ID with my name, I opened up my laptop and showed him the screen. "Meet Chad."

"This little shit is really starting to piss me off," Phoenix said. "Basically, we know what he looks like but have nothing new to help us find him, correct?"

I nodded. "Pretty much. We could have somebody keep an eye on Lawrence's hospital room in case he tries to visit him."

"Might as well. We've got eyes on Gabby's house and Lauren's hospital room. Can you think of anywhere else he might show up?" Phoenix asked.

"Maybe my house, if he thinks Gabby's there," I suggested.

Phoenix nodded. "Shaker, you and Ranger hang out

at Byte's place today. Take his truck so it looks like he's there."

I frowned but held out my keys for Shaker. I understood why Phoenix didn't send me to watch over my own house, but I still didn't like it.

Shaker took my keys and clapped me on the shoulder. "Take care of my girls."

"Of course," I said and turned back to Phoenix. "Was the detective able to get anything out of Lauren?"

Phoenix shook his head. "No. Apparently, she isn't as stupid as we'd hoped. He said she started saying 'lawyer' through her closed teeth the second he entered the room."

"Maybe Carbon should try to talk to her," I suggested, only half kidding.

Phoenix laughed. "I'm sure he'd be happy to give it a shot, but I'd prefer it be somewhere with less of an audience."

"What about Lawrence? Any chance we could get someone to talk to him?"

"I'm sure Luke could get in to see him. Do you think he knows something?"

"He has to. He called Gabby six times yesterday right after Chad visited him. I doubt he suddenly had the urge to say hello after all these years. She said she didn't want to know what he had to say, but I think it's worth checking into."

"I agree," he said and reached for his phone. "I'll give Luke a call. Anything else?"

"Is anybody free to hang out at the diner?" I asked. "I know there's a slim chance he'll show up

there, but I'd like for Irene to have some help in case he does."

He nodded. "I'll send one of the guys at Gabby's house to the diner."

"Thanks, Prez," I said and got to my feet. "I'm going to keep digging. I'll let you know if I find anything."

"Are you going to be here all day?" he asked.

"Well, since you sent Shaker and Ranger away in my truck, I don't really have a choice in that."

"Oh, right," he laughed. "I'll find you after I hear from Luke."

I stopped by the common room on the way to my room to find Keegan heading for the front door with her keys in her hand and her purse on her shoulder. "Where are you going?" I asked.

"To pick up the bidet that I ordered for your bathroom."

I shook my head. "Send someone else."

"Are you serious?"

"Shaker asked me to watch out for you and Gabby while he's gone. This is me doing that," I said.

"Fine," she huffed.

"I'll go," Flint volunteered.

"Thanks, man," I said.

After Flint left, I joined Keegan and Gabby at their table. Gabby was still working on her breakfast, and I could tell she was frustrated. It took her longer to eat, but she was managing better than I expected.

"Have you had anything to eat?" Keegan asked.

"I'm about to," I said and started for the kitchen.

"Will you refill my coffee?" Gabby asked.

I picked up her mug that was half full and looked at her in confusion.

"It's cold," she grumbled.

"Can't I just reheat it?" I asked.

Keegan's eyes widened like I had said something sacrilegious in the middle of church.

"I'd rather have a fresh cup," Gabby said politely.

Keegan looked at her and pretended to be shocked. "You're not going to give him your dissertation on the horrors of reheated coffee?"

Gabby narrowed her eyes as if willing her sister to shut up. "I'm trying not to be too picky when I'm being waited on."

"I'll get you a fresh cup," I said and headed for the kitchen before their pending argument could escalate.

When I returned, I placed a stainless steel insulated mug full of fresh coffee in front of Gabby. "It should stay warm for hours in this. I dropped a few ice cubes in it so you can drink it right away without scalding your mouth."

"Thank you," she beamed.

We were finished with breakfast but still sitting in the common room when Flint returned with the bidet.

"You want to help me install it?" I asked.

"I'm not very familiar with plumbing, but I can try," he said.

By the time we were finished, it was well after lunch, and I never wanted to see another bidet again.

"I thought that would be easier," Flint said.

"It was the first time I did it," I grumbled. "I'm not sure why this one was such a pain in the ass."

"At least I know why plumbers are so expensive now," Flint joked as we headed to the common room for lunch.

We were just finishing up when Phoenix joined us. "I spoke with Luke. He's going to send someone to talk to Lawrence. It'll probably be sometime tomorrow."

"Thanks, Prez," I said and tried to hide my disappointment, or perhaps frustration. I was tired of waiting for something to happen. I just wanted the situation to be done and over with.

"Flint, I want you to head over to Byte's place after dinner and spend the night there with Shaker and Ranger. Check in with them and see if they want you to bring anything over before you go," Phoenix said and got to his feet.

"Will do," Flint replied and stood to leave with his dad.

Keegan dropped into Flint's vacated seat and propped her chin on her hands. "Want to build a robot?"

25

FLINT

I left the clubhouse after dinner and headed to my apartment to grab a few things before I went to Byte's house for the night. Thankfully, everything Shaker and Ranger requested was in their rooms at the clubhouse, saving me from driving all over town. Not that I would have minded. The driving part wasn't the issue. I wasn't exactly comfortable going into their homes and going through their personal belongings.

When I pulled into my designated parking space in front of my apartment, I immediately realized something was off. It took me a few moments to realize the welcome mat my mother bought when I moved out was folded over on itself like someone tripped on it. Then I saw movement through the blinds. Someone was in my apartment, and I had a pretty good idea who it was.

I pretended like I was looking through the center console for something while I quickly placed a call to Shaker instead of my dad. I knew Dad would tell me to

leave or wait for the club to arrive, and I didn't want to take a chance of this prick getting away again.

"Hey, Flint," Shaker answered.

"I don't have time to talk. I'm at my apartment, and I'm pretty sure Chad's inside. If I'm right, we'll be headed your way shortly. Be ready," I said and ended the call before he could utter a single word.

I took in a deep breath and got out of my truck before I could really think about what I was doing. Then I unlocked my front door and stepped into my apartment. I was right. Chad was sitting on my couch with a pistol aimed directly at me.

I tried to play the part of an unsuspecting victim and raised my hands in front of me. "Who are you and what do you want?"

Chad snorted. "You know who I am."

I shook my head. "No, I don't." And that was the truth. I had no idea who he was. None of us did.

He gave me an appraising look. "I suppose that's true, but you know what I want."

I wanted to roll my eyes. I wasn't interested in playing his games, but I also didn't want to let on how much I knew. And I didn't want to piss him off and get shot. I was already walking a dangerous line.

"It'd be easier if you just told me," I said carefully.

"It'd be easier if you just told me," he said in a mocking voice.

Instead of responding, I remained silent with my hands still in the air and waited for his next move.

He huffed and walked over to where I was standing. "Turn around and put your hands behind your back. If

you even think about trying anything, I'll put a bullet in your brain."

I did as he said and wondered if I was making a colossal mistake while I willingly let him tie my hands behind my back.

"Where are the keys to your truck?" he asked once he had my hands secured.

I wanted to tell him he should have asked for those first and checked me for weapons. Instead, I said, "In my right front pocket. It's a fob, not keys."

He quickly retrieved the fob and turned me toward the door. "Let's go."

In any other situation, I would've been praying one of my neighbors would see what was happening and call the police. But as I dutifully walked to my truck, I hoped no one was watching.

He tossed me into the back seat with a command to stay down and hurried around to the driver's seat. Once he was in, he didn't waste any time and peeled out of the parking lot with squealing wheels. He was either a total dumbass or didn't care about attracting attention. I voted for total dumbass.

I thought about trying to maneuver my hands to my front and then using my bindings to strangle him from behind, but that would likely result in him crashing my truck or shooting me since his hands were free. It went against everything I'd ever been taught, but I stayed quiet and patiently waited for us to arrive at Byte's house. Since I'd been there so many times, I could tell exactly where we were without being able to see out of the windows. I

almost sighed in relief when he turned into Byte's driveway.

As expected, he dragged me out of the back seat and used me like a shield as he positioned himself about twenty feet away from the front porch. Once he was where he wanted to be, he yelled for Byte to come outside.

Shaker opened the door and cautiously stepped out onto the porch. "What in the hell is going on out here?"

Chad pressed his gun to my temple. "Where's Gabby?" he demanded.

"She's not up for having visitors right now," Shaker said.

Chad tensed, and I could practically feel the rage rolling off of him. "I'm not fucking around!" Chad screamed. "Send her out here, or I'm gonna kill your friend!"

Shaker raised his hands in a placating manner. "Hang on a second. Let's talk about this."

"Send her out here! Now!" he yelled and pressed the gun harder against my head.

"I'm sorry, I can't do that," Shaker said and made eye contact with me. He glanced to the ground and then back to me before he returned his attention to Chad.

"I'm fucking serious, man! If she's not out here in the next five seconds, your friend is dead!"

Shaker looked directly at me and said one word. "Drop."

I did exactly as he said and crumbled to the ground in an instant. The crack of a rifle sounded through the

air not even a second later, followed by a dull thud that I felt more than heard.

Shaker leaped off the porch and pulled me to my feet. He wrapped me in a bear hug and started patting me down to check for injuries. "Holy fuck! Are you okay?"

"Yeah, I think so," I stammered.

Before I could give it any more thought, Ranger came through the front door with his trusty rifle in his hand. He walked right over to Chad, or what was left of him, to inspect his work. "Yep, I still got it."

"Was there ever any doubt?" Shaker asked.

Ranger shrugged. "No, but I try to be modest." He clapped me on the shoulder. "That was a pretty ballsy move, son. You okay?"

"I'd be better if one of you would untie me," I said.

"Oh, shit," Shaker said and pulled out his knife. "Sorry about that. Turn around."

I rubbed my wrists once I was free and was surprised at how sore they were even though I wasn't restrained for very long. "It'll take a day or two for the soreness to go away," Shaker said in a way that made me think he knew from experience. Before I could ask, the sound of motorcycle pipes and sirens approaching filled the air.

"My dad's going to be pissed," I said.

Shaker nodded. "Your dad will be, but your president will be proud. How'd you know he was in your apartment?"

"The welcome mat my mom gave me was all messed up, like someone tripped over it."

"The one you complained about?" he asked.

"Yep, that's the one. And now I'll never hear the end of how the ugly-ass welcome mat she got me saved my life, as well as yours, Ranger's, and Gabby's."

The club arrived first, with my dad leading the way. He barely managed to get his kickstand down before he was off his bike and in front of me. "You scared the shit out of me," he said as he engulfed me in a hug.

"How'd you know?" I asked.

He stepped back and shook his head as if I should've already known the answer. "I was on the phone with Ranger the whole time."

Before he could chastise me for putting myself in harm's way, Byte was shoving him out of the way and hugging me. "Thanks, brother. I fucking owe you."

"I'm just glad it worked out the way it did," I said.

"You got lucky," my dad said.

"I know," I admitted. "But I didn't have much time, and it was the only plan I could think of. I knew Ranger would have his rifle and would be able to take him out.

"I get it," he said. "I don't like it, but I get it."

"Did he say anything to you?" Byte asked.

I shook my head. "Nothing of significance. He told me not to do anything stupid, tied my hands behind my back, and drove me here. Then, he demanded they send Gabby outside. That was it."

"So we still don't know who he is or what he wanted," Byte said.

"Nope, and we can't ask him," I said, and gestured to the mess that was once Chad. Ranger had taken him out with a shot to the head and the end result was the most disgusting thing I'd ever seen.

"Do we really care?" Ranger asked.

"No, I suppose we don't," Byte said. "Gabby's safe, and that's all that matters."

One of the police officers approached with a friendly smile. "Hey, Phoenix," he said and held out his hand. "Are your guys ready to give statements?"

"Sure," my dad said and turned to me. "Tell them everything."

26

BYTE

It took forever for the cops to finish processing the scene. I was anxious to get back to the clubhouse to tell Gabby everything, but I also wanted to stay to make sure they didn't miss anything.

The detective who seemed to know Phoenix came over to where we were gathered on the porch. "You said this guy's name was Chad Higgins, right?"

"That's the name he gave Gabby," Phoenix said. "Why?"

The detective opened the wallet he was holding and pulled out multiple IDs. "Looks like 'Chad' may have been involved in identity theft. It might take a bit for us to verify his true identity. Is there anything else you can tell me that might help?"

"No, I don't think so," Phoenix said.

We'd already told them about his association with Lauren and Lawrence. I knew one of the IDs had my name and address on it, but since I wasn't supposed to know that and hadn't found out legally, I kept that

information to myself. I also didn't want them looking into my information while they were trying to identify Chad. "Can we take a look at those IDs to see if we recognize any of the names?" I asked.

He shrugged. "Sure. Why not?" he said and handed over the small stack of licenses. I slowly went through them and waited until the detective looked away to slip the one with my name and address on it into my shirt sleeve. When he turned back to me, I handed the IDs back to him. "Sorry, I don't recognize any of those names."

"Thanks for looking," he said. "We'll get it figured out."

I knew they would, and it really chapped my ass that I hadn't been able to. I silently seethed about that until they finally left.

"I saw that," Phoenix said knowingly.

"I didn't care if you did," I said. "I was only worried about the detective."

Phoenix laughed and clapped me on the shoulder. "Do you need any help with that?" he asked and gestured to the large blood stain marring my otherwise clean driveway.

"Nah, I have a pressure washer."

"Where is it?" Ranger asked. "It's my mess to clean up."

"I'll take care of it," I said.

Ranger shook his head. "I'm getting up there in age. I might not have many more opportunities like this."

"Okay," I said slowly, while Phoenix and Shaker laughed.

Ranger was in rare form as he washed Chad's blood and brain matter from my driveway. He smiled the whole time and may have even been whistling at one point.

"He's doing that for you," Shaker said.

"What?"

"Showing you how happy it made him to get rid of someone who threatened Gabby."

I shook my head and laughed.

Shaker's hand landed on my shoulder. "Welcome to the family."

* * *

IT WAS LATE WHEN WE FINALLY MADE IT BACK TO THE clubhouse. Gabby and Keegan were asleep in my room. Instead of waking them, Shaker and I decided to let them be. He went to his room, and I went to one of the empty rooms to sleep. Despite the events of the day, I couldn't fall asleep. I tossed and turned all night. I couldn't stop thinking about Chad. I knew I was missing something, and it was driving me crazy. I finally gave up trying to sleep and got out of bed around six in the morning.

The common room was quiet, and I assumed I was the first one up. I went to the kitchen to make myself a cup of coffee and almost jumped out of my skin when I turned around to find Keegan standing behind me. "Holy shit," I breathed. "You scared me."

She huffed and placed her hands on her hips. "You deserved it."

"Why? What did I do?" She was obviously upset, but I had no idea why.

"You didn't wake me up to tell me what happened."

"We couldn't wake you without waking Gabby. And you said yourself she needs her rest," I explained.

Keegan grumbled something I couldn't hear and stepped forward to help herself to my cup of coffee. "I'm awake now."

"I'll tell you after I make myself some coffee," I said and turned back to the machine. When I heard her make a noise of discontent, I stifled a laugh and refrained from telling her she deserved that.

I'd barely taken a sip when she demanded, "Now, tell me what happened."

I thought about making her wait until Gabby was awake, but I could tell by the look on her face she wouldn't find it as funny as I did. "Fine," I said and filled her in on everything that transpired at my house.

"He's dead?" she asked.

"So dead," I confirmed.

"Is Gabby safe now?"

"She should be. Chad's dead, Lauren's in police custody, and Lawrence will either die or go back to prison," I said.

"Do we know who stabbed him?" she asked.

"No," I said. "Do you want to know?"

"I don't necessarily want to know, but I feel like something's missing," she said.

"Yeah, me, too," I shared. "Let me grab my laptop."

I carefully opened the door to my room and tiptoed inside to get my laptop without waking Gabby. I froze

when she repositioned herself, but thankfully, she stayed asleep.

"All right, let's see what we can find out," I said when I returned to the common room. It took a little longer than I thought, but I finally located the information. "Okay, Lawrence was stabbed by Todd Orson. He's a thirty-six-year-old serving a ten-year sentence for identity theft, cyber crimes, and financial fraud. He's about a year and a half into his sentence."

Keegan started typing on her phone. "Do you have a picture of him?"

"Yeah, his mugshot," I said and turned my screen to give her a better view.

"Great," she said and took a quick look at his picture before returning to her phone. I was about to ask her what she was doing when she gasped.

"What?" I demanded and leaned over so I could see her screen.

"That's Chad," she said and showed me a picture posted on one of Todd's social media pages. According to the caption, the photo was of Todd and his brother Brett.

I returned to my computer and typed Brett Orson into the search bar. Plenty of information came up immediately. Then I went back to the prison records and looked at the visitation log for Todd. I opened another tab and pulled up Lawrence's visitors. "I think we might have some answers. Look at this. Brett was visiting his brother when Lauren went to see Lawrence for the first time."

"That must be how they met," Keegan observed.

"Oh, and look at that. 'Michael Fuller' also visited Todd Orson the day Lawrence was stabbed."

"I bet Brett asked his brother to do it."

"But why?" she wondered.

"I can answer that," Phoenix said and joined us at the table. "Luke was able to get someone in to talk to Lawrence yesterday. He called and left a message, but with everything going on, I didn't check my messages until this morning."

"What did he say?" Keegan asked impatiently.

"He said when Lauren first started coming to see him, she said it was because she wanted to get to know him. After the first few visits, she started asking about what happened to his assets. Then she started asking about Gabby. He said she became increasingly more demanding each time. At the visit before her last one, she gave him Gabby's phone number and asked him to contact her. She wanted him to convince Gabby to cooperate with her and give her half of her inheritance. During her last visit, he told her he hadn't contacted Gabby and had no intention of doing so. He said Lauren was furious. She told him she would get what was hers without him, and that he would be sorry for not helping her. Then he said a man he didn't know came to see him the day he was stabbed, which we now know is Brett. Brett told him what happened with Lauren and Gabby and said he would finish the job. Lawrence didn't know exactly what that meant or if he was serious, but he tried to call Gabby to warn her, just in case. He was going to try to call her again, but Todd stabbed him before he had the chance."

"Why would he want to finish the job for Lauren? What did he get out of it?" Keegan asked, though I was wondering the same thing.

"I'm not sure we'll ever know, but if I had to guess, I'd say money. She probably promised him a hefty sum if he'd help her get her inheritance from Gabby," he said.

I nodded in agreement. "That makes the most sense. He probably learned some of his computer skills from his brother."

"If that's the case, why didn't he just hack into her bank account and take the money?" Keegan asked.

"He probably didn't know how. Hacking into a home security system is a lot easier than breaking into someone's trust fund. Even if he knew how to get in, he likely didn't know how to take the money and cover his tracks so he didn't get caught."

"I still can't believe either of them thought Gabby had his money. I mean, look at every drug lord or Mafia boss that's ever been busted. Their family didn't get to keep their money and their mansions," Keegan said.

Phoenix shrugged. "People are stupid."

"Yeah, they are," I agreed.

"Does Gabby know yet?" Phoenix asked.

"Do I know what?" Gabby asked from behind.

"Have a seat while I get you some coffee," I said. "Then I'll tell you everything."

She took the news in stride. She listened to the entire story without much of a reaction. I was just as confused as Keegan was, but it was Shaker who seemed to know what was going on.

He sat down beside Gabby and gently wrapped an arm around her shoulders so as not to jostle her injured shoulder. "Is this about Chad's death, or is it about Lawrence actually trying to do something good for once in his life?"

"Both," she said quictly.

"It's okay to be happy Chad's gone. It doesn't mean you're celebrating death. It just means you're happy the threat to you is over. As for Lawrence, it's okay to feel however you feel about him. If you want to thank him for trying to warn you, you can. Or if you want to move on and not acknowledge him, that's okay, too."

"Thank you," she said and rested her head on his shoulder. Then she smiled. "I like things just the way they are."

27

GABBY

Three weeks had passed since Papa shot Chad, and it finally felt like things were getting back to normal. Due to my extenuating circumstances, I was granted an extension to finish my clinical hours. Patch assured me we would get my hours in, but, with the extension, we didn't have to rush. I had a feeling Gigi had something to do with my special treatment, but she wouldn't admit to anything. I thanked her anyway.

I also received a letter from the nursing board. I thought for sure it was the letter notifying me of the complaint against my license and the investigation they planned to launch. To my surprise, it was a letter telling me they were dismissing the case. I wasn't sure how that happened, but I called Tina and thanked her profusely.

The best part of those three weeks was getting the bandages removed from my hands. Since the fractures weren't complete, meaning the bones were cracked versus broken in half, they didn't take as long to heal. My hands were still sore and stiff, but I could use them

to do things for myself. Things that I'd always taken for granted, like washing my hair and buttoning my jeans. I insisted on driving home from the doctor's office, much to Byte's dismay.

Once we were home, I assured him I would be fine by myself and shooed him away to do his thing at the clubhouse. Then I called Flint and asked him to come over.

"What's going on, Gabby?" he asked when he arrived.

"I need your help with something, but it might mean you have to keep something pretty significant to yourself depending on the outcome," I said.

He gave me a skeptical look. "I'm not sure about this."

"Let me explain," I said and gestured for him to have a seat on the sofa. "Well, let me ask you something first. What do you know about Byte's past?"

"More than I should," he said. "I overheard my dad talking about it."

I exhaled in relief. I wouldn't be breaking Byte's trust by talking to Flint since he already knew. "I want to know if Byte was ever a suspect. He never wanted to know, but I thought I could look for him and maybe give him a chance to have his life back."

"What if he was a suspect or is wanted for murder?" Flint asked.

"Then I'll never say a word about it."

"I don't know, Gabby. This is a slippery slope to go down," Flint said.

"I know, but I can't do it without you. I know Byte's

been teaching you computer stuff. You're the only other person I could ask besides him. Well, the only other trustworthy person," I said. I knew I was asking a lot and wouldn't be upset if he said no, but I really hoped he'd say yes.

"I guess I could try," Flint said reluctantly.

"Great," I said excitedly. "What do you need to know?"

He snorted a laugh. "Pretty sure I already have that information. Blake Williams from Nebraska, right?"

"Right," I confirmed. "I don't know what his mother's name was, but I think the stepfather was named Glenn."

While Flint started searching, I got up and went to the kitchen to make us some coffee. When I returned to the living room, Flint turned the screen to show me a news article he found.

"Search continues for missing boy after parents found murdered in their home. It is unclear at this time if fourteen-year-old Blake Williams was kidnapped or murdered. Police are asking anyone with possible information regarding the case to contact them immediately," I read aloud.

Flint clicked to a different tab. "Here's another one."

"Gambling debt probable motive behind double homicide. Teenage son missing and likely in danger." I turned to Flint. "They think someone else did it. They think he was a victim."

"There's more," he said. "I saved the best one for last."

"Bookie Johnny Jenkins found guilty of murdering

eight people who owed him money. The victims were," I read and skimmed over the names until I saw two that seemed pertinent. "Glenn Dodson and Sheila Williams." I couldn't believe what I was reading. "Someone else was convicted for murdering them?"

Flint nodded. "Yep. I found some other articles that say his prints were found inside the house. He denied killing them, but he also denied killing the other six people."

"Can you send me the links to those articles?"

Flint laughed. "Sure, but he'll be able to find them and more on his own once you tell him."

"Crap," I said. "Now, I have to tell him." I knew he'd be relieved in the end, but I wasn't sure how he would initially react.

"It'll be fine," Flint said. "Just tell him the main point, and don't beat around the bush."

"Thanks, Flint. I really appreciate your help."

"Yeah, about that. Maybe don't tell him I helped you," he said.

"I won't," I promised.

It was all I could do to contain myself after Flint left. I couldn't call Byte and ask him to come home without him thinking something was wrong, and I couldn't show up at the clubhouse without garnering the same response. Plus, neither one of us needed an audience to witness what could be a disastrous conversation. When he finally got home, I was ready to burst.

"How was the rest of your day?" I asked.

"Fine," he said and gave me an appraising look. "What's going on with you?"

"I have to tell you something, and I'm afraid you're going to be mad at me, but it's actually a good thing," I rambled.

"Just tell me," he said calmly.

"Johnny Jenkins was convicted of murdering your parents. They thought he kidnapped and killed you but couldn't prove it," I blurted. "I'm sorry I went behind your back, but I wanted you to know if it was good news."

"And what if it wasn't?" he asked.

"Then I wouldn't have told you," I said quietly.

"How did you find all this out?"

"Uh, Google," I lied.

"Google?" he asked, and I could tell he didn't believe me.

"I mean, that's where I started. I'm not sure how I got from point A to point B, but that's not important. Where's your laptop? You can see for yourself." I was nervous and doing a piss-poor job of explaining myself.

"Okay," he said with resignation and sat down with his computer. "I'll be damned," he muttered a few minutes later.

I wanted to say, "See? I told you so," but decided against it and sat quietly beside him while he read through the articles. I was dying to know what he was thinking, but there was no way I was going to ask. I'd wait until he was ready to tell me.

He spent a while longer clicking through pages and reading articles before he closed his laptop and got to his feet. "Shadow probably needs to go out," he said. I

watched from the window as he took Shadow outside and tossed the ball for him.

When he came back inside, I was almost finished making dinner. I didn't know what to say, so I didn't say anything. And neither did he. We sat down to eat in silence. After the fifth or sixth bite, I couldn't take it anymore. "I'm sorry!" I blurted. "I shouldn't have done it."

Byte turned to me with a look of confusion on his face. "What?"

"I'm sorry for looking into your past. You've done so much for me, and I wanted to do something for you in return. I didn't know it would upset you this much. Please forgive me," I blabbered.

"I'm not mad at you," he said.

"You're not?"

"No," he said with a slight smile.

"Then why in the hell haven't you said a word to me since I told you?" I demanded. He might not have been mad, but suddenly I was.

"I haven't?" he asked.

"No! You said you were taking Shadow outside, and that was it."

"Oh," he said. "I guess I was lost in my thoughts. I didn't realize you thought I was mad at you."

"What was I supposed to think?" I asked.

"I don't mean this the way it might sound, but I wasn't really thinking about you," he admitted. "You dropped a major bombshell on me, and I needed to process it."

"Have you done that?"

"What?"

"Processed it," I said and tried to hide my exasperation.

"Yeah, I think so. I mean, it's good to know I don't have anything to worry about, but it doesn't change anything. It's not like I can suddenly start living as Blake Williams again."

"Why not?" I asked, slightly disappointed. One of the main reasons I wanted to find out about his past was so he didn't have to hide his true identity anymore.

"How will I explain where I was if someone asks? Or how there's no trace of my existence for almost two decades?"

"Who's going to ask?"

"The police department in my hometown. I was, or am, a missing person. I'm sure they have something set up to alert them if I resurface," he explained.

"I just wanted you to have your name back," I said.

"It's just a name," he said. "It doesn't change who I am."

"No, it doesn't," I agreed.

"Thank you," he said quietly. "I never would've looked into it on my own. Even though it doesn't really change anything for me, it's nice to know I don't have anything to worry about."

I exhaled in relief. That's why I did it. To give him some of the peace he'd given me.

EPILOGUE

GABBY

Eight weeks after the shooting, Patch insisted on returning to work, against the advice of his colleagues and club brothers. He promised to take it easy, and I made sure that he did. When I completed my clinical hours a little over four weeks later, he offered me a job at his practice.

"Shouldn't you wait until after I pass the boards?" I asked.

He shook his head with a smile. "I know you'll pass. You're welcome to work here as a nurse until then, or you can enjoy some time off and start after you pass the exam."

After giving it some thought, I asked if I could work part-time as a nurse until I passed the nurse practitioner boards. I'd had plenty of time off while I was recovering from my injuries, but I wanted to make sure I had time to study, as well as spend time with Byte and Shadow.

I was still staying at his house, though I'd migrated

from the bedroom upstairs to his bedroom downstairs. We hadn't talked about our living arrangements. I wasn't sure why he hadn't brought it up, but I was waiting until I finished school and had an idea of where I'd be working to make any plans, which is also why my house in Cedar Valley was just sitting there.

When I got home from the office, there was a note on the table telling me to come to the clubhouse after I'd showered and changed. I smiled. Byte knew me so well.

Once I was dressed and ready, I drove to the clubhouse. I was pretty sure I knew why I was being summoned, but I tried not to think about it.

When I walked into the clubhouse, I was greeted with various shouts of "Surprise!" and "Congratulations!" The entire club was there, as well as Gigi and Papa Ronan. I was surprised to see a few of the employees from Patch's office, Irene, and a girl I didn't know. She looked to be around my age, maybe a few years older, and was huddled close to Irene.

I made my way around the room to speak to everyone and thank them for coming. When I reached Irene, she introduced me to her friend. "This is Evie," she said. "She works at the diner with me and is new to the area. I dragged her along with me so she could meet some people her age in the area."

"Hi, Evie," I said and held out my hand. I noticed Edge standing off to the side with his eyes fixed on Evie and briefly wondered why he was staring at her so intently. "I'm Gabby. It's nice to meet you."

"Nice to meet you, too," she said softly. "Congratulations on finishing school."

"Thank you," I said. "How long have you been in town?"

Before she could answer, Keegan and Annabelle entered the room carrying a huge cake. "Come blow out the candles," Keegan said and waved me over to the table.

"I thought candles were for birthday cakes," I pointed out.

"I tried to tell her," Annabelle said.

Keegan sighed in exasperation. "Just do it," she said.

"Fine," I said and blew out the congratulatory candles.

Byte came up behind me and slid a hand around my waist. "What'd you wish for?" he asked quietly.

"Nothing," I smiled. "I've already got it."

* * *

Three Months Later

I SAT AT A TABLE IN THE COMMON ROOM WITH MY LAPTOP and clicked refresh. Again. I was not so patiently waiting for the website to update with my exam results.

Keegan laughed. "Be careful. If you keep refreshing the page like that, you're going to cause it to freeze up."

I didn't take my eyes off the screen and said, "There are plenty of other computers around here I can use if that happens."

Byte stood behind me and rubbed my shoulders.

"That's one of my laptops. It can handle her rapid clicking."

"Please don't encourage her," Keegan said.

"What is taking so long?" I asked no one in particular. The results were supposed to be available at noon. It had been seven minutes since the clock struck twelve, and they still hadn't been uploaded.

"Maybe you should take a break and check again in a few minutes," Keegan suggested.

"I can't," I said and continued to obsessively refresh the page. I realized I probably resembled an addict looking for their next fix, but I couldn't stop myself. I'd worked so hard to become a nurse practitioner, and it was all riding on the results of one exam.

"Are you sure they said noon?" Keegan asked. "Maybe you got the time—"

Her words were cut off when I let out a scream and jumped to my feet, causing Byte to stumble back a few steps. "I passed!"

Keegan and Byte hugged me at the same time while the room erupted in cheers. When they finally released me, the handful of people hanging around came over to congratulate me.

"I knew you could do it," Keegan said. "I'm so proud of you."

"Thank you," I said sincerely. "I couldn't have done it without all the love and support you and Jacob gave me."

"I love you," she said and hugged me again.

"I love you, too," I replied.

Keegan released me and took a step back. She

glanced at her phone, looked at the front door, and then back to me. "Well, you should probably get going."

I laughed. "Are you trying to get rid of me?"

"Yes, I am," she admitted and shooed me with her hands. "Go."

Byte took my hand and led me toward the front door.

"I'll see you tonight," I called over my shoulder.

"Pretend to be surprised so you don't ruin it," she said.

"I'll do my best," I returned. The surprise would have been if they weren't planning to throw a party for me. Whenever there was something to celebrate, the club had a party. And after everything I'd been through, I felt like celebrating. Chad was no longer a threat to me, Lauren was behind bars and would remain there until she was sentenced, Lawrence succumbed to his injuries about a week after he was stabbed, my license had been cleared, I finished college, and I passed my exam.

"Now that you're officially a nurse practitioner and have a job in Croftridge, can we talk about your living arrangements?" Byte asked.

He'd brought it up several times since I graduated, but I always put it off. I didn't want to make any decisions until after the exam. Perhaps I was more superstitious than I thought, because I felt like I would jinx myself if I let my house go before I took the test. So, ever since the shooting, I had been "staying" at Byte's house, not living with him.

"Sure," I said. "What do you want to talk about?"

He laughed. "You know exactly what I want to talk about."

"You're going to have to ask me. I'm not going to invite myself," I teased.

"I want you to live with me," he said.

"That's not a question," I pointed out.

"Gabby," he said with a hint of exasperation.

"Fine," I said. "I'll live with you."

"It's about damn time," he said. "Do you know what you want to do with your house?"

"I was thinking about keeping it and renting it," I said. "If Jake or Quincy go to college in Cedar Valley, they could stay there if they wanted to. Or any of the club kids. What do you think?"

"I think that sounds like a great idea," he said as he pulled into his driveway.

"I'm glad we got that settled," I said and made a show of stretching and yawning. "I'm ready for a nap."

"Your nap will have to wait," he said.

"What? Why?"

"Because you need to pack."

"For what?" I asked.

"We never got to have our long weekend at Badger's cabin. I figured we should take the opportunity before you start working full-time," he said. "We can spend the night at the clubhouse tonight after the party and leave first thing in the morning."

"Really? Is Shadow coming with us?"

Byte laughed. "Doesn't he always?"

"You're the best."

"I'm pretty sure that's you," he said. "Love you."

"Love you, too."

ABOUT THE AUTHOR

Website/Newsletter Sign-up

Facebook Reader Group

Signed Books/Merchandise

ALSO BY TEAGAN BROOKS

Blackwings MC

Dash

Duke

Phoenix

Carbon

Shaker

Badger

Blackwings MC Box Set

Blackwings MC - Devil Springs

Copper

Judge

Savior

Batta

Bronze

Bear

Coal

Game

Devil Springs Box Set Volume One

Devil Springs Box Set Volume Two

King Mountain Shifters

Slade

Standalones

Beached

Christmas in Tinsel Town

Printed in Great Britain
by Amazon

57601050R00165

Printed in Dunstable, United Kingdom

81388976R00184

Also by Ki Stephens

Coastal University Series

Spring Tide

Fault Line

Ripple Effect

Coastal Rivals Series

The Trade

Close Call

High Hopes

Coming Fall 2025

Game On

About the Author

Ki Stephens is a romance enthusiast who finds comfort in the happily-ever-after . . . with just a little bit of angst along the way. She has a special interest in works that include neurodivergent characters like herself. When she's not daydreaming about books, Ki enjoys working with kids, creating art in her backyard studio, and spending loads of time with her baby girl, her husband, and their three pets.

She released her debut novel, Spring Tide—Book 1 in the Coastal University Series, in December of 2022.

www.kistephens.com